CHARLOTTE BINGHAM

The Nightingale Sings
'A novel rich in dramatic surprises, with a large cast of
vivid characters whose antics will have you frantically
turning the pages'
Daily Mail

To Hear A Nightingale
'A lovely sprawling saga with a heroine you can't fail to love'
Prima

The Business
'The ideal beach read'
Homes and Gardens

In Sunshine Or In Shadow
'Superbly written . . . A romantic novel that is romantic in
the true sense of the word'
Daily Mail

Stardust
'Charlotte Bingham has produced a long, absorbing read,
perfect for holidays, which I found hard to lay aside as the
plot twisted and turned with intriguing results'
Sunday Express

Nanny
'It's deckchair season once again, and Charlotte Bingham's
spellbinding saga is required reading'
Cosmopolitan

Change Of Heart
'Her imagination is thoroughly original. This book has a
fairy-tale cover containing a fairy tale, which is all the
more delightful as it is not something one exp
a modern novel . . . It's heady stuff'
Daily Mail

Debutantes
'A big, wallowy delicious read'
The Times

Grand Affair
'Extremely popular'
Daily Mail

Love Song

Charlotte Bingham

BANTAM BOOKS

LONDON · NEW YORK · TORONTO · SYDNEY · AUCKLAND

TITLE: LOVE SONG
A BANTAM BOOK : 0553 50501 7

Simultaneously published in Great Britain by Doubleday,
a division of Transworld Publishers Ltd

PRINTING HISTORY
Doubleday edition published 1998
Bantam edition published 1998

Set in 11/13pt Palatino
by Phoenix Typesetting, Ilkley, West Yorkshire

Bantam Books are published by Transworld Publishers Ltd,
61–63 Uxbridge Road, London W5 5SA,
in Australia by Transworld Publishers (Australia) Pty Ltd,
15–25 Helles Avenue, Moorebank, NSW 2170,
and in New Zealand by Transworld Publishers (NZ) Ltd,
3 William Pickering Drive, Albany, Auckland.

Reproduced, printed and bound in Great Britain by
Cox & Wyman Ltd, Reading, Berks.

For Terence
my favourite singer of my favourite songs

A special thank you to:

Malandra Burrows, Brian Rawling, warner.esp,
Martin Craig, Judd Lander.
The lyrics of "Love Song (Don't Leave Me)"
featured on pages 555–6 appear by kind
permission of Rive Droite Music.

The action of this novel takes place in
the late nineteen eighties

PROLOGUE

Their voices came towards her on the quiet afternoon air, across a garden bathed in a golden sunlight. It was a light that seemed to her to be painting everything with a tender glow – touching the trees and the lawn with strokes of warmth, the kind of warmth that seems unimaginable when winter comes.

It was, too, the kind of day that she had once thought might never come again, when a dog shifts itself lazily, a baby sleeps, and someone, somewhere, calls out to someone else to 'come and see'. A day filled with those sublimely unimportant tasks that make up the best of life.

In this mood of contentment she turned, feeling someone behind her, smiling. She found no-one there, yet she knew just who it might be.

PART ONE

When you were there, and you, and you,
Happiness crowned the night.

Rupert Brooke, 'Dining Room Tea'

Chapter One

Hope had thought she was doing the right thing having a spring baby until she stepped into the hospital and saw how many other women were also doing the right thing. It was April and there seemed to be dozens of women arriving with their suitcases, all having babies. Hope had no suitcase. Everything had started to happen too quickly, in the Café Firenze of all places, right in the middle of a tea to celebrate Claire's birthday, just as the tall glasses with the frothy milk shakes had arrived and Donna Maria the café owner was discreetly lighting all the candles on the freshly made chocolate gateau which was not just the café's speciality but Hope's youngest daughter's birthday cake.

'I'm so sorry, Claire. What a time for it to happen!'

'Don't worry, Mums. If you hang on until after midnight,' her third daughter had said as cheerfully as she could, 'at least I'll have no trouble remembering its birthday!'

Hope checked in at the maternity wing and then, the pains having stopped as abruptly as they had arrived, she called her neighbour to ask

3

her to bring round the suitcase whenever she could.

'Fingers crossed!' said Imogen.

Hope moved away from the phone booth and was surrounded once more by the chaos on the maternity ward, more like a station in wartime than a hospital. Husbands and grandfathers, boyfriends and sons, small children who would have to be left with neighbours, neighbours arriving with small children who had already been left. And so many pregnant women coming and going, some with suitcases, some like Hope who had not had time to go home and were now queuing for one of the telephones to ask someone at home to bring in the carefully packed case with the talcum powder and the fresh nightdress, the bedroom slippers and the teddy bear.

The ward sister beckoned to her, and then, seeing Hope lean forward and give an involuntary gasp, caught her by the arm.

'Follow me, Mrs Merriott,' she said, looking back and smiling at the eternally moving but strangely quiet mêlée behind them. 'Spring bulge,' she added with a laugh. 'But Mr Macleod is here today, so you're in luck.'

Hope gasped. Luck. Of course. That was just what she needed.

In another five minutes she would be born.

Claire checked her last birthday present from her father to make sure. Five past two and counting. Another four minutes fifty-two seconds and – *wow!* – she would be coming into this world, exactly fourteen years ago.

'Claire?' her sister Rose groaned from under her duvet. 'Put out the light, OK?'

'No.' Four minutes and forty-seven.

'Put the light *out*!' Rose pulled her duvet higher over her mane of long dark hair and groaned again. 'Every year it's the same,' she complained. 'As if you were the only person in the whole world ever to have been born, for heaven's sake.'

'Three minutes.'

'Think of poor Mums.'

'She can do it in her sleep now.'

'I remember Mellie saying you nearly killed her.'

Melinda put her head round the door. 'You did, Claire, you nearly killed her.'

'Two minutes forty-eight seconds.'

'You arrived feet first.'

'I turned round at the last minute – just in time – two and a half minutes . . .'

Rose stood up. A tall, dark-haired girl with long legs and dark eyes, she made a terrific sight with a duvet wrapped around her. Even Claire, in the middle of her counting, could appreciate that.

'I'm going to sleep in Mellie's room, Claire. It's like sharing a room with the speaking clock being in here with you.'

'It's where you should be sleeping anyway.' Claire prepared to get out of bed to commemorate her arrival into the world. 'I don't mind if you want to go and sleep with Mellie.'

'You wanted me to sleep in here! You were the one having bad dreams!'

'Shush.'

But it was not another interruption from Rose that broke the silence but the sudden ringing of the telephone.

'God!' Rose, who had climbed back into bed, now sat bolt upright again. 'That might be Dads!'

'You go and see,' Claire suggested. 'I've still got just over a minute.'

'Verna will answer it.'

'Verna never hears anything.'

'God.' Rose sighed dramatically, jumped out of bed pulling her duvet around her, and staggered off to answer the telephone. 'Mums's probably nearly died again or something.'

'Forty-three seconds!' Claire's eyes narrowed. 'Forty-two forty-one forty!'

'Hello? Two six three oh?'

Melinda was by Rose's side. 'I'll take it—'

'Shhhh. It's Dads.'

'I'm born!' Claire yelled joyously from behind them both. 'Happy birthday to me! And not only am I born but I am fourteen at last, goodbye thirteen. Wow!'

'Shush! I can't hear Dads!' Rose turned to Melinda. 'He wants to speak to you.'

'Happy birthday to me! Happy birthday to me!' Claire sang, dancing round the landing.

'Shut it, Claire, OK?' Rose insisted, frowning hard. 'I'm trying to hear.'

'What is it? A boy or a girl?' Claire asked, coming to her sister's side and adjusting her wire-sided spectacles.

'Neither,' Rose replied, staring at Melinda who had lost all colour from her face. 'Yet. It's turned itself and got stuck.'

'It's nothing to worry about, darlings, really,' their father assured them on his end of the line, running a hand back through his thick dark hair. 'Really. Just remember, darlings, Mums's had one before. No, sorry, two before – or is it three?' he added, joking. 'Anyway, much better to give her another Caesarean, Alistair Macleod said. I'll explain it all when I come home, my angels. So. Really, there's nothing at all to worry about – nothing at all. They're doing it first thing in the morning, so go back to bed, and I'll wake you up with the good news.'

Alexander replaced the telephone and smiled wanly at the man, obviously yet another father, standing behind him. He hoped to God he had reassured them at home. He knew how much they worried, bless their cotton socks. They had all been knitting and sewing – in careful primrose or aquamarine, or navy blue – baby clothes for months. None of them minded in the least if it was a boy or a girl, *just so long as Mums's all right*. Nowadays fathers and children knew all about the risks of childbirth, not like in the old days, when it was all kept a mystery, and babies arriving seemed simply a matter for midwives and boiling kettles.

'I've never been able to understand that Catholic thing,' Alistair Macleod said the following morning to his anaesthetist, as the surgeon cut his way neatly across Hope's abdomen. 'Saving the baby and not the mother. It just doesn't make sense.'

Hope heard nothing of this. She was far away flying over beautiful green meadows filled with wild flowers while the medical staff drained off her amniotic fluid through a suction tube and began to ease the baby out through the eight-inch incision in her flesh.

A minute later the surgeon handed the newborn infant, still attached to its mother by the umbilical cord, to the nurse. They both looked down at the baby, registering its presence in this world, and wondering.

'Number four,' Alistair Macleod told Hope, an hour later, making sure to sound as cheerful as possible, as he placed her newest daughter in her arms, while Alexander stood with his back to her, staring out of the window.

'She has a beautiful face,' said Hope, at pains to sound as cheerful as the surgeon, yet in reality appalled at herself, at how she felt as she looked at her newest daughter. It was ridiculous. She felt as if she had done something terribly wrong, as if it was her fault that she had given birth to another one of her own sex.

'Wonderful to have a perfect baby . . .'

Hope nodded. 'She has a beautiful face,' she said again, and after a while, because there really was not much more to say, the surgeon left the three of them together. 'Hasn't she a beautiful face, Alex?'

'Absolutely beautiful, just like her mum.' Alexander leaned over and kissed his wife's oddly cold forehead. 'And, darling, you are not to worry about a single thing. Verna, the new Australian girl – she's a real goodie. So really, there's nothing to worry about at home. Nothing.'

Hope smiled, feeling that she wanted to go back nine months and start again.

She looked up at her absurdly handsome husband who was smiling down at her with such sweetness and warmth while he brushed some strands of her long blond hair away from her face. Alexander was so comforting. She was so lucky in him. Even so she stared out of the window, past him, unable to stop looking back. Before the baby everything had seemed so simple, but now it seemed suddenly far from so.

'Darling, all that matters at this moment is that the baby thrives and you get better.' This time Alexander leaned over and kissed Hope on the mouth. 'I'm just going to pop home and tell the girls – I think it's important that they don't hear from anyone else. Then I'll come back and look in on you before I toddle off to work.'

Hope nodded and then stared once more out of the window as Alexander went. It was so different for men. They could 'toddle off'. She thought of the girls at home, all waiting to look after the new baby, and the thought of them comforted her. It seemed to her that she could already hear them squabbling over who should feed their new sister. Everything would go on just as it had before – they would all just go on being as happy as they had been before, surely?

'Mr Merriott?' Alistair Macleod hailed Alexander as he walked across Reception. 'I was waiting in the hope of catching you.' The consultant gynaecologist smiled. He already knew Alexander by sight since they played tennis at the same club. He also knew he was what was known by other men's wives as 'quite a dish'. 'You already have, what is it? Three children, I believe?'

'Why?'

'Why indeed.' The surgeon took Alexander by the elbow to draw him aside. 'I'm sorry, Alexander – you don't mind if I call you Alexander?'

Alexander shook his head and smiled. Macleod was a nice man. Decent.

'In a way this should wait, but then it's going to have to be said some time, and the facts aren't going to alter in any meantime. The fact is, I doubt very much whether your wife – whether Hope – I would say, it would be – let us say *inadvisable* for her, in my view, to have any more babies after this. I mean, put it this way, if she was my wife, I would say, really, that this would be the time to stop. I'm sorry, but previous scars et cetera would make it quite unwise. I know you were both really longing for a boy, she told me, but really . . .' He tailed off.

Alexander tilted his head to one side and stared at the surgeon, only vaguely hearing him. 'When will you be certain?'

The surgeon stared at him. 'Not when, Mr Merriott, I *am* certain. I think you would find that anyone else you consulted would say exactly the same.' He cleared his throat and smiled. 'I mean, I know there is a woman in Ireland who holds the record at the Rotunda of thirteen Caesareans, and my wife has a cousin who has had six, but I would not swear to the poor creatures' quality of life, I really would not. Quite honestly, I would say that your wife, if she was my wife, deserves a rest now. Even though,' he ended with an attempt at a joke, 'it's not in my own interests to tell you so.'

That evening Alexander drove home in a hailstorm which he barely noticed. Poor, poor Hope, what a thing to happen. After such a long wait since Claire they had pinned so much on the baby's being a boy. Everything suddenly seemed to have gone pear-shaped.

'It doesn't matter, Dads, another girl doesn't matter,' Melinda said later, sensing her father's sadness and hugging one of his arms. 'Come on.

You know we shall love the baby anyway. Even more, probably.'

'Poor Mums.' Rose frowned. 'She is all right, isn't she?'

'She's fine. Just fine.'

'I don't think I shall bother having babies,' Claire said, taking her glasses off to clean the lenses on the hem of her nightgown. 'I really don't think I shall.'

'I shouldn't,' Alexander joked, suddenly smiling. 'I mean, look at you lot.'

With his arms round Claire and Melinda and Rose leading the way, they proceeded into the warmth of the long narrow kitchen where Melinda offered to make them all a hot drink. Alexander kissed her on the top of her head and demurred, fetching down a bottle of brandy instead.

'It's the man's fault if it's a girl, isn't it? The men determine the sex, don't they?' Rose asked her father.

'It isn't anyone's *fault*, darling,' Alexander smiled, pouring himself a glass of brandy. 'It's just what happens, that's all.'

'You know it's my birthday?' Claire asked him suddenly. 'You realize I am fourteen and baby is twelve hours or something, all at the same time? That means always sharing a cake with her – but I don't mind.'

'Really, Claire? Your birthday? I thought it was last week.'

'You are rotten, Dads.' Claire pushed her

spectacles up her nose, and then said with a happy smile, 'Aren't you going to wish me happy birthday?'

'No.'

'Oh. Why not?'

'Because I don't want to, Kipper.'

'Dads . . .' Melinda cajoled, because it seemed to her that Claire was about to take their father seriously, 'Claire is fourteen today.'

'I don't want to wish you happy anything, because I hate you.' Alexander growled like a dog, but opening his arms he hugged Claire to him. 'Happy birthday, Kipper.'

Melinda found Claire's presents and cards where Hope always put them once they were wrapped and written.

As Alexander piled the six parcels one on top of the other to carry them downstairs he felt a twinge of conscience that although he had signed the labels when Hope gave them to him, he had no idea what was inside.

Claire threw her arms round her father's neck to hug and kiss him while her sisters examined the book on Renoir and his paintings that he had apparently bought for her.

'It's just the book I wanted – absolutely.'

'That's two books on Renoir you've got now, Claire,' Rose said, starting to plait her dark hair rather tightly. 'You should be on "Mastermind" any day. Imagine, you may be the first really brainy blonde in this family.'

Melinda glanced at Rose. It was an old joke between them all that Claire was so bright and Melinda a bit of a plodder, but since it was her birthday she smiled at Claire before holding up her own present to her and urging her to open it.

It was a beautiful red blouson jacket from *Cache*, a shop in the high road, with a zip up the front and a fabulous padded black lining.

'How did you know, Mellie? How did you know I wanted this more than anything in the world?'

'Perhaps because you kept stopping in front of the shop and staring at it about a thousand times a day? It really is cool, though, right?'

'Cool, Mellie? It is *super-superior*-cool—'

'*And* super-expensive.'

Alexander's daughters were so close in age that they often reacted as one person. Now they all stared at him, frowning as one.

'You know I've been working at the café at the weekends, Dads.'

'Here's mine—' Rose quickly offered Claire her present to cover their embarrassment at Alexander's remarking on the cost of Mellie's gift.

At once Claire ripped off the wrapping to reveal a cap to match the jacket.

'Oh *yes*, Rose! Brilliant. Really brilliant! Thank you – thank you!'

She sprang up and down the kitchen to show

off how she looked, pretending to model the jacket and cap to the music on the radio.

As he sat drinking and watching his daughters, it occurred to Alexander that there was nothing they liked better than to make each other laugh. It was a charming sight. When all was said and done, he was very lucky, really.

'I'm off to bed, my darlings,' he announced with a sudden yawn and another look at his watch. 'Just the idea of being father to four beautiful daughters can tire a chap out, you know!'

They stopped laughing at this and kissed him goodnight, each in turn.

'My angels.'

The following morning as Hope lay still attached to drips and trying to get to grips with the pain of her latest Caesarean, Verna, their newly hired Australian nanny, cooked Alexander and the girls a perfect breakfast, and Hope's friend and neighbour Imogen paid her an early visit.

'Do they always give Caesareans a private room?' Imogen asked wonderingly, at the same time looking round for something to tidy in the already immaculate cubicle. 'Mind you, it's only sensible, I suppose. I say, love, do you think that drip should actually be like that? Half out of your arm? I'll ring for a nurse. I was reading some stats in the paper about how many accidents – fatal most of them – occur in hospital due to exactly this sort of thing.'

15

Before Hope could protest, Imogen had rung the bell for a nurse.

'It's only a saline drip, Imogen,' she muttered, trying to fix the wayward needle herself.

'How do you know?'

'Previous experience let's say,' Hope said, staring down at her newest baby in her cot, and making up her mind to love her as much as, if not more than, the others.

'Yes, well, you would know *rather* more than me about such things, Hope.' Imogen laughed, showing immaculate and healthy white teeth. 'Hope four, Imogen nil.'

'You don't want babies, do you, Imogen?'

'Not yet I don't. I don't even want to get married until you can predetermine the sex of babies. Any minute, though, they say, and we shall all be choosing. Alexander was longing for a boy, wasn't he?' She stopped, and seeing Hope's face she reddened and turned her attention to the small bunch of freesias she had brought in for the patient.

'What I mean was having babies needn't be – shouldn't be – such a lottery. Not nowadays. Not given the amount of engineering and mucking about they can do. Working mothers should be able to say – OK. What I want is two m one f, or one m one f – or whatever – and go for it. Rather than playing Russian roulette. Do you want a drink or anything? Some more juice? You're looking a little peaky, sweetie – ah, and here's the nurse. Nurse—'

Imogen pointed out what she considered to be the ill-fitting drip, only for the nurse to demonstrate that the drip was still properly in place and that it was only the sticking plaster that had come off.

While the two women fussed over her, Hope turned her head away and stared at the wall, thinking about her new unnamed child, yet another little girl. She remembered Alexander's words – *Darling sweetheart. Just this once – this time let's find out the sex – it's not as if it's going to spoil anything? Please?*

But Hope had refused to have the baby's gender disclosed. After so many miscarriages, after all those years of trying between Claire's birth and this one, it had seemed utterly wrong to care a jot what sex the baby was! All that had mattered to her was that it should be well, and whole, and be born with all its fingers and toes, and have a happy, healthy life.

It was only when she was well into her pregnancy that she had discovered just how much it meant to Alexander that this baby should be a male. For some reason, perhaps because she herself had just been so pleased to be healthily pregnant at last, she simply had not seen what she could now see, all too clearly, in retrospect. Alexander had not, as she had, longed for another *baby*, he had quite simply wanted a boy.

'Hope?'

She felt Imogen's hand on her shoulder and turned back to her.

'It was OK. At least the nurse said it was OK, but she still had to check the drip. Don't worry, your proto-feminist friend is on the case, OK?'

Hope smiled weakly at her neighbour, finding herself wondering idly what on earth *proto-feminist* actually meant, just as she sometimes wondered, admittedly without a great deal of interest, what on earth *post-modernism* could possibly mean. Then she told Mogs – as Alexander liked to call Imogen behind her back – that she was feeling a little tired and would like to rest.

'I haven't really seen baby, have I?' Imogen protested into her huge leather sack of a bag as she double-checked her belongings. 'Can I just have one proper peek before I go, Hope?'

Hope smiled her assent and, leaning over to the crib close by her bed, took a look for herself at the peacefully sleeping infant.

'Pretty, pretty – no, not just pretty – *beautiful*,' Imogen whispered as she stared into the cot.

'Goodness, I am tired. I think I'm getting too old for this lark.'

'Of course you're tired, Hope darling. Still,' Imogen straightened up, 'not as tired as if you'd had it normally, of course. None of that awful pushing and shoving, just a nice slice and out for the count, and all better now.'

Hope nodded, wondering how anyone who had not had a Caesarean could possibly say *all better now*. This was her fourth Caesarean, and just at that moment it felt like four too many.

'I'll look in again later if I can,' Imogen said, straightening Hope's sheets. 'And I'll pop in and say hi to the children. Meanwhile I'll say 'bye, love.'

As she went clattering out of the room Hope found herself fleetingly envying Imogen her independence, her smart clothes, her career, no operations. Really, when she thought about it, Imogen did not have to be a boy, nor did she have to give birth to them – she had it all.

Rose too had often thought that she was meant to have been a boy. Not from anything either of her parents had ever said, but because it just seemed so obvious. Melinda was the first-born and their parents would have accepted the fact that she was a girl with a good grace – but when their mother had become pregnant again it was obvious that she and their father would have been hoping for a boy. It was only natural. She and Mellie had often talked about it, wondering what difference it would have made.

Not that they minded about it or anything, and not that their parents seemed to mind either, and not that they thought their life needed changing in any way since they were so loved by both their parents, but every now and again they couldn't help wondering exactly what it might have meant had Rose been born *Robert*, which was

19

the name they had found underlined in the baby book Hope had bought before she was born. Robert. Rose was tall. She would have been a tall Robert. And dark like their father; and he would have taught her to play cricket, not taken her to dancing class.

'I feel so sorry for Dads,' Melinda sometimes said. 'I'm sure he'd like a boy – someone to kick a football around with, or whatever.'

'Except Dads doesn't like football,' Rose always reminded her.

'That's true,' Melinda had replied. 'And now I think about it, girls play football now. Do you still want to be a ballerina?'

'Yes. Why?'

'Nothing. Just that the other night Dads said Mums wasn't all that keen. She thinks it's a very demanding and difficult world, and she's not sure she wants you growing up in it.'

'Doesn't sound like Mums.' Rose pulled a face. 'I mean, it's because Mums was a dancer herself that I was so interested in the first place. That can't be right, surely?'

'I'm only telling you what I heard Dads saying.'

'But Mums only gave up dancing for us. To have us, rather. She loved dancing at Covent Garden.'

'I know.' Melinda shrugged. 'But people change.'

'But I've got my audition coming up for the school. If Mums wasn't keen, surely she wouldn't be putting me through all this – auditioning and getting my hopes up and everything, not if she's planning on turning round later and saying *I don't think I want you dancing after all, Rose*. I mean – you know me, Mellie! It's like you and horses! Dancing's everything to me – it's all I've ever wanted to do. And just the thought of not being allowed to do it – I'd kill myself.'

'Of course you wouldn't, Rose,' Melinda sighed. 'But I know just what you mean.'

'Perhaps it was Dads?'

'Dads?' Melinda stared in astonishment at her sister. *'Dads?* If you wanted to – I don't know – what's the worst thing in the world to want to be?'

'A prostitute?'

'No,' Melinda said slowly with a smile. 'No, I don't think even Dads would wear that – but you know what I mean. Dads wouldn't stop any of us from doing something we *really* wanted to do. I mean Dads is brilliant like that.'

Imogen had asked Alexander next door for a 'kitchen supper' and plenty of wine and sympathy. Hope knew all about it, Alexander knew all about it, they had all planned that Imogen would 'look after' Alexander when Hope was 'taken in'.

'I suppose you mind dreadfully, you poor sweetie? About having yet another girl?'

Imogen had always fancied – a very Imogen word – Alexander. Ever since she had moved in next door to the charming Merriott family she had kept a firm eye on him. Tall, ridiculously handsome, and in the habit of smiling at the world as if he was a lazy tiger and the planet his basket, he had been earmarked, all along, for what she thought of as 'her moment', and once she saw Hope pregnant, nine long months ago, she had planned that moment. And tonight, thank God, was it.

Different, of course, if Hope had given birth to a boy – in that case the outcome of this evening would be far from a foregone conclusion. But, bless her cotton socks, Hope was now out of the picture, lying in hospital half a mile away, all doped up after her operation, while Imogen was lying across her Victorian chaise longue in a crushed velvet dress with a thick black ribbon round her throat and soaked in *Heartless* by Ramona Lacache. There was simply no contest, but even so she had to be at pains to look sympathetic and loving, most of all towards Hope.

'And I suppose Hope, although she is being *so* brave about it, I suppose she minds too dreadfully too, though she won't say, because, let's face it, that's Hope.'

'What difference does minding make, Imogen?' Alexander wondered, smiling. 'Minding hardly ever changed the course of history.'

'Even so, I remember you saying that you were praying for a boy, you told me yourself.'

'There was always a fifty-fifty chance it would be one or the other, and it turned out to be the other. Still, we can always try again.'

Alexander looked across at their neighbour. Imogen – so opinionated, at times horrendously so – had always rather bored him, but this evening, what with Hope in hospital and yet another girl to bring up, he somehow could not remember how irritating he had always found her. Particularly not after two martinis.

'I've cooked your favourite supper – chilli con carne with sour cream and grated cheese. Hope gave me the recipe months ago, and I've been practising.'

Imogen's scent floated across to Alexander. It was exquisite, musky and subtle.

'What is that perfume you're wearing?'

'*Heartless.*' Imogen looked down at her victim for a few seconds, and then threw back her head and laughed.

As she did so Alexander could not help noticing the little bumps under her velvet dress where her suspenders were, doubtless, holding up her stockings.

'*Heartless,*' he murmured, after she had left the room. And he too laughed, the martinis and the fire making the name of the perfume seem strangely amusing, like an 'in joke' that only Imogen and himself could appreciate. '*Heartless,*' he repeated, and once more the name appealed as being inordinately funny.

Imogen's kitchen, like the Merriotts', was at the back of her semi-detached house, but unlike the Merriotts' it was spanking new, brimful of the latest magazine ideas. Following her from her all-white drawing room, Alexander appreciated all the more the tasteful pale aqua paint and the units especially carved by Selward and Brimley, the most modish of all kitchen designers. The basket drawers, the old Victorian clock above the small cream Aga, and the array of gleaming copper pots on the shelves above – her kitchen was utterly devoid of homework, nannies, cats and ringing telephones. It was also, thankfully, devoid of girls. Here Alexander could speak and be heard, and goodness Imogen listened. She listened not just with her ears, but with her whole face and body, and Alexander felt grateful to her.

She *understood* him, she really understood him. She understood what it was like to get out there and really, really have to struggle – something Hope could not truly understand, because she had never had to do it. She had never had to *get out there*.

Imogen kept using the phrase as she poured wine into Alexander's very tall, very large glass. They both knew what it was like to *get out there*. The supper was quite excellent. Despite having cooked it, even Imogen was enjoying it, and what was more, in the candlelight, Alexander was looking even more handsome than usual, so handsome that whatever he was feeling for her, she was melting.

'Oh, but should we?'

'Oh, yes, yes, yes!'

It was the moment that Imogen had imagined for nine whole months, and now it was upon her. Alexander and she were kissing, and then they were undressing, all the way up the stairs and into her incredibly sexy bedroom with its black iron-work four-poster bed, its white drapes – she loved white because it showed up your clothes so beautifully – and its polished Italian tiled floor which had been so expensive, but worth it.

Just as Alexander's love-making was worth it. Every single second was just as she had hoped, and feared. He was fantastic. He made love as if it was the first time for him, and for her, and she knew that she would never meet another man with so much to give. She would never have believed it possible, but it was true.

Imogen lay back against her pillows.

It had been worth waiting for this. Every single solitary day of the nine months Hope had been pregnant had been worth it.

Out of the darkness of her satiated state she heard Alexander saying as he started to dress once more, 'My God, Imogen, I should never, ever, have done this!'

Imogen could not have agreed with him less.

Hope returned home with her new baby after a week in the hospital, collected by Imogen in her immaculately clean black VW Golf GTI. She sat in the back with the baby in her arms, trying not to breathe in her overpowering scent – *Restless* or whatever it was called – a passion for which Hope could not share.

'Decided on a name yet?' Imogen asked, never taking her eyes off the road in front.

'Oh, the girls and I will do that,' Hope replied, closing her eyes so as not to see the risks Imogen was taking. 'And Alexander, of course.'

'I hear Alexander was thinking of "Letitia",' Imogen said thoughtlessly, then glanced quickly in her driving mirror, seeing Hope catching the look. 'At least, when I popped in to see the girls the other night, that's what they said.'

'I like "Letitia",' Hope said, and she smiled, knowing that Alexander must have been at her book of baby names, since Letitia had been one of the many names three-starred for Claire, the last time. 'I had a great friend at— an old friend of mine was called "Letitia".'

'At where?' Imogen persisted, on to the fact that Hope was covering up. 'School, you mean? A school friend, was she?'

'Yes.'

'Which school did you go to?'

'Royal Lodge.'

'God – the ballet school, of course. I keep forgetting. You were at Royal Lodge.'

'That's right.'

'I'd forgotten you were going to be a dancer.'

'No, I actually was a dancer, actually!'

Hope saw Imogen glance up again into her driving mirror.

'Bus,' Hope called, holding her newborn tight. 'Turning out in front.'

'It's OK – I saw it. No panic. Thanks. No problem. How long – how long did you dance? For?'

'Long enough.'

'I'd just forgotten you used to dance, that's all.'

'Of course – why should you remember?' She yawned, putting her hand in front of her mouth. 'Sorry!'

'Hope, darling, please! You've just had a baby!'

No I haven't, Hope thought. *I've just had yet another little girl.*

Chapter Two

'Everything in its own time, darling.' Alexander smiled at his wife, who had just asked whether 'Letitia' should be christened 'Letitia' or 'Daisy', the corners of his eyes creasing as he spoke.

Like most things about Alexander, his even-featured face, white teeth, and slim figure, Alexander's smile was perfect – a mix of lazy charm, sweet good nature, and beguiling humour. When he had first smiled his perfect smile at Hope – eyes first, then a slow widening of that perfect mouth, finally showing a set of perfectly even snow-white teeth – Hope had fallen instantly in love. She worshipped smiles, probably because when she was growing up her father had rarely smiled and her mother never, at least not at her. And of course her ballet training had encouraged such a serious attitude, while at home her father, once her mother had run off with a publican, had never smiled again; small wonder, therefore, that when she met the handsome, charming and above all laughing Alexander Merriott she had fallen immediately and hopelessly in love.

Alexander leaned over and kissed Hope long and lingeringly, feeling, if anything, more passionately affectionate towards her than ever, suddenly wondering whether his male friends were not after all right in their frequent assertion that a 'little fling', as they always called it, made them feel even more loving towards their wives.

'I'll leave all that to you, darling. You're wonderful with the girls, really you are.'

Hope nodded, and then, looking down at the tiny child in her arms, wondered aloud, yet again, about a name for her.

Alexander got up from off the bed and stretched. 'Diaspora,' he announced. 'I like names ending in "a" best.'

'Oh, Alex! You say that every time the subject comes up. We must decide on a name for her, or people will feel we simply don't care, that we were counting on having a boy, and didn't want another girl.'

She looked across at her elegant husband, who was now gazing at his own reflection – as well he might, she thought affectionately, because when it came to Alexander's looks they were both ardent fans.

'Thank you, darling,' Alexander said, talking to her through the mirror. 'If there's one sure fire way of killing a joke for good it's to point out that it is old.'

But, seeing the defeated look in his wife's eyes, he immediately sat back down on the bed and, with a sigh, took hold of one set of Hope's toes through the bedclothes and wiggled them affectionately.

'No, I mean it. I don't know how you put up with me.'

Hope looked at him. 'It doesn't really matter, does it?' she asked. 'About her being a girl? It is still wonderful to have a new baby after all this time. Isn't it?'

'Of course it is.' Alexander squeezed her toes and got up once again from the bed. 'Anyway – c'est la vie. These things happen, darling. We're just getting someone else's share of girls. Now. I have to go out. I have an appointment with a man who I've been told has money to burn. Wants in on the trout farm in Scotland, I'm happy to tell you. I just hope he never takes the night train to Oban and finds out the problems. You are going to be all right now, aren't you?' He said this last as a question but did not wait for any reply, because he was already late, and awfully afraid that the man concerned was merely playing him along.

'You are going to be all right?' he called once again from the door.

Hope smiled at him. He always asked that question before he left the house. It was one of his most endearing habits.

The question Alexander asked his father's lawyer the following week was altogether different.

'That is the way it was ordained, Mr Merriott,' came the reply. 'Whether one considers it fair or unfair, mad or wise, that is the way it was

30

ordained – and there is precious little one can do to effect any change.'

'Meaning there is nothing one can do about it, Mr Wilson – full stop.'

'Exactly so, Mr Merriott.'

'One lives in hope that there will be a change – that something will change. That somebody will come to their senses about this matter.'

'Isn't it a little too late for that, Mr Merriott?'

'It is never too late for anything, Mr Wilson. The goalposts are being moved all the time in our country, everywhere. Particularly in cases as absurd as this.'

'It might seem absurd to you, Mr Merriott. It might seem absurd to me. But to your respected father it obviously makes perfect sense.'

'One has heard of wills being . . . re-written, even after death.'

'Not in cases like this, Mr Merriott. No, no – I am very much afraid not. Besides, it is not the practice here. Your family – the Merriotts – have been looked after by us for many years now.'

Alexander pushed his chair back, putting his hand up to his mouth to stifle a yawn. 'Excuse me. New baby.'

'Having never had that problem, Mr Merriott,' Mr Wilson replied, getting to his feet, 'I can only say I envy you, whatever the outcome.'

Alexander thought of his house teeming with young girls, of his newest and most beautiful daughter, and yet again sighed inwardly. It was not that he did not love his daughters, all of them, it was just that his own father did not like them. That was just how it was. Merriotts had to be male to inherit.

'What a pretty little baby,' the elegant, red-haired woman exclaimed as Hope carefully placed Letty's carrycot on the floor beside her chair in the highly polished hallway. 'How old is she?'

'Six weeks,' Hope replied, sitting back and brushing her hair from her eyes. 'Thank you. Yes, she is a pretty little thing, isn't she?'

'I have two little girls,' the woman volunteered. 'Jemima and Rosanne.'

'I have a Rose,' Hope told her. 'In fact it's Rose who's here. To audition.'

'How old would Rose be?'

'Rose is fifteen. Here she comes now.'

Rose appeared from the changing room opposite, dressed in a black leotard, pale tights, and new pink ballet shoes her mother had given her for her birthday and with her ever growing long dark hair tied up on the top of her head by a black velvet ribbon. Hope picked up the cross-over cardigan she had left on the chair and draped it round Rose's shoulders for her. Rose was tall, dark and beautiful, and never more so than when she was as anxious as she was now.

'What is your daughter going to dance for them?' the red-haired woman wondered, most of her attention still on Letty.

'What everyone is, I imagine,' Rose muttered nervously, with a look to her mother. '*The Dying Swan.*'

'It doesn't matter. It's how you dance it that counts. They're not judging you on the music. You didn't write the music.'

'I know, Mums. But Miss Somerville said everyone will be dancing it.'

'It's the piece you do best. That's what counts.'

'Oh – what a dear little hand!' the red-haired woman exclaimed to Letty.

'Rose Merriott?' a voice called from down the hall.

'Good luck, sweetie. Blow them away.'

Rose managed a tight smile in return, slipped her white cardigan from her shoulders, and pattered her way down the shining corridor to where another woman was waiting at an open door.

'You have to feel sorry for them,' Hope's neighbour said. 'No-one knows what they go through, poor kids.'

Hope was about to say that, having been a dancer herself, she knew just what Rose would be going through, but remembered how such an admission usually led to a lot of awkward questions about why she had not continued with it. Instead she picked up a book and started to read.

'So you have two girls, like me.' The woman could not leave the subject alone.

Hope looked up, finally fed up. 'No, *four*, actually.'

'Four! Oh dear, your poor husband! He must get terribly teased at the pub.' As Hope looked openly bewildered, she added kindly, 'Don't you know, love? If men only have girls, it means they're not *real* men.'

Alexander sat drumming his fingers on the chrome bar top and looked at his reflection in the mirror behind the row of bottles. As always the sight of his own image cheered him immensely, and only yesterday Imogen had told him that he was one of those lucky men who got even better-looking as they got older.

Not that he was going grey at the temples yet – far from it. His hair, which he wore swept straight back, was as black and as thick and lustrous as ever, but at thirty-eight his face was just beginning to show experience. In his twenties he always thought his boyish good looks counted against him, since in the final analysis a lot of his women admirers failed to take him as utterly seriously as he had wanted them to, feeling – he always reckoned – that because he looked so absurdly young it must follow that he was feckless. But now that lines were appearing at the corners of his eyes and interesting dark shadows under them, and his cheeks had hollowed out so satisfactorily, Alexander looked much more the part he was intent on playing – part gambler, part roué.

The only thing which was spoiling this otherwise perfect moment was that she for whom he was waiting was late, so late that he had actually had time to enjoy a fantasy or two about some of the pretty women who seemed to be intent on passing by his part of the bar. Sirens all of them, but very pretty, or so it seemed to a bored man fresh from his father's lawyer.

'Another glass of white wine,' Alexander ordered, 'And this time I would infinitely prefer if it were properly chilled.'

When she finally arrived ten minutes later, Alexander was pleased to see Imogen was wearing a long dark brown light wool dress with some sort of honeycombed texture bodice, which showed off to perfection the soft roundness of her stomach and her small firm breasts. She swung into the bar with the easy gait of a woman who knows that the man will wait for her, and wait for good and long if she so wishes. As he watched her Alexander wished that she was not looking so terribly attractive, but fresh from the office of the wretched Mr Wilson and his interminable intransigence, he felt like going to the devil in the arms of a passionate woman. Mr Wilson would have that effect on a saint.

Imogen was Alexander's first affair, and he had not expected to be so hooked by it – not, of course, that he *was* hooked by it, but really he had never realized until now that he was *quite* so attractive as she had made him feel, or *quite* so handsome as she kept insisting that he was. He could not help realizing, much as he tried hard not to, that after he had been with Imogen he felt – what was it that Melinda would say? – he felt he was the *cat's pyjamas*.

In fact he had promised himself, after that first evening, that he would definitely not continue the affair. He loved Hope and he loved his daughters, and he certainly did not need another woman in his life. But it was not as easy to give up an alluring and beautiful woman as he had first hoped. Particularly not one who lived so nearby and was so chic, so *soignée*, so full of sympathy, and, most of all, understood his world, and his problems. How terribly, terribly difficult it was to make money – money enough to house and feed not only three girls, but four.

And then again West Dean Drive now seemed to be teeming with babies and nannies – not to mention teenage daughters who were all busy growing so fast that sometimes he thought they would grow straight through the roof like shot plants in a greenhouse.

And to cap it all he had not been able to make love to Hope for six whole weeks, and might have to wait even longer, the doctor had said, so – well, so it was nice – to make love was so *nice*. And Imogen had fallen into the habit of booking hotel rooms so that they could carry on their affair near to her office, and there was something about hotel rooms that was so conducive to affairs, their anonymity, their pristine cleanliness, the room service that just came and went so silently leaving lovers to be so intimate, and, sometimes, so daring. They had been to an hotel only the week before that Imogen had told him was designed *only for that*, and it had been – well, delicious really. And Imogen, being a professional woman, had paid, which was also delicious, as well as a change, to have someone pay for him rather than having always to be putting his hand in his pocket.

'You look very good indeed, Mogs. In fact you look altogether perfect,' Alexander said, appraising her. 'From that dear little velvet cloche hat—'

'It's wool felt actually,' Imogen corrected him, rummaging in her handbag.

'To those very sexy boots.'

'They're Peruvian, actually.'

Alexander called for his tab, spreading some money out on the counter.

'You may not have noticed, Alex, but I have only just arrived.'

'Thirty-five minutes late.'

'The traffic was terrible.'

'I got here on time. Now come along.'

He took her arm on the rise, steering her towards the café door as the barman muttered dark imprecations behind his back at the lack of any gratuity.

'Where is the *fire*, Alexander, please?' Imogen insisted as she pulled her arm free from his hold.

'In the Hotel Utopia, I hope,' Alexander replied, scanning the street for a cab.

She stopped and sighed, staring at him in a challenging manner. 'I would quite like to talk, actually.'

'We can talk in the taxi.'

'About us.'

Alexander frowned and looked round at the tall, slender woman beside him. *Why – he wondered – are so many good-looking women born with no minds? Or is it perhaps because they are born beautiful that they never bother improving their grey matter?* Deciding the latter was most probably the case, he pulled the cab door open, gave the driver directions and climbed ahead of her into the back.

'Thank you,' Imogen said pointedly, although she did laugh.

'You're a feminist, Imogen,' Alexander reminded her, smiling. 'This is the last of the eighties, remember? You are meant to be a proto-feminist career girl with plenty of attitude and a briefcase with your initials on who has it *all*. That sort of thing not only doesn't matter any more, you are meant to prefer it.'

Imogen eyed him and smiled, for Imogen, almost demurely.

'I really do think we should talk,' she said, taking out a paper tissue and lightly touching her nose with it, more to gain time to think than anything else.

'You haven't got a cold, have you?' Alexander enquired. 'I can't risk catching a cold, not with a new baby.'

'I have not got a cold, Alex, and I am not even getting one. This is simply the result of traffic fumes. You know that. They always have this effect on me.'

'I didn't know that – I really did not know that.'

Alexander pushed himself deeper into the corner of the cab and watched a particularly pretty brunette in a long red suede coat sashaying into Harrods. Had the taxi not still been moving he realized to his utter amazement that he would have climbed out of it and followed her.

'We have to talk about you and Hope,' Imogen was saying. 'Or rather we have to talk about you and Hope and me. You owe it to me, I owe it to you, we owe it to each other. We should really put our relationship on some sort of firm footing, don't you think? Not that I want to rock the boat—'

'In this case don't you mean cradle?'

'You know where I'm coming from,' Imogen said and she gazed into his eyes in a way that Alexander suddenly found embarrassing, just as, equally suddenly, he found her perfume cloying, suffocating, and the nails of her hand which was pressing his arm were no longer long red-painted shiny nails but talons.

'I know where you're coming from,' Alexander mused, gazing out of the window as the taxi stopped again just beyond Brompton Road tube station. 'But the trouble is I don't know where I'm going to – but it can't be here. Look, we'll have a really long talk about how we are, and how we may be going to be, but – my God, I've suddenly remembered my meeting!' He waved his leather organizer at Imogen. 'Look, sweetheart, let's meet tomorrow, all right? You know, same time, same place, only this time be on time!'

At which he jumped out of the mercifully unsecured taxi, closed the door, and was gone across the road and through the traffic and into the entrance of the tube station before Imogen had the chance to follow, waiting just inside the subway until he was sure it was quite safe to re-emerge. Once reassured, and back in daylight, he sauntered across Hans Place and into the side entrance of Harrods.

He had no idea what he was doing other than escaping from Imogen, so he wandered aimlessly around the ground floor of the shop looking at everything from food to men's clothing with absolutely no interest. At the back of his mind was the very faint hope that he just might bump into the luscious brunette in the red suede coat but of course he did not, finding himself instead at the end of his short odyssey looking for a place to sit at the little coffee bar in the corner of the food halls.

'Excuse me,' he said, standing by an empty stool. 'Is this taken?'

'I wouldn't say so, would you?' an American voice replied. 'If it was I doubt it would still be here.'

As he sat Alexander took a glance at his neighbour. She was a tall redhead dressed in what looked like only a fabulous phoney silver fox fur coat, since he could see no sign of any other garment apart from stockings and bright red leather shoes. He put her in her late thirties and, from her expensive accessories and jewellery, very rich. She even smelt rich – probably some perfume privately mixed especially for her. But what took his fancy more than anything was what she was reading, propped up against the sugar bowl in front of her – a book of poetry.

'A jug of wine, a book of verse,' he said casually.

'I'm not reading Fitzgerald,' she replied. 'Robert Frost as it happens.'

'Only thing I know about Mr Frost was that once apparently when he was watching the sunset from his veranda,' Alexander said slowly, examining the menu card, 'a young woman exclaimed, *Oh, what a lovely sunset!* To which your poet friend replied, *I never discuss business after dinner.*'

He knew the woman was looking at him but he paid her no attention, putting down the menu card and nodding to the waiter instead.

'I feel like a drink,' he heard her saying, before he could get his order in. 'You know? Do you know where the Carlton Hotel is? Care for a drink?'

'Yes, but I shouldn't,' Alexander said, with only the suspicion of a sigh.

'Sure you shouldn't,' the woman replied. 'That's why you will.'

He followed her until they came to the exit into Brompton Road, always just a step or so behind her. For her part she never looked round at him once.

'Don't you want to do any more shopping?' he asked, once he was beside her, both their hands on the doors to the street.

'Afterwards,' the woman answered. 'If I shop before I have a drink I look at all the price tags. Afterwards, I don't give a goddam.'

Amazed at the change in himself Alexander realized that she was not the only one not to give a damn. As he followed her out into the rain-sodden afternoon, neither did he.

'They want me to come back again next week for the second lot of auditions, so I'm still in with a chance,' Rose called to her mother before she had even reached Hope's chair, sliding the rest of the way on the flat of her ballet shoes.

'But that's wonderful, Rose,' Hope said, kissing her daughter. 'Well done. So *The Dying Swan* wasn't such a dead duck after all.'

Rose looked at her mother with a frown. 'You really are pleased, aren't you?' she asked. 'I mean you really want me to go on dancing?'

'Of course I do,' Hope answered, only half

listening. 'You know I do. Now on with this cardigan – and your leggings. We don't want you getting cramps.'

'Can we ring and tell Dads that I've been asked back?' Rose asked, turning a pair of anxious dark eyes on her mother.

'Later, sweetheart. He's got important meetings all day. And if you're going to get in here, they're going to have to be successful ones too. Places like this cost money.'

And the Lord alone knows where that's going to come from. Hope had long given up any attempt to try to persuade Alexander that they simply could not afford to educate the girls privately, because Alexander would hear none of it. As far as he was concerned the girls were Merriotts and Merriotts were educated privately; every one of his children should be given the best, up to and including their boy, when they had him.

Hope, like many women married to men who play the money markets, had no clear idea of what her husband's work exactly entailed. Ever since they married Alexander had taken over the running of their financial life entirely. All she really knew was that he worked with money – or rather *in* money, as Alexander called it – as a money broker at first, which was way beyond her financial comprehension, then as an investment adviser which she found a little less obscure, scheme-brokering to be precise, which it seemed meant finding the money to put into other people's

43

notional businesses. Finally he had graduated to something they called *market-monitoring*, which apparently involved listening to the financial bush telegraph and buying not just early, but before anyone else was even half awake.

Originally he had worked from an office in a large block in a newly developed portion of the City, but Hope had never been there, and indeed by the time she suggested meeting Alexander at his office for lunch one day he told her that he had moved to another job in yet another large building, this time on some upwardly fashionable wharf where he had a telephone line, a fax and a secretary who answered his phone.

At least the modernization of the five-bedroom semi-detached Edwardian house they had bought four years earlier was now practically finished, but here too Alexander had not skimped on the work, never once stopping to query the cost of anything. The result was a house which some of their older neighbours had more than hinted had no *place* in West Dean Drive, something which whenever they repeated it to each other always made Alexander and Hope laugh.

It had all started off quite simply with a plan to convert the house with one eye on sympathetic restoration and the other on their immediate environment and growing family. Alexander, however, being Alexander, soon forgot all about his good intentions and proceeded to throw an inordinate amount of money at what was after all only a modest sort of house, built at the turn of the century for retired gentlefolk, not for Mrs Thatcher's brat-packers. Within sixteen months they had added a hand-built and expensively tiled conservatory, put a pine-clad studio cum office in the roof, built on a morning room extension to the kitchen, knocked the two reception rooms into one large one, walled and floodlit the garden, painted the house bright yellow, sunk an illuminated ornamental fishpond in the front garden, replaced all the charming old leaded lights with picture windows and installed large pull-down striped awnings above them. Privately Hope felt that they had gone too far, spent too much, but to Alexander his house was a status symbol, and if he could not live grandly in an expensive house then he had to live grandly in a cheap one.

Not that Alexander would not have far preferred to live in a large detached house with a swimming pool, and extensive grounds, and indeed, Hope realized long afterwards, he had, when he married her, believed that within a few years that would be the case. Since Hope was the only surviving child of her parents' marriage, Alexander had taken it for granted that his wife would inherit all her father's money. Hope's father was a wealthy man, having himself come into a not inconsiderable sum from his own father, who had been a self-made businessman.

To give him his due, Alexander was no snob,

and had no prejudice against inheriting his father-in-law's money from wherever it came. What mattered to him was that it was safe to assume that even were Hope perhaps not to be left the whole of her father's fortune, she must at least expect a reasonable inheritance, and – when the size of the family fortune was taken into consideration – one surely large enough to pay for many of the things they found so hard to pay for now.

So when Hope's father had died prematurely only two years after she and Alexander were married, having long ago divorced Hope's mother on account of her sudden and scandalous adultery, while she mourned the passing of a man who had hardly ever addressed a civil word to her, Alexander began to count his chickens. Unfortunately for them both, they did not hatch.

Hope's father left her nothing, or near to nothing compared to her husband's expectations, but willed the bulk of all he had to his eldest nephew, his fortune therefore returning to a male, in line, it seemed with his own father's wishes.

Consequently, although to Hope it came as no surprise when she was told that her father had made no provision for her in his will other than a small bequest, Alexander was actually outraged. He urged Hope to contest the will, but there was little point in doing so, as their lawyer pointed out, since the will was in perfect legal order.

'My father wanted a son, not a daughter. So why should he leave me his money? In fact I'm astonished he left me anything at all. What was his was his to do with as he wished. None of it by *right* belonged to me. I was only his daughter.'

Publicly Alexander had pretended to understand but privately he had been infuriated, because although he had truly fallen in love with Hope, who was as intelligent as she was pretty, and whom he had loved and did love with all his heart, his attraction to her had been more than doubled by the apparent promise of a large inheritance to come.

In fact so great had been his private anger that for many weeks after her father's death, Alexander considered pursuing a claim against the estate on Hope's behalf, and was finally only prevented from doing so by the death of his seemingly indestructible old grandfather. When his will was duly read, it emerged that he had left a fortune to Alexander's father, who would duly pass that fortune to Alexander himself – but only upon the birth of a grandson who would continue the Merriott name.

'Supposing Hope and I can't have a son?' Alexander had wanted to know. And in the long silence that followed he had heard himself finally filling it with, 'Well, if that happens, I suppose I could always divorce her, and try again?'

'The Merriotts do not divorce, no matter what the fashion. There has never been a divorce in this family.'

'So what next – just try again, I suppose?'

'If you have twelve daughters, they will all be down to you. Produce a son and the money will pass to you. That's how it is. The Merriott name goes on through the male line – the Merriotts have sons.'

Alexander never told Hope of the condition in his father's will, his private excuse being, as daughter after daughter was born within three years of each other, that it might put too much pressure on her. Besides, he loved her too much to want her to know just how much future financial happiness might be riding on the sex of their next child. He had reasoned to himself that it was bad enough having a baby; and since her refusal to contest her own father's will he felt in some ways that she had forfeited the right to know about *his* father's will. It was not exactly a revenge, but it was not exactly not a revenge either.

Even so, his approach to this last pregnancy had been very different. This time he had tried to make it quite, quite clear that after such a long gap a son was very important to him, although he still did not think it right to indicate just *how* important, or just *how* much money might be riding on his wish for a male heir. Not a kingship perhaps, but an awful lot of money.

'Guess what – Rose got called back!' Hope told Alexander when he walked into the house an hour late for dinner.

For a moment he stared at her blankly, not just

as if he had no idea what she was talking about but – worse – as if she was a total stranger, before suddenly focusing himself, shaking his head and smiling his beautiful smile.

'Darling – forgive me,' he said, picking a cashew nut out of the dish Melinda had just brought in for him. 'I have so much on my mind – and it really has been one of those days. The consortium I thought I had all nicely set up has gone cold on the project.'

'Which project?' Melinda asked, sitting down cross-legged on the floor in front of him.

'Nothing you would understand,' her father replied, holding up a nut and then throwing it to his eldest as if she was a dog.

'Try me,' Hope suggested before putting up a hand to stop Alexander throwing her a nut as well. 'No, I didn't mean that, Alex. Tell me which project is in trouble.'

'Oh, it doesn't matter,' Alexander sighed, before grinning boyishly. 'There'll be another one along in a minute.'

'Project? Or consortium?'

'Both. Tell me about Rose.'

Hope began to, but Alexander's eyes shifted restlessly after only a few seconds. He always found it very difficult to concentrate on any interests other than his own, and even as she was speaking his mind was shifting back to the wondrous afternoon he had spent with the woman in the phoney fox fur coat. A fantasy, a pure fantasy, had actually happened to him. The kind of fantasy that he had always thought never would happen, for he had married young, and until Imogen it had never occurred to him to have affairs. Now suddenly a whole new world seemed to be opening up for him out there, a world where, he realized, women did actually find him irresistible.

'Early days still,' he said, as Hope finished speaking. It seemed a pretty safe thing to say. 'And I mean,' he went on, quickly realizing that more was obviously needed, 'I mean, that's only one audition. And the competition is fierce.'

'Still. I think Rose deserves to be congratulated.'

'I think she deserves a medal,' Melinda said. 'I think things like that must be gross.'

'Gross?' her father wondered, lightly sarcastic.

'Gross,' Melinda repeated. 'Having to dance cold like that. Uninspired. In front of a lot of people who are probably half asleep. I mean I think that's pretty gross.'

'Try another word, Melinda, something more fitting? Less *gross*.'

'OK,' Melinda shrugged. 'Obscene?' As Alexander shook his head, 'Er – *seriously* gross?'

Alexander sighed and raised his eyebrows at Hope as if it was her fault that Melinda could not think of more decorative words. 'What, I wonder, has happened to our lovely language?' he asked, his voice still light, his mind already straying back to the afternoon.

'I know, Dads, but it actually is gross,' Melinda insisted. 'Having to dance like that. I don't think that's the best way to choose who's good and who's not, asking them to dance "cold".'

'Is that so?' Her father nodded thoughtfully, then threw a nut up in the air for himself, caught it in his mouth and smiled at his eldest daughter. 'But then life is notorious for not being fair, is it not?' he asked, and looked at Hope, and then towards Letty who was sleeping outside in the garden in her pram, before reaching behind him for a bottle of whisky off the sofa table, at the same time asking Melinda to fetch him a glass.

'Hmmmm,' he mused some more, chewing another cashew before turning to ask his wife the date of her next visit to her gynaecologist.

Hope looked astonished. 'Macleod? Next week. Why?'

'Just curious,' Alexander replied, with a smile, as Melinda returned with a glass. 'No, Mellie,' he scolded. 'A *whisky* glass.'

Hope followed Melinda out, in order to bring Letty in from the garden. As she leaned over and looked in the pram her heart sank, as for one shaming moment she found herself wishing that the little baby looking back so sweetly at her over the edge of her covers had been born a boy – because there was no point in self-deception. It was patently obvious that Alexander was thinking of getting her pregnant yet again. Why otherwise should he have mentioned Mr Macleod?

Chapter Three

As always when something very important was being said to her, Hope was finding it difficult to concentrate on the real meaning behind the words.

'I think you must consider that, given your particular history, all in all it would be better if there were no more children,' the consultant told her. 'I'm sorry, but that's how it is.'

'You mean I can't have any more?' Hope asked. 'Or shouldn't?'

'You could conceive again, but it would be inadvisable, to say the least.'

'Mr Macleod, I know that it isn't what my neighbour would call *politically correct* to say so, but – my husband is very keen to have a son. Really keen.'

'I know, Mrs Merriott, I am very aware of that fact. But each time you become pregnant, each time you try for a boy, the risks become greater.'

'Of losing the child? Or risky for me?'

'For both of you, really. The number of Caesareans you have had to undergo – that alone increases the risk factor. It's bound to, I'm afraid. And unfortunately your first section was not very tidy, not a good job at all, I have to say. I've tried to tidy you up a bit since then, but a certain amount of damage has been done that cannot be undone. So all in all, were you to ask my advice, I would say that another pregnancy would be highly inadvisable.'

'But I am still able to conceive?'

'Of course you are – I would just recommend you not to consider doing so. It really isn't worth the risk. I could make certain you don't, if you like.'

'By tying my ends up?'

The consultant nodded. 'Better to be safe in this case. Believe me. Particularly when fathers become so insistent on trying to achieve what is after all just some sort of ego trip. In my opinion, there are more important things in life than just reproducing ourselves, and I speak as the father of three girls.'

'I'm not sure this particular father would thank either of us for thinking that.'

'Well, quite, but it's not this particular father's body, is it? Or life. I could have you admitted straight away for this little op, which would end all your problems. You'd be home the next day.'

'Thanks, but I think I'll take the famous rain check.'

'Of course. But in the meantime do keep taking the pill. I'm serious. Either that or advise your husband to have a vasectomy. It's vital you do not have any more children. Really.'

*   *   *

Alexander was home early for once, anxious to know every last detail of her consultation with Macleod. Hope gave him the sanitized version.

'How long do we have to wait?' Alexander enquired when she had finished her short résumé. 'Exactly how long?'

'Does it matter, Alex? There's not a clock on it, is there?'

Alexander smiled and stroked her hair, a habit of his which Hope loved. 'In a way yes, my darling, there is a clock on it. There's a biological clock.'

'Mine's still fully wound up as far as conceiving is concerned,' Hope replied. 'It's just there are obviously certain difficulties, after so many Caesareans. Five is not quite on, according to Macleod. In fact he actually advises that you have a vasectomy.'

Alexander had not thought of this. He laughed, making sure to sound quite at ease with the idea, while all the while his heart quickened at the suggestion, and the lost fortune that would result from it.

'Of course, darling, but from what I've heard at the club, Macleod advises all the men to have one. He has a bee in his medical bonnet about it. It comes of seeing too many women having too many babies. He thinks Britain is going to end up like China – you know, chucking out all the unwanted baby girls, that sort of thing.'

Alexander laughed but at the same time, to calm

himself, he wandered around the kitchen fiddling with the inevitable bric-a-brac that had been left on the sides, tidying some items, straightening others which were already straight, while Hope started preparing the evening meal. Finally Alexander sat down in the dining area of their kitchen overlooking the garden, his drink in front of him, and turned to stare out of the window, losing himself in his thoughts. It had not occurred to him that Hope would be advised to persuade him to have a vasectomy.

He was after all a Scorpio, and as such he relished intrigue and subterfuge, which was why he could not help himself enjoying the fact that Hope did not realize how much depended on the fruit of her womb, that she naively thought because his father lived very simply that he was not a rich man, and that Alexander merely wanted a son so that he could have someone to play cricket with. Much as Hope's goodness sometimes irritated him, and difficult as he found her to understand, he nevertheless had to admire her lack of guile. The idea of divorcing her to produce a boy was not only against his father's moral and religious code, it was against Alexander's finest feelings. Despite his recent infidelities, he still loved his wife.

He looked back from the window at her. She was as usual busy cooking for her ever growing family, and now that she felt him looking at her she looked up and smiled at him. She was a very pretty woman, she looked after herself – Alexander noted that her figure had already more or less returned to its normal slender pre-pregnancy shape – and there was no doubt at all in his mind that he still loved her. Even if his father had been less intransigent towards the idea of divorce, Alexander knew he would still be more than reluctant to give up Hope.

'Dinner's ready,' Hope announced, going to the door to call her daughters to table while Alexander finished his whisky. 'And what are you smiling about?' she asked, although she too smiled.

'Nothing. Just happy.'

'I like to see you smiling.'

Perhaps if she had known quite what Alexander was smiling about, Hope would have thought differently. Alexander, and he could not have said why, all at once had a good feeling about the future.

'Will you at least think about a vasectomy, darling?' Hope said, finishing an earlier conversation.

'Of course, sweetheart. I will think about it, soonest.'

Hope kissed him tenderly on the mouth, and Alexander pulled her closer, wishing that they did not have to hold back so long after babies. The wait seemed interminable, but – and he could not prevent the idea coming into his head – he still had other avenues open to him.

* * *

56

Some months later a letter arrived in the post for Alexander written in a beautiful old-fashioned hand, formally addressed to 'Alexander Merriott, Esq.' After he had picked it out of the basket on the front door he opened it as he headed out to keep yet another sexual assignation with Imogen at the newly built Ilchester Hotel in South Kensington.

Hope passed him on her way in from the shops, noticing the letter he was now standing reading on the doorstep.

'Would you believe it?' he said. 'It's from my old Great-aunt Rosabel – and you know what? She's only asked herself for Christmas.'

'We've hardly got over last Christmas yet,' Hope called back over her shoulder as she hurried inside out of the rain. 'Besides,' she added, laughing, 'you said your Aunt Rosabel hated you, ever since you married me!'

'She seems to have forgotten that she does, because it appears that there is nothing she would like better than to come and stay at West Dean Drive.'

'You can't be serious, love?' Hope wandered back to the doorway. 'She's terribly grand, far too grand for us, and besides, with all the girls, where on earth are we going to put her? She can hardly have the bottom bunk.'

'You know, I think we should invite the old lady, if she really wants to come.'

Alexander returned to the subject that evening

after he had got home, pouring them both a glass of wine and smiling at Hope.

'Alex – you hate her. She hates you. Hardly very Christmasy for everyone. I really don't see the point.'

'Maybe it's time for us to stop hating each other. And what better time than the season of good-will?' He did his innocent act, holding up his hands like a martyred saint. 'Look,' he continued, 'if she wants to come, why not? What harm? After all, I used to be her favourite great-nephew – not that she has any others. And she's old, and lonely. I'll write to her, and see if she was serious.'

The reply, however, was addressed to Hope, since it would appear that the old lady assumed, since Hope was the cook and hostess, it would be more proper to address her rather than her favourite nephew.

How *very* kind of them to ask her, she wrote, ignoring the fact that she had asked herself – how *very* kind of them to have asked her to spend Christmas with them. Generally she spent it with her cousin Bobs, but as it so happened this coming Christmas Bobs had been persuaded to visit her daughter and her grandchildren whom she had never seen, in Canada, so Aunt Rosabel would be only too delighted to come and stay with them in London and to meet Hope, whom she had after all not had the pleasure of seeing since their first and only meeting before she had married Alexander, as well as Alexander's little girls, who must be quite big by now.

'You look a little down in the mouth, now that she actually is coming,' Hope remarked after Alexander had finished reading his great-aunt's reply. 'After all, it was your idea to say she could come.'

'I thought I could effect a U-turn. I tried to arrange it so that she'd ask us all down to Hatcombe. I mean it's a huge house and there's just her rattling around there.'

'Maybe she wants it cosy,' Hope replied in her ever practical way. 'If she asks us all down there, think of the work. She's an old lady, Alexander. A big family Christmas she doesn't need.'

'Listen to you,' Alexander sighed. 'You're beginning to talk television speak. *A big family Christmas she doesn't need* indeed.'

Hope laughed, and then turned back to her cooking, but Alexander was all too occupied with his own feelings and would not let it go. 'Slovenly speech is not good in any of us.'

Hope looked at him, head on one side, eyes sympathetic. 'OK, sweetheart, to use yet more television speak – want to tell me about it?'

Alexander turned away, sighed, shrugged his shoulders and raised his eyebrows as high as they would go but finally said in a low voice, 'The trout farm scheme's down the tubes.'

'Oh, Alex, I am sorry.'

But even as Hope put her arms round him and showed him all the kindness and sympathy she could muster, she felt anxiety once more engulfing her as if someone had thrown a heavy velvet curtain over her, and all her old worries about security began to surface once more.

'What next then, darling?'

'Wait and see,' he said. 'Just you wait and see.'

Hope did wait and see, and unfortunately she did not have to wait for very long. She was alone in the house, with Verna out walking Letty in the park and the other three girls still in school. She wasn't expecting anyone, so when the doorbell rang and through the double glass doors she saw two very large men waiting to be let in, not unnaturally she hesitated.

'Yes?' she asked, having let herself into the porch while still keeping the outer door shut and bolted.

'Mrs Merriott?' the larger of the two men enquired loudly, holding up a white business card. 'Swaine Debt Collection, madam.'

'I don't think you have the right house,' Hope replied. 'We don't have any debts. I'm sure we don't.'

'I'm very much afraid you do, madam,' the man replied with a smile and a tilt of his shaved head. 'At least Mr Merriott does.'

Hope hesitated.

'If you don't let us in, Mrs Merriott, we can get quite loud,' the man assured her. 'And streets like this have a lot of ears.'

'To whom does my husband allegedly owe money?' Hope asked as she opened the door, still leaving it on the chain.

The second debt collector pulled an invoice from his pocket, holding it up for Hope to see. It was headed Bridge Street Garage. Seeing the letterhead, Hope slipped the chain and stood to one side, allowing the two men in.

'Very sensible if I may say,' the first one said, coming into the hall and looking round him. 'Nice place.'

Uninvited, he wandered into the double drawing room, followed by his stooge.

'Yes, very tasty indeed,' he said, looking closely at the fixtures and fittings. 'Very classy. I can tell classy, Mrs Merriott, because we see a lot of interiors in this line of work, you know. And do you know what I say? When I see a place like this, I say I don't get it. Grot, yes, OK, so they stretched themselves, got into too much debt – but when we come into houses like this I just don't get it. I really don't.'

'Could you just tell me what this is about, please?' Hope said. 'My husband isn't in at the moment—'

'Your husband is as slippery as the proverbial eel, Mrs Merriott. He doesn't answer his phone, he doesn't answer any letters—'

'Just tell me what this is all about.'

The stooge produced the invoice once again, this time handing it to Hope who read it carefully.

It was for the fourth time of asking, the sum in question being £745.25 inc VAT for repairs to Alexander Merriott's 1968 Mercedes 280SE coupé.

'There must be some mistake. I'm sure my husband paid this.'

'If he had done so, Mrs Merriott, we would not be here, I most earnestly assure you,' the first man said. 'And I'm afraid our orders are not to leave here without being paid. If you won't pay us, then we shall have to collect in kind.'

'You can't possibly do that. I happen to know my rights. You don't have the authority to do that.'

The man in charge gave her a patronizing look. 'You have some very nice things here, Mrs Merriott,' he said, leaning his hand on Alexander's prized Queen Anne bureau. 'You wouldn't like anything to happen to them, I feel sure.'

'Are you threatening me?'

The man shook his head. 'Simply stating the obvious. People who have nice things don't like nasty things happening to them. I would hardly call that a threat. Like I said, a statement of fact, that's all.'

Panic struck at last, Hope tried to reach Alexander on both his numbers but he was at neither one.

'We don't mind waiting, Mrs Merriott,' the stooge said. 'You get to be very patient in this job.'

Knowing her children would be home any moment, Hope asked them to wait while she ran upstairs to get her personal cheque book. With a hand that shook with the worry and tension of it all, she wrote a cheque for the full amount, leaning on her dressing table before hurrying back downstairs.

'We do normally prefer cash, Mrs Merriott,' the head man said, 'but seeing as you're obviously a lady, we'll make an exception.'

The stooge took his cue, replacing a statuette he had been examining back on the china shelves and smiling at Hope.

'Just as well you weren't in here a moment ago, Mrs Merriott,' he said. 'I as near as dammit dropped that lovely little piece.'

'If ever you or your hubby needs help *collecting* the rent, Mrs Merriott, just say the word,' the leader said. 'I've left my card on the mantelpiece.'

Hope said nothing. After all, when all was said and done, there really was nothing left to say.

She closed the front door behind them and leaning against it let out a sigh that as it ended sounded more like a sob.

Naturally Alexander protested vigorously when Hope related the afternoon's events to him, swearing that he had paid the account and ordering her to stop her cheque. For her part Hope doubted very much that any mistake had been made, advising Alexander first to check his bank statements and if he did find any anomaly to make representations to the garage in question.

Finally Alexander muttered something about

the state of the post nowadays before pouring his inevitable whisky and going to stare out at the rainsodden garden through the conservatory windows.

'I didn't know you had a private bank account!' he called after Hope as she headed past him for the kitchen. 'That's a bit underhand, isn't it?'

'It's only that little bit of money my father left me. That's all I have in it, just to help out with small things. We agreed that when I was left it, remember? Or perhaps you don't.'

'I do now, darling. But if you'd only reminded me we had something put aside—'

'I never thought you would need it so badly.'

'I could have used some of that, Hope. Saved us a little embarrassment.'

'You should have told me you had got into debt. That might have been a much bigger help all round. To know where we stand.'

'Trout farms! I can't look at fish at the moment,' Alexander muttered, clearing some condensation off the window in front of him. 'It was the blasted trout farms that did me.'

'Alex?' Hope came back to his side and slipped her arm through his. 'Talk to me. Tell me about it.'

'How much money do you have?'

'How much do you need?'

Her husband turned and looked at her, then after a moment shook his head. 'I wish you would leave these things to me,' he said, and he looked irritated. 'It really isn't your worry, really. You get on with your things, and I'll get on with mine.'

'We have school fees to pay, Alex. We have to buy all sorts of new stuff for Rose, and Mellie needs some shoes – so does Claire. There are obviously other bills that need paying, so it is my worry too – I need money for my *things*, as you call them, as well, you know.'

'It's OK, darling,' Alexander said, with his bravest smile, putting an arm round Hope's shoulders and hugging her to him. 'We'll be all right.'

'Are we always going to live this hand to mouth, Alexander?'

'When I make a strike it won't be hand to mouth any more. You just wait. It just needs one scheme to come good . . .'

'How much do you need meantime, Alex?'

Alexander breathed in deeply and sucked his teeth. 'Five grand to be going along with,' he said. 'I'll let you have it back.'

Once Hope had written the cheque and done her subtractions, she discovered that she was left with just three and a half thousand pounds of her rainy day money; just three and a half thousand pounds from her small bequest.

As she put her cheque book back in its secret place, Hope wondered how long she'd be able to hold on to the remainder. Obviously if she wanted to keep a hold on any of it, the most sensible thing would be for her to go out and get a job of some kind. Melinda already had a Saturday job, and

Claire was talking of taking a computer course so that she could work as a 'temp' as soon as it was possibly possible – so why not her?

The following evening when Alexander was out at a business dinner and the girls were in bed and asleep, Hope sat herself down at the kitchen table with a mug of hot chocolate, a plate of biscuits and a copy of the local paper.

There were so many situations vacant it made her head spin, and of course nothing suitable. She was above office cleaning and below accountancy, not trained in office work and unsuitable for bar work. She was too fastidious to become a 'masseuse' and certainly not desperate enough – and had far too much of a sense of humour – to become a 'kissogram'. She was nearing the end of the paper when at last her eye was suddenly caught by something for which she really could be suitable. She sighed with relief. *Wanted*, it read. *Trained dancer to teach ballet to infants*. It might be that her much despised *hoofing*, as Alexander called it, was going to pay off after all.

Chapter Four

At first Alexander was not pleased. The way he saw it was that for his wife to be going to work meant a certain amount of loss of social face. It meant that he was not doing as well as he would have people believe, and – worse – it meant that Hope was not always at hand when he needed her.

But as winter set in and Christmas with all its expense approached, Alexander realized there were advantages as well as disadvantages, and not all of the advantages were monetary. One of the main ones, in his eyes, was the fact that if Hope was out working, and therefore absent at regular times, he could pop next door to Imogen and save on the hotel bills. Hope's working could be a saving all round. As long as Verna, the nanny, did not come back too early and find out he was next door, everything in the garden would be pretty perfect.

Then again, Christmas was coming up in two weeks, and there was a goose to be plucked – not one for the table but one up from the country.

The girls needed to be briefed about Great-aunt Rosabel. None of them knew anything about her, except that Hope had only met her once before her marriage to Alexander, and had possibly not been approved of by the old lady since she had never met her since. Nevertheless Hope did her best to paint a sympathetic picture of their father's ageing relative, not wanting them to be put off the undoubtedly grande dame that she remembered. Most of all she wanted them to recognize that Rosabel Williamson, wife of the late Harold Fairfield, came from another era, an era with different rules, and quite different attitudes.

The little that Hope herself knew of the old lady led her to believe that Alexander's great-aunt was, whatever else she might be, most definitely formidable. She had been successfully married to a much older, and very rich, man. Harold Fairfield had been one of the country's leading archaeologists, as a result of which, Alexander teased the girls, Aunt Rosabel was prone to start every sentence, *As you may well know, it was a common habit among the ancient Egyptians* . . .

Still, the old woman exercised a sort of fascination over the imaginations of both Hope and the girls, not least because she lived in a large house in the Vale of Pewsey in Wiltshire to which they had never been invited, but about which they loved to fantasize. Alexander, remembering Hatcombe from his boyhood, often described idyllic holidays spent there when he had used to go visiting in a pony and trap down the English country lanes, and he spoke of the house as being beautiful and classically set in lovely countryside.

'Perfection,' was how he finally described it.

'Classical Georgian, those lovely long sash windows down to ground level, south facing – wonderful grounds. It could be one of those perfect English country houses that everyone wants and never can find.'

'Why doesn't she ask us down there for Christmas?' Rose grumbled when Hope had finished instructing the girls on how not to behave in front of the old lady. 'Such a large house, and just her!'

'From what Dads says it's really formal and starchy. You'd have to be on your best manners all the time. Think of that!'

'We wouldn't mind. Besides, we could help her, and everything. Dads said she has a great library, full of fantastic books.'

Hope sighed and patted Claire on the head. Claire was blond and a bookworm. Somehow, she did not know why, it seemed an unexpected combination, Hope thought, looking down at her second youngest daughter.

But there was something so special about Claire. Of all of them she was the most original, seeming always to burn with something which had not yet found expression. For Claire's sake Hope longed for that moment to arrive, knowing as she did that talent realized, wherever and whenever it found expression, made for contentment.

'You can help me here!' she told them all. 'We have to smarten up a bedroom for Aunt Rosabel, and make sure that everything is just as it should be, because she is used to a much grander life than we can offer.'

Normally Hope loved Christmas, every last inch of it, from the moment she climbed up into the attic of West Dean Drive to find her precious collection of tree ornaments right down to when Claire insisted on handing out the presents from under the tree, reading out the labels with conscientious attention to the exact wording of the messages, labels that Hope kept for years afterwards.

'*Darling Dads, something that you will recognize! Lots of love, Mellie.*' '*To Mums, with all our love Wonder Woman, Rose and Claire. PS Ha, ha, ha, you thought we didn't notice you wanted it, didn't you!!!!!!*'

But all the normal relaxed and sentimental feelings that Hope felt at this particular time of year had flown in the face of the arrival of Alexander's stately relative who, if she did not approve of Hope, would certainly not approve of West Dean Drive after the great house in which she had lived for the best part of her life. No amount of fresh flowers in the newly decorated room, so recently vacated by Rose to make way for their guest, no amount of copies of *Country Life* or *Harpers & Queen* by the bedside, would induce the grand Aunt Rosabel to imagine that she was staying in a place that was compatible with her status.

'When's the elderly person arriving?' Alexander wanted to know.

The answer was at eleven twenty at Paddington, and since he was busy at the office it was up to Hope to meet the train, a faded photograph of the old lady in her pocket.

Needless to say the train was late, it was raining, and the station was so crowded that Hope lived in dread that when it did arrive, not knowing what the old lady looked like, she would doubtless miss her. To pass the time she phoned Melinda to warn her that she would be back much later than she had originally anticipated, and then, for want of something better to do, decided to take a short walk. Venturing out of the station into grimy, dirty side streets housing squalid little hotels very soon convinced her that the area around stations the world over was always the same, not really very inviting to a woman alone, even in daytime.

So instead of wandering and window shopping where there were no decent windows she returned to Paddington and finally found a bench where she sat down disconsolately, watching the people ebbing and flowing around the refreshment booths, travellers arriving and departing, bag women enviously eyeing other people's laden shopping bags, and everyone, it seemed, discarding sweet papers, cigarette packets or drink cartons on the already litter-strewn concourse. Most of all she watched everyone looking, and yet seeming to be noticing nothing.

To pass the time Hope imagined how it would be if she and the girls were arriving at the station, along with so many others, to catch a train *to* Pewsey, not waiting for an old lady who was coming *from* Pewsey. It seemed to her that it would be very exciting if they were all in their best going down to stay with a rich old relative who lived in a beautiful house called Hatcombe in Wiltshire.

There would be a great fire in the hall when they arrived, and a kindly housekeeper who would take the girls straight up to see their rooms, which would be furnished with pretty chintzes and have flowers on flounced dressing tables and Scottish shortbread in tins, and grapes by the bedside.

The kindly old great-aunt would have borrowed ponies for Melinda and Claire to ride out accompanied by an old groom in weathered old-fashioned riding breeches and a faded cap from under which his shrewd blue eyes would be twinkling. And of course Christmas dinner would be perfect, a meal of the tenderest home-bred turkey cooked to perfection, which they would all enjoy in the elegant dining room where portraits of benignly smiling ancestors stared down. The napkins would be so starched it would be difficult to pull them apart to put them on their knees, and the crackers would be luxurious ones from Harrods, the super-de-luxe kind that always had wonderful presents.

Hope would wear a new, very chic, long black evening dress which would be teamed with an expensive glittering evening jacket of the kind that everyone was wearing in glossy magazines; and during the day she would wear a marvellous new blue suit in the shade of sapphire that showed up blue eyes so well, while the girls would all have those Fair Isle jumpers and chic little skirts and dark stockings and shoes, with their hair tied into black velvet ribbons. At the head of the table Great-aunt Rosabel would be smiling and laughing, enjoying her first *un*-lonely Christmas since she could remember – and all thanks to Alexander and his family of laughing, chattering girls.

Just in time Hope awoke from her daydream to hear the announcement of the train from Plymouth's late arrival at platform eight. Hurrying the wrong way through the crowds, Hope reached the barrier and stood waiting anxiously for sight of the old lady, but there was none.

Finally, as it seemed the last disembarking passengers hurried by her, Hope ran onto the platform, fearing that Alexander's elderly relative might have plunged off in the wrong direction or unbeknownst to her headed straight for the taxi rank.

She had not. Last of all the passengers descending from the train came a tall, beautifully dressed old lady, her long white hair neatly twisted into a French pleat and secured with tortoiseshell pins, her excellently tailored tweed suit showing beneath a swagger coat with a back belt and full pleats, her small velvet hat pulled down to just the right angle.

'Great-aunt Rosabel?'

'Ah, my dear. You're Alexander's wife, are you not?'

Great-aunt Rosabel smiled down at Hope, for, elderly or not, she was still taller than her hostess.

'That's right.'

'How very kind of you to meet the train.'

Hope took her small crocodile leather suitcase from her, realizing as she did so that it must be pre-war luggage for it was very heavy, and the initials on it so small that it breathed monied discretion.

'So kind, so very kind,' Rosabel murmured again, following Hope down the platform. 'A very crowded train, but that did not matter because I had a very nice window seat. And there was excellent coffee, so the delay passed quite comfortably, I am happy to tell you.'

Hope smiled back at her, full of relief that she had found her at last and that she was so charming and kind, not alarming at all. 'We have been so looking forward to your coming.'

'And I to meeting you all. So kind of you to ask me.'

Arriving at West Dean Drive Hope could not remember when she had last seen Alexander on such superb form. From the moment he greeted his aged relative he was the personification of charm. Hope could not help but be impressed by the way her husband beguiled his relative. He was both attentive and skittish. He teased her and laughed with her, he sat in front of the fire and placed a tray of superb sandwiches and a glass of sherry in front of her. He told her that she looked seventeen not seventy – knowing that she was well over eighty.

Aunt Rosabel clearly loved everything and said so. Her room, the house, the welcome, Alexander, everything seemed to please her above and beyond any possible expectation.

And the girls – dressed in the kind of clothes that they normally only wore for birthdays or parties – were also on their best behaviour, practically curtseying every time the old lady came into the room, and staying quiet where they would normally have been tumbling over themselves to chatter. Hope puzzled over this sudden change in their outward demeanour and then realized that they were, quite literally, awestruck by Aunt Rosabel, the old lady having been a name around the house for such a very long time that her belated appearance in person must be like some kind of hologram come to life.

But, more than that, Hope could see that they really liked her.

'Ah, Melinda, there you are. I have brought you down some photographs of some polo ponies that Uncle Harold bred. I knew that would interest you, because I remember hearing, long ago, that you were interested in horses. And for Rose, a theatrical book to look at, very old, as you can see, even older than myself. Now, you are Claire, I know, and the baby is Letitia. A Fairfield name, I am proud to say, and one of the nicer ones too. Uncle Harold would be pleased.'

From the moment she sat among them they were all in her thrall.

And far from being frightened of babies the old lady insisted on sitting next to Verna and taking the baby's hand and holding it tight, while hearing all about Letitia's progress and how she was taking to solid foods, asking of the nanny everything that was appropriate and interesting. In this way the time between lunch and tea passed very pleasantly, finishing with Aunt Rosabel telling the girls about something called *It* which, when she was young, it was the ambition of every young *gel* to possess.

'I can see you all have *It*,' she told the girls, smiling round at them. 'Not just beauties, but beauties with something *extra*.'

Of course they were all fascinated by the idea of *It*, and even Verna confessed to wanting to possess it, so that as Hope, in happy mood, served tea and cake before the crackling fire it occurred to her that far from spoiling Christmas Aunt Rosabel was bringing something extra to their house, something that only an older person could bring, some depth that just her presence, redolent of the undoubted charm of the old days of faithful servants and great houses, of old mahogany and rooms with ornate plaster work, of family pride which had stood the test of a thousand years, could conjure up.

Hope was not alone in her feeling that Aunt Rosabel had brought some sort of special quality to their Christmas. Melinda felt so too, and as Christmas morning came round and found them all in their best, the fire once more lit and the tree looking prettier than ever, she would not have swapped places with any other girl enjoying Christmas with her family. West Dean Drive seemed to be the very best place in the world to be.

Besides, the lunch was cooking and smelling wonderful, the table was set, and so far none of the younger ones had got over-excited. In fact everything was shooting along and everyone really enjoying themselves.

To begin with Rose and Melinda had accompanied Aunt Rosabel to a most enjoyable family service at the church at the end of the road, where for once Melinda had done her best to concentrate on the sermon which she had then determinedly discussed on the way home, awarding the vicar good and bad points for what Rose called 'his performance'.

'But that is exactly what church is, my dear, a theatrical performance,' Aunt Rosabel had agreed. 'But just like the *the-ate-er*, one must never ever go backstage and meet the actors. My father used to say that after every Christmas service. He never went backstage to meet the *actors*.'

'Do you know that Rose is named after you, Aunt Rosabel?'

Aunt Rosabel paused in the road to stare round at her tall, dark great-great-niece.

'My dear! No! No-one ever told me. Do you intend to dance under my name? Because if you have been named after me, then it would be more fitting were you to use my entire name. I shall suggest that you do. To your father. *Rosabel Fairfield*. I can see it in lights already.'

After which she gave such a happy laugh that despite not quite agreeing with her, Rose could only smile in return. As she said later to Melinda, 'She's so *sweet* – there was nothing I could say.'

Before lunch, while Hope put the finishing touches to the table, Melinda set about opening the champagne. Each year that was her self-appointed task at midday, but this year, as she brought the first bottle in, Aunt Rosabel stiffened and said, 'I am afraid I am rather gun shy when it comes to bottles.'

However, when the first bottle had been opened silently and expertly by Mellie under a tea towel, she was reassured – so much so that after the first glass she forgot all about noises and corks and once more fell into happy conversation with Verna, telling the young Australian all about the war when she was in the WVS and working under Lady Reading, and how she and her committee had to find homes for evacuee children in their area, all of whom had screamed in terror when they had first seen a cow, convinced, she told the incredulous Verna, that it was a wild animal and that they would be eaten by it.

As always at West Dean Drive, no matter what the state of their finances, there were plenty of presents under the tree, beautifully wrapped by Hope and her daughters, and each bearing a carefully thought out message. There was even a gift for Minou, their much-loved Burmese cat. This year, of course, there were even more, Aunt Rosabel having carefully placed her presents in the pile along with the rest. She sat back with a look of some contentment to watch 'the young', as she called the girls, unwrapping her presents first as a compliment to her and, as Hope said, 'before the room becomes awash with paper and ribbons'.

'Oh, but this is beautiful, Great-aunt Rosabel,' exclaimed Melinda.

'*Sexy* . . .' Rose began facetiously, looking at the silk shawl her sister was holding up, but then she stopped and added quickly, 'Gosh, that's beautiful, Mellie, really beautiful.'

Melinda wrapped the old shawl round her and then, reaching forward, she kissed the old lady's cheek, noting her skin felt just like a fine china teacup.

'Aunt Rosabel!' Rose exclaimed after opening her own present, which was labelled *Fragile* most carefully. She held it up for all to see, a pretty piece of old porcelain.

'Really one should have given you a ballerina, had one known of your dancing. But the Spaghetti Seller is very special,' the old lady told Rose. 'Very special. It is not an English piece, do you see? It is German.'

Then it was Claire's turn. Her present from Aunt Rosabel was discovered to be a finely illustrated book on Old Masters, with beautifully coloured reproductions.

'However did you know, Aunt Rosabel?' she wondered, leafing through the book. 'That this is my thing?'

'Your *thing*?' Aunt Rosabel repeated.

'She means her latest interest,' Alexander explained, winking at the rest of the room.

For Alexander himself there was another silk scarf, but this time the sort that people like Noel Coward used to wear with a Sulka dressing gown, as Aunt Rosabel told him, in case he did not know. Which indeed he did not, because, as Hope always teased him, he really had not the slightest interest in anything unless it had just been on the news.

'And from Dads for – Great-aunt Rosabel—' Claire began, only to be stopped by the old lady.

'*Aunt* Rosabel. No need for the *Great*.'

'Sorry, Aunt Rosabel.'

'I only think of you as Rosabella,' her great-nephew told her, teasing her and playing the gallant to her fair lady, which made the old lady laugh and smile, and turn to Verna with a murmured, 'He's *such* a tease.'

The delay had given Claire just enough time to re-read the labels on the remaining parcels under the tree, and she realized in an instant that there was nothing from Dads for Aunt Rosabel. Her loving great-nephew, having announced that he would be buying his great-aunt 'something special', had, in the Christmas rush, obviously completely forgotten to do so.

For a clutch of seconds that strayed into a minute, Melinda and Claire stared at each other. Nothing could be worse, they knew, than that their father would not have thought of giving a present to his aged relative.

'Take our label off, and just give him ours to give to her.'

Melinda stared down at the carefully wrapped parcel. It had taken all of them hours to prepare the gift. It had been Mums's suggestion, and they had gone along with it willingly, but they knew that the whole day would be spoilt if Dads had nothing to give Aunt Rosabel.

'It doesn't matter who it's from, Mellie, just so long as she gets something from Dads. That's all that matters really, isn't it?'

Noting not just the delay, but the expressions on their faces, Alexander walked over to them.

Reaching out blindly, as he was so used to do, he took the package from his daughter and handed it to his great-aunt himself.

'And this, my dear Rosabella, is from me,' he said.

Rose and Hope watched in astonishment as it was unwrapped. Rose, who had not been paying much attention, was just about to protest that there had been a mistake when Claire put a warning finger to her lips.

'When you think of the work we put into that . . .' she muttered.

When the girls had heard that their father's aged relative was definitely coming for Christmas, at Hope's suggestion they had spent hours and hours of their spare time in preparing an illustrated scrap book all about their family, cutting out things from old family papers, sorting through old photographs in dusty boxes that they had found stored away in the attic, finally laboriously captioning every illustration with special lettering purchased with the last of their Christmas pocket money, the very last few pounds left to them after splashing out on the expensive mock leather album that they had chosen as the binding for their surprise.

'So what are *we* meant to be giving her now?' Rose went on under her breath, as Claire valiantly continued to read the labels and hand out the rest of the presents from under the tree.

'I'll ask Mums,' Melinda said, getting up from where they had all been kneeling on the floor.

'She always has an emergency store.'

But Hope had already realized what had happened, and was slipping out of the door unnoticed as Melinda caught up with her.

'I've got some things at the top of my wardrobe . . .'

Hurrying upstairs, Hope prayed that she still had something suitable. As luck would have it she found something not only suitable – an elegant pack of expensive soaps and bath oils she had been given by a grateful mother from the dancing class – but appropriately old-fashioned too, the whole being made by Bonnier & Castleman, an Edwardian company who still knew their lavender from their rose geranium. She hurried back downstairs where, with well-practised maternal skill, she managed to smuggle the gift back to Melinda with whispered instructions to 'lose' it under the tree.

'Oh, Claire, look,' Melinda said at the appropriate moment, having saved the label from the other parcel. 'You've forgotten to give Aunt Rosabel our present.'

But their house guest was far more interested in Alexander's supposed gift to her, having now carefully unwrapped the book to examine its contents with the aid of her reading glasses.

'Alexander, dear boy,' she exclaimed. 'But this is a work of art – I could not be more astonished and delighted. The work you have put into this! One is at a loss for words.'

Slowly the old lady turned the pages, lingering over each image, finding herself in an old sepia photograph as a small child leaning one plump hand on a cushion while looking seriously at the camera, then dressed for her presentation at Court, later on her wedding day to Uncle Harold and finally in her WVS uniform during the war.

'Where in heaven's name did you find all these, Alexander?' she enquired with a laugh. 'Where were they?'

'I keep everything about our family, Rosabel dear,' Alexander replied, sitting on the arm of her chair and helping her turn the pages. 'I don't throw anything out. I've kept all these things, family things, treasured things, all this time.'

Hope smiled to herself as she heard him, remembering how Alexander had needed to be persuaded not to junk stuff he had described as boring old rubbish about boring old people, but said nothing, concentrating instead on opening her presents from her daughters. And as she kissed each of them in gratitude for their gifts, Hope made sure to give them an extra hug too, because she was so proud of them for not giving the game away.

Because she always opened the youngest's first, she opened Melinda's present to herself last, taking out a large paperbacked book entitled *Drawing With the Right Side of the Brain*.

Alexander looked over her shoulder as Hope was starting to read through it, and took it out of her hands to examine the title. As soon as he saw it he wandered off laughing.

'Nice thought, Mellie,' he said. 'But surely in order to be able to utilize it, you have to be blessed with a brain in the first place!'

'Take no notice of Dads. It's a simply wonderful present. And so imaginative. You know how much I want to be able to draw.'

'Right. Soon as I read about it I said, "That's for Mums!" Apparently everyone can draw by using this other part of your brain – the artistic side or something. A bit that we don't use at all, you know? And apparently if you follow everything it says anyone can do it – look. Just look at the results.'

Hope and she leafed through the book, and Hope promised to read a little bit every night before she went to sleep.

'That way, Mellie,' she added, 'I can start to practise drawing in my head too, you know, using the other bits. By locking it all in my head before I go to sleep.'

'And then you can show me, right?'

'You don't need to be shown, Mellie, you're as bright as a sixpence.'

Later, while everyone was busy exclaiming over their family presents, Hope slipped out to check that everything was set properly in the dining room. It was only when she was there, quite alone, that she sat down and, taking one of the carefully ironed napkins from the table, suddenly pressed it to her face.

She was not at all sure what had caused the feeling – all she knew as she sat there with a napkin covering her eyes was that she had never felt quite so dejected and fearful in her life. As if her life was about to change for ever, and not for the better. She suspected it might be something to do with Aunt Rosabel, but at the same time reason told her this was absurd.

But then, as she well knew, not everything could be explained away or rationalized. Many things in life were born from mere sensations, and there were indeed such things as bad omens. And however much she tried, Hope could not dismiss the idea that from the moment she had collected the old lady from the station, despite all her charm, all her undoubted delight in coming to West Dean Drive for Christmas and the girls' delight in getting to know her, all their lives were about to change for the worse.

The day after Boxing Day Alexander volunteered to run his great-aunt to the station. After kissing the children and shaking Hope's hand, the statuesque old lady folded herself into the front seat of her great-nephew's old Mercedes coupé.

'What a wonderful Christmas! I cannot remember enjoying myself so much in an age. Your girls are the most delightful, the best mannered, and the sweetest that I have ever come across. And the baby – a delight. Letitia. I am so pleased – Uncle Harold would be so pleased – that you have given her a Fairfield name. He would be delighted, really he would.'

She patted Alexander's hand and he smiled but said nothing, just as he did when he returned from seeing his great-aunt safely onto the train. In fact if anything his smile was even bigger and his silence even deeper, and for a long time after Christmas, long after the tree had been thrown out, when all the little tags were once more hanging as souvenirs from the kitchen message board and Hope was proudly wearing the lambswool twinset that he had given her, nothing and nobody could rouse him from his state of almost euphoric calm. It was as if he had retreated from the world to a much higher plane. Or, like some great beast of the jungle who has killed and eaten, as if he was lying eyes half closed basking in the shadows, knowing that there was yet more of that which he so desired, just around the corner.

Chapter Five

'We have been invited to Hatcombe for the Easter weekend,' Alexander said, passing the letter to Hope.

This was the second letter he had received from Great-aunt Rosabel since Christmas, the first one having been a thank you note addressed to Alexander alone, in which their house guest had described the celebration as a quite splendid festivity and had thanked him warmly for making her feel a part of what was obviously such a happy family.

The second letter was also addressed only to Alexander and seemed to be further to certain conversations which had already passed between Aunt Rosabel and her great-nephew on the telephone. For such an inhibited personality as Rosabel Fairfield, the whole tone of the letter was effusive and affectionate, leaving Hope only to wonder at the power of her husband's charm.

'I suppose it's because I make her laugh. We all have these preconceived ideas about each other, half the time forgetting there's a real human being lurking in the psychological undergrowth. Rosabel was famous when young for being quite a spark and a bit of a goer, so if we've unthawed her at last it's not really that surprising.'

'If *you've* unthawed her, you mean,' Hope said, smiling and folding up the letter. 'I've never seen such a transformation in anybody. You are brilliant, darling.'

Easter was early that year, and after what had seemed to be endless grey February, at the beginning of April the weather suddenly relented, becoming quickly bright, breezy and sunny, the clouds clearing and a blue sky hinting at the golden days of summer which lay ahead.

To the Merriott girls sitting in the back of their father's gracious old German car with little Letty on Melinda's knee, the Wiltshire countryside was as unfamiliar as London suburbia was familiar, and as they passed trees already budding with spring green they stopped chattering and fell to silence in keeping with the quiet of the life that they sensed lay outside the car windows.

None of them was at all familiar with the countryside, not even Hope, who, having been born in Norfolk where many of her relations still lived, had moved to London when she was only a small child. Apart from the occasional weekend away with Alexander when they were first married, and family holidays taken in North Devon, she knew little about the west country, and nothing at all about Wiltshire, the county towards which they now were headed. To her surprise it was much more beautiful than she had expected, particularly once they entered the Vale of Pewsey with its picturesque whitewashed and thatched cottages lying in the folds of the majestic Marlborough Downs.

To please the girls Alexander took a brief detour to show them a little more of the downland. Melinda fell into a deep and reverential silence, assuming what Claire always called 'Mellie's Buddha expression', while Hope held little Letty in her arms and Alexander leant on a field gate and stared at the miles of green silence surrounding them.

'Rather more beautiful than London, I think you will agree?' As he spoke, Alexander breathed the air as if he was drinking a glass of morning champagne.

'Are you thinking of moving us to the country?' Hope looked up at him anxiously, feeling her heart sink at the idea of leaving West Dean Drive.

'How does the way we live compare with this?'

'All I can see are fields. I don't see a way of life.'

'I can work from anywhere, Hope darling, anywhere. Besides, England is its countryside, and we should enjoy it while we still have it, and so should our children. With communications now—'

'I know, I know. You can work from your car.'

'Would you mind it so much? Would you mind living in the country?' Alexander asked as Verna and the girls all bundled happily back into the old Mercedes with its noble symbol and its leather seats.

'I don't know, Alexander. I just don't know. It would be such a disruption at this point in our lives. Especially for the girls, and Rose in particular, now she's got her place at Park Lodge. She's all set, and I'm so happy for her.'

'It's just an idea . . .' Alexander sighed, but his eyes lingered on the quiet of the green fields and the trees in early leaf, the beauty around them, mentally comparing it to the noise and dirt of the South Circular Road, the shops and schools that were at once too far to walk and too near to ignore, and the many mediocre restaurants all of which served moderate food at moderate prices. To him there was no comparison.

In London he felt he had no individuality. There were so many other 'Alexander Merriotts' living in other houses just like his, whereas if he lived at Hatcombe he would be Alexander Merriott Esquire of Hatcombe House in the County of Wiltshire. Hatcombe was somewhere to which anyone would aspire – no, to which *everyone* would aspire.

After their short stop Hatcombe was still another twenty minutes' drive, lying west from where they had stopped and to be found at the end of a tortuous network of farm lanes; and whereas Alexander's mind was still caught up with the romance of the countryside around them, and the possibility of possessing some of it, Hope seemed only able to dwell on practicalities.

'How does Aunt Rosabel manage?' she kept

wondering, as Alexander missed a turn yet again. 'She doesn't drive, and the main road is what? A mile back at least.'

'She has a housekeeper who lives in a cottage in the grounds.'

'Is that all?'

'She's still with us, isn't she?' Alexander smiled as at last he saw the gates of the house ahead of them at the end of a no through road. 'If she hadn't been able to manage she wouldn't still be around, I shouldn't have thought.'

'But she must get lonely.'

'She's lived here for ages, ever since she was married.'

As they headed up the pot-holed drive Hope could not see what Alexander had meant when he said the house was probably in a state of some disrepair, for from the bottom of the drive, looking up towards its elegant façade, it was clear that Hatcombe was as beautiful as West Dean Drive was ordinary. It did not boast Gothic windows, or an ornate *cottage ornée* in the grounds, because, clearly, it had no need of such flights of architectural fancy. It was, quite simply, perfect. A perfect, simple Georgian house set in a lovely old garden with a drive leading to a front door with a flight of steps and a terrace with a balustrade.

Hope looked round at Alexander and he returned her look with a smile.

'*Charming and much sought after eighteenth-*

century rectory,' he quoted, '*possibly in need of some modernization.*'

'It's so pretty . . .' Rose sighed.

'Has it got stables?' was all Melinda wanted to know.

'Half a dozen, as far as I remember,' Alexander replied. 'Cobblestoned. With big heavy doors.'

'Awesome.'

'Look!' Claire exclaimed, pointing. 'There's a cat! And it hasn't got a tail!'

'She's always had tailless cats running about the place. They keep the rats and mice down,' Alexander observed, parking the car by the elegant stone steps. 'Or maybe they're her familiars.'

Melinda and Rose laughed, but Claire remained silent, impressed by the whole look of the place despite the missing tiles and flaking window paint, already wondering which room housed Aunt Rosabel's books.

'What a beautiful house, don't you think?' Verna asked Letty, holding the baby up to see the house and laughing as she waved to the approaching figure of Aunt Rosabel. 'You remember your great-aunt – well done, Letty!'

Aunt Rosabel smiled delightedly at everyone but said, 'I thought perhaps something had happened to you. So worried – other drivers, you know,' as she proffered everyone her cheek.

'I didn't think we set a time.' Hope gave Alexander a worried look as she reached over to take Letty from Verna's arms.

'My dear, it could not matter less, really. Come in, come in. Mrs Lander has lit a fire in the drawing room, and there is lunch soon, and ginger beer, and heaven only knows what treats and things. And how are you all?' she asked the girls, smiling. 'Tired out after that horrid long journey, I imagine.'

'No, we're fine thank you, Aunt Rosabel,' they chorused, Claire adding, 'Just hungry, actually. Wish you hadn't mentioned lunch, as a matter of fact.'

'You have been warned,' Alexander told his relative with a laugh, putting his arm round her. 'Girls? Why don't you go and find the stables yard? If that's all right?'

'By all means.' Aunt Rosabel nodded, smiling at him. 'So sweet of—' She looked suddenly at Hope, obviously suddenly blanking on her name. 'So sweet of you to bring them all down, really so sweet of you, and such a compliment that you thought you could.'

Hope started to walk with the girls towards what she imagined were the stables, pretending not to notice that Rosabel had not been able to remember her name, but Melinda had also noticed and caught her mother by the arm.

'It's OK, Mums. It's when Dads can't remember your name that you should start worrying!'

'Come with me to the library, Alexander dear,' Hope heard Aunt Rosabel say, and turning she saw Alexander take his great-aunt's arm as they walked together up the old, crumbling flight of steps to the double doors of the beautiful eighteenth-century house. 'Mrs Lander is serving sherry and biscuits for us there.'

'You don't like sherry, so that's all right,' Melinda muttered. 'Come on – let's go and see the stables.'

The stables were magnificent, built around a cobbled courtyard. The boxes were made of wood and iron, and the ceilings were high and painted cream. The girls and Verna, pushing Letty in her pram, started to explore them, fantasizing about the horses they might one day own, but Hope, overcome with curiosity and an insatiable desire to see round the interior of the house, slipped off on her own. Feeling a little like a burglar she crept through the courtyard, past the old well and the bell pull that looked a little like something more suited to a church, and in the back door of the house. The old kitchen was stone-flagged, polished to a high degree, and again painted a light cream, with an immaculate pre-war Aga standing where once there would have been a fire burning and a spit set in place. Looking round, Hope could see that there had been a cook at work in this kitchen for many years, however old-fashioned, for there were dried herbs in glass-stoppered jars near to the solid fuel stove, and a log store handily placed, and bowls set with muslin bags full of curd dripping on a far table, and apples in the dark larder stored on brown paper, and marmalade, home-made and dated.

Leaving the kitchen area and wandering quietly through the shuttered and darkened rooms, well away from the distant sound of conversation in the library, Hope soon became accustomed to the darkness of the as yet unlit house. She made out furniture which, if not carved by Chippendale, must at least have been fashioned by men who admired him, chests and tables, and chairs which when picked up she knew would prove to be surprisingly light, so beautiful was the workmanship, and so balanced their design.

The downstairs cloakroom was also revealed to have a flagstone floor, and boasted two beautiful eighteenth-century Hepplewhite chairs set with old silk pads, correctly piped, which, when turned, revealed a vibrant yellow, now long since faded from their uppers. It was a beautiful room, shutters palely painted, its centrepiece a mahogany throne, its old basin made of marble and magnificently marked with the name of its Victorian manufacturer and crowned by old brass taps which ran water that at first was a little brown.

Hope stared at herself in the cloakroom mirror and slowly brushed her dark hair, the thick, fine hair that, like her dancing, Rose had inherited. The mirror must have been silver-backed because Hope could see that it reflected a much prettier version of herself than she imagined herself to be, eyes large and clear, skin pale and without blemish, head set just a little proudly on a fine neck which made her look taller than she was.

For a second she imagined herself living at Hatcombe. Rising every day to the sound of the birds, visiting this cloakroom, looking into this mirror, perhaps dusting those chairs – it seemed just a little too good to be true. Hatcombe was too real to be perfect, and too perfect to be real.

Later, after what Aunt Rosabel described as 'prep school boys' favourite lunch' in the eau de Nil dining room, hung about with portraits of horses and dogs from other eras – roast chicken followed by the best bread and butter pudding that anyone had ever tasted, delicately flavoured, deliciously light – Aunt Rosabel and Alexander once more closeted themselves in the library to talk business while Hope beckoned to the girls and Verna to follow her up the stairs with their weekend luggage, and find their bedrooms.

Room after room displayed the same perfect taste as the house boasted in its downstairs rooms. Graceful silk furnishings in delicate colours, high-backed beds and old wood floors set about with rugs, curtains trailing to the floor and looped and pleated in effective folds that showed off inner silk linings of contrasting shades. And in all the rooms there were watercolours of flowers, or country scenes, depictions from long ago, acquired because the buyer liked them, and not with investment in mind.

Aunt Rosabel's own room, very much

sequestered from the other bedrooms and next door to a large Victorian marble bathroom with a tub set in the middle and large windows giving onto a magnificent view, was dominated not by a watercolour but by a portrait in oils of the kind that is normally found in dining rooms. Unable to resist a closer look at the painting which had caught her eye from the moment she pushed open the old painted door with its eighteenth-century panelling carved in six, Hope tiptoed across the room and gazed up at it where it hung above the old carved and painted chimneypiece.

Now she could see it at close quarters she realized that her first impression was right – this masterpiece had to be of the young Rosabel. As she stepped back from the portrait to look at it once more, she saw that the eyes staring out at her from the beautiful young face above her were precisely the eyes that had stared so luminously out of the old lady's face downstairs. The same penetrating, unswerving gaze, the same sense of having been put on this earth for a purpose, and perhaps even knowing just what that purpose might be.

'So,' Alexander said to Hope as they prepared for bed on Easter Monday night. 'Isn't Hatcombe just as beautiful as I have always told you?'

'Well, it is a fairly magical place, outside. Stables, barns, a lake – horses in the next field, all sorts of wildlife and wonderful walks.'

'Could you live here, darling?'

'No, and nor could you. You'd be bored in a minute.'

Alexander shook his head. He'd given the matter a lot of thought – more thought than he normally gave things, since his declared attitude to life was to fly by the seat of his trousers – and he had reached the conclusion that Hatcombe House would be the answer to his own particular everything, in all ways, bar none.

'But it's academic anyway, darling,' he heard Hope continuing beside him as he reached over to turn off his light at the on-off switch hanging on a nearly bare wire. 'I mean, for one thing we couldn't afford a place like this and for another—'

'We might not *have* to afford a place like this, Hope.'

Hope turned round on her pillow and stared at him in the half-darkness. 'What do you mean?'

'Just a feeling I've got, that's all. But I'm not going to say anything more because you're forever lecturing me about raising false hopes. And you're right.'

As Hope saw Alexander fall asleep and heard his breathing become slow and regular, it occurred to her that she had never seen him do so as quickly, nor look so relaxed. In contrast, Hope herself found that she could not sleep, but lay staring at the dense, still, black darkness that is so characteristic of the countryside at night, unlit as it is by street lamps, the fields resounding not to the comforting sound of distant traffic but to the call of hunting owls.

Only the wind rattling the doors of the old house gave her a strange feeling of comfort, as if it was reassuring her that it too was awake.

'Our worries are over!' Alexander shouted from the hallway, just over a week after their return from Hatcombe. 'I told you so! Didn't I tell you so?'

'Not exactly,' Hope replied as Alexander came into the kitchen re-reading the letter in his hand. When she saw the small light yellow paper with the beautifully formed handwriting she didn't even have to ask who it was from.

'Has she sent you some money, Alex?' she asked. 'Is that what this has all been about?'

'Better than that, Hope darling – a lot, lot better than that. Here – read it for yourself.'

Hope read it standing up, then she sat down at the table and re-read it. Then she shook her head and handed it back to Alexander. 'Don't even contemplate it.'

'She has left me the house, Hope. She is leaving me Hatcombe.'

'Noticed anything, Alexander?'

'Such as?'

'Rosabel Fairfield is still alive, Alexander. She is not dead.'

'She is leaving me Hatcombe in her will.'

'That, Alexander darling, is the way people normally get left things.'

'So?' Alexander shook his head in slow wonder at Hope. 'Don't you realize what this means?'

'All too well, Alexander,' Hope said, and then she added flatly, 'It means you intend to move us to the country.' She got up from the table, picked up the pile of ironing she had just finished doing, and started to stack it away carefully to air on the shelves above the boiler.

'But we agreed!' Alexander protested. 'We agreed that Hatcombe would be a wonderful place to live. And what a background for the girls.'

'No, we did not, Alex. All we agreed was that it was a lovely part of the world. We never agreed to move to that terrible old house.'

'Terrible old house?' Alexander echoed, then frowned dramatically. '*Terrible old house?* A Grade II listed Georgian rectory in Pewsey Vale? Have you seen what those places go for?'

'Alex.' Hope put her laundry basket back down on the table and looked her husband in the eye. He started fidgeting the moment she did so, just as he always did when she pinned his wings. 'Alex, the best thing you could do, believe me, if and when Aunt Rosabel dies—'

'There's no if about it. Death is life's only great certainty.'

'When your great-aunt does finally die, and *if* she has left you the house—'

'Of course she'll have left me the house! You read the letter, didn't you? How you and I and the girls have brought sunshine and light back into her life! How much she loves having her great-nieces round her! How—'

'Alexander?'

'Yes?'

'What is it that you always say – there's no such thing as a free lunch? Don't you think it applies most of all to families, darling? Really?'

'What's got into you, Hope?' Alexander groaned. 'You complain when things don't go right—'

'I do not complain, love. When have I ever complained?'

'You complain when something goes wrong with my business—'

'I don't—'

'And then when at last we get a real chunk of good fortune, you complain about that as well!'

'No, I don't – I just think that we should what Mellie calls *get real*. We are fine, for the moment. We can't change our whole life on the promise of a will, really we can't.'

But Alexander just sighed and took the whisky bottle off the nearby worktop.

'And it's no good just sighing. She might not leave you the house.'

Having poured himself a drink, Alexander looked up at his wife. 'She will if we go and move in there now,' he said, screwing the top back on the bottle.

Hope said nothing.

'Look,' Alexander began again. 'She's a lonely

old woman, and that is a very big house—'

'It might need things done to it,' Hope insisted, hating to hear the rising panic in her own voice. 'I mean, we know nothing about the house.'

'If it needs anything done to it, or we want to alter it to suit our needs, she will pay for whatever needs doing, she said so.'

'Really?'

'We certainly discussed the matter when we were down there at Easter. And when you think about it, it's only common sense. Since her son was killed in the war, she's been living there on her memories. This way, if we move in with her, there will be a family there again.'

'We've barely finished converting this, and it's hardly, you know, *Interiors* standard—'

'Let me finish for once. Look. Just suppose – that's all I'm asking you to do, suppose – just suppose we did go and live in Hatcombe. Great-aunt R says she's perfectly happy to move into a wing and let us have the rest of the house. We can change whatever we need to change, at her expense, and when the old lady pops off either we sell it and realize a tidy profit or we go on living there. Either way it's not going to *cost* us. She's leaving me the house, Hope. That's the point, she is leaving me the house.'

'How do you know how much money she's got?'

'She told me. No – all right – she showed me.'

'She took the sock out from under the bed?'

'She told me she has over two hundred and fifty thousand – and another quarter of a million in stocks and shares.'

Hope frowned deeply, not at the amount of money but at the look in Alexander's eyes. 'It's not our money, Alexander,' she said wearily. 'It's *her* money and her house.' She sat down and started folding some napkins she had forgotten to include in the ironing, thinking for a moment. 'What about this place? What about our home here? This is our home, not just a house.'

'The girls will like living in Hatcombe even more than here,' Alexander replied. 'And what *about* this place? This may be home to you, Hope, but to the rest of the world it is merely a little piece of suburbia with a long narrow front room and a long narrow back garden and, let's face it, a shabby sort of road with down at heel housing at the bottom half and hardly better at the top. Anyone can live in this sort of house, but it takes someone particular to live at Hatcombe.'

'I realize it must seem mad to you, Alex, but I really don't like the idea of living somewhere like Hatcombe. All the responsibilities of a great big house just make me panic. I like being normal, and ordinary, and here.'

'Hope, Hatcombe is hardly Kensington Palace. And look – if the worst came to the worst—'

'Which when other people's families get involved it invariably does—'

'We can sell Hatcombe and always buy back.

This is the chance of a lifetime. Do you know what a place like that would be *worth* properly modernized? Five bedrooms, four reception rooms, separate granny wing, staff cottage, over ten acres with stables and paddocks?'

'No,' Hope said quietly. 'And I'm not sure that I really want to know.'

'Six, seven – eight, nine – hundred thousand pounds – and that's a conservative estimate in a bad market.'

Hope nodded, got up again, and added the folded napkins to the rest of the laundry she was airing because there was no point in continuing the argument. The trouble was, in a way Alexander was right. It did make perfect sense.

If everything went according to plan, not only would they have a lovely home, a background for the girls as they finished growing up just as Alexander had said, but with one move they would be out of debt. If on the other hand everything went pear-shaped, then they would hardly be any worse off than they were now, namely facing some sort of Alexander-induced ruin.

For once Alexander would have a cast-iron opportunity to make some money without any enormous risk in a market which was regarded as the most secure of all, the property market.

'OK,' she heard herself say, finally closing the boiler cupboard doors. 'OK – you had better start talking formally to Aunt Rosabel, if she really does mean it.'

'Hope darling,' Alexander said, taking her in his arms. 'You won't regret this, I promise. This has to be the best thing that ever happened to us.'

That night when everyone was asleep Hope slipped out of bed and went down to the kitchen, a habit of hers when she was anxious. As quietly as possible she made herself a hot drink and with mug in hand went into her back garden and sat down on the bench under the little cherry tree which she had planted when they first arrived in West Dean Drive.

Minou, the girls' little Burmese cat, appeared from nowhere and ran up the tree behind her, pausing to sink her claws in and out of its bark, purring loudly as she did so, while Hope stared up at the night sky, oblivious of the cold air. If she was at Hatcombe she knew she would be able to see a sky studded with stars and seemingly aglow with light, but from West Dean Drive very little of it was visible, while ever more aeroplanes dropped low on the flight path approaching Heathrow, it being still the Easter season.

Yet these were some of the many things that she liked about where she lived, its smallness, its ordinariness, its proximity to everything else. She even liked the sound of the night flights returning from exotic places about which she had only read, the rumble from a distant city that never slept, the hum of traffic from the South Circular Road at the end of the Drive. The very sense of all the other people living or sleeping, of life going on, in a neighbourhood without pretension or grandeur, pleased her and gave her a feeling of content.

Most of the people who lived around them thought of themselves as ordinary, and perhaps even took pride in so doing; but Hatcombe was the very opposite. Hatcombe was everything West Dean Drive was not, graceful, grand, even a little imposing. She knew she should feel hopeful about the change in their fortunes, yet for no reason she could name she was filled again with that same senseless dread she had experienced at Christmas.

'How soon do we have to be out of West Dean Drive?' Hope asked as they stopped off for lunch at a pub, on their way to make a closer inspection of Hatcombe House. 'If we do decide to sign? How long, Alex darling?'

'Three weeks.'

'Three weeks?' Hope echoed disbelievingly. 'You've just given me a heart attack. That just isn't possible.'

'It's a buyers' market, Hope darling. When they say jump, you jump. Ask the estate agents. You know with the slump and Black Monday, and Black Wednesday, everything's pretty – black,' he ended, joking, because he felt so light-hearted. He was all right. He was going to be all right. The rest of the world might have jumped out of various windows, but he was going to be all right, thanks to Aunt Rosabel.

'Three *weeks*.'

'Foreigners buying for employees, the estate agent told me. Nowhere to sell, they can move straight in. The company they work for want them up and running within a month.' As Hope continued to look aghast, Alexander put his head to one side and said to her as soothingly as he could, 'Come on, Hope, it isn't as if we don't have anywhere to go.'

'What about the kids' schools? We can't just pull them out weeks before the end of term, Alex.'

'We pay the fees. We can do what we like, I'd have thought.'

'And Rose? We haven't really discussed Rose.'

'We've been through all that, Hope darling.'

'What about what Rose wants?'

'Rose is a girl, she'll soon forget about being a ballet dancer. Inevitably she'll marry and have babies. Ballet won't be a full-time career thing for her, really.'

An unsaid *Just like you, darling* lay between them and Hope felt a burning sense of the futility of it all. Why should Rose's life just be like her mother's? Why should she be forced to choose between marriage and dancing, for that matter?

'You don't want Rose to be a dancer because it doesn't fit in with your plans, Alex,' she finally said, in a quiet voice. 'That is the only reason, nothing to do with her having babies, or getting married, or anything.'

'I don't want Rose to be a dancer . . .' Alexander

took his wife's hands and looked into her eyes. 'I don't want Rose to be a dancer? Sweetheart, it has nothing to do with what *I* want, or do not want. It is a fact that I am talking about, Hope, and that fact is, darling, she is going to grow too tall, so why let her go on hoping and sweating on the line, believing she will become something that she will never in reality be able to become, through no fault of her own?'

'At least we should give her the chance to follow her bliss.'

'Of course she should follow her bliss, darling, we all should. But being too tall for something that you want to do is not going to make anyone *happy*, and who is to say that her bliss, as you so sweetly call it, is not ours? Who is to say that moving to Hatcombe will not make her happy, away from sniping dance masters?'

'I think we should give Rose the chance to see how good she is. She's earned it. She won that place over hundreds of other applicants.' Hope turned to look pleadingly at her husband. She could not stop thinking of that moment when Rose won her place, how her eyes had shone.

'Look – I do not want Rose to go on with her dancing only to end up on the scrap heap. The rest of the family understands that, but because you were a dancer and it came to nothing—'

'I loved dancing, and it only came to nothing, as you call it, because I married. Besides, I'm still teaching, and you know, Alex, it may not seem much to you, but going back to teaching dance has done so much for me—'

'Even if I changed my mind, Hope darling, there would still be the question of the fees. I simply can't afford those fees, not on top of everything else.'

'You never mentioned there was a problem with the fees before. You said you'd borrow the money from your father until this latest scheme of yours came good – you told Rose that was what you would do.'

'That's not such a good idea any more, and anyway – it's academic.'

'I want Rose to go to Park Lodge, Alex, I really do. I want her to have the same chance as I had. If she decides to give it all up, of her own accord, well – that's another matter.'

'I do not want her to be a disappointed dancer.'

'And I do not want to move.'

Alexander stared at her again. 'Look – what is all this about, please? I thought we had discussed all this. I mean, it's all a bit late, isn't it?'

'I do not want to move, Alex. I've told you over and over again. Not only do I not want to move, I do not want to move in with your great-aunt. It just does not seem a healthy kind of thing to do, whatever the financial advantages. I really do feel that. We'll muddle through at West Dean Drive, we always have before. Really, we'll be all right. I find I keep saying *yes* to all this when I really mean *no*.'

'As I said, she's an old woman, Hope. Try to be a bit more understanding.'

'And I'm still a young woman, Alexander. I still have life in me, more perhaps now I've finished having babies, and I am really worried about moving to Wiltshire. All those country women – I just won't fit in.'

Their conversation had continued from the pub to the car, and on from there, but now as they passed increasing expanses of green fields and there was a sight of woods in the distance, and imperceptibly everything outside the windows of the old car seemed to be becoming lighter, and the air clearer, a silence fell between them, leaving only the wipers and the engine to break the pause which had turned into a battle of wills.

'I don't think you realize that whether you like it or not, we have no choice. I mean, we really have to do this, Hope,' Alexander said finally and quietly. 'We have no alternative.'

'There's always an alternative, Alexander.'

'Fine. So there is an alternative, Hope.'

'Which is?'

'Bankruptcy.'

At last Hope recognized the dead end to which they had finally come.

On this visit Hope looked at the house with quite a different eye. This was going to be her home. She must now try to think of what it would be like to run it, day by day, week by week. By prior arrangement Alexander left her and Aunt Rosabel alone in the library with a tray of tea while he took a surveyor over the place.

'Lovely spot,' the surveyor said, and then, 'Beautiful house.' And finally, 'Hope it's not in need of what I think it is.'

'Which is?' Alexander asked, following him out into the courtyard, and then back again into the drive, and then right round the outside, and then back that way too.

'Underpinning.' The surveyor rolled his eyes. 'Not good. And that's not all . . .' He appeared to be enjoying himself enormously at Alexander's expense, so Alexander was determined not to show any outward emotion. 'And once I've had a dig in the attic and had a floorboard or two up, I fear I will find worse. Dry rot.'

Other defects became all too apparent when, after climbing up into the attics, they found that part of the roof in one of the wings had collapsed. What was more, although outwardly the house seemed dry enough, the cellars were in a state of semi-permanent flooding, the influx of rainwater and seepage from the surrounding lawns and paddocks being only just held at bay by a Heath Robinson type of pumping device; as a consequence of which there was at least six inches of water in the basement at any one time.

'This is a lot of work, Mr Merriott. To put this right is a *lot* of work. My goodness, I don't envy you at all,' the surveyor concluded, smiling.

'Fine,' Alexander said, apparently unworried, also smiling. 'So a ball park figure then. To put it all right.'

'A lot of money.'

'Which means?'

'Fifty, sixty thousand – underpinning alone will eat up thirty thousand, I would say. Oh, yes, definitely thirty thousand.' He smiled again.

'Oh well,' Alexander said after a moment's pause, his good humour restored. 'Not to worry. The old girl's loaded.' But later, as he drove Hope back to London, he said, 'Nothing much wrong, I think you'll find, from what the surveyor has just told me. The place is in fine form. Nothing much to do, really.'

Hope murmured, 'Oh good,' and then she stared ahead into the darkness. She had liked sitting with Aunt Rosabel in front of the fire in the library and hearing her talk of the old days before the war, when her son was young, and her husband bred polo ponies. Hatcombe had suddenly seemed a refined and gentle place to be, and leaving West Dean Drive not so bad.

Chapter Six

When Rose discovered that she was not going to be allowed to go to ballet school she shut herself in her room.

'This must be you,' she said to her mother, when Hope broke the news. 'Just because you failed as a dancer, you don't want me to succeed!'

'Rose,' Hope began, but Rose was already halfway up the stairs and in spite of everyone's intercessions she refused to come down to tea or supper, nor would she accept the food which Melinda took up for her.

'Dogs and children never starve themselves.' Alexander stared unconcernedly at the tray when Melinda returned with the unwanted food. 'At least that's what my father was forever saying when I was growing up.'

'Even so, I think I'll go up and have a word with her.'

'Your supper will be ruined, Hope.'

'Mellie can put it in the oven.'

Rose was sitting on her bed up by the pillows, looking out of the large picture window onto the garden, when Hope came in.

'Rose—'

'You know how much I'd set my heart on it. How could you stop me?'

'I'm not stopping you from doing anything,' Hope said, sensing betrayal.

'All those things you said to Dads about dancing, and how they treated you at ballet school – you knew, you knew what his reaction would be.'

'Well, yes, I admit it is a very hard discipline, but I told you that – '

'You didn't have to make it a reason for me not going on – I mean how could you! How could you let me go through all those auditions!'

'But, Rose – believe me, this has had nothing to do with me, really—'

'You don't want me to dance,' Rose said suddenly and very quietly, and she bit her lower lip. 'You don't want me to dance in case I'm better than you.'

'Don't be silly, darling.' Hope reached out a hand, but Rose snatched hers away.

'It's true. Dads is right.'

'I don't understand. What's Dads got to do with it? What did he say to you?'

At that moment Alexander put his head round the door and smiled at Rose. 'All right, sausage?' he enquired. 'Everything all right here?'

'Alex—' Hope turned.

'Fine, thanks, Dads,' Rose said from behind her. 'If someone will just leave me alone, I will be fine.'

After taking one last look at her daughter, Hope followed her husband out of the bedroom, Alexander shutting the door behind them.

'What is this all about Alex?' she asked him, dragging him by the arm into their own bedroom and shutting the door. 'What have you been telling Rose?'

'Don't you see? It made much more sense to give you as the reason,' he said. 'What other possible reason could I give her for not wanting her to go to ballet school? At least one that she'd believe? While doing it this way, since you've actually been a dancer—'

'Rose will hate me – don't you see? This will turn her against me for ever, Alexander!'

'Of course it won't turn her against you. It's different with mothers – girls can take things from their mothers they couldn't possibly accept from their fathers – you know that. You're a girl.' Alexander stopped and held up his hands with the open palms facing her, as if stopping a runaway animal. 'It really does sound much more plausible coming from you. You know about these things – and let's face it, you're always telling the poor kid what a tough time you had when you were dancing. It just made more sense, that's all.'

'Thanks. Thank you very much.'

'Just one thing though, Hope. Don't blow the whistle on me. Because that really is the cardinal sin between couples.'

'What?' Hope stared at Alexander, totally baffled.

'I'm serious, Hope. Believe me – we must stick together on this one, I mean it, otherwise Rose will only become confused. Not that Rose would believe you anyway, if you told her *I* wanted her to give up, and that's a fact.'

Alexander placed his hands on the tops of her arms and squeezed them, then sauntered out. Hope watched him go, and after a few seconds she realized, to her surprise, for she was not an angry person, that anger actually was a very little word compared to how she felt.

Melinda came up to see her mother later, long after Hope hadn't come back down for her own supper but had sat staring listlessly out of the window, torn between self-hatred and despair at her inability to cope with her life and somehow make what she wanted to happen, happen.

'Don't say you're throwing a wobbly as well.' Melinda gave her mother an affectionately patronizing look and sighed, sitting down next to her on the edge of the bed.

'No, I am not throwing a wobbly,' Hope replied carefully. 'I am simply calming down, that's all.'

'You're not the one banned from going to ballet school.'

'No – apparently I'm the one doing the banning.'

'But why?'

'Melinda.' Hope looked at her eldest daughter and this time it was her turn to sigh. 'Do you really think I would stop Rose going to Park Lodge? After all the encouragement I've given her?'

117

'Dads said—'

'Dads says a lot of things, many of which he simply does not realize are . . . inaccurate.'

'But he's right though, Mums. Remember? I mean remember how you hated ballet school? You're always telling us how you got slapped at the barre if your leg wasn't high enough, and how that awful teacher humiliated you—'

'I told you those things because I think illusions are dangerous. I didn't want Rose to have any illusions, but I would never stop her doing what she wanted – just as, please God, I would never stop any of you doing what you wanted, ever. Why should I? God knows I've done little enough myself.'

'No, but it's pretty clear to all of us now that you don't want her to go to Park Lodge at all.'

'According to Dads?'

'That's what he said. He said you were the one who was so keen to move us all to Hatcombe, give us some sort of *background*, whatever that might mean.'

Hope sat for a moment deep in thought, nodded once, then got up off the bed. 'OK,' she said. 'If Dads said I did, what chance have I?'

Melinda frowned at her, puzzled. She had never seen her mother like this before. She hurried off to talk to Rose, hoping against hope that everything would calm down soon. As she opened Rose's door she heard her father let himself out, as he so often did, out on business again in the evening.

She sighed and wished that they would all move to Hatcombe, as soon as possible, that Aunt Rosabel would turn out to be a fairy godmother, that Dads would not have to work so hard to keep them all, that life was, or would soon be, just a bit more of a bed of roses.

Hope went to Park Lodge at the earliest opportunity, only to find that she was already too late. The Principal's secretary informed her that Mr Merriott had telephoned first thing the previous morning to tell them that unfortunately their daughter Rose would not be in a position to take up their offer of a place.

'I understand you are moving,' the woman said. 'To the country. I must say, from what Mr Merriott said, it does sound lovely.'

'Yes, but we've had a rethink since all this came up,' Hope replied. 'There's no reason why Rose can't board, not now we have really thought the thing through. Rose can board with some friends of ours round the corner—'

The secretary smiled but at the same time shook her head. 'I'm afraid your husband said it was a past the post decision, as he called it, so because the waiting list is so long and there's such a demand for places the Principal thought it only proper to offer your daughter's place to the next girl in line.'

'I see. So that's that, really? I suppose that is really that?'

'I'm afraid so, Mrs Merriott. Such a pity because, as you yourself must surely know, your daughter showed signs of a very real ability, not to mention her dedication, which is well above average. Never grumbles, loves her dancing so much. Such a pity, but there.'

When she finally had Rose to herself and they were able to talk rationally Hope found she was too late on that front as well.

'You don't have to explain,' Rose sang out, pretending to tidy her room. 'Really. It's fine. Dads has already told me.'

'May I know what? What he's told you?'

'About you cancelling my place. You couldn't wait, could you?'

'Rose,' Hope said, having drawn a long deep breath. 'That might be what Dads has said to you, but this morning I went to Park Lodge to try to persuade them to change their minds.'

'And?' Rose turned from her pretence at tidying too quickly for Hope not to realize straight away just how much she would like that decision reversed.

'They can't – not at the moment.'

'I see.' Rose dropped her eyes and turned back to the ineffectual sorting of ballet shoes that would no longer be needed. 'Lucky thing, the girl who got the place. Lucky, lucky thing.'

Seeing her daughter's lips suddenly trembling

Hope thought her heart would break for Rose. She of all people knew only too well what Rose had gone through to get that place, but she also knew that she couldn't betray Alexander to his daughters, and that's what Alexander was banking on. He was playing on the fact that Hope well knew the rules of the married game. They'd been drummed into her hard and long by her father, and for as long as she could remember. Any matter for dispute was to be conducted between husband and wife alone.

'Rose, please listen to me, and don't walk away when I'm talking to you.'

'I'm walking away because I don't have anything to say to you.'

'I do to you, Rose. You see, we always agreed that we would never send any of you girls away to school, and now that your – now that we have decided to take this opportunity to move to the country, had you gone to Park Lodge you would have had to board.'

'And now we're moving to the country, guess what, Mums, I'm going to have to board anyway!'

'Not necessarily, Rose. Look, all is not lost. The Principal at Park Lodge was so impressed with your talent that she's taken the most unusual step of recommending you to a very good ballet school in Devizes, which isn't really very far at all from Hatcombe. Isn't that great?'

'Mums—'

'I can drive you there every day, darling. And if you really are as talented as they think you might be—'

'Mums – there's no point, right?'

Hope stopped and looked at her daughter, to find her staring back with grim determination.

'Of course there's a point. Why shouldn't there be?'

'Because,' Rose said, frowning and narrowing her dark eyes, 'because I don't want to be a ballet dancer any more, that's why. OK? I realize just how much it means to you that I don't compete with you, Dads has already explained all that to me, and it's OK. It's cool.'

Another person who didn't like the idea of the Merriotts' moving was Imogen who demanded to know what *she* was supposed to do.

As always when he found a question fatuous, Alexander treated it with undue seriousness, considering the problem for an inordinately long period of time before simply throwing it back in the asker's face.

'What are you supposed to *do*?' he echoed. 'Pass.'

'With you moving to the country. What am I supposed to do?'

'Stay where you are. You don't have to move.'

'What about you and me, Al?'

'What about you and me? And don't call me Al.'

'When am I going to see you?'

Alexander shrugged. 'I don't know, Mogs, really. We'll have to put our diaries together and work out some dates. But if you think about it, we're going to be able to spend even more time together than before.'

'The point was,' Imogen reminded him, 'since Hope couldn't have any more children—'

'That was your point, Mogs,' Alexander corrected her. 'My father won't stand for me divorcing Hope. I hope that is quite clear.'

'Your father isn't the issue here.'

'He's an old man, Mogs. And not a very well one. Be patient.'

To stop any further argument Alexander then made what he considered to be pretty good love to his mistress, and since for once she was completely silent afterwards, on reflection he felt his opinion was fully justified.

The person who finally took the most persuasion, surprisingly enough, was Claire, her problem being that she had settled so well into her new school and made so many friends that she was not looking forward to starting all over again at a place which she might not like nearly so much.

'I know what you're going to say before you say it, Hope, so don't bother,' Alexander had remarked lightly as they drove back home from a friend's birthday party. 'I assure you it will be worth it, in terms of lifestyle, quality and worth. No-one brought up in the country ever regrets it –

the country is an education in itself. That's a known fact. And the other known fact is that kids are made of rubber. They bounce. Just you wait. Before the removal men have even finished unpacking, unbridled joy will be the order of the day.'

It seemed that Alexander was right, because even before the Mercedes had left West Dean Drive for the last time the excitement emanating from the back seat of the old car was palpable. As the girls all fell asleep during what they called the boring motorway bit, Hope's thoughts strayed back to her old house, and she found herself staring at the cars going in the other direction, back to London, with envy, knowing that many of those people in their vehicles would be going back to their comfortable lives in various versions of West Dean Drive.

Even so, as Alexander drove them further and further away from their old, happy, home, she realized that her unshakable sense of foreboding must seem pretty strange to anyone else. It was as if she was moving towards self-immolation, not into an old, enviably beautiful, eighteenth-century house.

After all, the girls had been awestruck when they first saw Hatcombe, and, when it had finally sunk in that the country house with its acres of parkland was actually to be their new home, the problems which had been dividing the family seemed to melt away and they could not wait to leave London. Even Rose seemed to have become reconciled to the idea and Claire had long forgotten the possible misery of starting at a new school. So why did Hope feel as she did?

Because she didn't trust what was happening? Because she felt it was all slightly unreal? Or was it, as Alexander had said to her late one night, because she had had no real say in the matter? Was she really what he, jokingly, called a control freak? Was she actually resentful of this golden opportunity which was being afforded her family because it had nothing to do with her?

'You are a walking womb,' Alexander loved to tease her. 'Not just down there, up here. In your head. You are the giver of life, you like to be the creator. Actually, you are a right little deity in your own way, do you know that? And like all little gods, you move in some *very* mysterious ways.'

However, as with most new enterprises the initial euphoria of novelty finally overcame any doubts or worries that might have beset a family moving from the warmth and security of their familiar home to the uncharted territory of a dilapidated old house deep in the heart of rural Wiltshire. Besides, once Hope had made up her mind to do something she was not someone who would permit herself to give in to despair.

The glorious weather certainly helped, but mostly it was everyone else's enthusiasm which finally carried Hope along, so that on arrival at Hatcombe she determined that the first thing she would set her mind to doing was making sure that everyone was as comfortable as possible, and that Aunt Rosabel was not disturbed in any ways that she might not like.

With that in mind, as soon as they arrived and even while the removal men were still unpacking the pantechnicon Hope set about looking for the most waterproof outbuilding on the estate, somewhere where, as she said, 'the girls can play music and camp out for the rest of the summer while we unpack and sort out the rooms the way that will be best for everyone'.

Leaving little Letty in charge of Verna, who was more than delighted to be left to spread out a rug and open a picnic for the girls in one of the back meadows – summer having moved in so fast on spring that the bluebells in the wild woods beyond the garden were only just discernible – Hope started to explore the outbuildings around the house.

She finally decided that, since among other things it had electricity and was dry enough to store the straw and hay, the upper room in the main barn in the stable yard had to be the best site.

'Where is Mrs Lander?' Hope asked Aunt Rosabel once she had directed the girls towards their new 'camp'.

'With you all here I have no need of her, not for the moment anyway.'

Aunt Rosabel smiled with real warmth, at the pantechnicon, at the summer coming in, at the spring departing, at the blue sky, at the few flowers on the climbers that were wearily making their aged way up the façade of her house.

'Does she have somewhere else to go?'

'Of course. She has gone to her sister. Housekeepers always have sisters. Usually in Seaford, I think you'll find.'

That was the end of that particular conversation for the time being as Aunt Rosabel steered Alexander away with her to have a private talk, leaving Hope in charge of the removal men. The good news was that Alexander and Hope could move into the housekeeper's temporarily vacant cottage until such time as they had all sorted out where everything should be, how Aunt Rosabel wanted them actually to use the house, how happily she could put up with the girls living with her, and how little she minded.

'And that is all any of us care about,' Alexander told her, putting his arm round her shoulder, 'that we should not disturb you.'

His great-aunt beamed at him. She had done nothing but smile and laugh since their arrival. It was as if she had been born again, she told Alexander, or as if she and Uncle Harold were once more moving in themselves.

Meanwhile, Hope and the three girls had set up camp in the main barn.

'This is going to be fun,' Claire announced. 'I think I'm going to really love being here, you know, even if it does mean changing schools.'

''Course you are, you dork,' Melinda replied, pinning her long blond hair back up on top of her head during a pause in the spring cleaning. 'And just you wait till the stables are full of ponies and horses.'

'You might have a bit of time to wait till that happens,' Hope warned. 'We have to move into the house first.'

'Aunt Rosabel has promised us some ponies straight away,' Melinda said dreamily. 'She says it would be great to have some horses here again. She said she couldn't wait to hear the hooves rattling over the cobblestones in the yard, and to be helping us bring them in from the fields, and we talked about how sweet grass-fed horses smell – the sweetest smell in the world, Aunt Rosabel said.'

'Never mind, anyway, first things first,' Hope commanded. 'First we make this place fit for human habitation, and then we'll see about horses.'

During the next weeks, as the summer weather turned from warm to hot and Verna and the girls lived outside, swimming in the lake and picnicking in the fields, Hope found herself driving round the neighbourhood researching the various schools that might have vacancies for the girls in September. She finally found an old-fashioned but charmingly situated establishment on the north side of Marlborough which agreed to take all three Merriott girls.

'But why do the gels have to go to school?' Aunt Rosabel wanted to know at dinner in the cottage that night. 'Should they not be educated at home, at Hatcombe? I know all Uncle Harold's sisters were educated at home, as I was. Gels did not go to school in our day. Boys, certainly, but not gels.'

There was a stunned silence around the table as the 'gels' digested this riveting fact. Claire immediately thought *Whoopee!* and, given a little more time, Melinda and Rose's reactions were finally not dissimilar to their younger sister's. The very idea of not going to school was bliss to Melinda, who immediately imagined herself going to work in a racing yard, or making a stables at Hatcombe which she and Aunt Rosabel would run jointly, Aunt Rosabel knowing really quite a lot, having bred polo ponies with Uncle Harold.

Seeing the excited looks being exchanged between her daughters, Hope felt she ought to say something, and, having first glanced towards Alexander, she plunged in. 'I don't think the girls would be happy just being educated at home, Aunt Rosabel. We're not that sort of family, really. This school – I've heard awfully good things about it, and Mrs Robins the headmistress seems to be a very nice person. She has also been running the school for over twenty years, which just about says everything nowadays,' Hope continued. 'Most other head teachers seem to change every three or four years.'

Aunt Rosabel nodded at this, and said, 'Quite

so,' but Alexander touched her hand as if to say, *I agree with you, but what can I do?*

After that there was a short silence before Aunt Rosabel announced sadly to Hope, 'I am afraid I am not particularly partial to minted chicken. Not that it is not well cooked, it is simply not to my taste. Mint should be kept for new potatoes and that is all, in my opinion.'

She pushed Hope's carefully cooked food away from her and before Hope could say any more Alexander had done the same. 'I agree with Aunt Rosabel, I'm afraid, darling. I find this dish just too sweet.'

Aunt Rosabel smiled warmly at him and put her hand on his arm. 'Perhaps we should discuss the menus together in future, Hope?' she suggested gently.

The old lady rose from the table, dressed as always for dinner in a beautiful short cocktail dress of black taffeta. Alexander put out his arm for her and they walked slowly out of the small dining room to the sitting room.

'Don't worry, Mums, we'll finish theirs,' Melinda said to comfort Hope. 'We're all starving.'

Hope looked at her eldest daughter and smiled, although Melinda was sure that for one awful minute she had seen tears in her mother's eyes.

'Stupid thing is,' Claire whispered, *sotto voce*, as the other two quickly picked the rest of the minted chicken off the discarded plates, 'she's probably right. I mean we could learn just as much here at

Hatcombe as at school, I should have thought.'

'And save the fees,' Rose added, her spirits lifting at the idea of never having to sit at a school desk with 'normal' girls.

'They haven't even had their pudding,' Hope said, looking round at the sideboard at last. 'I did home-made raspberry jellies with lemon mascarpone.'

'Don't worry, Mums,' Rose told her. 'We'll eat their share. As Mellie said, we're still starving.' She smiled and put a hand over her mother's, and they looked at each other in the way that they had always used to do, sending Hope off to the kitchen greatly cheered.

'As soon as you've finished pudding you can push off to the barn and have a good game of ping-pong,' she told them on her return. 'I bought some balls and ping-pong bats when I was in Wharton, cleaned up the old table and mended the net, so off with the lot of you.'

'Great, Mums.' Melinda grinned. 'This is good.'

As they went they all kissed her, and Rose made sure to give her an extra hug. Indeed it meant so much to Hope that they had all wanted to show her that they were on her side that she left the washing-up and walked out of the cottage by the back door, leaving Alexander and Aunt Rosabel to their murmured conversation while she walked round and round the grounds to think, and be quite quiet.

The light of the moon was brilliant, and the stars

131

too, and what with the sounds of the girls' happy shouts coming from the barn, not to mention the now familiar hooting of the owls, combining with the noise of passing tractors returning late to their owners' farms, for the first time since they had arrived Hope felt quietly at ease with Hatcombe, her sense of dread quite vanished. She knew that old houses, like old ladies, were difficult, and resisted change, and that it would take time for both Hatcombe and Aunt Rosabel to get used to them all, but suddenly she had a feeling that they well might and, that being so, they would be happy in their elegant new home, as happy as they had been in dear old familiar West Dean Drive.

It seemed that Hope was not alone in that feeling, for in no time at all Hatcombe was becoming both a haven and a heaven to them all, even to Rose, who appeared to have either sublimated all her ambitions to become a dancer or rejected them. Outwardly anyway they were a happy bunch, all of them busy dreaming of what the house was going to become, and how their own lives would change. Even the beauty of the weather helped, wooing them all into a false sense of security, as if life at Hatcombe would always be, and had always been, so blessed.

One afternoon Melinda borrowed her mother's little automatic camera and set about recording that day, quite simply, from every one of its beautiful angles. The handyman in his straw hat who had come from the village to help in the vegetable garden, Verna pushing the baby down the drive towards the lake, where she would be photographed again as she sat rocking the old Victorian perambulator found at the back of one of the stables and watching dragonflies swooping, daringly, over the water. And then again Claire climbing the ladder to the apple loft where she loved to dream and read, and Hope spraying a rose in one of the borders.

'This is truly excellent, wouldn't you say, Aunt Rosabel?' she asked when she had finally made her way round to the old lady's side, where she sat in her chair on the daisy-strewn lawn staring back at the house with its pale apricot climbing roses and its lavender bushes edging the flower beds.

'Oh yes. *Truly excellent*, as you say, Melinda darling. Just such a day as Uncle Harold and I would enjoy, always saying to each other, *A day away from Hatcombe is a day wasted*.'

When they had first seen it at Easter they had all reckoned Hatcombe was the most beautiful house they had ever seen, with its tree-lined drive, the beautiful walled garden, the long sweeping lawns. All it needed was a touch from a magic wand to make it all come alive. For Melinda naturally the stables had been the place to centre her dreams, whereas for Claire it was the library or the lake where she liked to sketch, while Rose found herself drawn to the ancient forage barn, a fine timbered building imbued with an atmosphere which quite intoxicated her.

'We should build a theatre here,' she said one day to Claire. 'It's absolutely ideal for that. And we could put on plays, and have concerts in aid of charity. This place just cries out to be a theatre.'

'It once was,' Aunt Rosabel informed her when the subject came up. 'When the family first came to Hatcombe, every year there would always be a concert or a play or some such event – usually Gilbert and Sullivan or an Agatha Christie. It was very much the cultural hub of village social activity. It was even used on many occasions for weddings and dances.'

'I think we should return the barn to that,' Rose announced. 'I shall make it my task.'

'While your task, Melinda, would seem to be recording the works going on at present for posterity,' the old lady remarked one fine evening when once again she encountered Melinda busy taking pictures around the grounds.

'Ssshhh, Aunt Rosabel,' Melinda whispered. 'For once I've caught Mums sleeping and I don't want her to wake.'

She pointed out Hope now fast asleep in a wooden liner chair under the big tree, in a white dress with her straw hat tipped slightly down over her face, an open book on her knee and beside her a basket full of flowers which she had just picked for the house from the still unkempt herbaceous border.

'If this comes out,' Melinda whispered, 'I'm going to sell it to a postcard company.'

'Ah, now that would be something.' Aunt Rosabel slipped her arm through Melinda's and, leaving Hope still peacefully asleep, they walked down the lawn towards the house as swallows dipped and dived above them.

'These pictures of yours – just think, they will always be here. We should not forget that, Melinda. You and I gone, but your pictures still here, so that other people can remember this day with us, even though we won't be here.'

As she finished speaking, Melinda looked round and thought that even if her photographs never came out she would always remember these first days at Hatcombe as blissful. A summer garden droning with bees and pungent with the rare scents of truly old-fashioned roses, and the whole place full of birdsong. She sighed with contentment, but a little part of her felt sad for Aunt Rosabel, who, as they had walked down the lawn in the growing dusk, she had felt was thinking back to the past, to Uncle Harold, to the times when they had walked down the lawns together and the house had echoed to the shouts of their only son and his friends, every single one of whom had been killed in the last war.

When Aunt Rosabel had disappeared into the house Melinda took herself off to photograph the stable block where she had already been at work. Entering under the clock tower and crossing the cobbled yard she tried to imagine what it must have been like in the days when the yard was full of hunters, carriage horses and polo ponies, instead of just rusting old machinery and discarded furniture. She could almost hear the clatter of hooves, the ring of the farrier's tools, the whinnying of the horses and the voices of the riders returning from a hack round the parkland or the rumble of coaches making ready to leave. Just as Rose had ambitions to restore the barn so Melinda had ambitions to restore the stable block, until it was rebuilt and refurbished down to the last water bucket and manger, and looking just as it was in its heyday in some of Aunt Rosabel's old sepia photos.

But before all that could happen Aunt Rosabel had promised her a horse of her own next Christmas, which added an even greater urgency to each passing day and week that brought her, or so it seemed it must, to that wonderful moment when she could settle back in a saddle of her own, on the back of a horse that would actually be hers.

Unsurprisingly, in the weeks since they had first moved to Hatcombe, Melinda had grown not just to respect Aunt Rosabel, but to love her. She was old and snobbish certainly, and sometimes Melinda could see that she was even a little pettish, but having never really known either of her grandmothers – Hope's mother having run off with a lover, and Alexander's having died before any of them were born – Melinda found that getting to know a relation from so far back in the past was like following a maze, picking up certain threads in her conversation and trying to understand how much things had changed since she was just their age.

But Melinda was not alone in loving to be with her. Claire was also discovering that Aunt Rosabel too had loved drawing and she seemed to think that Claire had a natural gift for it. Back in West Dean Drive she had used to spend hours drawing by herself, but now she would spend those hours not just drawing but painting with an old set of watercolours given to her by Aunt Rosabel.

'Used to be Uncle Harold's,' she had murmured, handing the lovely old wooden box to her great-great-niece one sunny morning after breakfast. 'I suddenly remembered where it was, in the night. He was very good at watercolours. But you must make sure you can sketch first, before you try to use them. You have to be able to draw before you attempt watercolours.'

Claire did make sure that she did plenty of drawing, but after a while the lure of the watercolour set was too much, and it was with great excitement that she started to use them. Seated on a folding stool she would attempt to paint the lake in all its moments, gently passive at early morning, shimmering beneath a warm sun, or darkly inviting at dusk, fish jumping, wrens sleeping. After that she would move to the orchard glistening with its summer crop, the house at twilight, the landscape which stretched beyond the park up onto the Downs – all became subjects for her sketchbook.

'Coming on very nicely, my dear,' Aunt Rosabel would say, looking at her work. 'I don't think you're ever going to make the National Gallery, but you certainly have a feel for it.'

Rose added, 'I expect it makes a change from just reading about painters, Kipper?' at which Claire smiled.

Rose was right. It did make a change, but what was better was taking her work to Aunt Rosabel for her comments – comments which were always 'quite nice' or 'coming along' or 'pretty good'. Somehow her clipped little compliments seemed so much more genuine than those of someone saying in a *pretend* interested voice 'great' or 'brilliant' or 'fantastic' and then just walking off.

At the end of the month, before school was due to start, Alexander took his great-aunt to London at her own request. They were to do business, Rosabel to see her lawyers and bankers, and Alexander to get back 'on track', as he called it. They would be away overnight, Aunt Rosabel staying with an old friend who still lived in Mayfair, and Alexander with a colleague while he conducted negotiations with the family lawyers and tried to sort out his business affairs.

Hope found herself suddenly alone, and feeling strangely free, something she took some time to appreciate until she realized that, until they came to settle at Hatcombe, never before in the history of their marriage had she spent so much concentrated time with Alexander.

It wasn't that she had discovered that she loved him less because of it, but that because he was so demanding in his own way she was exhausted by him, finding that she never had any real time to herself. So when Alexander rang only an hour after he had reached London to say that he had already found he had much more to do than he had anticipated and as a consequence would be spending a few extra days up in town, Hope could not help feeling secretly delighted.

She at once planned a trip into Marlborough for herself and the girls, making an appointment to get her hair done properly for the first time since moving to Hatcombe and intending to buy her daughters some much needed new clothes. But before they could leave for the town, someone called.

He was a tall man, white-haired, and smartly dressed in a dark suit and white shirt with a tie of a discreet navy blue. He looked like a businessman but when Hope shook his hand she realized that he was an artisan, for not only was his hand rough to the touch but both his thumbnails were partially blackened, as if the hands had been in the wars many times, and his fingers were no strangers to the odd missed hammer blow.

'Mr Frances, ma'am. I expect your husband warned you that I was coming?'

'No, I am afraid he didn't, but can I help you?'

Standing in her light cotton blouse and blue and white skirt, Hope raised her hand to her eyes and smiled up at the tall man standing in front of Hatcombe's delicate façade.

'If Mr Merriott is not home, then perhaps I could speak to Mrs Fairfield?' he said, nodding towards the house windows as if he was quite sure that Aunt Rosabel was in and waiting for him.

'I am afraid they have both gone to London.'

'Ah, I see. Well, that's a bit awkward, seeing,' he said, smiling, 'that we have to start work on the house tomorrow.'

'Work?'

'Yes, ma'am.' Mr Frances nodded. 'Mrs Fairfield and Mr Merriott have engaged us through Mr Lambert, the surveyor. We do a great deal of work together on these sorts of houses, in this area. Yes, indeed. But I expect you know all about it?'

It was the cellars which were to be the object of their attention, although as Mr Frances began to talk his way through the problems that lay there Hope got the feeling that this was not the subject at the actual forefront of his mind.

'You really think that will solve the problem with the flooding, do you?' Hope asked superfluously, since Mr Frances had already assured her that digging a three foot deep by six foot square sump below the present level of the cellar floor and installing an automatic pumping device would most surely do the trick.

'It will indeed, Mrs Merriott,' the tall, shock-haired man replied. 'It will cost a little extra, of course, because we hadn't allowed for either the size of the pump or the increased depth we shall now have to go to – but all indications are that from now on these cellars will be dry enough to store anything you like from antique furniture to fine wines.'

'Excellent,' Hope said, beginning to make for the stairs. 'Jolly good, Mr Frances.'

'There is just one other matter,' the builder said to her as he followed her up the stone steps. 'I hope you don't mind my mentioning it, but we are due to start tomorrow . . .'

They had reached the top of the cellar stairs and were standing in the hallway, and Hope stopped and looked at Mr Frances enquiringly.

'We still haven't been paid for our materials, Mrs Merriott,' Mr Frances said, rubbing his chin. 'I know it's not down to you, ma'am, but the contract quite clearly states . . .' He stopped, looking anxious, his soft west country accent making him sound even more worried than he perhaps felt.

'I don't understand,' Hope interrupted. 'Sorry – but what do you mean?'

'I understand it's complicated,' Mr Frances replied. 'Your husband said that all the bills for hirings and materials were to be invoiced to Mrs Fairfield, which we have indeed done, but they have remained unpaid. And of course the contract is with the old lady as well, but when we approached her in person she told us that she had given power of attorney to your husband and he was in charge of everything.'

'So what happened when you billed my husband?'

'Well – nothing, really. He said papers were being drawn up with the lawyers and that these things took time – as I know they do. But he promised that we'd have the money we're owed by the end of that week, which was last Friday. And now here we are Thursday and still no cheque. We do have a great many costs on a job like this as I'm sure you understand – only being a small firm.'

'Of course,' Hope said, with what she prayed was a reassuring smile. 'Look, I'll go and call my husband at once. I know one of the things he and Mrs Fairfield planned to do was to see her lawyers, so I'll get it sorted out and if necessary write you a cheque myself while the funds are being transferred.'

'That's very kind of you, Mrs Merriott. I'm really sorry to have to bring this matter up, but we have to pay our suppliers. And you know what a dog eat dog world it is nowadays.'

There was no reply at any of the direct numbers Alexander had left her.

Hope then tried to reach Aunt Rosabel at her lawyers, only to learn that the appointment was not scheduled for another four hours. She left a message for Alexander to ring her before trying one other connection where she thought he might be, also drawing a blank.

Fortunately, before she had time to panic, Alexander called her back and Hope explained what had happened. He laughed, then sighed, and explained that the transfer of money from Aunt Rosabel's bankers and trustees to Alexander's account had been delayed.

'Pay him whatever you have, and tell him I'll give him the rest on Monday. That should keep him happy over the weekend at least.'

'Alexander—' Hope began.

'I'll pay you back then as well. In full. Promise, darling, really. Believe me, I will pay you back, everything.'

Hope replaced the phone and stared ahead of her. She had no idea if Alexander would ever pay her back, and, she suddenly realized, it hardly seemed to matter. She put a hand to her head, which was throbbing with the anxiety of it all. All the money she had saved from her teaching job in London had gone, and with this large payment the bequest from her father too would have disappeared. She knew that she should believe Alexander when he said he would pay her back, but the trouble was he never had.

She went back to the hall where Mr Frances was still waiting for her.

'I'll just go and fetch my cheque book, Mr Frances. I am sorry to keep you, but I had to just find out what had gone wrong, you know?' She made out the cheque and handed it to him.

'I am ever so sorry to have to call like this, Mrs Merriott, but it's just that with such a huge undertaking we do have to insist on some sort of down payment,' the builder said apologetically, and he shifted from one foot to the other. 'We have to put up the scaffolding tomorrow, see.'

'Scaffolding?' Hope turned to look at him as she opened the front door once more and he stepped out into the drive.

'Underpinning and dry rot, they're not going to take five minutes, as I am sure you appreciate, Mrs Merriott. I did warn your husband and his aunt, but they said that was perfectly all right, and you would be living in the housekeeper's cottage while the work was taking place.'

Mr Frances smiled affably and stretched out his hand once more. Hope smiled back and shook the large, rough hand while hoping that her eyes did not register the shock she was feeling. Even she knew that 'underpinning' and 'dry rot' could cost a fortune to make good. And she had just handed over all her savings, every single penny of them.

'I can't quite remember how much your estimate was in all, Mr Frances . . . ?'

'Well in excess of fifty thousand, I'm afraid, Mrs Merriott, well in excess.' He climbed into his car and drove off, leaving Hope to stare after him realizing that Alexander had talked her into a Hatcombe that might well turn out to be as costly to their security as his varied investments.

True to his word, Mr Frances and his men started on the house next day, and when Hope had packed up Aunt Rosabel's clothes into cases and moved the greater part of her personal belongings into the housekeeper's cottage, while scaffolding went up against the old house, Hope once more tried to ring London, but neither Alexander nor Aunt Rosabel could be found on any number. Either they were 'in a meeting' or they had 'just left' and so, since there was nothing more she could do, and remembering how much they had banked when they sold West Dean Drive, and thinking that not even Alexander could have spent that much money in the few weeks they had been at Hatcombe, Hope shelved her anxiety and turned her attention to the house.

Three days later as the building works began in earnest she found him standing in the hallway. She glanced at the stranger anxiously, and then outside to his car, and then to what he was wearing. Taking comfort from his expensive clothes and air of easy charm, she forgot to ask him how he came to be where he was.

'Strewth,' he said, shaking his closely cropped head. He looked up and around as he spoke. 'I mean we had problems at the Mill House when we moved in, but not like this. Underpinning, the builder just told me, definitely not something I envy you.'

'I don't envy me either,' Hope replied. 'I mean when they said *underpinning* I never realized that it meant leaving the literally sinking ship!'

'Be careful,' her visitor said. 'I mean it. Old houses – once they start to shift you could find yourself floating out to the lake.'

Hope laughed, but the stranger just looked at her and nodded knowingly. 'No joke, is it?' He grinned affably, and held out a slim hand. 'Jack.'

'Jack?' Hope asked, wiping her dirty hand on her jeans before shaking his.

'Just Jack.' But as Hope waited patiently for him to give his full name he gave in and added, 'Tomm. Abbreviated from Tomaso. De Tomaso, as in the motor.' Hope pulled a face and shook her head to illustrate her ignorance, so her visitor went on to explain. 'There was a motor called a de Tomaso. Italian job. Nothing to do with my family, unfortunately, but there you go. I dropped the a s o when I started doing my own thing, and not the family's, which was ice cream not engines.'

'And yours is?'

'Was. This and that, really.' He stared around the hallway. 'This is a beautiful house. Rumour told me it was really rather exquisite, and—'

'Rumour was right,' Hope said.

He had a firm handshake, not a bonesqueezer, the sort Hope hated and could never understand why some men thought it necessary to practise on women, but a strong grip, holding her hand for a second or so after he had finished shaking it, but thankfully without looking deeply into her eyes while he did so which she always found acutely embarrassing. Instead he seemed to have forgotten about her as soon as he looked up at the plasterwork above him.

'Beautiful plasterwork. There were some Italians employed by Lord Jessup at Ardington Court very near to here, and rumour had it that when the old boy didn't meet his debts they left and found employment in smaller local houses in order to earn the money for their journey back to Siena. Just think! *Eh, Gianni, I 'ear 'Atcombe 'Ouse no plasterwork!* So that's how this kind of detail came into these sorts of houses, or – rumour again – so rumour has it.'

'Do you – would you like to see round the house, before it all becomes chaos here? They've only just begun, you know, and I don't know about you, but I love seeing round other people's places. It's nosy, I know, but it is fun, don't you think?'

Jack looked down at Hope. She was small, slender and pretty, but she exuded anxiety. Yet that was perhaps part of her charm, her anxiety to please, her wish to make whatever was so wrong with everyone else right. Perhaps because, if he was correct, there was something very wrong in her own life. He wanted to put out a hand and touch her on her arm, and say, *It's OK, kid, don't let it get to you*, but of course he could not. He hardly knew her. They had only just met, so he smiled down at her instead and murmured, 'Great.'

He followed her up the wide, shallow stairs, and onto a spacious landing which was dominated by an elegant eighteenth-century brass lantern converted from candle holders to electricity but still retaining that old air of light gently diffused on a world that had been both more real and more elegant than their own.

'All the rooms are beautifully furnished. Aunt Rosabel has exquisite taste, doesn't she?'

As they moved in and out of the perfect rooms, and Jack admired the simplicity of the architecture combined with the elegance of the furnishings, he again wanted to take Hope by her hands and say, *Relax!* Since he could not, and since he also did not want to leave her, he found himself asking to see round the attics, wanting to delay the moment of finishing the tour, so that he could go on listening to her voice, which had been both gentle and kind.

'Well, funnily the attics are rather marvellous,' Hope admitted, laughing.

And so they proved. More wide shallow stairs led up to a great room which in a larger house would have been called the 'Long Gallery' but at Hatcombe was just 'attics'.

'It's got all its original rafters,' Jack said, as his eyes ran over the roof. 'Common rafters,' he went on, 'butt purlins, struts, collars – all original, says a lot really, just a pity about the subsidence, yes? Expensive business, subsidence.'

Hope looked quickly past Jack as he said this. It was as if she was turning away from a book that she did not want to read, or an ugly painting, a moment that Jack, after twenty years in the music business, could not miss. It was strange, he had often thought, just how observant 'the business' had made him. Writing a song was one thing, surviving the business was quite another.

They returned to the hall and there was yet another silence as Jack looked round the elegant reception area and sighed inwardly for the days when such beauty was merely an everyday matter.

Finally he nodded. 'Right. I got two boys and one girl, which is really why I'm here. It's my daughter's birthday Sunday, and we all suddenly thought of you. You see, there aren't too many kids their age round here at the moment, in fact there's a dread dearth of them. Now your eldest—'

'Melinda—'

'She's what age? Cyndi, our Cyndi as in Cyndi Lauper, she's sixteen—'

'Melinda's seventeen and a half.'

'Next?'

'Next is Rose and she's sixteen, like Cyndi, and then there's Claire who is fifteen – and after her a long gap until Letty the baby who's one point three. All girls, you see.'

Thank God he did not say *Bad luck* or *Didn't anyone tell you the special way of making sure it's a boy* or

How awful for your husband, a house full of girls, as most people did. Instead he just nodded and smiled, seeming if anything only too pleased that a clutch of girls had moved into the neighbourhood.

'Right. Our Josh is twenty-one, and then there's Tobias – dread name. His mother's idea. I call him Toby – or Tobe usually. Tobe's eighteen—'

'Perfect. Now all they have to do is hate each other on sight.'

Jack smiled then explained exactly where he lived, a converted mill about six miles away, down a hard-to-find lane.

'Best if I come and pick 'em up before the party, perhaps?' he said.

'No really, Alexander can bring them—'

'Is he around?'

'He's in town on business, actually.'

'Weekender?'

Hope shook her head. 'Family business. Do you weekend?'

'No way. Full time yokel, me,' Jack said with a grin. 'Can't you see the straws in my hair? So what does your other half do, then? If he doesn't commute?'

'This and that. He describes himself as an indie.'

'Yeah? What tribe?'

Hope laughed and began to walk across to the cottage. 'He's an independent business consultant—'

'I know. Seat of the pants pilot.' Jack grinned. 'He who dares wins.'

'What do you do, Mr Tomm?'

'Mr Tomm! Jack.'

'Jack . . .'

There was a short silence as they walked on and Hope noticed how clean and crisp his shirt was and the way his blue cashmere jumper was knotted stylishly around his broad shoulders and how comfortingly tall he was, and the merciful fact that he did not smell of some overpowering aftershave and had what Melinda would call *really neat* shoes on, and that he had hands with long fingers and properly trimmed nails.

Jack for his part noted that Hope was more than pretty. She was quite beautiful, in her cotton skirt and crisply ironed blouse, with her freshly washed brown hair caught back by two tortoiseshell combs. Mercifully she had not adopted some awful overdone 'country look' and her sandalled feet had very pretty toes, which Jack had often found to his dismay was most unusual in women. He increasingly did not want to leave this petite and charming woman with the sad eyes and the grateful laugh.

'So what is your – what is your main thing?'

'Music, I suppose.'

'You play? You write? What exactly? You know so much about old houses I thought you might be an architect.'

'No, I'm not an architect.' Jack thought for a moment, the way he normally did when asked the question, then decided on what he always called

151

his 'number two answer' – at this stage anyway. *Maybe when I get to know her better*, he thought. *If I ever do, that is*.

'I teach music. Freelance.'

'Really? What instruments?'

'Keyboard. Guitar.'

'Claire wants to learn the piano.'

'Well – there you go.'

'Are you frightfully expensive?'

'Frightfully.' He stopped by the chaos left by the builders outside the gutted kitchen and looked at his lovely, sad-faced companion. 'I'm not at all expensive,' he said, suddenly feeling sorry for her without knowing why. 'Not at all. And if one of your kids is really serious, I'll teach her.'

'That's very kind of you, thank you,' Hope replied, feeling herself blushing. To hide the fact that she had coloured she immediately turned away and pretended to look at something of interest in the builders' skip.

'Got time to walk round the grounds?' he wondered. 'I mean this is some setting. No kidding.'

'What's it like where you live?' Hope wondered, falling into step alongside him.

'Nice. Not grand like this – but nice. Millpond, stretch of river, bit of garden – yeah, it's nice. Good. We like it, all of us. Nicer than I ever thought I'd own. Still, there you go.'

He turned and grinned again, a most beguiling boyish grin, in such sharp contrast to one of

Alexander's slow smiles. Hope had only just thought this when she frowned, suddenly realizing that she was thinking of Alexander as if he was someone in her past – a schoolteacher, a family solicitor, a bank manager, someone she no longer really knew.

'Where did you think you'd end up?' she asked. 'When you say where you live is nicer than you ever thought you'd own?'

'Certainly not where I started.'

'Which was?'

'Not like where I am now.'

Again he smiled at her, this time as if in challenge, but Hope pretended to ignore it, leaving the gauntlet where it lay. Instead she pointed across the fields where she could see three girls running towards them, laughing and talking.

'I'd have liked to have three girls,' Jack said, watching them approach.

'You like the *thought* of having three girls,' Hope corrected him, laughing.

'You'd rather not have had 'em, Mrs Merriott?'

'No, I love them. But then, I'm a woman.'

She introduced her daughters as they arrived breathlessly at her side and as one they all fell silent and started automatically to tidy their hair and their clothes before shaking hands very seriously, while Hope told them of Jack's having invited them to his daughter's party.

'I am sorry – I've suddenly forgotten your daughter's name.'

Jack laughed. 'It's OK – I forget names all the time, Hope,' he said, using her name with perfect ease, as if they had known each other some time instead of being strangers. 'Cyndi. C y n d i.' He smiled at the girls. 'As in guess what?'

'Cyndi Lauper?' Rose replied.

'She was christened Cindy with a y, then along came Ms Lauper.'

'And your wife's name?'

'There isn't one. We split. We're divorced.'

'I'm sorry.'

'I'm not.' Jack laughed in a carefree manner which made the three girls smile in a shocked sort of way. 'I'd be a whole lot sorrier if I was still married to the— to *her*. Name of Davina.' He pronounced his ex-wife's name in a deliberately mock-upper class way, pulling a little snobby face as he did so which made the girls smile again. 'I used to call her Dave. Didn't like that a lot, I can tell you.'

'How long were you married?'

'Ninety-eight years. And every day seemed a year too long.'

By now the three girls could barely contain their laughter.

'You'd all better go and get changed. It'll soon be time for lunch,' Hope told them, suddenly remembering they had rescheduled the postponed shopping trip for that afternoon. The girls ran off still giggling, and Hope watched them for a moment. 'Like a bunch of fillies in a field,' she said to Jack, shaking her head. 'All legs and tossing manes.'

Jack seemed to want to go on talking so they wandered on round the grounds, stopping every now and then as they discussed some aspect of the lovely old house, or an old tree that would have to be removed, and Jack continued the story of his marriage, seeming almost anxious to do so.

'I was married nine and a half years. We really should never have married in the first place. I mean talk about not meant for each other. I only wanted to play music and she only wanted to have babies. Then one day she decided she preferred music after all and ran off with my drummer. I got custody of the kids, which is what I wanted – and the rest, as they say, is history. It was a while back now – an age, or that's the way it seems. Haven't heard from her or of her in years. They went to America apparently – and I never did meet a woman, to tell you the truth, who in the end had so little maternal feeling. I think she would have eaten her young, if she could have, which was all the more bewildering since they were all her idea in the first place.'

'How very odd.'

'You said it. Odd and scary. I lost three stone after she left, and of course the children – well, I thought they would be devastated, you know, but after a while they were fine. Great, in fact, once they got over the initial shock. They took it in their stride, realized it happened to other children so why not them. That's when I gave up performing and stayed home to compose and teach, all that, so's I could be with them. Never regretted it.'

'You were a performer?' she said. 'A singer? Or what?'

'Or what,' Jack replied, realizing he'd unbagged the cat. 'Another time.'

Hope was about to show Jack round the interior of the old stables when he looked at his watch.

'Look, I can't quite make the full tour,' he apologized. 'I must pick up young Tobe from the stables and Cyndi from her friends – so all right if we make it another day?'

Hope agreed. They parted, smiling, and she watched him drive off in a big black four wheel drive before she turned back to the house. He had said the party for Cyndi was on Sunday – in which case she had better get organized.

The crisis with the builders, although temporarily resolved, had left Hope with only a few hundred pounds. It was enough for the shopping trip to Marlborough, but not much more, which was why she found herself trying to steer the girls towards clothes which she thought would be useful for many different occasions. Needless to say her efforts were met with derision by all three.

'It's a party, Mums!' they kept reminding her, over-patiently. 'We've got to look cool.'

In the end Hope relented, allowing them to

choose pretty rather than practical, paying for the treat from what remained of her little nest egg. She salvaged part of the cost by sacrificing her hair appointment, privately resolving that since she wasn't going anywhere she might as well wash it at home with the aid of the rubber-hosed shower extension in the cottage. Who would notice the difference?

Alexander finally returned from London late Saturday afternoon with a strangely elated Aunt Rosabel in tow. Hope had expected the old lady to be exhausted after her protracted stay in London but far from it. She and Alexander were like a couple of school kids who'd been allowed to spend their entire half term in London unsupervised.

But the biggest surprise of all was the method of transport by which they returned. Gone was Alexander's much loved old Mercedes 280SE coupé and in its place stood a shining new silver-blue Mercedes Benz estate car.

'Whose is the motor?' Hope asked, never for a moment expecting the answer she was to receive.

'Mine,' Alexander replied, smiling. 'Or rather ours.'

'Alex—' but he already had his hands up to stop her.

'She insisted, didn't you, Aunt Rosabel?'

'I insisted,' the old lady replied warmly. 'Of course I did, but it was your choice, Alexander darling, and very comfortable too.'

'I loved that old car, Alex.' Hope dropped her voice. 'And so did you.'

'The two doors were very awkward for Aunt Rosabel. She insisted on replacing it with whatever we would like. Sweet of her, don't you think?'

'I hope you kept the old one.'

Alexander shifted awkwardly and opened the fifth door of the Mercedes. 'Here,' he said, handing Hope three very expensive-looking boxes. As she took them Hope could see the back of the estate was piled high with more shopping bags and boxes. 'For you.'

'From?'

'From Aunt Rosabel. And girls?' The girls all gathered closely round him, having collected to inspect the shiny new car. 'Aunt Rosabel hasn't forgotten you lot either.'

'Hey,' Melinda wondered as she saw the Harrods bags. 'I mean – what is this?'

'Check this out,' Claire whispered, looking inside hers and seeing silk and sequins.

'This I do not believe,' Rose said quietly, pulling out a sparkling and obviously very expensive top. 'This I just do not believe.'

Hope stood back for a moment, watching Aunt Rosabel watching the children as they dived in and out of the collection of shopping bags, holding up shoes, skirts, tops, bottoms, and bits of glittering paste jewellery with a variety of delighted gasps. Nothing she saw except the paste could have cost under a hundred and fifty pounds,

158

making the clothes she had bought for them earlier that week look like offerings from a charity bazaar.

'Aren't you going to open yours, Hope darling?' Alexander asked, taking out a set of large boxes and piling them up in her arms.

'Clothes for you as well?' she asked.

'Aunt Rosabel insisted. She thinks we're too scruffy!' he added teasingly, and turning back to his old relative he winked.

'Not *scruffy*, Alexander, dear boy. I just thought it would be fun for you to choose them all something glamorous, and *expensive*. After all what is money for but spending?' Aunt Rosabel exclaimed, laughing delightedly.

Even as she spoke Hope suddenly found herself determinedly replacing the unwanted boxes on the open tailgate of the forty-thousand-pound car, unable to control the flood of furious jealousy coursing through her, ashamed of how she felt, and at the same time helpless to stop herself.

'Mums!' Melinda exclaimed as she saw what her mother was doing, and she sidled up to her out of Aunt Rosabel's hearing. 'What do you think you're *doing*?'

'These are really too expensive for us to accept, Mellie,' Hope told her quietly, in sudden desperation. 'It's very sweet of Aunt Rosabel, but we really cannot accept.'

'*Mums!*' Both Claire and Rose now joined the chorus.

'We can't accept such generosity—'

'Mums, these are presents!' Melinda pleaded with her mother in a low tone. 'You can't take away our presents from Aunt Rosabel, it will hurt her feelings!'

'Of course she can't,' Alexander said, over-hearing and taking the bags back from Hope and handing them to his daughters. 'She's just being polite.'

Giving his wife his best hard look, Alexander made sure the right parcels were returned to each recipient while Hope waited to take him aside, walking him away from the rest as the girls tumbled over each other to rush off to the barn to try on their new clothes.

'Just tell me you didn't sell Brünnhilde?' Hope pleaded quietly, using their pet name for the car they had owned since they were married. 'Please tell me that you kept her?'

'She's already done one head gasket. Remember? Too costly by half.'

'But Alex—'

'She was a car, a piece of metal, that's all, Hope. Don't sentimentalize, will you, not now, not when Aunt Rosabel has just spent forty thousand pounds of her money buying us a beautiful motor car that few people could afford.'

'But why should she buy us such an expensive car?'

'Never heard of generosity, Hope? Of people

finding they have money and wanting to do something useful with it?'

'This isn't what this is about, Alex.'

'And you – you are about something else altogether!' Alexander walked away from Hope, shrugging his shoulders. 'Really, you astound me. You want one thing one moment and the next . . .' He raised his eyebrows and shook his head in despair, then turned and entered the housekeeper's cottage. In a moment, Aunt Rosabel came out to talk to Hope.

'I must speak with you, my dear. I perfectly understand how you feel. Perhaps I should feel as you do if I were in your position, but I do assure you these gifts are given in good faith. I only want to spend my money before I die, see people enjoying it, and enjoy it with them, that's all. And what better way to do that than to give it to you and Alexander and the children? Money is for enjoying, and now that you have come to live with me, what better way to spend it than on you? And, too, you must always remember that Alexander is not just a Merriott. His mother was a Williamson, and he likes nice things, it is in his blood. It is in all our blood. Perhaps you do not understand, because you are not a Williamson, but never forget that your children too have Williamson blood. They too will grow up to want good things, and to want to mix with distinguished people – they too are looking to make the best possible lives for themselves. And lastly, if a very old lady may give you some advice – we must always, all of us, be at pains to look – and be – gracious.'

She turned on her heel once more and Hope watched her elegant, upright figure disappearing into the old cottage. Seconds later she heard Alexander and the old lady laughing and joking with Verna. Together with the joyous shouts from the barn the sound seemed suddenly to isolate Hope from everyone at Hatcombe.

Late that night, as Alexander lay sleeping, Hope slipped out of bed and crept off to the downstairs back room, the sitting room next to the dining room, where she proceeded to unwrap the clothes that Aunt Rosabel had shamed her into accepting.

As soon as she undid the silvered paper in the boxes in which they lay Hope immediately saw that the clothes were beautiful. Not only that, they were clothes she could never, ever have imagined owning. They were clothes of which to dream, and she knew at once just from the look of them that they had been chosen by Alexander, who always did have such a good eye for lovely things. That had been yet another of the characteristics which had attracted Hope to him, besides his easy charm, his handsome looks, his lustrous dark hair, his apparently wicked gaze and his extraordinary poise. He had an unerring eye for the sort of clothes which would look good on her, and, though they had always shopped on a shoestring, whenever Alexander was with her he managed to choose clothes for Hope which made her look like a fashion model.

But the clothes he had brought her back from London were something else again. There were three outfits, a black wool suit by Chanel, a red silk party dress by Armani, and a cream trouser suit with the palest of pale blue silk chemises by Caroline Charles. Shoes as well, two pairs, both by Manolo Blahnik, elegant, sexy and the height of fashion, one pair in a light slightly mottled tan, the other black and classically so. Overcome, Hope closed the door and tried on each and every item, having to stand on the sofa in order to catch a sight of herself reflected in the oval looking-glass hanging over the fireplace. When she had finished her luxurious session, she folded the clothes up as well and as dexterously as they had been folded by the shop assistants, wrapped the exquisite shoes in their fine tissue papers and returned them to their boxes. Putting the lights out and closing the door silently, she took them all upstairs again with her, and left them in their shared wardrobe, ready to wear, some day soon, when she was feeling – what was it Aunt Rosabel had called it – *gracious*.

The next day was Cyndi Tomm's party, for which, for no reason she could imagine, Hope still thought her daughters would elect to wear the clothes they had all chosen together, with the last of Hope's savings, in Marlborough that happy day.

Leaving Alexander, Aunt Rosabel, Verna and the baby to have a buffet lunch on the lawn in the shade of the old yew trees, Hope wandered off to the barn to help the girls dress, taking with her a holdall filled not just with the clothes she had bought them, but with the usual beauty aids that they had nearly always lost, misplaced, or broken, such as a hairdryer, pins and clips, ribbons and bunches. Everything, in fact, that they could possibly want or suddenly think that they might want, up to and including perfume and lipsticks, sparkle for the eyes and cheeks, and face paints.

Hope often thought that the time before a party – the excitement of dressing and criticizing each other's choices, bathing and snatching, shouting and powdering, teasing out hair, or putting it up, or down, or bunching it, tonging it, frizzing it or spraying it, the time of borrowed tights or pull-ups, skirts or shirts, lost and found shoes, near delight and near tears – all these moments added up to three-quarters of the fun of going out.

'Hi, Mums—'

'Hi, Mums—'

The sudden quiet, the looks thrown and caught between them, the total silence that greeted the appearance of the clothes she produced from her holdall and laid out on Melinda's bed, the utter astonishment when she put out ribbons and bunches for their hair, all carefully chosen to go

164

with their clothes, should have told Hope which way the land lay, but it did not. And the reason it did not, she realized afterwards, was because she had still clung to the idea that for her sake they would wear the clothes that she had spent her hard-saved money on, rather than the ones Aunt Rosabel had bought with money that had come to her from anything or everything except her own toil.

'Mums.' Melinda took her hands and, having given the other two an anguished look, said, 'Er, Mums – we're going to wear the – er, you know, designer things, if you don't mind.'

'And sequins on our faces, you know!'

Hope stared first at Melinda and then at the other two. How ridiculous to even suppose that they would not be wearing the *designer things*. But even so, she opened her mouth to say, *Oh, for God's sake, you will look ridiculous at a country party with lots of kids who won't possibly be able to afford those sorts of things*. She stopped herself in time, remembering Aunt Rosabel's warning – no, she must be gracious, she must, whatever happened, not have a chip on her shoulder. Just because she could not afford to buy her children expensive clothes did not mean they should not wear them.

'Of course,' she murmured, and was suddenly glad of the old lady's advice when she saw the girls' faces. 'Of course you must wear what you like. You can keep these other things for the holidays, or something.'

She turned away, swallowing the unwelcome lump in her throat, unable to come to terms with her feelings, which were quite out of proportion with the moment. Gracious – she must be *gracious*.

Hope had arranged for Alexander to take the girls to Cyndi Tomm's party, and Hope and Aunt Rosabel and Verna and Letty gathered to wave goodbye to the three teenagers, all of whom, climbing into the back of their father's forty-thousand-pound Mercedes, looked as if they were about to pose for *Vogue* or *Town Magazine*, so glamorous did they look, and so chic.

Later Alexander collected the glamorous Merriott sisters from the party, and, as it transpired afterwards, stayed on for a drink with Jack. Hope could not wait to hear all about everything and so was waiting by the front door of the cottage as soon as she heard the new car arriving back. Seeing her three leggy daughters scrambling out of the car and walking silently off to the barn in the dusk Hope called to them to wait for her, which they quite obviously were not intending to do.

'Hey, Mellie darling, Rose – wait. I'm just dying to hear about it all, darlings, do tell. Was it great fun? It sounded as if it was going to be a corker.'

'Oh, yes. The party was. Yes, it was great fun,' Melinda admitted.

Hope put her arm round Claire. 'Was there dancing?'

'Yes, there was dancing.'

'And a group?'

'Yes, there was a group.'

'And . . . ?'

They were all back upstairs in the improvised bedroom of the barn, and Melinda and Claire were taking off their shoes, seated on the edge of their beds, while Rose, having put on a tape of her favourite ballet music, proceeded to dance carefully around the room in her flat ballet shoes.

'It was terrible, Mums,' she said finally, as she turned and turned to the music, making Hope feel dizzy just watching her as her dancing took her to the end of the barn room and back again. 'Just terrible.'

'We should have listened to you,' Claire mumbled. 'We looked like – well, I don't really know what we looked like.' She turned to Melinda for help. 'What did we look like, Mellie?'

'Tarts!' Melinda put her head in her hands and started to rock with hysterical laughter.

'Yes, she's right. We looked like teenage tarts!'

'And what's so funny,' Rose said, stopping her dancing plum in front of her mother, but then seeing Hope's genuinely horrified face she too started to laugh. 'What was so funny, Mums, is that Aunt Rosabel's most worst word, if you know what I mean, her most worst word – and she's always saying it – is *tarty*. You know? *So tarty, Rose dear, so tarty, just like on the television, not that I would ever own one.'*

'No, she watches Mrs Lander's instead!'

'Oh dear, you should have seen how *stupid* we looked . . .'

The relief they all felt at being able to laugh at how they had looked was second only to the relief that Hope felt as she watched them laughing.

And she would not have been human if she had not also felt relieved that it was they who had chosen to wear their overly expensive clothes, and not Hope. She joined in their laughter, and then they all carefully hung the designer clothes on hangers and went for a long soak in the downstairs bathroom next to the kitchen in the housekeeper's cottage and Hope sat down to watch Mrs Lander's television with Aunt Rosabel, despite the latter's revulsion for the medium.

'How was it?' Aunt Rosabel wanted to know, and she and Verna turned expectant eyes on Hope.

'Oh, a great success,' Hope murmured, and smiled briefly at them before picking up her tapestry frame.

A week later, putting their *great big wham, bam, thank you ma'am flop party* behind them, as Melinda said, they all started their new school, and Hope was left alone for long stretches at Hatcombe with only Letty, Verna, Aunt Rosabel and the builders, Alexander taking himself off more and more frequently, it seemed to Hope, to London in his shiny new car on increasingly long business sorties, leaving Hope in charge of the building works.

'If there are any difficulties and you can't get

hold of me, you and Aunt Rosabel decide, but there really shouldn't be too many more *'ere-come-and-look-at-this-will-you?*s. Anyway, you have a whole set of numbers where you can reach me.' He kissed her lightly on her cheek and climbed thankfully into the Mercedes.

'What exactly is this great new venture, Alex?' Hope had enquired, shutting the heavy door. 'I mean things are really bad out there, aren't they?'

Alexander had given a little sigh before starting the engine. 'Don't worry, Hope darling, things will come round, they always do. My backers may have got cold feet but just wait – I'll bet you anything some brave entrepreneur will run with one of my ideas this time, and I'll clean up.'

'You haven't put any of our house money in this venture, have you?'

'Really, darling, please try not to be so *suspicious*. Oh, and by the way, I am going for that little operation Macleod recommended after Letty was born. You know the one? Where they give you a head graft?' he ended, teasing, but whispered, 'I'm going for the vasectomy, so that should put all your fears at bay, yes?'

'Alexander! But shouldn't we at least talk about it?'

'Nothing to talk about, darling. I've given it a great deal of thought, and I must have it done. It's up to the man to do these things nowadays. For you it's one hell of another operation, while for me it's nothing. Hardly more than a toothache, the clinic told me. So next time I'm down, watch out! Wish me luck!'

Seconds later he was gone with a wave from the car window, disappearing in a cloud of dust past the piles of rubble which still surrounded the house.

Hope gazed after him. They had not made love for many weeks now, but there was no getting away from it – the idea that she would never, ever get pregnant again, or have to live in fear of it, was too wonderful to even think about. And not only that, but when she returned to the cottage she found that Alexander had left a cheque for her. He had paid her back. Things had to be looking up, surely?

'Mogs? It's me,' he said into the car phone as soon as he could get enough cells. 'Alexander.'

'Alexander! Where are you? You never said you were coming up?'

'I'll be with you in no time at all, and guess what? I have a pink ticket for the whole week. I'll tell you why when I see you!'

Replacing the car phone he took a quick look at the expensive stereo on the dashboard and pressed the play button for the compact disc mode. A moment later the car was flooded with the sound of Joe Cocker singing 'Up Where We Belong'.

The following days passed in a sort of haze of content for Hope. The builders were rebuilding, and although the autumn leaves were definitely beginning to fall she found that the silence of the countryside no longer frightened her, nor even the darkness, and going for long walks with Verna and Letty in the absence of the rest of the family allowed her at last to appreciate where she had, with such reluctance, come to live. Now she no longer missed the noise of aircraft, or the sounds of neighbours, but walking among the colours of autumn allowed her eyes to try to pick out each one of the thousand colours that made up the season.

'Did you know that Van Gogh used eighteen versions of the same yellow?' Hope asked Verna one afternoon, but Verna, although pretending polite interest, was much more taken with Letty who was pointing and saying 'Glugg, glugg, glugg' to the ducks on the pond that they were passing, a reaction that Verna was stoutly maintaining was actually 'Ducks, ducks, ducks'.

Hope sighed with happiness whenever her eyes fell on Letty's ravishingly pretty face. Naturally to her all her daughters were beauties, but there was no doubt that out of all of them Letty was the most astonishing to look at, with her large blue eyes and her already thick wavy blond hair. Little wonder that whoever they passed on their walks always turned to stare at her.

'She's going to be famous, mark my words, a great beauty like Lily Langtry. People will stand on chairs to watch her pass,' Aunt Rosabel announced when they returned from their walk, and she kissed the baby's hand. 'Although one hopes that she will be a wife rather than the mistress of a king or a prince,' she added, with a roguish look at Verna.

Verna laughed good-humouredly as she whisked Letty off for her bath. She liked Mrs Fairfield, 'one of the old sort', she would insist to Hope.

Seeing the old lady through the Australian's eyes, Hope's vision of Aunt Roṣabel had mellowed in the same way that her vision of Hatcombe had mellowed, so much so that the two of them had become indivisible, and she now thought of them as one. It was as if in restoring Hatcombe she was also restoring to Aunt Rosabel the life that she had once enjoyed. That she might even, with the house, become modernized was too much to ask, but she did look rosier, and altogether happier, and here again Verna had a theory.

'Young people give off an energy that old people can feed from. They don't realize it's happening – I mean it doesn't make the younger people weak or anything, but they do most certainly give off an energy that helps the older, weaker ones. That's why lumping old people together in a home isn't right. Families were meant to be together, not herded according to their ages. And the same goes for schools – nothing mellow to calm them all down, nothing but children bullying each other.

That's not right either. We've got it wrong.'

One thing Aunt Rosabel had not got wrong, however, was the date of her annual tea when, as she told Hope, 'the Old Contemptibles come to see me, and we talk about John, killed in Italy, you know. Northern Italy.'

She glanced up as she said it to the painting of a little boy pushing a wheelbarrow that hung above the fire, the only possession that she had not put in store when she had moved into the housekeeper's cottage once the underpinning had begun in earnest.

'Yes, they all knew John. Tanks, the cavalry of World War Two. Not much chance, you know, not much chance if you were in a tank, as Harold used to say, but there – one of these days I will see him again, and we will all be together, the three of us, I am quite sure.'

As the old lady finished speaking, and the fire crackled and snapped with the damp of the logs freshly brought in, Hope could hear Letty laughing and gurgling in her bath. Happy sounds of babyhood, and above them Verna singing in a reedy Australian voice, 'Nelly the elephant packed her trunk and went right off to the circus.' What a pointless thing to have given birth to a baby who would grow into a child who would grow into a man to be blown into a thousand pieces. Was that what boy children were for? Just to be killed? Was that why they were so important to everyone?

*   *   *

They arrived one by one driving modest cars, and soberly dressed in dark coats and scarves covering tweed suits which had been teamed with gleaming shirts and regimental ties. And the moment they saw Rosabel Fairfield, their faces lit up.

'Not in the big house any more, Mrs Fairfield?' they teased her as they trooped into the house-keeper's cottage. 'Coming down in the world, we see?'

They shook hands at the door, where the same safe old phrases of welcome rolled out as must have rolled out in previous years. 'You haven't changed at all since last year!' 'I'd have known you anywhere.'

Yet there was no sense of awkwardness when they sat down, crowding the little sitting room as Hope and Verna hurried about with plates full of finely cut sardine sandwiches, and little iced cakes, and fruit cake, and chocolate fingers that melted a little by the end of tea but were appreciated none the less. And out came the photograph albums, and the air became filled with 'ah yes' and 'well, well' and 'well now, fancy that', old-fashioned sounds that did credit to the listeners and the speakers alike, waiting as they did for each to speak in turn.

Aunt Rosabel's face became quite pink from the heat of the fire and the excitement, and when they all finally stood up to go it was evident that, as always, they were as reluctant to leave her as she was for them to go.

'Till next year,' they told her.

'Indeed, indeed,' she agreed, but when they had gone, and Hope and Verna had finished waving to their modest, unassuming cars, which were so utterly in keeping with their characters, she turned away to stare at the painting of her son as a small boy, and stayed in front of it for many minutes.

Chapter Seven

Hope and Aunt Rosabel had become more than friends. They had achieved an understanding, possibly from being together so much while Alexander was away in London, possibly because they, and Verna and Letty, were all living in such close proximity with the builders still hard at work on the main body of the house. Their afternoons were spent out walking together by the lake, or sometimes, if Aunt Rosabel was feeling up to it, to some nearby woodland where they carefully picked their way through the crackling dead branches of last year, and marvelled at frost sparkling like the tiniest blue diamonds on dead leaves.

Aunt Rosabel loved nature and she had always lived in the country, although not always in Wiltshire, having been born and brought up in Sussex – *the poet's county*, she called it.

'A wonderful childhood full of the sound of laughter, and of course, my dear, we never left home. Can you imagine? There we were with our parents and the servants, and the next moment we were whisked up to London, popped into a white dress, presented at Court, had our photographs taken at Lenare, and then walked up the aisle to

the usual strains, and we did not know a *thing*.'
Hope heard this last many times, and never tired
of it.

Once, probably because they both knew what
Aunt Rosabel meant by saying that they *did not
know a thing*, Hope asked her how they had coped?

The old lady stopped and with a curiously theatrical gesture of the hand she laughed and said,
without embarrassment, 'Well, my dear, it was
just as the nursing sister said to me when
John was born – *You'll manage!* And we did. But,
do you see, the boys – English boys – were so
ignorant, they were often petrified too, and many
a honeymoon went by with only *vingt et un* being
played, and dancing to the gramophone, and such
like!'

Hope left it at that. That Aunt Rosabel liked to
tell her little snippets, or to pass on small items of
gossip about people long gone, made their time
together fascinating to Hope, because she had
known so little of her own mother's past. But other
than that one enquiry, she far preferred to listen to
Aunt Rosabel than to question. In the same way,
although she offered her arm to Aunt Rosabel over
the rougher terrain, if she did not wish to take it
Hope would leave her alone, imagining that it
must be irritating to be over-protected, and that
the old, like the young, asked for help when they
needed it, and if they did not ask it was best to let
them make their own way.

Perhaps this last walk together had been a little

too adventurous for the old lady. Hope castigated herself, too late of course – that she had taken them on a new route through the woods. Aunt Rosabel was hobbling back, leaning hard on Hope, and not able to go more than a few paces without stopping.

At last they reached Hatcombe again and Hope called the doctor, who, as it transpired, was about to come out on another visit and would be passing by their door. He bandaged the twisted ankle and prescribed a mild painkiller, as well as sleeping tablets in case the pain kept his patient awake.

'My, my, Mrs Fairfield,' he teased her, 'you really must stop running marathons on such frosty ground!'

They all laughed and at the end of the evening, after a convivial supper in the kitchen, Verna and Hope managed to help Aunt Rosabel up to her room and settle her for the night with what she always called 'a nice cup of cocoa' but was actually drinking chocolate made by Verna and finished off with a little sprinkling of cinnamon, which was delicious.

Hope put out her own light and settled down to the kind of sound sleep that a cup of chocolate and country air always seemed to bring about. She was awakened, she did not know how many hours later, by the sound of someone in her room.

Terrified, she sat up and put on her bedside light to find herself staring into Aunt Rosabel's eyes.

'You must help me,' she told Hope. 'The house is on fire. I must rescue my son.'

Hope was out of bed in a second and pulling on her wool dressing gown. Running into the corridor to call to Verna, she peered out of the window at the façade of Hatcombe. But there was no sound or sight of a fire, and besides, she suddenly realized, Aunt Rosabel's sight was not so good that she could have seen a fire at the main house from her bedroom window. Nor could she have smelt it, for again, the house was too far from the housekeeper's cottage.

'Mrs Fairfield!' Verna was out of her room and giving Hope 'leave her to me' looks for which Hope felt intensely grateful. 'Come with me to your room, Mrs Fairfield, and I'll stay with you until you have calmed yourself.'

Aunt Rosabel suddenly turned a face of panic on the young Australian nanny. 'But – but what am I doing here?' she asked. 'Why aren't I in my own house?'

'Your house is being repaired, Mrs Fairfield, and when it's all finished you will be there again. Nothing to worry about.'

Verna looked back at Hope and nodded at her, and in an attempt to reassure her mouthed as silently as possible, 'Probably had a bad dream.'

'You're going to be all right. Don't you worry about a thing, Mrs Fairfield, Nanny's here. Remember the joke we were having yesterday? Nanny's here?'

Hope waited and then hearing them laughing together she went back to bed. Verna was probably right. Aunt Rosabel must have had some terrible nightmare. But the next morning Verna, whose patience seemed endless, and whose kindness was bottomless, shook her head.

'No, Mrs Merriott, I was thinking about it. Normally she sleeps so well. No, I would say the pills that the doctor gave her brought about some sort of confusion. This happens with old people. I mean,' she added, joking, 'until the old lady decided to go jogging with you, she really was very fit. And she will be again, don't you worry.'

But Alexander was not so sure. He worried aloud on the telephone from London that Hope had been encouraging his elderly relation to do too much.

'I don't want her going before her time,' he said sternly.

'She's not going before her time, Mrs Merriott,' Verna laughed when Hope confided Alexander's worries to her. 'Great heavens, she's fine in every way. She's just turned her ankle, that's all. But to make our sleep patterns just a little easier I've thrown away the sleeping tablets – mild though they were, I think they're just not what was needed. Painkillers, yes, but not both. So many doctors are such junkies, really they are. I've some homoeopathic tablets that will be very soothing, and if she takes them with a hot drink she won't know anything until morning!'

Hope looked after Verna's bustling figure as she put Letty in her pram and pushed her out of the cottage door and onto the path that led to the gates and the road. She would gamely walk her down to the village shop some three miles away, coming back with fresh loaves and farm butter, and anything else that Hope needed. Hope did not know what life would be like without her, but her wages were now being paid out of the sale of West Dean Drive, not out of Alexander's earnings, because there were none. Yet he was so convinced that his many ugly ducklings were about to become swans, Hope had to believe him. Or at least, she wanted to believe him, because only by believing him could she go on with her quiet life at Hatcombe, with walks and talks with Aunt Rosabel and watching Letty growing day by day more beautiful.

She turned back to the cottage and saw Aunt Rosabel's upright figure leaning on her stick, waiting for her. As soon as she drew near her Hope could see that the look in her eyes was the same as in the night, and knew that it would take all her courage to deal with the old lady on her own now that Verna had disappeared to the village with Letty.

'Aunt Rosabel?' she called to her. 'Isn't it a lovely morning? Winters nowadays are definitely becoming warmer, wouldn't you say?'

Aunt Rosabel's brilliant gaze was turned on Hope, but her words were strangely pathetic. 'I cannot understand it,' she told Hope sadly. 'He's normally in for dinner, but look, he's not here. What can have happened to him, do you think?'

'I expect he'll be back soon,' Hope heard herself saying. And then, 'Come inside and wait for him. You'll see, he'll be back soon.'

Once inside, Aunt Rosabel went and sat by the fire as if nothing untoward had been said.

This time, instead of issuing dire warnings for the safeguarding of his great-aunt, Alexander had no time to listen.

'It's just the pills,' he said dismissively, 'as Verna said. Just stop giving her the painkillers and you'll find she'll be right as rain. If you hadn't insisted on taking her walking she'd be perfectly all right.'

He rang off after only a minute or so. Putting down the receiver with a sigh, Hope asked Verna, 'But supposing it's not the pills?'

The handsome Australian girl continued to give Letty her tea, but as she did so she looked at Hope in a worried way. They both knew the problems if Aunt Rosabel's mind was beginning to go, and it would be all too heartbreaking.

'I'll wait until she's fallen asleep tonight, and then I'll remove her cup from her bedside and lock her door. I'm always up with the lark, so I can return the key before she discovers. At least this way we will be able to get some sleep, not lie awake worrying if she's wandering about the cottage or on her way down to the lake, Mrs Merriott. Can't have all of us doing without our shut-eye.'

Hope could not help wondering what she would have done if she did not have Verna. She would be all alone in the countryside with only the baby and an old lady whose mind might be beginning to go.

'What does Mr Merriott say about his great-aunt?'

'He doesn't seem very interested.'

'No, well, that's normal, if you don't mind my saying so, Mrs Merriott. Men don't like this kind of thing, it frightens them.' Verna looked across at Hope but Hope said nothing, simply because there was nothing to say. 'At least the house is getting along fine,' she went on brightly. 'Mr Frances told me he would have finished the first part of the building works very soon – sooner than he had scheduled, in fact, which must be a first.'

Hope nodded, but again she remained silent, because a terrible thought had occurred to her. Later she tried to ring Alexander, but once more he was not obtainable at any of his given numbers, and so she was left with Aunt Rosabel who, to her relief, seemed once more quite her usual self.

She continued to behave normally when Alexander and the girls came home for the weekend, so that Alexander teased both Hope and Verna that they were hysterical women with too little to do. The girls appeared to notice nothing until on Sunday evening, just before they were due to be driven back to school by Alexander, Melinda caught her mother by the arm and said, 'Is everything all right with Aunt Rosabel, Mums?' And then, in answer to Hope's enquiring look, 'It's just that she woke up suddenly this afternoon and told us that she was going to join the WVS and nothing we could do or say would stop her. And she kept calling Rose by her sister's name – Victoria. Verna says it's what is called a time lapse but, I mean, is she *all right*?'

Hope nodded as cheerfully as she could. 'Good heavens, yes,' she said, her heart sinking. 'Perfectly all right. It's just as Verna says – a sort of time lapse.'

After that, with the girls back at school once more, it was difficult for Verna and Hope to go out together unless Aunt Rosabel accompanied them. Otherwise one of them would stay behind to sit with her.

Hope found herself worrying about Aunt Rosabel more than ever in the next few days, until Jack phoned and asked Hope and Alexander over for lunch. There was a pause while Hope's gaze wandered around the kitchen, to the jug of flowers she had just arranged, to the rough brown loaf she had baked that morning, to the ingredients of the salad waiting on the side to be mixed.

'We'd love to come,' she heard herself saying and her heart seemed to stop with the knowledge that Alexander would almost certainly be in

London, that she was telling a deliberate lie, and worst of all that she really wanted to have lunch with Jack Tomm alone. Which was wrong. But as soon as she had heard his voice she had not cared. She wanted him to herself.

For the next few days she lived in terror that something would go wrong between her present and that future for which she now found herself living. The future which was to hold *lunching alone with Jack*.

Once or twice she told herself that she should really back out of the date, but then the glorious realization would come to her that, lunching alone with Jack, she could be someone else. That from the moment she stepped from Verna's car she would no longer be the mother of four daughters, the wife of Alexander, the friend of Verna, the carer of Aunt Rosabel. She would be, quite simply, Hope.

And so the excitement grew in her mind, and secrecy added to that excitement, so that she could hardly eat, and she seemed to be washing her hair five times a day in order to style it as beautifully as she could, make it look polished and gleaming, and have her combs at just the right angle. Even as she realized what a fool she must look to anyone else, the excitement would not go away. She would be lunching with Jack, alone.

But then of course Alexander, who now hardly telephoned during the week when he was in

London, perhaps by some second sight, phoned Hope just as she was leaving the cottage, hair done, and wearing a navy-blue pullover with matching corduroy skirt and what Verna called 'cute boots'.

Hope was just about to say 'I'm out', but before she could Verna handed her the telephone. Crossing her fingers that Verna, who had disappeared upstairs to see to Letty, would not hear, Hope told Alexander her second lie. 'I'm going shopping and then having my hair done in Marlborough,' she told him, and then fled the housekeeper's cottage leaving Verna to give Aunt Rosabel and Letty lunch.

I should not be doing this, she told herself as she drove Verna's car over to Jack's house. *I should be staying at home with Aunt Rosabel, but I have been cooped up in the cottage at Hatcombe for what seems like weeks now, and I would like to see Jack's house. I am only going to see him out of curiosity*, she added, continuing to lie to herself. *Just curiosity, that's all.*

'I'm afraid Alexander could not come. He's been detained in London,' she explained as Jack came out of the Mill House to meet her.

'Oh good,' Jack said, without any attempt at pretence. 'I was hoping it might just be the two of us. Much more fun.'

He tried to look contrite but seeing Hope burst into laughter at the audacity of his honesty, he smiled. He could not help being honest, just as

Hope could not help laughing at his truthfulness. It was breathtaking, and somehow shocking too. And although Hope felt a momentary twinge of guilt that her laughter might be betraying Alexander in some way, she nevertheless found that she almost floated ahead of Jack into his house, still feeling as if she had suddenly been freed from prison. She realized it was wrong, but at that moment she simply did not care.

She stood in the hall of the Mill House and knew at once that it was everything that everyone would want. Not grand and elegant like Hatcombe but simple and welcoming, and glowing with colours – as in a sixteenth-century painting, vibrant reds and dark greens. It was a man's house and a family house, and both at the same time.

'Of course, you haven't been here. I keep forgetting.' Jack nodded and indicated that Hope should go ahead into the sitting room. 'It's a mill house, as you can see, fourteenth century originally, part timbered, part stone, and part old red brick. No. Stop. I'm being a building bore. They're even worse than jazz bores!' He went to the drinks tray. 'Wine?'

Hope drifted past the crackling log fire and gazed out of the sitting room window, which overlooked the millpond outside. The pond lay dark and calm, populated by a clutch of what she recognized as Muscovy ducks, all of which were busy catching insects. Inside, the colours of the sitting room were cream and amber, the paintings few and modern, and Jack was bringing through a tray of smoked salmon and chicken and mayonnaise sandwiches for them to eat in front of the fire, 'just cosy'.

'Do you like it – do you like my house?'

'I was just thinking, it's everything that a house should be.'

She looked at him and wondered how his wife could possibly have left such an attractive, kind and intelligent man. At the same time, Jack looked at her and wondered why this slender, beautiful woman with the sad eyes should be abandoned all week by her handsome, pompous husband.

'There's no way that a house can lie, is there?' He sat back in his winged armchair and smiled at Hope. 'Whatever you are, from wherever you've come, wherever you're going to, your house will always tell the truth about you, don't you think?'

'Oh yes.'

'And so, Mrs M, what does this house tell you?'

Hope put down her wine glass and immediately stood up, eager to rise to the challenge that she could hear in his voice.

'Right, you've had it now,' she joked. 'There is no way that I am going to show you any mercy. You know that, don't you, Mr Tomm?'

'I don't want any.'

Hope did not turn and look at him, knowing just by that remark that certain territories that had lain between them were now crossed, but she continued as if she had not noticed. 'Yes. So. The man who owns this house is certainly a very strong character, we can see this from this lovely amber colour he has used, and he is not afraid of contrasts either because suddenly there is red too, on the reverse of these cream cushions and in the folds of the pelmets of the curtains. That he loves art is also obvious. Here is a David Tindle, and there an Edward Piper, and a John Piper and a . . .' she leaned over the sofa staring at yet another signature on an exquisite drawing, 'and a drawing by Nicola Hicks. All these choices show very good taste indeed, I have to tell you.' She turned and looked at Jack with a 'Shall I go on?' look in her eyes.

'No, it's OK, I love talking about me. Go on about me – especially the bit about my great taste.'

'Right. Now the piano. A Bechstein grand and to the side a metronome, and a stave – I think that's what a music sheet waiting to be marked up is called – and pens and pencils. Well, now, let me see, could it be that this is the house of a musician? And not only a musician, but perhaps a *composer*? Even perhaps the composer of a certain "Meadow Grasses", a song that went to the top of the charts about five years ago?'

Joining in the fun, Jack let his head drop into his hands and pretended to groan while saying, 'Oh, no, no, I am discovered. You have uncovered who I am!'

'Music teacher! Who did you think you were kidding? And anyway, did you really think you could keep your fame from Ben the local postman whose ears and eyes are super-powered and whose bicycle wheels carry news faster than a wire service? But never fear, Mr Tomm, your secret is completely unsafe with me. I shall tell the whole of Wiltshire not just who you are, but what a lovely house you have.'

Hope sat down again, leaving Jack laughing and applauding her performance before he disappeared in search of coffee, after which Hope demanded to see the rest of the house.

He led the way upstairs, and as he did so they passed pieces of sculpture, well placed on window sills and shelves, and other larger pieces set in alcoves along the landing. When they came to the bedrooms he seemed to take great delight in showing Hope the two rooms which were rumoured to be the oldest in the house, small cell-like chambers with stone-mullioned windows, before leading her to his own bedroom, a magnificent room which faced south and overlooked the millpond, the stream and the meadows beyond.

'I masculinized it, if there is such a word,' he told Hope, as they both stared at the steel bed and then up to the concealed modern lighting, at the leather chair at the desk in the corner, and at the dark colours of the furnishings, the lack of anything at the windows except the simplest, darkest blinds, the cupboards of dark wood.

And there was a small silence which Jack filled by going on to explain, 'After Dave, as in Davina, left, I ripped out the rubbishy phoney four-poster and all the frills, and the dressing table and the chintz-covered chair, and I gave them to the local Oxfam shop. I don't think they knew what to do with it all, but who cared? After that I felt much better. As if I'd got rid of her myself, not that she had left me, which, after all, was the truth. But, well, now of course—' He stopped. 'Now of course women look funny here, at least so I'm told. Out of place.'

It was his way of saying that he had not been a monk after Dave as in Davina left, and Hope was grateful to know, although she took care not to look at him, not even a glance as he spoke, preferring to pretend to be more interested in the view, and after that his paintings, and the family photographs – his boys with a kite, his daughter Cyndi in a long flowing velvet cape and carrying a bunch of wild flowers.

'I took that,' Jack said as Hope leaned forward to appreciate the photograph on the wall in its modern silver frame.

'Very talented photographer. Is there anything you can't do?'

Jack took Hope's hand and kissed it briefly. 'Plenty,' he said, sighing and turning away. 'But most of all too much that I shall never do, and that sometimes makes me sad.'

'What sort of things will you never do?'

'Paint a really good picture, pilot my own plane – oh, you know, those things – I mean the way our kids talk we must seem like Victorians to them. Helicopter pads are everywhere in these parts now, you know, as strange to us as *motor stables* as garages used to be called in the old days must have been to our great-grandparents, but our grandchildren will be going to school in them. We'll be saying *Whatever next?* as they pop off to the moon for a quick few days the way we might pop to Paris.'

Hope turned back to·Jack, smiling, but as she did so her eye was caught by something that Jack, who had his back to it, could not see.

'Anything the matter?'

She continued staring ahead but eventually turned her eyes back to Jack's and shook her head. 'No, why?'

'Are you sure?'

'No, really.'

'It's just that you looked so strange suddenly, as if you had seen something.'

'No, it was nothing. Just a shadow.'

She passed quickly from the room, and Jack followed her, and moments later they were laughing and she was looking at her watch, and murmuring about staying too long, but with her heart sinking, and feeling wretched, because she knew that she had to leave the Mill House and Jack and head back to Hatcombe, and that her one day of being just 'Hope' was over.

'It's been so lovely—'

'*You've* been so lovely—'

'You're being direct again.' She turned and smiled, feeling safe to tease him as she climbed back into Verna's little car.

'I'm going to be even more direct. It's been so – such – well, why not come and have lunch again tomorrow? Please?'

Hope meant to say, through the open window of the car, *I can't, really*, even *I really shouldn't*, but instead she heard herself saying 'Where?' and even as she said it she knew she should quickly alter it, but that was impossible because the look in Jack's eyes was such that she could not go back on that single 'Where?' despite its having taken her one bridge far too far.

'Stourhead. Let's take the day out and go to Stourhead.'

'I'm not sure I can get away for the whole day—'

'Try. The weather's meant to be going to be fine, and I want to take some autumn photographs for the cover of my new album coming out next year. The colours there at this time of year are out of this world, literally.'

'What shall I tell them?'

He knew at once what she meant by *them*, and in knowing she felt that in some way they were already making love, by his understanding look, by the way he had put his hand into the car and covered hers.

'At home? Tell them – tell them, I know, tell them I need you as a figure in the photograph. It's true. Bring a dark coat.'

Hope nodded, but she drove home trying not to realize that because of the last few hours her life had been transformed for ever, and she would never be able to go back to the old one. Try as she might, she knew that this feeling that nothing was going to be the same again had to be faced.

Not home, not children, not husband – nothing to which she was returning would ever look the same, sound the same, or be in any way similar to how it had been before she set out a few hours earlier.

But she was a wife. She was a mother. She could not contemplate any other relationship, and to do so would be to be quite wrong, and yet, even as she went in the cottage door, she knew she was already planning her next lie, yet another small, artless lie, which Verna and Aunt Rosabel, who both knew how much she was looking forward to Melinda's being able to keep a horse at Hatcombe, would believe without question.

The next day out came that second lie, and it was breathtaking how artless she was able to make it sound, how amazingly truthful, even to herself, who knew it was a lie.

'I have to go over to Sherborne to see a second-hand saddle for Melinda. It's a secret. I'm planning it for her birthday.'

'Oh. She will be thrilled!'

Verna looked up from her ironing, and Aunt

Rosabel lowered her copy of the *Daily Telegraph* and smiled.

'The old place will soon be just as it was in Uncle Harold's time,' she murmured, and went back to the newspaper with a small but happy sigh.

If they had not been so kind and understanding about her lie, if they had not wanted her to find Melinda a good saddle so much, if they had not waved her goodbye so happily, Hope might have felt better, but as it was she felt terrible. And as she turned Verna's car onto the main road which would lead her eventually to Stourhead, and lunch with Jack in the pub on the old estate, she knew she should turn back, but she was as capable of stopping herself heading for that part of Wiltshire as she had been of stopping herself waking early that morning to think of him, and only of him. Of his tall, rugged looks, his close-cropped hair, the way he laughed, his voice. Everything about him filled her with a wonder that she had never felt before.

He was already in the car park, his dark cashmere coat tightly belted, his thick, short dark hair brushed back and his eyes searching impatiently to see the little Renault turning in to park beside his old Range Rover in the shadow of the former coaching inn.

'What kept you?' he wanted to know. 'I thought my heart would stop. You're two minutes late, for God's sake.'

Before Hope could say anything he laughed at

the surprise in her eyes, and then went on to explain, 'My father used to wait thirty seconds, and then that was it, off he'd go. Didn't matter where or how. It taught us all to be on time – boring man. And now I'm boring. I have become a boring man like him. How about you? Do you feel you've become like your mother, say?'

Hope shook her head as she locked the car. The whole meeting was so *Jack*, she knew that already. They had been together a matter of a minute and he was already demanding to know more about her.

'No, well, at least – I don't know, really. You see my mother ran off when I was quite young, and I've never seen her since, and to tell the truth, I'm too old to be able to adjust to how she would be now. And having grown up without her, and my father having died as a result, really – I put her out of my mind. Just never wanted to do that to my children. And yet—'

Jack took Hope's hand. 'You won't have to.'

She looked away knowing that no matter what he said, if she told herself the truth, she was about to tread precisely the same path as her mother.

'This is not a place I should be, Jack,' she said, after a few seconds. 'I should not be here with you, I really shouldn't have come. I can't stay.' She did not add, *Because I have just remembered my mother ran off with her lover at exactly my age and ruined my father's life*.

'Pub lunch then photographs, then home,' Jack said quickly, sensing she was about to head straight back to Hatcombe. 'Pub, photo, home, pub, photo, home. Right?'

'That's all.'

But of course it was not all, and although it was not much either, yet it was everything, for as soon as they went into the pub they became a couple, two people alone at a table with no-one to look at but each other, no-one to distract them, and that in itself, for both of them, was startling and strange.

Being seated opposite Jack was magical and Hope forgot all about home, and all those things that wives and mothers are meant to remember all day every day and all night every night of every week and every month and every year, and all she could see was how masculine Jack was, and how easily he laughed, and how he looked after her, paid attention to what she said, was not dismissive.

At what moment she knew that they would have to make love Hope never could remember. Later, back at Hatcombe, she tried to recall when it was. Was it, she wondered, when the clock on St Peter's church had shown the time to be two o'clock? Was it when Jack called 'Look here, Hope' and smiled before taking the photographs, or was it when he pulled her coat tighter and kissed her on the forehead?

Somehow, afterwards, she fooled herself that if she could only have recognized *when*, she might have been able to stop what happened next. That she might have been able to put a hand up as someone who puts a hand up to cover a lens on a camera will stop the next photograph being taken, might have been able to stop the '*if* we make love' turning to '*where* shall we make love?'

And yet at Stourhead they had only talked and walked, and she had posed for him with her dark hair touching the velvet of the collar on her coat, and her face turned away, not really identifiable, Jack said, to anyone but herself and him, so far away would the figure be. And what with the mist rising from the lake and the late afternoon sunshine, and the rust red, russet, terracotta, Titian and henna of the leaves wrestling the coming dark of the early evening, as if in some final colourful fling they could defy the gods to bring on winter, it could all have been so innocent, just lunch, and a photograph, until Jack kissed her.

A kiss was a kiss was a kiss. So he had kissed her? So what? Lots of people kissed and forgot.

And yet.

There was no way that Hope could describe that kiss, no words which could convey the thrill as Jack's lips briefly touched hers.

She had been astonished, overwhelmed, enraptured, made speechless. She was not just weakened by the kiss, she was made infirm, ill, sick.

She lay on her bed, upstairs in the cottage, after she returned home – feigning a headache, reliving that brief moment again, and again, and again, pining for it, longing only to go back to that moment.

And this was just the result of one kiss, one not very long kiss, just one brief kiss in the shadows of the rustling trees, as swans passed on the lake below and she heard the murmur of other visitors' voices passing up and through the gardens. The winter sun had long moved from overhead, but a light brush on her lips had brought the radiance of summer to Hope.

Lying in the darkness of her room, her heart throbbing with the reality of the knowledge that was slowly coming to her, Hope raised both her hands, palms downwards, and stretched out to reach the memory of that warmth once more, before suddenly putting one hand down quickly to cover her mouth as the wonder of what had happened to her enveloped her. She had fallen in love.

Of course, after that, the lies accumulated, as they had to do, and they found Hope in strange places, away from Hatcombe and the cottage, standing in large department stores where no-one knew her, and no-one could overhear their telephoned conversations.

'Come to my house. The kids are all up in London next week.'

'I can't, not in your house . . .' Hope stared despairingly round at the shoppers outside the phone booth where she was standing. Ordinary, nice women, ordinary nice women who would never – or so it seemed to her – would never think of taking a lover, of risking whatever a love affair with a man not your husband put at risk. Those wives and mothers with their pushchairs and their shopping would never surely dream of planning what Hope was planning?

She turned back to stare once more into the booth, unable to observe their innocent interest in a beauty demonstration taking place only yards away, or see the simple unaffected looks that they gave each other, or their husbands, or their children, without being overwhelmed with guilt. She knew she was about to leave the company of those everyday saints who were only interested in making themselves look nice for their husbands. She knew she was about to cross the floor and change for ever, and the worst thing was that she could not find it in herself to care.

'Where then, where would you like to go?'

Jack's voice sounded so kind, thank God, it made how she was feeling seem normal and sane once more, not wrong-headed and deceitful.

'Somewhere where no-one knows either of us, somewhere that is away from everything we know, somewhere that will make me feel I am not me at all, but someone else.'

'But I don't want you to be someone else.'

Hope paused, and then she said passionately, 'I do! And I want it so much. I no longer want to be Hope Merriott, not any more. I just want to be your lover.'

INTERIM

There is only one happiness in life,
To love and be loved.

George Sand

At last they were running away together.

Hope looked in wonder at the November weather, wet, grey, raining, but to her it might have been bright sunshine and blue sky, so great was her euphoria. She was running away with Jack to a house where, Jack said, the beds were old-fashioned and set about with thick eiderdowns, where log fires burned in every grate and no-one would know where they were or who they were.

She continued to stare out of the window as they drove steadily on, further and further away from Hatcombe.

'Don't agonize, will you?' Jack looked at her briefly as he drove on up the motorway. Hope turned to smile at him. She would never ask anything more of life, she thought with a sudden passionate intensity, than this moment in time, Jack driving, the sound of the rain, a tape playing Jack's music.

'Why should I agonize?'

'People do.'

'There's no point, now. Even if I wanted to.'

'I just wanted you to know that I knew it was a great deal more difficult for you to do this than it is for me.'

'Set against the last twenty years what is three days?'

Jack glanced at her again, but this time he gave his own familiar wicked grin. 'Was it difficult? To get away?'

'No.' She smiled, but shook her head, not wishing to elaborate on how she had won her three days. She did not want to talk about 'back there' any more. Back there was her other self, the Hope that had married Alexander to get away from her father's brooding presence in her life. The Hope that ran after life, always a little too late, it seemed to her now, or a little too early, for everything. Now at last there was one thing happening to her for which she was determined that she would be on time – for Jack, for love. No, the one thing she was not going to do was stop and *agonize*, as Jack called it.

The house that Jack had borrowed was in Worcestershire on the outskirts of a remarkable village set about with the black and white timber-and-plaster houses typical of the area. It seemed that originally, hundreds of years before, there had been a castle built to guard a road, but the castle had long gone, and now there was only an enchanting village, and a road leading into it lined with a scattering of elegant houses, and an old stone barn, past which Jack drove before eventually reaching the house where they were to stay.

All Jack had said was that he had hired a house for them which was a nice, comfortable place with central heating; not that it was a former medieval great hall converted in the eighteenth century, and then again in the early part of the twentieth to become an enchanting small house with pale-washed stone and Tudor-style windows and a river running through the grounds which led back to the village, along which were perched many square-built cottages with a ribbon of green threading its way past their doors, their frontages reflected in the water of the river.

'I want to live here!' Hope turned and laughed up at Jack.

'You can – I'll buy it for you, if Landed Heritage will sell it!'

He meant it, which was probably why Hope laughed again, not believing him, and yet believing him too.

There was nothing she could say or do now. Any moment when she could have turned her back on Jack was well past. She could only step into the future and give him her hands, go with him upstairs to a large white room with a patchwork quilt, high-ceilinged but warm with the late morning sun, and as they set down their cases and turned to each other it seemed to Hope that never had making love been so extraordinary. Here at last she was making love *with* someone else. There were two of them with their hands stretched out to each other, there were two kissing, and two falling onto the bed, and Hope was no longer anxious, the way it seemed to her that she had always been before, but a lover in her own right, and nothing could go wrong; and nor did it.

Later when they went walking they wanted to talk of nothing else except the wonder of what had just happened, of how they had been before, in such contrast to how they were now.

'It seems so unfair. Why did I marry Alexander, why didn't I wait until I was older and then meet you, and why did you marry Davina and not wait for me to come along? Then there would be no-one else in the world who could be hurt by our happiness—'

'Shut it.' Jack stopped, and kissed Hope's hand. 'We promised, remember? In the car coming here? No agonizing.'

'I'm sorry. You know.' Hope shook her head. 'To meet with love now, at my age, at our age—'

'Means that we will never not appreciate each other. Means that we will never be careless of how we feel. Means that we will never willingly hurt each other's feelings. Means that we will always think of each other, every hour, every minute, every second. Means that we will never not be making love. Means that whatever we say, when-ever we say *How are you, are you all right? You look wonderful. Would you like a cup of tea?* even that will be making love. Touching your hair, I will make love to you. Holding your hand, I will make love to you. Just thinking of you, just thinking of your reality, will mean I am making love to you. And nothing else matters, not time, not place, nothing, just that I love you, and will always love you. That it just happened, or that it happened thirty years ago, that we have only three hundred or three days together, matters not a damn. We may be stars destined to burn out, or souls destined to live for ever, it's of no importance compared to this one unalterable fact – that we love each other.'

Hope turned to look up at him. It was true. All that did matter was that they loved each other. She put up her arms and held Jack to her, and it was as if, standing together in the shadow of an old tree down a country lane in Worcestershire, they were the only thing on earth that counted, and the least thing too. It was as if in being irreplaceable to each other, the world might at that moment come to an end and they would, at the last, find that that too was unimportant, because that was how important love was – beside it, nothing else mattered in the least.

'Let's go back to the house.'

With this new love-making Hope discovered that Jack was right, and that, strangely, afterwards she could remember nothing. So different was their love-making, so much part of everything else, that it was not one thing on its own, but all things making up their time together.

And she saw that he was right, that their love was one whole, nothing separated. The big white room that was their bedroom, the drawing room downstairs, playing Scrabble in front of the fire, buying food at the village shop, bicycling into the Malvern Hills over dead leaves and crackling ferns. Playing darts in an old pub tucked away from all but a few locals, hidden from main roads, small roads, lanes and byways and only reached on foot or horseback, by wandering lovers such as themselves pushing their bikes – everything was one whole, as Jack had said, everything, that is, except their parting.

On the last night he found her staring into the darkness, unable to sleep for the anticipation of the pain that she knew was to come. He put on the light, and laying her head on his shoulder he nursed her to sleep again with the sound of his voice telling her that they would be together again soon. And when they were together again it would be for ever.

PART TWO

Must it be?
It must be.

Beethoven

Chapter Eight

With the money repaid to her by Alexander it was now possible for Hope to buy herself a car instead of always having to borrow Verna's old Renault. She bought herself a second-hand Morris Traveller of great lineage but recently restored so that its wood shone, and its maroon paintwork looked as near to that of an old coach as was possible.

Aunt Rosabel approved of her choice – *very discreet* – but for Hope, newly returned from her three days away, which were meant to have been spent quite alone resting in Worcestershire, Aunt Rosabel's choice of words seemed horribly apt.

Very discreet could only too easily apply to a love affair, a love affair which, Hope realized, was becoming all too central to her existence.

Not that she and Jack were able to see each other very much – no parents with children are able to conduct love affairs easily – but just the thought of him kept her swinging through the day.

And then there were the phone calls. Calls that she still made from roadside telephone boxes, or large, anonymous department stores, or small teashops such as were still found in the country and to which she could be quite sure that no-one she knew would go, places which sold small packets of home-made fudge where the drinking of tea was a great deal noisier than any of the whispered conversational exchanges.

'There's a Celtic saying *We saw the two days – the good and the bad,*' Jack said at one moment. 'We had the three days – and they were out of this world. I can remember each hour, each minute and each second of all three of those days. I can remember how you felt and how you looked, and what you wore, and how your voice sounded, the very scent of you – everything. And now nothing seems to matter beside those three days, not now, not the rest of my life. Because I have known you, everything's all right. All my bitterness over Dave's leaving me and the children, all the confidence that her departure took from me, it's all healed. Every day I get up and I think, *I am all right because I have Hope.*'

Neither of them discussed what they should do next because somehow for the moment it did not seem to matter. Sometimes as Hope drove through the country lanes around Hatcombe she found herself imagining what Hatcombe would be like if she and Jack were living there. She could not stop herself from imagining how it would be, walking through the gardens on a summer evening with Jack, talking and laughing. And because she had never done anything like that with Alexander her daydreams seemed all the more real, just as the wonder of Jack in her life seemed all too unreal.

Nevertheless, careful as she was only to telephone Jack away from home, she knew that she must be equally careful not to think about him in front of Aunt Rosabel. Having grown so close to her, Hope was frightened that the old lady might somehow be able to sense something different about Hope; afraid that the old, like the young, being somehow removed from that state of involvement from which the in-between ages suffered, were able the more easily to sense feelings and read thoughts that were not their own.

As something of a distraction to both of them she set about encouraging Aunt Rosabel in her criticisms of the modern age.

'Oh, my dear,' Aunt Rosabel would say, with that curiously theatrical gesture that was so characteristic of her, the hand first raised, and then dropped as if she was starting a race. 'Do not, I beg you, start me on modernisms.'

'Oh, but please, Aunt Rosabel. You know how much I love to hear what you think.'

Then Hope would pick up her tapestry and start sewing, something which seemed to soothe Aunt Rosabel and give her the energy and confidence to express herself.

'Oh, very well. Let us talk about *voices*. Why must they always be raised so, for instance on the wireless? Why so dreadfully harsh? And the sounds they make, they split the ear. And who taught the young to say die-rect instead of di-rect, nee-ther instead of nei-ther? It is so appallingly ugly to the ear. English, if it is to be spoken and written correctly, must start off with a standard. Then – and only then – there can be diversifications, embellishments, modern argot, development, but there must be a decent standard from which to work. It is precisely the same with art. Do away with drawing by all means, but only once you can draw. Develop the singing voice along the classical lines and then ask of it what you will. Draw the lines of a garden so that its outlines are quite clear, the bones are there, and only then, after that, fill it with what you will. Everything will then work.'

After these small lectures Hope would turn away, longing sometimes to be back in some more classically minded era and at the same time ashamed for the era in which she lived which seemed to have destroyed itself, its eyes fixed only on money.

Certainly, and the thought was unavoidable, Alexander seemed to have spent his whole life being interested in nothing but money, whilst at the same time hankering after a lifestyle which he had not yet been able to support. To say that they had, of late, grown apart, would be to miss the point – they *were* apart. He was in London all the time, she was at Hatcombe, they hardly saw each other except at weekends, and then only to find themselves surrounded by other people. And yet, ironically, Hope who had dreaded moving to Hatcombe now loved living there, whilst

Alexander seemed only too bored by Sunday evening and only too anxious to leave it.

At least the building works were at last completed, the dry rot eradicated, the underpinning finished, and she and Aunt Rosabel could set about apportioning rooms to each of the girls, and planning their redecoration on a major scale.

It was entrancing for Hope to be with Aunt Rosabel in a furnishing shop and to hear her discreet reactions to the wallpaper and curtaining samples in front of which they would be seated by some uninterested and half-trained assistant.

'My dear, too awful – Hope ducky, look at this! I mean to say! The vulgarity of those swirls. Have they no taste!'

At the end of one of these sessions they might come away with perhaps a small scrap of material or a paint card, and in the end too, little by little, Hope came to appreciate Aunt Rosabel's discerning eye for colour, her understanding of how to put subtle tones together and yet not make them shout or over-state, for decoration in Aunt Rosabel's era had been a much less fleeting matter, a serious matter that when undertaken it was assumed would set the tone for the next generation.

'The painters would arrive in their striped trousers and their black coats, looking much as perhaps only bank managers do today. And they would set up their paint pots in the pantry or the scullery and mix for you there, my dear. No question of bringing home some little pot to try out. You spent the morning with them, and in general, providing there was a modicum of taste about, the result was quite good.'

Certainly the results in the girls' rooms were spectacular, and in a matter of a few weeks under Aunt Rosabel's guidance Hope was able to see that essentially taste was a matter of discretion and discipline, and decoration should be in keeping with the building in which it was set, and she looked back on her and Alexander's naive efforts in West Dean Drive with embarrassment.

Light too came into choices, and it was at one such moment, when she was holding up a swatch of cloth at a window so that Aunt Rosabel could judge its folds, that Hope saw a man down below, staring up at the house, obviously waiting for someone to come to the door.

For no cause that she could imagine Hope felt her heart sink. It was unreasonable, particularly since he looked respectable, suited and hatted, and wearing the kind of topcoat that usually inspires confidence. And yet there it was, her sense of someone down there who might so easily be something to do with Alexander and his ugly ducklings that had still not yet turned to swans.

'I'm sorry, Aunt Rosabel, I must go to the door. There's someone down there. The bell can't be working.'

She hurried down the stairs and opened the first of the two main doors. The man, grey-haired and with a round good-natured face, smiled at her affably and, although Hope immediately recognized him from his previous visits to Hatcombe, meticulous as always produced a card which read *Orphan Welfare Trust* with, at the bottom, a photograph of the gentleman who was now standing in front of Hope.

'Mrs Merriott?' he asked her, beaming. 'How nice to see you again.'

'Mr Bell – how are you? Goodness, is it really a month since you were last here?'

Hope smiled and shook his free hand, the other being weighed down by his old-fashioned leather briefcase.

'No, indeed, Mrs Merriott, I was in fact here just a fortnight ago – or was it only ten days? At any rate Mrs Fairfield wrote and asked me to call again today to discuss the Trust and other matters of concern to her.'

Hope showed Mr Bell into Aunt Rosabel's drawing room. He was a nice man. Every inch the country gentleman. It was typical of Aunt Rosabel to forget, she thought, as having called her she left them together and hurried off to fetch what she thought might be suitable refreshment for such a charming old-fashioned pair – namely, sherry and biscuits.

As she pushed open the drawing room door in an equally traditional manner – using elbow, backside and foot in neat transition – Hope heard Mr Bell saying, '. . . but such generosity deserved a personal visit, Mrs Fairfield. My only regret is that you cannot personally see all the good your tremendous generosity has brought about, all the immense good. There are still, alas, in our society, too many Oliver Twists, too many children at risk from the fiendish Fagins of this latter part of our century. By helping them we cut down on so much evil, so much wickedness.'

Hope served them both sherry and small sweet Italian biscuits and then left them together, smiling as she went, because what with Mr Bell's immaculate moustache and Aunt Rosabel's silk dress and white hair the two of them seated together would make a beautiful photograph. She could already hear herself telling Jack about it, and found herself wishing that he had been there to take it in the light falling from the window, the pale, faded blue silk of the drawing room covers, the old rose of the antique ornaments on the military chest, the sunlight making dusty patterns in the air.

Yet the covers and the ornaments were not the only faded elements in the beautiful room. Their voices too, low and intermittent, the sentences dovetailing each with the other, never hasty, they too were faded. Shutting the door on them Hope had the feeling that she was shutting the door on the entire century and that never again would she hear or see such niceties of behaviour.

But it was not only in her taste that Aunt Rosabel gave Hope a sense of something about to be lost.

When Alexander's great-aunt talked about her son, which she sometimes did on their drives in search of furnishings, Hope understood that the nature of people had changed. Gone was the unswerving ideal of dedication to duty and love of country, to be replaced by something more amorphous, and yet perhaps more urgent. Where now Hope's children seemed to talk of saving the planet, Aunt Rosabel had thought only of saving her country.

'We all knew there would be another war. Hardly had we put up the monuments to the dead from the First World War before we realized that there would be another. And those summers, you know, before the second war – they really were sunnier, and the voices on the air as we played croquet and swam and boated really were happier, because we still, despite everything, we still believed in the old ways, God, Church, that sort of thing, despite that terrible first war. Ridiculous when you think of it, but there. Perhaps we had to – perhaps there was no alternative? And of course we all wanted to give birth to sons, because if we did not every scrap of our world would be annihilated. As it is, now, there is still something left, don't you think? I look at your young and I think, *Yes, there is still something left*. Not that we were perfect, by any means, but I do think we might have been happier, or just simpler perhaps; perhaps less choice made us happier.'

*   *   *

Hope was at pains to try not to look different or happier to Alexander, but sometimes, on his brief weekend visits to Hatcombe, and together once more in the same house and the same bedroom, she thought she felt him looking at her in a new way, and she hated it.

That she should change so much, and in so short a time, shocked her. Time was when she would have given anything to have Alexander look at her with some new sense of appraisal, as if he had not really noticed her before, but now she dreaded seeing that appreciative look in his eye, and was grateful for the least distraction – Letty having a cold, herself having 'flu and a temperature, Aunt Rosabel having one of her little turns. Each weekend she would find herself praying that some small domestic drama would take her out of Alexander's range, away from the gleam in his eye which, rightly or wrongly, she was sure that she could see.

Jack did not have the same problem, since he lived with no-one but the idea of Hope, but he seemed to burn up with just the idea of Alexander coming home.

'It eats me up, Hope. The idea of his coming near you—'

'I know, Jack, but he is my husband.'

'What is to happen?'

'Something.' Hope turned to look at him. 'Believe me, something always does.'

*　　*　　*

However, happily for Hope, Alexander was far too involved in extracting himself from Imogen while at the same time plunging deeper into his affair with a newer, richer and far more interesting mistress to notice anything more than that Hope was looking younger and more attractive than he could remember her ever looking before. Naturally he put it down to her having settled into Hatcombe and enjoying country life at last, and flattered himself into thinking that with this knowledge of his wife's new contentment he could enjoy his life in London even more. Her obvious happiness seemed to justify his own pleasures and make his life more carefree, encourage him to take risks in his business associations, be braver than he had previously been.

Indeed as he went about London Alexander really did like to think of Hope being at Hatcombe. He found he could take a pride in his own unselfishness, because, after all, it had been his idea to go to Hatcombe, and Hope who had been insistent, to the point of boredom, that they should not take the gamble, a gamble which he had been at such pains, against everything she had thrown at him, to point out was non-existent.

But, in the event, how right he had been, and how grateful she should be to him for his foresight, which meant that she and the girls now lived in a beautiful house that at last gave them some status, meant that they were people of note, not crouching in some insignificant suburban semi.

All the more astonishing therefore to find that Hope, on his weekends home, always seemed to him to be carping on about money. Try as he might to reassure her, she seemed quite unable to accept that for once everything was all right, that Aunt Rosabel was paying for everything.

'Not everything, Alexander. I have had to pay for all the furnishings so far.'

'You?'

'Yes, out of my account and what you give me. You know how it is. She's really quite forbidding when it comes to discussing money, most of her generation are – and somehow or another I haven't dared ask her to pay me back. But now I must, simply because there's nothing left in the kitty. It's not her fault, it's my fault. I should have asked her sooner, and now it's getting to be just a little awkward.'

'Well, if you're stupid enough not to ask for your money back you can't expect her to be a clairvoyant, can you?'

Hope looked up from her sewing and stared at Alexander. She knew him well enough to be certain that he only became really vehement when he was deeply and truly worried. Most of life for Alexander was a question of coasting through and only coming to a shuddering halt when he met up with a concrete wall, or a mountain.

'I just said that, Alexander,' she said quietly. 'It

is my fault. But I mean, has she paid you for what you have paid for the building work? Has she paid you for what you handed over to Mr Frances?'

Alexander stood up and put another log on the fire, and then turned and smiled wearily at his wife. Really, Hope was so *boring*. No wonder he had to have a mistress.

'Of course she hasn't, why should she? I could well afford to pay for everything out of our house money, so I did and I know, absolutely, that she will pay me back.'

'Good.'

Hope looked down at her sewing and tried to think about Jack and what he would say or do, because she had a feeling that when it came down to it, much as he was always boasting about 'charming' Aunt Rosabel, Alexander was actually really rather frightened of her.

'As a matter of fact, before I go back to London tonight – after she wakes up from her kip – I will ask her for my cheque myself. And while I'm at it, I will also ask her for yours, since you don't have the courage to do it for yourself.'

'No, you're right. I don't have the courage.' Hope nodded her agreement. 'I don't have the cheek either.'

'What's *cheek*, as you call it, to do with anything?'

'It's to do with—' Hope stopped before starting again quietly, 'It's to do with thinking that we seem to be taking so much off her already – the use

223

of her house, this lovely place. I feel terrible asking her for money for furnishings for our daughters' rooms, for heaven's sake! And, as a matter of fact, I don't think I should, but if I am to go on paying Verna and buying the girls' clothes, and all those things, I have to. That little bit of money is all I have that is my own.'

'Ah!' Alexander smiled suddenly, his white teeth flashing really rather effectively, he noted as he looked at himself appreciatively in the mirror above the chimneypiece. 'In that case, why not leave it to your gorgeous husband? Leave it all to me, and I will charm our money out of her and be back to take tea with you in no time at all. Just watch.'

He was gone, and an hour later, having taken tea in to Aunt Rosabel in the room now used solely as her personal drawing room, he came back brandishing a cheque.

'There you are, you silly little thing, that's what a little charm, a little time, and a nice cup of Earl Grey tea can do. Let that be a lesson to you, Mrs Merriott.'

Hope looked up at him briefly, and although she did not say *Thank God for that* she certainly felt it.

Jack and Hope did not dare to meet either in London or anywhere close to Hatcombe, or at any venue where they might be recognized by anyone at all. If they wanted to hold hands, or go to a pub or have lunch out together, they had to meet miles away.

This particular day they had planned to meet in Bradford-on-Avon, and that was where they both fled, in separate cars, to huddle together in the back room of a wine bar. While driving rain outside flung itself against the windows, they were served fresh king prawns and home-made mayonnaise and thick brown bread that had been baked only an hour before, and white wine properly chilled, and then, the rain having ceased, to spin out their last hours together before what Jack called 'the dreaded moment of return' they wandered together round the antique shops playing 'guess the price' and marvelling at the audacity of what was being asked for what might indeed be fakes.

'When I think about it, some of Aunt Rosabel's furniture must be almost priceless,' Hope said at one point to Jack.

He nodded absently, because for some reason she could not quite fathom Hope had noticed that Jack, who had obviously earned and still did earn a great deal of money, never seemed to be very interested in its reality. In that he was precisely the opposite of Alexander, for he obviously enjoyed earning it, loved spending it, but never gave it another thought.

'My father worked in the City,' he explained, 'and he had such a thing about money, you know? I mean he ate, slept and breathed numbers but he never enjoyed it, never relaxed and let it roll in. Never spent it either, as a result of which when he slipped off to heaven the government took it all. What was the point of all that work? I mean you don't have to go mad, but enjoy it; or join a Buddhist monastery. We only pass this way once, if you notice.'

For some minutes Hope felt puzzled that such a philosophy should sound so appealing when expressed by Jack and so unappealing when expressed by Alexander, but then she realized that there was, in fact, a profound difference. Jack's money was earned from what he did, and not from gambling on what someone else did. Among many other wonders, she knew that she could love him for that alone.

And then it was time to part, and as always at such moments they clung to each other and wondered how they would be able to get through the next days.

'I keep trying to write a song to you, but every time I start all I can see is your face and all I can hear is your voice and then it seems to me that there is no point because nothing I could write would do justice to how I feel about you, nothing describe how you are to me, and knowing that you love me too is to stop and not be able to go on.'

Jack should never have written that to her, and Hope should never have kept the letter, but lovers *keep things. Most of all, they keep the look in their eyes.*

'What's this, he's writing a song to you? He's in love with you?'

'Alexander – I can explain!'

Hope woke up from her dream and gazed round her room with such gratitude that her bedroom could have been paradise itself. For a few minutes she lay in bed, alone, thanking God that she had written nothing down, and neither had Jack. There was no actual proof of how they felt. No-one else would know, so long as they never saw them together, no-one could even guess.

And yet. She covered her face with her hands. And yet she knew she must stop seeing him. It was impossible. She would have to tell him, next time she saw him or spoke to him, that she had to stop seeing him. It was no good, their relationship, the two of them loving each other as they did. It would all end quite terribly.

But when she phoned him to tell him exactly that, he sounded so buoyant, and so happy, that Hope found that the words simply would not come out, and all she heard was her own voice agreeing to meet him once again in the wine bar at Bradford-on-Avon, *our bar* as they were beginning to think of it, after only one visit.

After shopping and making her call to Jack, Hope went to the bank, realizing that although they were destined to meet in two days, and despite all her good resolutions, the time would drag until then. At the same time she felt guilty, because she knew that time should not drag when she had so much that any other woman would envy. A beautiful house in which to live, a delightful old relative to whom her husband was heir, four ever more delightful daughters. Time should not drag. And yet the truth could not be avoided either. It did drag when you were loved as she knew now that she was loved. Every minute and every second was a thousand times longer for not being with Jack, so that meant time dragged. It moved with leaden feet. It mocked and stared out at her, saying, *Wait, wait, wait, not yet, not yet, Mrs Merriott, still another twenty-nine hours* – Mrs Merriott – *until you meet your lover, still another whole twenty-nine hours.*

'Mrs Merriott?'

'Mmm?'

'Mrs Merriott?' The round-faced woman with dark-rimmed spectacles behind the security glass in the bank was staring at Hope and pushing Aunt Rosabel's cheque back towards her.

'Mrs Merriott, I'm afraid this cheque that you presented the other day has been stopped.'

'I'm sorry?'

The woman looked embarrassed, but she continued to push the cheque towards Hope.

'Yes, Mrs Merriott, I'm afraid it's been stopped.' She glanced towards the small queue, obviously feeling awkward for Hope, knowing that although they were lined up dutifully behind a notice they could all still understand what she was saying.

'But this is our great-aunt's cheque – Mrs Fairfield of Hatcombe House. Surely there has been some mistake?'

The woman smiled sympathetically at Hope, but since her eyes had started to stray towards the man in the queue behind her Hope had nothing to do but drift towards the exit, all the time staring down at the cheque and seeing Aunt Rosabel's signature on the bottom, the correct sum, and the correct date, as if in a haze.

She drove home as fast as she could, which on reflection she realized made no sense. Arriving back faster at Hatcombe did not mean that she would necessarily find a faster solution to the problem that faced her. In fact it would have made more sense had she driven more slowly and less dangerously and spent the time trying to work out what could have happened.

Finding Aunt Rosabel in high good humour eating lunch with Verna and Letty in the kitchen made the stopping of the cheque seem even more unreal, and Hope found that there was no point at which she could interrupt the fun they were all having with a casual remark such as *By the way, Aunt Rosabel, what happened to the cheque you wrote me?*

And since, after lunch, they all went for a walk, laughing and talking, wrapped up against the weather and looking every inch the ideal companions, Hope could only stare after them as they walked down the drive and wonder what she should do. The answer was that she could do nothing until Alexander phoned.

'Don't worry,' he said, sounding irritated and bored at the same time. 'It's just a cheque bouncing because she's probably drawn it on the wrong account, that's all. She has three or four accounts for different things, that's just her local one. Really, Hope, you're hardly going to starve until the weekend, are you? I mean I'll pay in a cheque if things are that bad.'

Hope could only agree that she was not going to starve until the weekend, but nevertheless she asked Alexander to pay some money into her account to cover her housekeeping and tide her through until he came down and sorted everything out.

But when he eventually appeared that weekend Hope took one look at his face and realized at once that far from having everything sorted out they were in a much worse situation than she could possibly have imagined.

Alexander walked her into the now vacated housekeeper's cottage. Following him, Hope could see that there were lines under his eyes, he had not shaved for at least a day, and his usually immaculate clothes looked as if he had slept in them, which perhaps he had for all she knew.

'She's only spent it all!'

'What all?'

'Her money. She's spent it all!'

But Alexander was wrong, in a way, for the fact was that Aunt Rosabel had not spent all her money. She had given it away. Every penny that her husband had left her had been made over to other relatives or to her favourite charities, and all that now remained to the old lady in the way of assets was Hatcombe itself.

'And you bet they've all cashed it. Cousins who have never seen her, relatives in America or South Africa, charities – dozens of those – they've all spent it, every last penny of it, and pronto. It's unbelievable. Hundreds of thousands of pounds, all gone.'

Alexander walked up and down the tiny sitting room, white-faced, as he spluttered out the news to Hope as if in some way, it seemed to her, it was her fault that the poor old lady's mind had obviously gone.

'The stupid old woman has made over hundreds of thousands of pounds to orphans, old-age pensioners, anyone and everyone except us. We who are here looking after her, we whom she has made to pay for the house she has given absolutely nothing to, and now she has no money whatsoever to pay us back!'

Hope stared up at Alexander and for a second – it was probably hysteria – she wanted to laugh. The situation was so terrible, and Alexander was so terribly furious, but somehow it was so *funny* too, just because it was so terrible. And also, and the thought would not be put away, she knew that if she was with Jack, and not Alexander, they would stare at each other and while still finding it all terrible they would have to laugh. Then she turned her attention back to the grim reality of the present.

'Alexander, let's not panic. We aren't ruined. We still have most of our house money, haven't we? The money from West Dean Drive?'

There was a long pause as Alexander poured himself a whisky and considered what Hope had just said. He drank the whisky, and then another, without thinking to offer his wife one.

'No, we have not got our house money, Hope, for the simple reason – for the very simple reason – that I *invested* what was left. How do you think I have kept going in the City these last months? No-one would invest in me, so *I* had to invest in me, and that is where the house money went. Helping me invest in my business ideas, invest in projects I really believed in.'

'Well, we can sell the investments, can't we?' Hope asked, determined to stay calm no matter what.

'No we cannot *sell the investments* as you so naively put it, and for a very good reason.'

'You haven't lost our house money, Alexander? Please tell me you haven't lost it all?'

'I haven't *lost* it, Hope. It's just that some of the

sure-fire investments I was advised to take on have not proved as sure-fire as everyone thought they would be. Believe me, I'm not alone. Everyone out there is having a seriously bad time, and it's not just trout farms and all that, it's everything. Black Monday, Tuesday, Wednesday, Thursday, Friday, black everything as far as investments go. But I've bought into certain areas while they're cheap, and they're going to come good, I know they are – it'll just take a little time, that's all.'

Hope stood up and wiped her hands down her skirt, because they were running with sweat as she understood just what had happened. She had trusted Alexander and he, in return, counting on the old lady's money, had gambled away all the money they had realized from the sale of West Dean Drive.

'You have yet again bought into all the wrong things, haven't you? That's why you've been in London for such lengths of time, and why you go back so quickly, because you've been having a bad time?'

'I have been *working*, which is more than I can say for you, Mrs Merriott. When did you last bring in a penny to the house?'

'I gave up West Dean Drive and my job because you told me to!'

Alexander leaned towards Hope and she could smell the whisky on his breath.

'You have never given up anything, Hope, not

a thing. You think life's just about staying at home and having babies and you couldn't even do that right. You couldn't even give me a son, could you? No, you had to trust to luck that you would have a boy instead of taking my advice. Had you had a son, we wouldn't be in this mess now. In fact Aunt Rosabel and her money wouldn't matter a tuppenny ha'penny damn if you had done what you should have done, just kept terminating, for God's sake, until you had a son. That way I would be rich now, not in this mess. And we would not be lumbered with this stupid old woman and having to make her sell her wretched house.'

Hope stared up at Alexander, appalled. That night when he had told her that he was to inherit Hatcombe she had known that nothing good would come of it. She had felt it so strongly, and yet there was nothing she could do.

'Well, so be it. She can sell Hatcombe and pay us back all that we have spent on it.'

'Try making her sell her house, Hope! Just try! Just try making her leave it to us, too! I've been talking to our lawyer about this. I said I'd have her proved insane, but it's not as easy as that. Believe me, it's not as easy as that at all.'

Hope closed her eyes. 'When has anything ever been easy with you, Alexander?'

She waited for him to say something but he merely poured himself yet another whisky and stared out at the darkness outside the cottage windows. For once he had nothing to say.

Hope eventually let herself out of the cottage and went to find Aunt Rosabel. That was all they could do now, all that was left to them, to find Aunt Rosabel, explain what had happened and try to get her to understand that they were all penniless, all three of them, and they would have to sell the house and move somewhere cheaper. She knew it was not going to be easy, but nevertheless it had to be done.

As she walked across the lawn to the main house Hope remembered the kindly man who kept calling from the Orphan Welfare Trust. No wonder he was so grateful to Aunt Rosabel. He must have taken thousands from her for his orphans.

She pushed open one of the double doors that made up Hatcombe's entrance and stepped into the hall.

'My dear!' Aunt Rosabel was waiting for her, and yet again she made that curiously theatrical gesture of hers, her hand dropping down in her excitement. 'Too wonderful!'

Hope stared at her. She was so sweet, despite all her comings and goings. Hope was always cheered by the sweetness in her face.

'Yes, my dear, too wonderful. I have just been told. The war is over!'

Chapter Nine

The next day found them all in Aunt Rosabel's drawing room.

'Right, now, Aunt Rosabel, we have to come to grips with things, business things.' Alexander was standing in front of a blazing winter fire, and she seemed to be listening and smiling, as he was smiling, but to Hope, who was serving tea at a far table and intent on bringing them cups and small side tables, it seemed that Aunt Rosabel knew about as much about *business things* as Hope did about nuclear physics.

'My dear boy, so sweet of you to take an interest, but you know Uncle Harold has always taken care of everything, and really it's terribly important to ask him too, because I have no idea about money, I really have not. Ask Victoria here.' She turned a laughing face towards Hope, who smiled back and placed her tea on the table beside her. 'Our father would hardly trust us with our pin money, let alone our inheritances. Originally our money came from linen, you know, in Ireland, and then I think we went into sheep, and of course that went at the beginning of this century – but at all events you know how it is, dear boy – men's palaver, that's what I call it – men's palaver!'

Alexander walked back up the room to Hope and taking her arm he marched his wife towards the French windows.

'How long has she been like this?' he demanded. 'And why didn't you tell me?'

'But we did, Alexander! Verna and I kept telling you, over and over, but you just said it was her pills or only to be expected because she was so old, and all that, that's all you said. And when I wanted to take her to see her doctor in London that time you said it wasn't worth it because he couldn't put back what had worn out, don't you remember?'

Alexander could remember many things over the past year, but he was damned if he could remember a thing about Aunt Rosabel going round the twist, or Hope ever telling him about it.

Seeing that he did not believe her, Hope added, 'Ask Verna, she'll tell you. It started ages ago.'

'But you must have been aware she was writing out cheques!'

'Absolutely not. She sat here, or in the house-keeper's cottage, and all we saw her doing was writing letters. We didn't know she was putting cheques in with them.'

This conversation was conducted in such low voices that when Alexander returned to Aunt Rosabel and the fire he felt quite exhausted from the effort of trying not to be heard. He sat himself down beside her on the Knole sofa and tried a new tactic.

'Darling,' he said, looking deep into Aunt

Rosabel's eyes. 'What I am about to say to you is pretty terrible, but you have completely mismanaged your affairs. Not through any fault of your own, just through misplaced generosity and others taking ruthless advantage of you, but as a consequence I'm afraid that you will have to sell your house in order that we can straighten everything out.'

Aunt Rosabel stared at him for a second and then, turning towards the small side table beside her chair, she picked up her faded flowered teacup and sipped at her Earl Grey tea as if she had heard nothing of what Alexander had just said. Alexander returned to his subject and began again, but this time he spoke in an altogether firmer tone, looking her in the eyes so that he could be sure that he had her complete attention.

'Aunt Rosabel, due to financial problems Hatcombe will have to go. I hate to be the one to tell you this, but it is a fact. Hatcombe will have to be sold, and soon. On the bright side, however, things are *slightly* looking up in the property market, so I am sure you will get quite a good price for it. So all is not, as it were, lost. But I am afraid that the house has to go. You and we have no alternative.'

Aunt Rosabel nodded sympathetically. 'Oh yes, I know, Alexander. I read the *Daily Telegraph* every day, don't I, Hope? I know all about the property market going flat.'

Oddly relieved that she was once more 'Hope'

and not 'Victoria', Hope smiled and came to sit near her. 'Of course you do, darling,' she said warmly, 'and the property column is always interesting to you because you've known so many of the big houses being sold. You've been to parties and dances and stayed in them. It's always fascinating to hear you talk about the old days.'

'Well, exactly.' Aunt Rosabel smiled across at Hope and then turned to Alexander. 'You know she is the best thing that has happened to you, don't you? I never had much time for you before, but since you came to live here and Hope and I became such friends, I've been happier than I've ever been since John was killed in the war.' She stopped suddenly. 'Oh, but good gracious. Now. Where was I, I wonder? I do ramble on so, don't I?'

'You were telling us all about your friends and their houses and so on.'

'That's right, I was, wasn't I? That's how I realized, through reading the paper, just how valuable Hatcombe is, and of course when that nice gentleman came back – you know, my dear, when you were in Worcestershire on your little break – the nice man from the Orphan Welfare Trust, and told me how really valuable Hatcombe was, I decided there and then to take his wise advice and I have sold the house to him. So you have no need to worry in the least. I shall be perfectly fine. He has bought Hatcombe from me for a very fair price, almost too fair, considering that Uncle

Harold only paid five thousand pounds for it in 1922 or thereabouts.'

She leaned forward and whispered to Alexander, 'He has paid me *one hundred and fifty thousand pounds* for this house. Imagine! I signed everything when he called again last week. Imagine! If Harold was alive he would never believe it. He has bought the house for his nephew, who lives with him, his nice young nephew whom he brought to see me when Hope was away on her little break. And so, as he said last week when he was here – or was it the week before? At any rate, he said that now I can move into a nice warm apartment at Bath and not be a trouble to you all after all. And you can all go back to London, which Alexander does so prefer anyway.'

'Where were you when this man kept calling for God's sake, Hope? I mean you must have suspected something, mustn't you? You must have seen that he was a suspicious character, surely?'

'But he wasn't. And he didn't just keep calling, he came once a month to have tea with Aunt Rosabel. I didn't know he came to see her with his so-called nephew when I was in Worcestershire.'

'Yes, I meant to speak to you about that—'

'Not now, Alexander—'

'How come you had enough money to go to an hotel in Worcestershire?'

'I didn't go to an hotel, I went to a Landed Heritage house – it's very cheap in winter.'

Alexander turned away, already bored with what she was saying. How tedious Hope was, and how virtuous. More than anything her virtue bored him. She had never had affairs, never really lived. Thank God, he at least had learned to live.

He moved away from her, and Hope noticed that the hand which reached towards the drinks tray was trembling and he looked flushed. He poured himself a drink, and started to walk up and down their sitting room.

'This man from this charity is obviously bogus. He has obviously duped the old woman out of all her money, and then charmed the house out of her for the princely sum of what a one-bedroomed flat in Bath would cost her. He's a crook, obviously. And we can sue him. We shall sue him. We'll sue him for everything he has, and more. What criminals these people who prey on old ladies are! But why, why in God's name you couldn't see this one coming I do not know. Why you couldn't have at least said something to me—'

'I tried to, Alexander. I tried to warn you that her mind was coming and going.'

'Did you? I don't remember your words of wisdom!'

Hope turned back to the window at which she was standing. Due to the gravity of the crisis Alexander had not returned to London so she had been forced to cancel her meeting with Jack in

Bradford-on-Avon, but Alexander was going back to London that afternoon and Hope would be meeting Jack the following day.

As she thought of him she imagined his face as she told him all that had happened, and wondered what he would say. It was nice to imagine being with Jack. It made whatever insults Alexander chose to hurl at her somehow pathetic and irrelevant.

'Yes, what we will do is sue Mr Bell. He obviously took advantage of your stupid trip to Worcestershire to get the old woman to finalize everything with him. My God, we will sue him, I will sue him, until the pips squeak. Watch it, Bell, because I'm coming for you. But really.'

'Bell?' Jack said. Hope nodded.

They were back in their favourite wine bar in Bradford-on-Avon, and although Hope knew that the prawns should not taste so good, or the bread quite so fresh, or the white wine so crisp, yet they did, because Jack was seated opposite her, and he was wearing his cashmere coat, and his thick hair was brushed back from his broad forehead, and although the look in his eyes was thoughtful it was also comfortingly unshocked, as if he was grown-up enough to know that while the situation at Hatcombe was grave, it was not the end of the world.

'I know Bell,' he went on. 'He comes from Bath. He's well known to move in on old ladies – and

242

gentlemen too, I might add. Charms the furniture out of them for his antiques business, or the money out of them for his Orphan Welfare Trust – rather misnamed, I should think – and he's also a sleeping partner in one of the solicitor's firms around here. These old firms can be hotbeds of God knows what, you know? Old family trusts are particularly their speciality, because the beneficiaries, usually at least one generation removed, all live in some far-flung spot and know nothing of what has been left to them, and half the time care less, so whatever the dear old family lawyer cares to throw at them they pocket all too gratefully. Fantastic how some of these west country firms have grown rich on so-called *trusts*. Misnamed again – or perhaps *well* named in order to avoid suspicion.'

'You mean he doesn't really collect for orphans?'

'Oh no, you'll find *that's* all above board and perfectly administered, until you look at the costs of running, that is, and then I think you'll find that surprise surprise those costs are all trickling back, one way or another, to you-know-who. He's going to be a very difficult fellow to sue. Good luck, but – well, in the meantime, what are you going to do, Hope?'

Hope gazed out of the window at the rain that always seemed to accompany their trysts, and shook her head.

'I don't know,' she said. 'All I do know is that I

was right when I said to you that time that we shouldn't worry about the future, because something always happens.'

Jack took one of her hands and kissed it, after which he held it to the side of his face as he stared across the table at her.

'Maybe something does always happen, Hope, but as far as I'm concerned the only thing that has truly happened is – us.'

Hope smiled. 'We had the three days, Jack, didn't we?'

Jack was silent, and then, 'We must have many more than three, or I will never believe in anything again.'

Now Hope was silent, seeming only to hear the ticking of her watch in her head. In another thirty minutes she must get up, go to her car and go back to Hatcombe, and poor Aunt Rosabel, and – everything.

'We must make love again.'

Hope looked at Jack. It was true. They must, but where, and when? And when it was all over, there would still be the going-back. There would never not, now, be the going-back. The going-back that seemed always to overshadow the going-to.

'My dear, I didn't think to see you here!'

By some extraordinary freak of fortune Jack had let go of Hope's hands, although his eyes had never left her face, and only now reluctantly, and almost lazily it seemed to Hope, raised themselves to Mrs Taylor-Batsford's face that was even now reflecting the story she would start in her circle as soon as she should be able to. *My dear, the awfulness of it, quite alone, and quite obviously together with that song-writer man and – you know – quite obviously.*

'You don't know Mrs Taylor-Batsford, do you, Jack?'

Jack's expression of utter resignation made it quite clear that he wished Hope did not either.

'Oh, but yes, I think my little gel is in the church choir where you teach once a fortnight, is she not? Mary Jane Taylor-Batsford?'

'Oh – MJ? She yours, is she? Nice little thing.'

'Well, well – I mustn't keep you.'

She nodded and passed on into the main part of the wine bar where Hope saw her raising a gloved hand to someone in greeting.

'Supposing—' Hope looked after her, frightened and guilty, but Jack merely shrugged.

'Don't worry,' he said, having stood up to watch the woman's progress down the bar. 'She's meeting a man friend herself!' He laughed and sat back down again.

'Probably her husband.'

Jack shook his head. 'No way.'

'How do you know?'

'He didn't kiss her like a husband, Hope.'

'How, then?'

Jack would not be drawn and shortly after, or so it seemed to Hope, their precious time together was over. Despite Jack's shrugging off the chance meeting with Mrs Taylor-Batsford, Hope drove home feeling uneasy, and sad, because she knew that they could never again risk going to Bradford-on-Avon. Whatever happened they would have to meet somewhere else. A door had shut, and for the first time it was not on Hope and Alexander, but on Hope and Jack.

Until the moment when Mrs Taylor-Batsford had happened upon them in the wine bar Hope had not, as yet, contemplated guilt. It was strange that she, who had known guilt at so many times in her life – when her mother ran off with her publican lover, when she herself married Alexander and left her father to fend for himself – with Jack had felt not a shred. She had allowed herself to be swept up into her relationship with Jack as carelessly as Alexander seemed to be intent on driving his helpless family into the darkest of times.

It was difficult to see how they would be able to survive the coming months. As Hope stared into the darkness of the winter nights that followed her lunch with Jack, for once she could see no way out, and her normal optimism was no longer there to be drawn upon.

The house was sold, and whatever the law said, it would be years before that particular battle was settled. And although Aunt Rosabel would no doubt continue to be as sweet as ever, Hope knew that the old lady would never be able to cope with the idea of living anywhere but Hatcombe. Indeed, now that she had gradually come to realize that her days at Hatcombe might well be numbered, the old lady seemed curiously uninterested in anything, and not even walks with Letty and crumpet teas by the drawing room fire could bring the old look back to her eyes.

Verna too, without being told, knew that the writing was on the wall, but busily pretended it was not so until the inevitable day when she came to Hope and explained that it was time for her to return to Australia, thereby letting Hope off having to tell her that they could no longer afford to pay her wages.

'I shall miss you all. You've been quite the happiest family I've ever been with. Such lovely girls, all of them,' she said sadly, which made Hope suddenly turn away, this time hearing the sound of not one door shutting, but many. 'But I must go home.'

From accidentally hearing her nanny speaking on the telephone Hope knew that Verna already had another family to go to, her trip home to Australia was only for a month's break, and soon there would be some new little Letty at the centre of her life, but nevertheless they both smiled, mutually thankful that a tactful way round the situation had been found.

'Letty will miss you.'

'I know, but it's probably best if I do go, before I can't!'

They both smiled briefly, once again mutually covering the agonizing heartbreak that those few words always embraced, and to cover the moment Verna took out some photographs from the summer and they immediately started to remember those sunny, happy days which suddenly, to Hope at least, seemed already very far away.

Afterwards Hope walked round the garden on her own, despite the growing dusk.

It was four o'clock. Everywhere children were being collected from their schools by their mothers. Her own three daughters would be sitting down to school tea, moaning about home-work, sharing jokes with friends from whom they would soon have to be parted, because Hope knew that, after this term, they could not possibly stay at the school any longer. They would have to come home and go to a non-fee-paying school and find part-time jobs in after-school hours. From now on what they did for themselves would be as important as what she could do for them. They would all have to look after each other, the way they had been becoming used to do at West Dean Avenue.

For perhaps the thousandth time Hope wished that they had not forfeited Rose's place at her ballet school, that they had never moved to Hatcombe. Yet another thousand times she wished that she could have the past year back again, that time could be returned for a refund and she could be allowed to put the past year in an envelope and get back a credit by return of post.

So irrational did her anxiety over the future make her that when she was yet again propped up against her pillows and staring out into the dark, once more wondering what she could do to save her family from destitution, she found herself hating Hatcombe and Aunt Rosabel, and wishing that the old lady had never come to visit them that Christmas, but had stayed in Wiltshire, had never come to inspect Alexander to see if he had changed for the better, had never promised him that she would leave him Hatcombe, had just left them all alone.

'Aunt Rosabel!'

Hope found herself whispering.

The old lady was lying against her pillows staring ahead. Dawn had long come and gone and with it any shred of desire for sleep, and so it was that as Hope had passed her door, on the way to make herself a cup of tea in the old kitchen below, she had noticed the light still burning, and, since both the light and the open door were unusual, had looked in on her.

At first Hope was sure that she was dead, such was the still look of her, the eyes open but not seeing, the beautiful old hands lying on the lace of her upper sheet quite unmoving, but as she hurried to the bedside she noticed that the old lady was still breathing, and it was with a strange feeling of gratitude that Hope found herself taking Aunt Rosabel's wrist, for whatever had happened or would happen to them all on her account, Hope knew at once that the last thing she really wanted was that the old lady should die.

'Just don't move,' Hope said, realizing as she did so how pointless and meaningless her words sounded as she tried to feel her pulse with the tips of her fingers. 'I'll go and ring the doctor straight away.'

And yet at the sound of Hope's voice Aunt Rosabel's eyes seemed to register her presence and she turned her head slightly towards the younger woman, and it seemed to Hope that she was trying to speak.

She quickly returned to the old lady's bedside and leaned her head towards her.

'I'm all right really . . .' Aunt Rosabel whispered, but her speech was so quiet it was hardly above the sound of a sigh.

'I know, you're fine, but even so I shall ring for help straight away.' Hope pulled the bedclothes closer around her and she noticed that the old lady attempted a smile before her eyes closed. Hope ran from the room down to the hall and the nearest telephone.

Please, please, don't die, Aunt Rosabel. I'm sorry for thinking bad things because of not having any money and you selling Hatcombe to the man from the Orphan Welfare Trust – please don't die and leave me all alone.

As the ambulance at last arrived and Letty was

woken by the sound of their activities and cried to be lifted, and Hope followed the men up to Aunt Rosabel's room, the thought came to her that she must be past redemption, for even as the poor old woman might be poised between this world and the next all Hope had been able to think of was herself.

But when she confided this to Jack, much later that day, he laughed a rich laugh that rang down the telephone with a warm reassuring acceptance of human frailty. 'Join the human race, Mrs Merriott,' was all he said, and then, more softly, 'Can you feel my arms about you? Shut your eyes. I am about to put my arms about you and hold you to me.'

Hope closed her eyes and for a few seconds she was able to fool herself that this was all that mattered, before replacing the phone and going to find Letty.

In hospital that evening Aunt Rosabel lay against alien pillows, not soft cotton with old lace like her own but stark white with *County Hospital* embroidered in red down their sides, and her eyes were closed. Hope found herself tiptoeing towards her bed, still afraid that she might not be sleeping but already gone from this world.

She must have sensed Hope's presence because she opened her eyes after a minute and turning towards her smiled in warm if tired recognition, and although it was obviously an effort she spoke. 'I had these pains in my chest in the night. It's my age, d'you see? I am so sorry, Hope, just when you have so much with which you have to cope.'

Hope said nothing, only lightly squeezed her hand, feeling absurd relief that she was not gone. She loved Aunt Rosabel, more than she could tell her, because they were both, in their way, shy of emotion.

Back at Hatcombe as the ambulance had driven her away, leaving Hope and Letty to breakfast alone together, the house had seemed to be leaning towards the departing vehicle with its flashing lights and whispering over and over, *Don't go, don't leave me alone with people who don't really know me.* And the flagstones that lined the halls and the corridors, they too had echoed to the sound of their two sets of hurrying feet with, *Where's she gone? Bring her back!* because until that moment even Hope had not realized just how much Hatcombe was Aunt Rosabel, or Aunt Rosabel was Hatcombe.

Looking round the house, Hope, with only Letty now for company, had seen that everything, from the delicate arrangement of the flowers in their silver and crystal vases, the seemingly casual little gatherings of the chairs and sofas in the drawing room, the Paisley throws across the back of an armoire on the landing, to the arrangement of the hand tinted flower prints in the bathrooms, was Aunt Rosabel, and really very little, if not nothing, either Hope or Alexander.

Try as they might to enter, reorganize and modernize her house, it had remained, ultimately, that of Aunt Rosabel. Hatcombe was where she and Uncle Harry had lived out their lives, and in some strangely spiritual continuity still survived, for it was they who had made the place what it was. In all humility, Hope realized that she and Alexander might have moved in and repaired it, but when it had come to adding actual quality to its old rooms, and that touch of magical lightness that only true good taste could bring, it was all Aunt Rosabel.

'So dull for you here visiting me, my dear. And what about little Letty?'

'Mrs Shepherd came in.'

'Of course – from the new cottages.'

They both smiled. It had become one of their little jokes. The 'new' cottages were actually Victorian. Very new as far as Hatcombe was concerned, but not quite so new in the late nineteen eighties.

Shortly after that it seemed a good thing for Hope to go but with promises of returning in the morning overriding mild protests from Aunt Rosabel that there was no need. It was quite obvious that there was every need, for she looked suddenly tired and unable to talk, but also lonely and frightened, so that Hope promised to arrange for her to come back to Hatcombe as soon as she could, the underlying understanding being that if she was going to die, she would prefer to die at home, at Hatcombe.

Of course Alexander had been informed, and was back at the old house the following day looking suddenly young and carefree, as if he had quite forgotten that his future inheritance had been sold to someone else, and that technically they were, in fact, now homeless, not to mention very nearly penniless.

They did not kiss exactly, for as soon as she saw him Hope realized that she could no longer bear to kiss him now – for a true kiss requires honesty and is real – so they bumped cheeks and Hope went straight back to the kitchen. Alexander followed her, interested only in hearing whether or not Aunt Rosabel was still alive, and looking almost openly disappointed when he heard that she was.

'Let us pray,' he intoned, accepting a cup of freshly made coffee from Hope, 'let us indeed pray that she is carried off to meet her maker very soon, for all our sakes, and then we can get on with our lives.'

'I didn't hear that.' Hope opened a fresh packet of biscuits and placed them on a plate in the middle of the table for Alexander and Letty. The little girl was staring up at her father as if she did not quite know who he was, as if he might be a man come to sell them something, or the vicar visiting.

'Is she all right without Verna?'

Hope half closed her eyes, her back turned to her husband. It seemed to her sometimes that he had a line in tactless utterances that had to be heard to be believed. The avoidance of Verna's name had been central to Hope's efforts to help Letty get over the sudden departure of her nanny.

'Biscuit, darling?' She quickly handed her youngest a biscuit to cover the moment, and tried to look across at Alexander in a new, calmer way, as if he was a lunatic friend who needed advice and help, nothing to do with her, someone quite other, someone of whom the girls might say, *Oh, not Alexander calling round again, poor Mums!*

'You do realize that if Aunt Rosabel dies it will be much, much harder to prove that she signed the house away when the balance of her mind was affected? I mean I suppose it has occurred to you that she is much better, from your point of view, alive than dead?'

Alexander nodded, turning away to avoid contact with Hope's direct, sometimes too honest, gaze. He had actually always hated the way Hope looked at him, he realized now, for she had a way of regarding him, so direct and the eyes so unwavering in their candour, which was utterly disconcerting, even more so now he knew that they were not, either of them, at all as they had been.

Certainly he could not tell Hope that since last week it did not matter to him in the least if Aunt

Rosabel came or went, lived or died, because at last, it seemed to him, he had sorted out a plan for their future. But it was not one that he could confide to Hope, not even whisper to her, Hope still being – in his eyes anyway – *hopeless*.

At the same moment Hope too turned away, suddenly chilled, realizing that she had just said to Alexander '*your* point of view' and not '*our* point of view'.

Alexander was the first to break the silence that had fallen, a silence filled only with a sigh of a relationship finally dying between two people whose backs were turned to each other, the sound of Letty sucking on a sponge finger and the click of the central heating system turning itself on.

'Look, let's all go and see her this afternoon, all right? Masses of flowers and those white chocolates that she likes, and then we can come back here and I'll stay on with you until we know one way or another. It's a bit quiet in London at the moment – although things are actually beginning to pick up. A small investment I made . . .'

Hope dropped her gaze and picked up Letty. Alexander's investments were not something that either of them should be required to talk about any more. But at least they could go to the hospital together. At that moment the telephone rang, long and insistent.

They both stared at each other. At that moment, as neither of them moved towards the phone on the wall that was ringing so insistently, on and on, and on until the sound was more like a woman screaming and neither reached forward or walked forward or even inclined their bodies forward to pick it up, Hope knew with absolute clarity why it was that she had felt no guilt about making love with Jack. It was because, undoubtedly, Alexander had already been unfaithful.

She knew this with a terrible certainty because she knew that at that moment he was petrified that the person who was ringing might be someone Hope should not hear, just as Hope was terrified that it was Jack ringing her and that Alexander would hear him calling down the telephone to her, 'Hallo, darling soul!'

Hope grabbed at the still ringing phone, already knowing that it was Jack, and preparing herself to sound confused and distant so that Jack, who was all too sensitive to voices and people, would know to sound the same in case Alexander might have moved closer to her to listen in on her conversation, which, chillingly, and for no reason she could imagine, he had.

But Jack knew at once because Hope answered by saying, as if she had been interrupted in the middle of something, '—it's sure to be for you, Alexander' and only then saying 'Hallo?'

'Bring the girls round when they break up from school? But of course I'd love to, Jack. Forgive me if I sound a bit strange, but it's Alexander's great-aunt, not too well, and you know – must dash. I'll ring back tomorrow, OK? Oh, and thank you.

Sweet of you to call about the girls, really.'

'Jack from up the way, huh? How is the ageing rocker?'

'Fine, I think.' But remembering the interest in Mrs Taylor-Batsford's eyes, she quickly added, 'Haven't seen him, really, except once we bumped into each other when I was picking up some spoons for Aunt Rosabel in Bradford-on-Avon. Letty, don't do that, darling.'

'Right, let's go then. Off to see the old bag—'

'Don't ever call her that in front of me, Alexander.'

'Oops, sorree, your ladyship, beg pardon I'm sure.' Alexander smiled, pretending to tease her in front of Letty, although his eyes were cold and humourless and his mouth tightened as it always did when he was corrected. 'You see, I thought – oh, never mind what I thought. Let's get going, shall we? This is becoming intensely boring.'

'You go ahead. I must take Letty to Mrs Shepherd. In fact you go on ahead in your car, and I'll follow in mine.'

'Oh, bring Letty, for goodness' sake.'

'No, hospital is not the place for littles. Besides, she likes going to Mrs Shepherd, don't you, darling? Because she has a kitten, and Letty is learning to make the word *kitten* with her crayon, and read it too. No. You go ahead to the hospital. Aunt Rosabel's in a private room. Well, the county hospital being the old cottage hospital, that's all there are, actually. And, Alexander, don't forget to talk quietly. She is very ill.'

As always when told to do or be something Alexander looked as if he was majoring in boredom and uninterest, but he nevertheless went on ahead, patting the sides of his navy-blue cashmere coat to make sure of his car keys and whistling slightly off key, which made Hope close her eyes as she realized just how used to Jack she had become, and how unused to Alexander. Jack never whistled, he sang. And Jack was always in tune, with her, with life, with everything.

Naturally, Alexander being Alexander, he overwhelmed Aunt Rosabel with flowers and chocolates, filling her room with expensive winter blooms, taxing the nurses with not having enough vases, while unwrapping her chocolates and insisting on her eating at least one, for him, threatening not to leave her until she did. And of course Aunt Rosabel being Aunt Rosabel could not resist being petted and spoiled and ate the chocolate, despite her weak state, and her lack of energy, and the look in her eyes that said, *I know you're a rogue, but you make me laugh.*

Hope left them together, having warned the nurses not to let Alexander tire his great-aunt. They'd promised to remove him after twenty minutes.

Unable to stand the sight of Alexander charming the woman whom he had been, only an hour before, so piously and sincerely wishing dead, she drove off from the hospital, intending to return to Letty, and the house, and some quiet, during which time she planned to compose what she had to say to Alexander.

But the relief of being away from the hospital and in her car quite alone was so intense that instead of turning towards home and Letty and Mrs Shepherd, towards Hatcombe and their future as a family, Hope took off in the opposite direction, driving blindly into a maze of country lanes, well away from anyone or anywhere she knew. And as she drove, the window down, the breeze blowing her hair, she tried hard to think of what to do, tried tò think out her irrational, unbelievable situation, somehow to make a rational, believable plan for them all.

Whatever happened, she decided, she must not do as she had read that so many other wives did, and that was to confront Alexander with her own infidelity. She had to continue to deceive him, even though she was convinced that he himself must have been deceiving her for heaven only knew how long in London.

Besides, the one thing that she did see quite clearly was that now was a time not for accusation, but for practicality. There was little point in looking to score points or find proof, about as much point as in trying to turn back the clock. This was the time for her to think of herself. Not of

Jack, nor of Alexander, but of herself and her daughters.

She could not, would never, turn to Jack for financial help. Not only was she too proud, she was too realistic. He had his own children, his own set of cares, which like herself he was only able to lay aside in the passion and romance of their relationship. And besides, what they had together was too precious to degrade with loans and payings back, and all the horrors that those situations so often brought.

She had parked the car overlooking a view of distant fields, and – as had happened to her before on the few occasions when she was swept away with feelings of misery and futility – it seemed to her that everyone and everything around her was happy and at ease with itself, and with nature. Nothing was stopping the cows wandering through their pastures, a cat from sleeping under the hedge, the postman jumping out of his van to unlock a box in a wall and pluck out the four o'clock letters – they were all just getting on with life while hers seemed to be grinding to a total, terrifying, halt.

Suddenly it seemed that there was no place for Hope, not even in her own life, let alone in the world. She knew now what it was to contemplate ending it all, to be brought to that edge of despair when nothing any longer makes any sense or matters in the least, and yet some remaining grain of sanity made her realize that she must not panic. She must not go home and confront Alexander with her love for Jack, or with his supposed infidelities. His reaction would be all too predictable – he would simply laugh at her.

He would laugh at her suppositions about his own life, and – which would doubtless be much, much worse – he would laugh at the very idea of her having an affair with Jack.

That ageing rocker!

As she sat facing the fields in front of her Hope thought she could hear Alexander's voice now, insultingly facetious, just as it had been earlier that morning.

Indeed as she sat watching the green of the fields that stretched out and away, running from in front of her up towards the sky as if running to touch the end of the world, and the view became slowly obliterated by a light rain, above the sound of the raindrops on her car roof, on the windows, she could hear, all too clearly, Alexander's mocking laughter, and all too easily imagine the kind of things that he would, or could, say.

He would stop at nothing until her tender love for Jack had been dismissed and derided, until it had been ground under the heel of his mockery and sarcasm, and within a very few minutes there would be nothing left at all, only a distant faint echo of Jack singing to her in the car, of their lovemaking, of the feel of his coat against her cheek, of the laughter they shared, the bicycle rides in the hills, the sounds of last year's leaves as they walked for miles into the woods, the feeling of secrecy, of being just two, and no-one else knowing.

His sarcasm always had been Alexander's greatest weapon against *Hopeless*. If he thought it necessary he would go on the warpath with it against her. He would, if expedient, work to get the girls on his side And, as he had done sometimes when they were growing up, encourage them to mock her.

Just imagine Mums with an ageing rocker! Your mother's having an affair with that old rocker up the way!

It would be terrible. But Hope knew, absolutely, despite all these predictions, that she had to have courage, she had to win against him, not for her sake, or for her and Jack's sakes, but for those same daughters'.

She had to be practical, she had to start where her problems had perhaps begun, she had to acquire the one thing which she so spectacularly lacked – namely, money. And it was as she thought about this that she realized that once a wife ceased to love her husband, that was all her life came to be about. That, and the protection of her children, shielding them, which was so strangely ironic, from the very man who had fathered them.

And so she drove away from the fields and the view knowing now that in fact she did once more have a place in life. Her task was to care and provide for her children, but alone, without either Alexander or Jack. And with this realization came another, more powerful and more glorious, and it was that she had finally overcome her fear of Alexander. At last he could no longer frighten her. Because Jack loved her, Hope was once more strong.

What was more, by rehearsing Alexander's mockery, his sarcasm, and his line in suppressed anger, she knew that she had utterly and for ever exorcised any future power that he might have had over her. He could not take anything from her any more. She could become herself at last. In some strange way she had a future which she could now see, a centre, independent of everything except her own feelings about life.

Yet, unafraid though she might now be of him, once she was certain that Alexander had been cheating on her, Hope herself began to feel like a criminal. She found herself not just spying on him, but planning to spy on him. And not in the usual ways that she had read other women spied on their husbands – looking through their pockets, or listening in to phone calls. All Hope did was to watch Alexander.

And of course the more she watched him the more he became what his great-aunt Rosabel would call an *adulterer*, and hand in hand with that fact came another more uncomfortable one, namely that Hope had been even more of a fool than she herself could have believed possible.

Why had she never noticed how often he absented himself to use his car phone? Why had she not noticed how many times certain numbers were recorded on the car phone bill? Why had she never realized how expensive were his aftershave lotions and soap and other toiletries, so expensive that not even Alexander would have contemplated purchasing them for himself, though a grateful mistress might? Even his haircut was of a sophistication which subtly proclaimed itself newly styled from a fashionable salon which would normally have been out of his reach.

Therefore, in the wake of having triumphantly thought that she had exorcised her fear of Alexander, Hope now acquired a new and worse emotion, that of self-contempt. And it was worse than anything that she had suffered before.

Much worse than the realization that Alexander was weak and a fool, or worthless, was the bleak truth about herself. The realization that she had been so stupid as to trust him, not to think at any point that he was capable of infidelity, that he might perhaps not have loved her as much as she had used to love him, these thoughts were a hair shirt against which Hope now placed the mind and the body that Jack had told her so very recently, over and over again, that he worshipped.

And so it was that day after day, night after night, Hope found herself unable to put aside the glaring knowledge of her own stupidity, the exact extent of the pathetic, foolish trust that she had put in Alexander's remaining faithful to her, and it seemed to her that this inglorious truth was far worse than any jealousy she might have once felt over some mythical woman, or women, with whom he might be, or had been, involved.

Dully the truth crept towards her in all its shabby reality. She had given up everything for Alexander, her dancing, her life, her body to have his children, what security they had once known – everything – and in return he had taken from her, deceived her, mocked her, and finally ensured, by his greed, that even their children might now be destitute.

She should have wanted to murder him, but because she was honest enough to desire only to see the truth about herself, Hope knew that what she wanted was to kill not Alexander but herself; and such was her renewed despair, she well might have done so, had Letty not been there, and had she not known how much the other three still needed her.

In the succeeding days, when she was on her own, she found herself wringing her hands in an anguish of worry, or leaning back against a wall somewhere in the house or garden while Letty was resting, her arm flung back against her head as if warding off a blow, as if she was being attacked by someone or something. These were long, hard, cold, comfortless days, days made longer and harder by Alexander's returning to

London, leaving herself and Letty quite alone in the great echoing house.

Now just going outside in the early dark of winter took all Hope's courage, and she found herself switching off the news on her radio, afraid that every reported murder would start to seem like something that might be about to happen to herself and Letty. She could not ask Mrs Shepherd who lived near to stay the night with her for Mrs Shepherd had her own family, and with Jack on tour there was nothing to relieve these dreary lonely days, the highlights of which were visiting Aunt Rosabel in hospital, or trying to contact Alexander in London, waiting all the time for some plan to suggest itself, some idea to come to her that would prove to be a solution to her difficulties.

It was in this frame of mind that, one bleak, dark night as Hatcombe's rooms and corridors echoed to the sound of doors and windows creaking and mice in what sounded like leaden boots scrambled through the attics and between the floorboards, Hope found herself peering at two men standing outside Hatcombe's unlocked double doors. Both were tall, brown-hatted and clothed in pale raincoats, and she knew at once just from the way they were dressed that they were total strangers to her, and so, cursing the fact that because she had been bathing Letty she had somehow forgotten to relock the doors after Mrs Shepherd had left them, Hope quickly crept off down the corridor in the opposite direction.

They, on the other hand, not receiving any answer to the old-fashioned bell that still rang somewhere in the cellar, started to rap repeatedly and, it seemed to Hope, a great deal too hard on the window glass of the upper doors. As the sound increased, Hope found herself trembling.

It was past seven o'clock, and dark, Letty was fast asleep after supper and a bath, Hatcombe was up a long drive, and she was all alone except for an old walking stick that had once belonged to Uncle Harold. As the men continued to rap, harder and harder, and her own heart seemed to be beating harder and faster in tune with the sound they were making, Hope picked up the stick from beside the downstairs cloakroom door and started to pray.

Chapter Ten

Jack must have had a premonition, or so it seemed to him afterwards, because, although he felt wiped out with fatigue, instead of driving back to the Mill House after a long hard tour of one-night stands – gigs in small market towns and large suburban areas with conference centres and small intimate theatres with audiences to match – he found himself turning his car towards Hatcombe, and Hope.

Of course the knowledge that she was alone with Letty, that the wretched Alexander was in London – and the fact that he had sensed a sort of despairing courage beneath the over-cheerful conversations that he and Hope had managed to snatch on the telephone – made his sudden change of mind seem logical, both at the time, and afterwards.

When he saw the car his heart sank. He knew just from its ordinariness, white and Japanese, that it could not belong to Alexander, the eternal car snob, and from its price range – well over fifteen grand – that it could not belong to a health visitor or a nanny, and so the thought came to him, and it burnt him up in a way that he would not have thought possible, that Hope was being unfaithful, not only to her husband, but to her lover too.

He would have liked to have jumped out of his own car and run towards Hatcombe, such was the irrational and furious jealousy that started to burn in him just at the sight of the car, but the wind and the rain had become so strong that he was forced to walk from his car in an unusually slow manner. His head bent, he did not run but struggled towards Hatcombe's graceful old double doors with their glassed uppers and lower parts carved of a wood that would have come from trees that were already two hundred years old when they were cut.

The doors were both wide open, and there were chairs piled each upon the other in the hall as furniture is when people are moving and it is due at any minute to be removed, and when he walked through the doors he could hear Hope's voice raised against a man's. He slammed the doors shut loudly before running up the wide staircase to the upper room from where it seemed the voices had drifted down into the hall.

Hope turned as he came in and Jack was shocked to see that her face was paler than he had ever seen it before. Her eyes were two large dark circles in what looked like a tiny heart shape, and it seemed that she had lost pounds in weight while he had been away. The moment she saw him, her face started to colour and the dull look in her eyes was replaced by one of relieved disbelief, and she flung herself towards him.

'Oh, Jack, these men, they've come to take everything, even Letty's bed. They say even that must go, and we must find somewhere else at once!'

Jack turned as a great bruiser of a man accompanied by another smaller type passed down the corridor outside carrying pictures and other items under their arms.

'They have a removal van coming to pack away all our stuff, everything, and they say they are from—'

'We don't *say* we are, miss – madam, we *are* from Elliots, Debt Recovery a speciality.'

Jack went straight to Hope and put his arms round her, and then turning to the now seemingly apologetic bruiser in the white raincoat he said in a deliberately tired but authoritative voice, as if he was well used to dealing with men like him, 'Why don't you get out? Really. Why don't you just go now and we'll sort it all out in the morning. Act like gentlemen, and let Mrs Merriott and her poor child alone, OK?'

'Can't, I'm afraid, sir. Nothing to be done. You see, sir, Mr Merriott—' He saw at once from Jack's reaction that he was no more Mr Merriott than he was himself, and so continued, 'Well, the fact is that we have written to Mr Merriott many, many times, warning him, and his lawyers, you see, sir, and the truth is our clients have been more than patient. I mean they have, legally, owned this place now for some time. They have every right to have the stuff removed. And Mrs Merriott with it. Every right, I'm afraid, sir.'

Jack looked down at Hope and knew at once why she had been sounding so brave and so resolutely cheerful every time he had telephoned on tour. It was because she had, somehow – he would discover how later – in fact, lost everything.

And the terrible irony was that because of Hope, Jack, having long ago lost just his nerve when Dave had left him, had himself regained enough confidence to go on tour in the first place, a tour which had taken him away from Hope when she must have needed him most.

You should have told me, his eyes told her.

Never. This is my marriage, not yours, her eyes replied.

'This does not look good for you, Mr Elliot, or whoever you are. Whatever the circumstances, whatever the legalities, this makes you look callous and brutal. You know that, don't you? I mean to begin with you are trespassing—'

'No such thing in English law, sir. And besides, this property has been bought by my clients, all legal and above board, and—'

'Yeah, well, be that as it may. The fact is I have a great many friends in the press, and, while I perfectly understand that there is the law and there is the – er – law, breaking into people's houses and molesting defenceless women on their own – not to mention trying to turn their children out of their beds – don't look good. Possession may be ninety per cent of the law, but I'll tell you what – the other one hundred and ten is the press.'

There was a small pause as Jack stared across at the bailiff, or whatever he was, or was not.

'You remember all the headlines that have ruined people and businesses overnight? Hallo?'

As he was busy talking Jack had been equally busy keying his mobile phone, happily aware that his oldest journalist friend, an old school chum with jazz-loving tendencies, was still employed on Britain's bestselling tabloid – much to his and everyone else's surprise since, after twenty years attached to a bottle of Scotch, he could hardly spell sun, or moon, and all too often saw stars.

'This is blackmail.'

'I know, old love,' Jack agreed, suddenly all affability. 'And of course what you're doing—Dee Dee – *hallo*. I say, is the boss with you? Oh, good.'

'All right. We'll go, but we'll be back.' The man turned and looked at Hope. 'It's only a matter of time, you know that, don't you? The house does not belong to your husband's family any more. And I happen to know that the old lady has agreed to go into a home. It's all above board – you know that, I know that. It's just a matter of time, Mrs Merriott, and you'd do best to make your plans immediately, for your own sake and that of your children. Really you would.'

To the sound of Jack's long, and falsely flirtatious, conversation with Dee Dee, whoever she might be, the men went, and quite quickly.

Leaning over the banisters Hope could see that

they had carefully and tidily left such furniture and pictures as they had been about to remove in the hall, and from an upstairs window she saw a removal van arriving and, after some consultation, departing. But even as she felt relief flooding her, and found herself running into Jack's open arms, she knew that the burly man in the white raincoat had been right. It was only a matter of time before they would be back, and she had to make plans to leave Hatcombe, not soon, but tomorrow.

As it transpired Jack not only saved Hope from the bailiffs, but he saved Christmas. Had it not been for Jack the Merriotts would have had no Christmas at all. Jack was Santa Claus. Very different from Alexander who, when he arrived from London feigning ignorance of their situation, made his unhappiness perfectly clear to everyone, including the girls. And much as they fussed over him in an effort to cheer him, even his daughters realized that, perhaps because of his long absences from Hatcombe, Alexander was becoming increasingly distant.

His silence was a blessing to a Hope torn between Letty and the still hospitalized Aunt Rosabel, not to mention Jack and their future. She too was more silent than usual, not just because she was worried and frightened for them, but also because when she witnessed Alexander's newly taciturn demeanour she could feel only relief.

They had no time to come to an agreement about how to act, but she could see that even Alexander was aware that telling their daughters about the sale of Hatcombe would be anything but easy, and that he too must have come to the same conclusion as herself, namely that it would be much better to wait until after Christmas to break the news to them.

But the Merriott daughters were more perspicacious than their parents perhaps gave them credit for, and long before the great family day was upon them, or they had learned of the perilous nature of their mutual future, or indeed that they would not in all probability be returning to their school, their studies and their friends, they were voicing their worries to each other.

'You don't think Dads is ill, do you?' Melinda asked Claire, as from their cosy eyrie in the barn they watched their father prowling around the grounds secretly smoking a cigarette before getting into his car and disappearing to some Wiltshire pub or restaurant.

'No.' Claire shook her head, while still watching the lights of the car disappearing down the drive. 'I think he's gone a bit mad. The worry of the builders all this time, and money, all that stuff. He's probably having what Aunt Rosabel calls a *nervous-breakdown-thing*.'

'You mean he's losing it! Oh, God, not someone else!' Rose threw herself dramatically backwards onto one of the old beds that were still in the barn and which now doubled as sofas. 'Oh, God, all the adults are losing it!'

'No, I don't think he's lost it.' Melinda looked down at her tall, dark sister lying chewing the end of her hair on her bed. 'No. I think he's lost everything. All his money. Everything. That's what I think.'

'Dad's always losing his money. He'll get some more, really he will, Mellie. He always does. He'll get some off Aunt Rosabel, just for starters.'

But Melinda looked so doubtful, and so worried, that Rose clambered off her bed and stared at her.

'Come on, Mellie. Spill it. Are we broke again? We can't be broke again?'

'I heard Mums talking the other night, and – well, it didn't sound good.'

'I hope we aren't broke,' Rose said, pulling her heavy cardigan around her shoulders. 'I'm quite enjoying school for once, and a change will not be as good as a rest. Not only that, but I'm not sure about going out to work plucking turkeys or something. Oh, Mellie, I don't really want to be poor. Not really poor!'

'I heard Mums say something about people coming in to take all the furniture and being sent off again. Bailiffs or something.'

'But that doesn't mean we're broke. Goodness. That means – like once at West Dean Avenue when Dad forgot to pay some bill, it just means they come for their money and as long as you pay them it's all right.'

Claire butted in, 'Oh, we know all about that. I remember Mums telling me about that. It sounded quite funny – but Mellie says this was much worse! You said, didn't you, Mellie, you said it was like Mums was suddenly losing the plot! All about Aunt Rosabel and the house, and stuff. Like she was going over the edge, you know, with the worry of it.'

Claire took off her glasses and whirled them in the air to take her mind off what she suspected, which was quite a lot, actually.

'Get out.' Rose's face reflected her disbelief, as she stared from one sister to the other. 'Mums and Aunt Rosabel get on like anything now, really they do, Mellie. Mums goes practically every day to see her. They're fine, really. And I mean Mums doesn't lose it. It's like when they keep saying one of those lumps of rock from space is going to collide with us – Mums would be the only person who wouldn't panic.'

'She'd be too busy making sure we'd flossed our teeth!'

Claire, who had been pretending to read, now put her book down again and stared at the other two.

'Seriously, you guys, we have to talk about this,' Melinda said. 'She was very tense, and I mean very very. And you know how it is, you can always tell with her, because her voice always goes all dead calm and flat.'

'Yes, but now the builders are finished, surely there's not much more to worry about?'

'That was the point, apparently. From what I heard Dads paid the builders and Aunt Rosabel was meant to pay him, but she hasn't – I couldn't quite hear the rest, and Dads kept saying, you know the way he does, *We've been over all this, Hope, what's the point? We've been over all this before!'*

'Yes, but Mellie—' Claire seized Melinda's hand in an effort to get her sole attention. 'What's all this stuff about the house?'

'As I said, it's to do with Aunt Rosabel and, you know, who she's left it to, and all that stuff. I don't really understand these things.'

'Well, you wouldn't, *Dobbin*, not unless it's got an open ditch in front of it.'

'How can Aunt Rosabel change her mind? She worships Dads and loves Mums.' Claire stared ahead of her, frowning, but Rose suddenly saw the point.

'OK, but what would happen to us, I mean if she turns against us or whatever? We'd have nowhere to live, and if Dads paid the builders, after all they've done to the house—'

'I expect she'd just pay them back, and we'd just have to buy another house, that's all. Perhaps go back to West Dean.'

'Yes, please!'

Rose turned and laughed with relief at Claire's

reaction. It was a private joke between them. She knew that Claire had loved their old life as much as she had, and sometimes, in the summer, to tease Mellie, she and Claire would stand sniffing the air saying, 'Oh good, I think I can just smell that gorgeous London smoke and grime from here. If the wind's in the right direction and the London train's going through – I think I just can.'

'Actually, as a matter of fact sometimes I wish we had stayed in London. Life seems to have become awfully messed up down here, as if no-one really knows anything about anything, nor what they all really want to do. And we never see Dads.'

'I suppose it would have been different if one of us had been a boy.' Melinda looked rueful and sighed.

'Why?'

'Why? Because I heard Dads saying as much – to Mums. He said it not once but two or three times. He kept saying, *If only we'd had a son, none of this would have happened!*'

'No-one listens to me! I seem to have spent my whole life offering to go for a sex change,' Claire grumbled, but she smiled. 'I mean. Since obviously I was meant to be a boy, of all of you I was the biggest let-down, wouldn't you say? I mean of all of us I should be the one to go for a sex change, shouldn't I? I saw it marked in the baby names book, I was meant to be called James. I know I was. Besides, you can get it done on the National

Health, a girl at school told me, you know. You can, for free. I could be the first sex change to inherit, and then I could give it all back to you all, and Mums. And Dads, of course.'

Rose had not stopped watching Melinda and noting her restlessness as Claire rambled on, so now she said, suddenly serious, 'Things are really going pear-shaped, aren't they, Mellie? I mean really, really pear-shaped. We should never have moved, should we?'

'Too late for that, Rose. We have moved and we're here, and now we just have to make something happen that will help us all. We have to kick on.'

Rose looked at Claire and raised her eyes to heaven and gave a small whinny before saying, 'OK, Dobbin!'

'Very funny.' Melinda too smiled, but even as she smiled she sighed too. 'The point is if there are going to be problems we'd better see what we can do to help.'

'Any suggestions?'

'When Aunt Rosabel comes home we had better do our Florence Nightingale bit. I mean, if you're right, she's the one with the power, isn't she? And the reason why we're all here in the first place, so that Dads could inherit Hatcombe? Because of us all not being boys.'

As arranged, once home for Christmas from the hospital, something which for some reason seemed to cheer their parents, Aunt Rosabel became the focus of the Merriott sisters' attention.

Not wanting to stay in bed any longer than was strictly necessary, the old lady was soon down and sitting in front of the drawing room fire in quite the old way, albeit much quieter and more given to falling asleep, and they were all able to agree that Aunt Rosabel seemed happier and more at ease than for some time.

A new routine became hers, part of which was being read to by Melinda in the afternoons, and it was during one of these sessions that she interrupted Melinda by saying suddenly, 'You look very much like my mother when you sit beside me reading by the fire, you know? Very much like my mother. Some sort of family likeness there.'

Melinda had not the vaguest idea what Aunt Rosabel's mother had looked like, but since the old lady was smiling in a warm sort of way she took it as a compliment, which was how she felt it was intended.

'Very pretty. Beautiful, in fact, small face, large eyes, very much the same type as Mamma.'

'Thank you.'

'You must remember to take care of your beauty. Never let anyone take it from you. Don't let them take those inner bits that make you beautiful away, Melinda. They count more than you can imagine. And of course, when you get to my age, they are invaluable. My mother married well. She lived in a house just like Hatcombe. So should you. Here would suit you. Now, where were we?' She looked pointedly at the book. 'I like to re-read *A Christmas Carol* every year at this time. It is a story of such genius. It never palls, does it? Never.'

Melinda picked up her book. 'Here's the bookmark, Aunt Rosabel, and if you remember we were just at the bit when Scrooge meets the Ghost of Christmas Future who shows him just what he could be like if he doesn't take care. I always like this bit.

'They left the high road, by a well-remembered lane, and soon approached a mansion of dull red brick, with a little weathercock-surmounted cupola on the roof, and a bell hanging in it. It was a large house, but one of broken fortunes; for the spacious offices were little used, their walls were damp and mossy, their windows broken, and their gates decayed. Fowls clucked and strutted in the stables; and the coach houses and sheds were overrun with grass. Nor was it more retentive of its ancient state within; for entering the dreary hall, and glancing through the open doors of many rooms, they found them poorly furnished, cold, and vast. There was an earthy savour in the air, a chilly bareness in the place, which associated itself somehow with too much getting up by candlelight . . .'

Melinda paused when she saw Aunt Rosabel's eyes closing, what with the warmth of the fire and the newly working central heating.

'No, no, do go on, please. You have such a pleasant voice, so unusual nowadays, if I may say so.'

'*They went, the Ghost and Scrooge, across the hall, to a door at the back of the house. It opened before them, and disclosed a long, bare, melancholy room, made barer still by lines of plain deal forms and desks. At one of these a lonely boy was reading near a feeble fire; and Scrooge sat down upon a form, and wept to see his poor forgotten self . . .*'

'Poor man,' Aunt Rosabel murmured. 'Poor man, such a wretched childhood. After such a childhood what could one expect? Only a poor wretched creature with miserly habits. Only to be expected in the circumstances, if one thinks about it, poor Scrooge.'

Melinda glanced at the old lady, who was frowning deeply as she spoke, and wondered whom she was thinking of. Perhaps Uncle Harry, or someone else that she had loved?

'Carry on, my dear, carry on.'

'*Not a latent echo in the house,*' she read. '*Not a squeak and scuffle from the mice behind the panelling, not a drip from the half-thawed waterspout in the dull yard behind, not a sigh among the leafless boughs of one despondent poplar, not the idle swinging of an empty storehouse door, no, not a clicking in the fire, but fell upon the heart of Scrooge with a softening influence, and gave a freer passage to his tears.*'

'Poor Scrooge,' sighed Aunt Rosabel, and for a

second it seemed to Melinda that he was not the only person with tears in his eyes.

Finally it was Jack who came to the Merriotts' rescue by playing Santa Claus. Before Christmas Day itself, before the last box on the advent calendar in the kitchen at Hatcombe could be opened and revealed to be a rocking horse with streamers, he had thrown a small family party at the Mill House for what he affectionately termed the *boppers*, and then again afterwards, for New Year's Eve, he arranged another event, a much bigger one, for all the young of the neighbourhood to come and enjoy themselves, thus not only giving them a good time, but freeing their parents to enjoy themselves in their own way.

Naturally all the girls were asked and, equally naturally, they all went, Alexander driving them while Hope stayed behind to look after Aunt Rosabel and Letty. Waving her mother goodbye Melinda felt a pang of guilt, but the Mill House was so packed with young people of her own age, all equally determined on enjoying themselves, that it was difficult to stay regretful for long. And besides, there was Josh.

As Melinda had previously noted, Jack's son was tall, dark, handsome, but strangely monosyllabic, always absenting himself from the room on the least pretext, and walking off towards the stables or down to the river which ran past the Mill House as if he had other, better things to do than to talk to people like herself. This had intrigued Melinda and also earned her admiration. Just as she instinctively liked animals because they did not waste time on anything that did not really matter, and showed their emotions with sincerity, so she felt for human beings who were the same. She liked people who did not want to socialize, who were loners, who, like Joshua Tomm, seemed to gallop off in the opposite direction.

Knowing all this already Melinda danced with everyone except their host's son, and as Jack and his group played for them all in the old barn that had been turned over to partying, naturally Melinda pretended that she had not really noticed Josh, any more than she had noticed anyone else, feigning to herself as to everyone else that she was just there to have fun, which was true, in a way, and untrue in another way, because she had every intention of making Josh notice her, if only because she was wearing her best velvet strapless bustier and had spent hours on her hair.

And when they ended up dancing opposite each other Melinda could not wait to show off just how good her dancing, under Rose's tuition, had become, just as Josh, it seemed, once on the dance floor showed none of the inhibitions that he obviously felt in company, when he left what Rose called *rabbiting* to his younger brother and sister.

Alexander was meant to be going to stay and enjoy the party with Melinda and the other two, while Hope, having put Letty to bed and seen to Aunt Rosabel's needs, was only too happy to be left alone, to sew, to listen to music on her old Roberts radio in the kitchen, to try to think about what had to be done, and to welcome in the New Year in her own way.

And so when she heard the all too familiar sound of Alexander's expensive car returning long before midnight – a car which she had every intention of making him put up for sale – Hope's heart sank.

Thinking the party must have been either a terrible flop or cancelled and that Alexander had returned early with the girls, Hope went at once to the front door and waited, suddenly feeling tired beyond reason at the thought that she could not even snatch a few hours of quiet after all the work and tensions of a Christmas where not only the turkey and the other food, but every present too, had been bought in the certain knowledge that all too soon she would have to pay the bank back with goodness only knew what added interest, and that she would probably have to sell her car, certainly whatever jewellery she still had, to repay everything she had spent to keep the girls from knowing just what was about to happen to them.

But when the front door eventually opened it was only Alexander, and he was quite on his own, and smiling, which made Hope frown.

'Is everything all right?'

He nodded. 'Yes, darling. I just came home to be

with you.' He smiled even more broadly. 'Came back to enjoy New Year with you, in our old way, the way we always used to in West Dean – remember?'

Hope stared at him, trying to remember and failing, and at the same time hearing Jack's voice in her head saying, as he had done when they were last together, *You know you've got to end it and come to me, don't you?*

As Hope tried desperately to recall how she and her husband had used to spend New Year when the girls were out partying she realized just how right Jack was. She had to end it. Now.

'Want to come to the stables and see our first rescue – c-case?'

Melinda was standing outside the now very hot barn sipping a cool glass of wine and lemonade. She stopped staring up at the clear, beautiful night sky and put down her glass without any hesitation.

'I'll get my coat,' she said, because they both knew what *our first case* meant without having to add any more, just as they both could appreciate the trust that such a very private sort of invitation implied.

Melinda grabbed at the new fleece-lined coat that her mother had given her for Christmas – which, since it must have cost a fortune, had gone a great way towards relieving any fears that Mellie might have been harbouring for the family's future – and hurried off towards the stables with Josh, both giving each other those particularly secretive smiles that people who share the same passion for horses will give, knowing just from the immediacy of each other's reactions that they would far prefer to be in the stables than in the barn, however enjoyable the music and the dancing.

Josh turned on the stable lights and led the way to the new horse's box. He turned and smiled at Melinda.

'Come – on – Mellie.'

That was all he said, but as he went to say something else and stopped Melinda realized just what it was about Josh that she had never realized before, and no-one had ever mentioned, probably because they must have imagined that she already knew. Why he had always, on previous occasions, and as soon as he could, just bolted out of doors and headed off somewhere on his own whenever they were all together. He had what Aunt Rosabel always tactfully called a 'hesitation'. Apparently the old gardener at Hatcombe had used to have just such a speech impediment, Aunt Rosabel had told Melinda once, and later, when the subject came up, long before they met Josh, she had instructed the girls never, *ever*, to try to fill in a pause, or butt in ahead of someone with such a problem.

'Hesitations occur far more frequently in boys than in girls, and need the most exquisite sensitivity at all times. They are not a laughing matter, although the Lord only knows there are all too many people quite capable of holding their sides laughing when they meet someone with such a handicap.'

Melinda had not really paid much attention to the old lady at the time, but now, as her heart went out to this tall, handsome boy with his long, faded green Barbour covering his purple silk party shirt who was trying so desperately to cover over his inability to speak fluently, Aunt Rosabel's words came back to her great-great-niece as if she had just uttered them, and Melinda waited calmly for his next words.

'She's called . . .' a long wait, and then finally but without a problem, 'Grey Goose.'

Melinda stared in at the mare in the box as Josh removed her rugs and stood back against the wall, waiting for her verdict.

'I heard she was a rescue job, your father told me before Christmas that he'd rescued a race-horse, but I didn't realize it was a mare. That makes it much better because she can have foals even if she flops at whatever you want to do with her.'

'Eventing.'

'She's in need of a bit more on top, isn't she?' Melinda eyed the grey mare appreciatively, adding, 'Yup, a bit more on her top line' – she patted the mare's quarters – 'and next stop Badminton!'

They both laughed. It was a joke. Imagine winning Badminton with a rescued racehorse.

But everyone can dream, and as Melinda started to help Josh replace the mare's rugs, she found to her surprise that she was no exception, and that by the time the last buckle was done up she could hear the cheers in her ears as she completed a clear run at the end of the three days. And as they both turned to check the bolts on the mare's stable door, she was quite sure that she could also feel Josh swinging her round, as, her clear round completed, she flung herself from the Grey Goose and into his arms.

Alexander had bought Hope and himself a secret picnic from a nearby delicatessen and was laying it out on the kitchen table in front of the old Aga.

'Just like old times,' he said gaily as he removed a ready-made game pie, a bottle of wine, some French bread and a wedge of Brie from their separate carrier bags. 'Do you remember our feasts once the children went back to school after Christmas? They were always such fun. I was remembering them only the other day, the good old days, at West Dean. How lucky we were to have that time.'

Hope stared at the picnic for two laid out on the table. It was a nightmare. Alexander, having behaved like a funeral director all over Christmas, was not only back in her life, but for some reason suddenly once more all sweetness and light and wooing her with gaiety and fun, while all the time she knew, absolutely, that she had to tell him that they must separate, immediately. That whatever happened he could not be part of her life again, or she part of his, that it was over, that she and the girls would make out somehow, that Jack had promised to lend her a cottage in the Mill House grounds. Part of her could not wait until the removal van actually did arrive for their things, but this time one paid for by her, because Jack, knowing how proud she was, had found her a job working as a personal assistant to a composer friend of his who lived nearby and was badly in need of what Jack called 'organization'.

It seemed that everything might be coming right for Hope at last, and it had all happened over these last days. In between the wrapping and the unwrapping, in between everything else, Jack had, since that awful night when he had found her with the bailiffs, stepped in and given Hope a torch to light her way out of the dark tunnel that she was in. The reason why she had so resented seeing Alexander coming back early from the party was because it meant that she could not start to make lists, to organize everything so that she could leave him as painlessly as possible.

At that moment, Hope, to her horror, found that she cared about the father of her daughters about as much as she might care about a stranger she had just read about in a newspaper, or some friend had told her of, someone of whom they would both say, *Thank heavens she had the courage to leave him*.

'You're looking really beautiful, do you know

that, Hope? Really lovely. I've been watching you all over Christmas and thinking how pretty you've become while I've been away so much. Country life seems to suit you. I'm amazed the difference it has made to you.'

Hope stared at the plate of food that Alexander was putting in front of her, knowing already that she could not possibly eat half of it, but also knowing, without any doubt at all, that somehow or another he had found out about her and Jack.

Alexander knew.

And she knew he knew, just as she had known that Alexander had been having affairs when he had not wanted to answer the telephone in front of her. In case. That was the trouble with knowing each other so well, despite all that had happened, or not happened, between them. Knowing each other as well as they did, it was impossible, finally, *not to know*.

Chilled at the very idea of how much else he might know, Hope raised her eyes to her husband's, and finding him smiling down at her she saw that she was right. He did indeed know *everything*, and this little feast that he had laid on for her was in some way a trap, and yet she still raised the glass of wine he had just poured for her to his, and even as her heart sank they clinked glasses, and smiled.

'Would you like to ride the Grey Goose, bring her on, eventing, with me, Melinda?'

If Josh had proposed marriage to her it could not have been a more exciting moment for Melinda. Nevertheless, out of long ingrained habit, she hesitated, knowing that she should really ask her mother before she accepted such an offer. She always did ask Hope about everything first. It was something she had always done, just as her sisters always seemed to ask Melinda herself for advice.

But there again, her mother was not present, and if she waited and asked her in front of her father, now that he was home, he might step in and say no for all sorts of reasons, and she would lose what she knew would be the chance of a life-time.

'Have you asked your father about this, Josh?'

Some strain of good sense, probably because she was the eldest of four, always reasserted itself, so that even when Melinda would have liked to say 'yes' she found she always played for time.

'Have I asked my father?' Josh turned and looked down at her. They were both poised on the threshold of the barn where Jack was still playing his heart out for the crowd of dancing, laughing teenagers. 'It was his idea! From the moment we bought this house he's always thought we should help to rescue horses who had been flung aside, you know, rejected by the uncaring world of racing, and as soon as he heard about Goosey, that was it. But the first person he thought of to bring Goosey *on* was you. He thinks girls are brilliant with sensitive horses, and people!'

Melinda looked across at Jack and then back at Josh. She could not imagine having a father who actually thought of doing things like rescuing horses. All her father ever seemed to think about was money. She smiled up at Josh. 'I tell you what, though.'

'What?'

'Nothing.'

'Not nothing.'

'Well.'

'Yes?'

'Swap you! My father for yours! No, I don't mean that. But I mean, he's quite something, isn't he?'

Josh looked proudly across at his father and smiled. 'Yeah, he's a good guy,' he agreed.

And then they moved forward into the main part of the barn, joining in and yet not joining in, because although they resumed the communal dancing that was currently so popular, in reality they both knew that they were really only dancing with each other.

'I – er – don't really think I had better have any more to drink, Alexander. Really.'

'Oh, come on, Hope. This is New Year's Eve, or whatever. The New Year coming in? The whole world is jumping around and all you want to do is sit with your crochet, or whatever it is you do.'

'Needlepoint, actually.'

Alexander always did get that wrong. They

were so different, crochet and needlepoint, so different. As different as Jack from Alexander, or Melinda from Rose, or Aunt Rosabel from Hope. She frowned, and put out a hand, too late, to cover her glass. She had to tell him.

'Alexander.' Hope put down her fork, and stared through the festive candles which Alexander had put about the kitchen table at his still handsome face. 'I have to tell you something. I should have told you before.'

Alexander nodded. 'Yes, darling?'

'I have to tell you that . . . I have . . .'

'More wine?'

'No. Really. Alexander. I have to tell you that I have fallen in love with someone else.'

Alexander stared at her, and actually managed to make his eyes fill with tears. As she stared into them, Hope thought she would end her life. She could not remember, ever, seeing Alexander cry. She stared down at her plate, and her own eyes filled with tears, and a lump came into her throat.

It could not be worse, telling him this way, after all they had been to each other years before. The years of fun and happiness, wrecked by her. No, not just by her – by both of them. But, even so, she had to share the blame. She had to shoulder her part of the failure. She had failed him too.

She started to cry uncontrollably. 'I'm so sorry, Alexei. I didn't want to fall in love with someone else. But I was alone here, in the country, with only Aunt Rosabel and Verna and Letty, and you were always away, and it just happened. I'm so sorry.'

She sobbed helplessly into her hands, hearing her own voice and her own heartrending cries, and there was nothing she could do to help herself, such was her sorrow, such was her grief.

As he laid her down on their bed and spread out her long hair around her face, for all the world as if he was her nanny and not her husband, Alexander stared down at his wife. God. The whole business had been so avoidable, that was what was so crass. As he gazed down at her he realized with a surge of passion that he still cared about Hope very much, despite everything. But it was just so much her *fault*. Not giving him a son, not doing what he wanted so that he could inherit his father's money, and now going and having an affair with that musician up the way. All this time she had been deceiving him with some old rocker, making love with him, perhaps in this very bed. All the time he was in London, working, thinking about their future, she had been deceiving him.

The foolish thing was that he would never have suspected a thing had Muffin Hatherleigh's best friend from her Pony Club days not been Poppy Taylor-Batsford who had, it seemed, witnessed the two of them lunching together in a wine bar in Bradford-on-Avon. Apparently they had not been able to pick up their knives and forks without holding hands, so blatant had been their relationship.

And of course quite suddenly, after Muffin had passed on the gossip to him, suddenly it had all made such sense! Particularly when Alexander came home and found Hope looking better than she had ever done. Suddenly her going off for a so-called 'rest' to Worcestershire, everything, had made such sense. Why had he not questioned her deep desire to go to *Worcestershire* of all places? Hope who had never wanted to move to the country, and whose first choice for a break must always have been London or Paris, Rome or New York, for God's sake? And who, most of all, had never before admitted to needing a rest.

But of course, he, Alexander, having been so hard at work in London, with so much on his mind, trying to make money for them all, had not once suspected Hope. Had it not been for Muffin, he would never have suspected her, not for one minute.

What he could not understand, and what he so resented, what made him burn up inside, was that Hope always seemed so innocent. Justifiable rage really seared him as he thought of himself in London, trying to keep them all, while all the time she was off with Jack Tomm! He stared down at her on the bed, and the thought of the two of them together, her and Jack, seemed to set fire to the alcohol he had consumed, jealousy now fuelled by righteous fury.

Well, as it happened, he was going to have to leave Hope for his new *amoureuse* Muffin

Hatherleigh anyway, because, quite apart from anything else, Muffin was just too rich for Alexander to resist marrying.

Over the past months Alexander had come to realize that the truth had to be faced. He had at last found a woman, a rich widow, who could actually, miracle of miracles, afford him. The icing on the cake was that Muffin was absolutely besotted with him. He could go and live with her and he would not even have to *sell his car*.

Everything was finally and absolutely over between him and Hope now, finally and completely. All he needed to do was leave a carefully written note to her saying goodbye, and go.

Hope was trying, as Melinda would say, to *get her head around* what Aunt Rosabel was saying.

'These gels have generally all had babies, you see, Hope. And someone has to bring them up, feed them, give them a home. So the women have now found this out, mostly to their cost – and the result? The result is that they have become hybrid creatures, unable to determine what determination they really have, or are, for that matter.' She paused and looked across at Hope. 'Do you get my meaning, my dear?'

Hope nodded. 'Of course. Things are really different now, aren't they? And with so many daughters you can imagine, Aunt Rosabel, I'm always thinking about these things. Is it right to marry and have babies and leave them to someone else, lots of other people, to bring up? Or is it better, if you want to work, not to have babies? I don't know, really I don't. It's something that really puzzles me a lot. I mean, I don't seem to have done very well myself, always betwixt and between, never doing anything really well, it often seems to me, so that I don't really feel I can pronounce.'

'Fiddlesticks!' Aunt Rosabel smiled and looked across at her great-nephew's wife. 'You have done excellently.'

Hope too would have liked to smile, but she found that all she could do was look rueful.

They were only a few weeks into the New Year. Outside the wind was not howling, it was screaming and tearing at the landscape, and if she stood up and gazed out of Hatcombe's windows she could see the rain coming in broad sheets, moving down the fields and the lawns towards the house as if being sent by God to cover the house in one long length of white-grey silk. Not far behind it came the sound of thunder and yet more sheets, but this time of bright white-yellow explosions of lightning.

As she stood looking out, a thunderbolt came to Hope, but not one that had anything to do with the weather. She turned. 'Excuse me while I fetch us some tea, Aunt Rosabel,' she said in a low voice. Walking as fast as she could, but not so fast that Aunt Rosabel would notice anything untoward, she left the drawing room and made for the downstairs cloakroom where she was heartily and gratefully sick.

Somehow she had known it. All along, since the New Year, through all the preparations for leaving Hatcombe, finding Alexander's letter, telling the girls that their father had left, arranging for them all to move into Jack's cottage at the Mill House, she had known with a dreadful certainty that there was something wrong with her, and that it was not 'flu, or measles, but something she had already experienced four times, and had been warned by Alistair Macleod she must never experience again.

Hope was pregnant.

Chapter Eleven

It seemed that no sooner had Hope's new pregnancy been confirmed than Aunt Rosabel was dead. It astonished Hope that she finally minded the old lady's dying as much as she did, and yet in another way it did not surprise her at all, for she had instinctively felt that Aunt Rosabel wanted to go before she was forced, one way or another, to leave Hatcombe. That being so, she had, in her own inimitable and elegant way, taken her leave once she knew that her own little world had finally come to a natural end. As Melinda put it, 'It's like that old actor guy said the other day, *The car has come for her.*' Hope could only be glad that Mr Bell and his so-called nephew's amiable plan to forcibly evict the old lady from her home had been unavoidably delayed.

Naturally, had they all still been living at Hatcombe the news of his great-aunt's funeral would have brought Alexander hurrying back from London, but as it was, with Muffin Hatherleigh waiting for him in Belgravia, her town house already filled with his clothes, her Scottish castle already changed to suit his needs, her private helicopter traded in for one which her new so-handsome lover preferred, Alexander had already said goodbye to Hatcombe, and written his farewell to Hope.

I hope you will understand that it is you, and no-one but you, who is utterly responsible for my being unable to carry on being married to you? Had you taken my advice before Letty was born and made sure of the sex of our child we would not only have been able to have a happy family life, we would have been able to afford it too. As it is, all that is now in the past, and all there is left to do is gather what we each can from the ashes and get on with the next phase. God help us all. But I am sure you will manage very well with Jack, and I am sure I can manage extremely well too. There is nothing more to say, really. Goodbye, Hope. Alexei.

Despite a throbbing head, far worse than she had surely earned from the few glasses of wine she had drunk, Hope had stared pitifully at Alexander's signature. It had been the final straw, somehow, his using Hope's love name for him – the one she had only used at intimate moments.

It was so cutting, and yet so fitting, and now 'Alexei' was gone for ever, and with him Alexander, leaving Hope and her daughters to attend his great-aunt's simple village funeral and give tea to as many of her old friends as were able to be present.

In fact, although thoroughly enthralled with Muffin, and perfectly happy to be her live-in lover and have her lavish anything she saw fit to lavish upon him, Alexander had remained in London rather than attend Aunt Rosabel's funeral not so much because he could not bear to stay away from his wonderfully wealthy new love and his equally new flamboyant lifestyle, as because he was far more interested in taking himself off to see the Williamson family lawyer and make enquiries as to the exact nature of the chaos in which his great-aunt's estate had been left.

'That, alas, would appear to be that,' the lawyer concluded at last, tapping the papers back into shape on the top of his polished partner's desk. 'Alas from your point of view, I mean.'

Alexander drummed his fingers on the over-new briefcase that Muffin had insisted on giving him, and, twisting his mouth into a sideways grimace, took a deep breath before speaking slowly and precisely, as if to a stupid person.

'Why?' he said, as calmly as he could. 'Why were her affairs allowed to get into this sort of mess, Mortenson?'

Mortenson stared at him, his expression filled with a most un-lawyer-like innocence while he practised a beautiful form of mental yoga which entailed thinking of flowers and night skies.

'Why, Mortenson? When I relied on you, we all relied on you – my soon to be former wife, my daughters, myself – not to let this sort of thing happen? We counted on you, Mortenson. We absolutely counted on you.'

'No-one can legislate for the failure of an old lady's memory, Mr Merriott, and the fact is that all is not yet lost. We are actually, as you know, in the process of taking that devious couple of gentlemen who talked your great-aunt into selling them her house to court, and I know we will win. It seems they have a history of this sort of thing – diddling old people out of their estates and hiving off a great deal not for their so-called charity – orphans, indeed – but for themselves. On the other hand, as you no doubt realized before you came to see me, it will take some time to sort out the various claims on the estate. I have little doubt that it will be sorted out, and of course there is a court order on the house, so Bell has not been able to take possession. If I have anything to do with it, he will never be allowed to.'

'I should think not! The balance of my great-aunt's mind was most definitely affected, as I can prove. She made out cheques here there and everywhere, some for thousands. I have medical proof that she was not in sound mind. Not only that, but she thought that the sum those two criminals offered her was the current market price. She was, in other words, duped.'

Rich though Alexander knew he would be the moment Muffin said 'I do' in Kensington Register Office – following what he devoutly hoped would be a quickie divorce from Hope – nevertheless he was more than reluctant to give up his claims on Hatcombe.

It was pride more than anything, as even he recognized. Even he knew, logically, that now that

304

he had Muffin and her millions, now that he had freed himself from all those daughters, he did not need Hatcombe at all; but since he felt he had been through so much for the wretched house Alexander had come to believe that, although he did not *need* the place, he nevertheless now *deserved* to live there.

He saw himself, but with Muffin not Hope, standing in front of Hatcombe's graceful double doors, saw himself striding across its fields, or standing of an evening in the old rose garden listening to birdsong. Not to give up Hatcombe to anyone else had become a principle of his that he would not willingly relinquish, a cause célèbre for him alone. He had been through too much to want to see anyone else – say Jack Tomm – living there and enjoying it. Hatcombe was meant to be his. It suited him. He had always thought so.

'Your great-aunt was duped,' the lawyer agreed, 'but I should tell you that when we have won this case – which I am sure that we will – you will find there are certain secret codicils to your great-aunt's will, codicils which I have to warn you, Mr Merriott, do not, I must tell you in confidence, include you.'

Alexander stared at Mr Mortenson. He always had got on his nerves, but never more than now. 'I beg your pardon?'

'Hatcombe is not to be left to you.'

Alexander's mouth opened and then shut slowly, and then opened once more to say, 'To whom then did my great-aunt leave her house?'

There was a short pause and then Mortenson shook his head. 'I cannot say, Mr Merriott. But it is perfectly clear that it was not your great-aunt's intention that the house should be yours. That is all I can tell you. And let us face it, given that you and your wife are divorcing, it cannot have come as the shock it might well have been before.'

'But when the will is read?'

'No-one will be any the wiser, no-one outside this office that is to say. Future ownership of the house is covered in a secret codicil which was the wish of my client, your great-aunt. In the meantime, until we have sorted out the other little complication, it is to be rented.'

Alexander stared ahead of him. 'I too have claims against the estate, Mr Mortenson. I poured money into that house, most of the profit on my own house—'

'Understood, Mr Merriott, and it will be heard in full, I promise you. But first things first. We must first go after these gangsters who duped your relative while the balance of her mind was disturbed, as I am sure you appreciate.'

Alexander tapped his foot, his mouth tightened, and he swept his fingers through his thick dark hair. What a pill! He would have to wait now, and for some time, until everything was settled, but no matter what the secret codicils he would buy Hatcombe back. In fact he would make quite sure that Muffin bought it back for him. She could well afford it.

'Oh yes, and one more thing. What about estate duty?'

The lawyer rose. 'I shouldn't concern yourself with that,' he said smoothly. 'Not much point, really, is there, Mr Merriott? Not considering.'

Alexander stood up. As the lawyer joined him on his side of the desk to escort him to the lift, he had the strangest feeling that Mr Mortenson did not really like him very much, and never had. Alexander frowned.

It did not occur to Alexander very often that someone did not like him. The last time it had was when he had returned home to Hatcombe and seen how far Hope – his own wife of all people – how far she had gone to avoid kissing him on the mouth.

'Goodbye, Mr Merriott.'

Mortenson turned back from the lift. Everyone in his office had succumbed to 'flu, his wife was away skiing with their sons, and he missed them very much. He had a pile of work that would take him into the small hours, but nevertheless Mr Mortenson's heart sang with the knowledge that Alexander Merriott would not after all be inheriting Hatcombe, and if this not-so-very-old family lawyer had anything to do with it, he never would.

'I thought as much.' Hope stared at the young woman gynaecologist. 'After four pregnancies you sort of know. And then of course when I did the test . . .'

Her voice tailed off.

'I expect, given your medical history, and the unplanned nature of the pregnancy, that you might be thinking in terms of a termination?'

Hope nodded. 'Yes,' she agreed dully. 'I am.'

'Your notes – you know, any new pregnancy, it is quite clear, would cause a great deal of worry. To have another baby would be to take a considerable risk. Your womb, previous scars, not really advisable, really, in the circumstances—'

'I know.' Hope nodded again. 'What a pill . . .' she started, and then, 'or lack of it!'

They both laughed with relief at Hope's joke, because in the circumstances, at that moment, anything was a relief.

'Terminations always sound so – terminal, don't they?'

'If I may remind you, you have your other children to consider, and in the circumstances, as you have outlined them, with your husband and you divorcing, you have to accept the fact that the child would be born into quite difficult conditions, really.'

'Yes, yes, I know.' Again there was a long silence, during which Hope could hear a patient murmuring in the next-door room, an ambulance siren stopping abruptly, the click of the gynaecologist's pen as she pushed the biro top nervously in and out, in and out.

It suddenly seemed so terrible to do away with

a baby who, after all, when all was said and done, had a right to life, surely? To Hope whose whole life had been devoted to loving life for its own sake, every form of life had seemed so infinitely precious to her, always. And yet now she was contemplating doing away with the beginnings of a baby. Did she have a right over the baby, or the baby over her? For no reason Aunt Rosabel's face came back to her. So serene! So enviably serene!

Hope continued after the considerable silence, 'Well, you're right, because there's more than that. There is the father. My lover.' She looked across the desk at the gynaecologist, relieved that she was a woman.

It sounded so strange saying that word 'lover', and yet exciting too, as if at long last Hope could be considered just like the rest of the world, flawed. No longer the upright woman who had never known a lover other than her husband, but a flawed human being, someone who could take, and had taken, a considered step towards her own personal happiness, away from the paths set by other people. Perhaps in some strange way she had, by her deception of Alexander, freed herself.

'My lover,' she said again. 'The father of my child. He already has three children, and, well, I have four. So he won't want any more, I don't suppose. In fact I'm pretty sure that he doesn't.'

'Does your husband not know about your pregnancy, then, Mrs Merriott? Have you not told him yet?'

'No. This baby could not be my husband's baby, so there doesn't seem much point in telling him something that is really none of his business, now. No, this is – this has to be my lover's child.'

There, it was out, and nothing to be done, but Hope was nevertheless grateful for the other woman's composure. Hope and Jack had met and made love over Christmas, rapturously, alone at Keeper's Cottage in the middle of sorting out all sorts of things, from how many new duvets the cottage needed to when to order the bottled gas.

They had not meant to, it had just happened. And now, unbelievably, she was having his child.

'Perhaps you ought to tell the father in that case? If you have a future together, you should perhaps tell your lover of your situation, Mrs Merriott? To be honest, in my experience it is usually much better, if I may say so, in these matters, to tell the father. Simply because if it should ever come out later, which it can – some moment of sadness revisited, too much drink, that sort of thing – well, then it can set up resentments, or worse, if these decisions have not been reached mutually. If the man and the woman haven't taken the decision together.'

Hope stood up. 'You're right,' she agreed. 'I must tell him. But I have to warn you, from what I know of him, if I do tell him I am quite sure that he will want me to keep it. He will see it as part of our planned future together. He – he's very romantic.'

'Well, then doubtless you will explain to him your medical situation. Or if you like you can come in here together, and I will explain it to him. At any rate – particularly since this baby, as I understand it, was not planned – I am sure he will see it as the wisest decision, given your medical records.'

A little touch of desperation had started to creep into the gynaecologist's voice and for a second Hope thought she could see the professional mask on the other side of the desk slipping, the doctor looking suddenly vulnerable as if she wished that she had not said anything about telling Jack after all. After some further minutes of discussion they both smiled and shook hands, but Hope felt the other woman watching her as she left the room. Her eyes had reflected such real anxiety for her patient as they shook hands that Hope almost felt sorry for her.

But she realized suddenly, with a blinding certainty, that it was too late anyway. Nothing that either of them could say now would change Hope's mind.

As she drove home Hope knew that an irrevocable decision had been taken. And it came to her that whatever was ahead did not matter now, and that whatever Jack had to say on the subject would not make any difference either, for in bringing herself to understand her own nature Hope had, come what may, determined that she should keep her baby, because she knew now that she loved Jack with all her heart, and that fact alone was enough to make her resist doing away with his child.

And so it was, as the trees flashed past her car window and the inevitable rain splashed against her windscreen and she wondered at the dark brown of the mud on the roads, not to mention the starkness of the leafless trees, that Hope came to her own decision, not to tell Jack about anything, not her medical record, not the gynaecologist's advice, nothing. And in realizing the risks that she was prepared to take for this new baby it came to her that when a woman loved a man as much as Hope now knew she loved Jack, more than anything in the world she wanted to have his child.

However, telling her daughters about their mother's new state would be anything but easy, and Hope was realistic enough to know it. Day after day she thought about it, and day after day she put it off. First she imagined writing to them, and then she imagined waiting until half-term to tell them all together.

And, yet again, she found that she could not face either option. When it actually came down to it, she could not bear to come face to face with them and tell them of her new condition; and considering all the talks that they had had together – talks about the insuperable difficulties facing girls who had babies and brought them up without fathers, about the necessity for each baby, if possible, to have two parents – Hope's embarrassment – for that essentially was what it was – was not really very surprising.

It was not as if she had not asked so much of them already. She had had to move them all into the little cottage near the Mill House and tell them that they could only stay at their school until Easter – and then only because Jack had offered to help fund them.

Despite the fact that they all loved Jack, and despite the fact that he was busy encouraging Melinda to ride his beloved 'rescued' mare, giving Claire piano lessons, and coaching Rose in her budding dramatic talent, telling them that this genial composer-philanthropist whom they all liked so much was also going to be the father of Hope's new baby was proving to be more than a problem. It was proving to be impossible.

'Don't tell them, then.'

Hope and Jack were out walking on the Downs, Letty running ahead, Jack's dog running still further in front, and although it was still winter the day was sunny and bright. Perhaps because of this, somehow Hope felt only optimism about the future, reluctant though she was to admit her pregnancy to her daughters.

'I must tell them sometime.'

'Yes, tell them you are going to have a baby, but don't tell them it is ours until afterwards. By that time they will have become used to the idea of us as a couple, and everything will be fine. You know how it is, with new babies, once they're born everything's all right and no-one really cares about who the father might be, least of all the baby!'

Jack put his arm round Hope and they walked on up the hill, Jack laughing, Hope smiling. She had not told Jack just what a risk the pregnancy would be for her. As far as she was concerned she wanted this baby, and she knew now that he too wanted the baby, and the risk was as nothing compared to those two factors.

Besides, Caesareans were growing ever less risky, and Alistair Macleod could well have been wrong about her.

'What a joy!' Jack sighed with delight at the thought of their future together. He picked up Letty and swung her round, putting her onto his broad shoulders and starting to trot ahead making 'horsey' noises. 'Of course, you know you won't get a look-in the moment he or she arrives? Not even a glance,' he finished, breaking into a canter to make Letty laugh.

Hope watched them going ahead of her, the wind blowing Letty's hair back towards her, Jack's strong form outlined against the skyline like a figure in a Stanley Spencer landscape, and as she did so she thought she could feel something. She did not quite know what it was, just a little kick, something that told her that what was happening inside her was just as important as what was happening outside.

'God bless you, Jack,' she murmured, trailing after him, her thoughts as always when she was with him turning to wondering, yet again, what would have happened to her had he not decided to call at Hatcombe that day. It seemed a hundred years ago now.

Silently she offered up a prayer to Aunt Rosabel, who she was quite sure was in heaven looking down on them all. *Look out for us all from up there, won't you?* she begged, and her eyes filled with tears as she remembered Aunt Rosabel entertaining the old soldiers who had known her poor dead son, her courage and gaiety with them, and it seemed to Hope that her situation was only lucky, and that she could never have been so brave or so resolute as Rosabel Fairfield who had lost so much, and yet retained herself.

Once Hope finally did pluck up courage and tell the girls of her situation, far from being upset or difficult they appeared to understand. Even though they did not know that their own father was not the father of the expected baby, they bravely accepted their strange new circumstances, adapting not just to the cottage but to Jack's place in their mother's life as if they had known all along where the problems with Alexander had been, from his constant absences, from his diminishing interest in them over the past year, and even his waning involvement with Hatcombe.

And, Hope realized, the truth might be that her

315

daughters were all secretly relieved that their parents had at last accepted what they had already guessed; or perhaps it was just that they liked being with Jack and his family, and found that they could be much more relaxed at the Mill House than they had ever been with Alexander at home. Whatever the reason, after only a few months it seemed to Hope that they were all looking forward to a future that seemed to beckon only too brightly. Until Hope had a dream.

Melinda was slowly coming to the conclusion that she and the grey mare, while suited to each other, needed someone besides Josh to help bring them on. As always, though, Josh seemed to be ahead of her.

'Found an old body called Colonel Simpson. He won Badminton in the Ice Age, but he's ready and willing if you are.'

Melinda's unspoken reaction was *I can't afford to pay for lessons*, whereupon Josh, having seemed to hear it, replied, 'It's all right, Dad's paying for everything, Mel, really. He's in such a good mood at the moment, since you lot came to Keeper's Cottage, I think he would buy your mum the world.'

There was a long pause during which Melinda found herself colouring with relief at being paid for, and at the same time feeling very much the poor relation because she had to be paid for. Josh looked over to her.

'It's all right, Mel, really,' he reiterated. 'Dad makes a fortune from his evergreens – some of his songs are never off the radio, in case you haven't noticed; and since your mum came into his life he's – well, he's a changed man. He really is. Not that he was ever nasty, or anything. He was just so worried all the time; and I mean really worried, what with me always behind at school, and our mother running off – well, you know the story. But since he met your mum and got his confidence back and went back out on tour, he's much more together. It's brilliant, it really is.'

'I just wish that I could pay for myself.'

'You are paying for yourself,' Josh insisted. 'You – are. You're doing all the work, riding, mucking out – everything – for free, see? So you are paying your way, OK?'

But when Colonel Simpson saw Melinda on Grey Goose, and had watched her showing off her paces for a few minutes, popping her over a practice fence, he said, 'The mare's got talent all right – or potential, anyway. Question is – have you?'

Melinda's expression dropped to the ground. She had worked her legs off on the Grey Goose the past few weeks, and had really felt they were both coming on in every area, particularly Goosey. And now it seemed there was a question mark not over the mare, but over Melinda herself.

'Wrong position, wrong leg position, wrong everything. You're holding her up, and unless you really pick yourself up and give yourself a shake you will continue to do so, and I shall have to advise Josh here that he would be better off getting another rider.'

Melinda felt her cheeks burning with the humiliation of it all. Josh was listening intently, could hear every word, and would surely report back to his father. She looked down into Colonel Simpson's hard, bright brown eyes. He had been in all sorts of 'hot spots' round the world, and had seen terrible things. It had made him hard, she could see that, just as she had been able to see, the moment she rode up to him, that he did not think her riding good enough and felt it would be better if she were jocked off in favour of some posh girl with a sponsor and a string of riding successes to her name.

'I have not had much time to devote to the Grey Goose because I've been at boarding school until now, Colonel Simpson, but next time I come you will see I am not the same rider at all.'

'No? Well, let's hope not. Now. Let's begin with your leg position, shall we? Old-fashioned and wrong. Don't know who taught you, but my grandmother rode like that. That is not how we ride today. And although your hands are, shall we say, sensitive, you should hold them much higher. Like this. And your head, up, up – that's better. Drop the chin, back straight. Well I never, Josh. Look. Thank you. Different shape, isn't she? And so, you will not be surprised to see, is the mare.'

Later, there was a long silence as Josh drove the

horse box back to the Mill House, and then Melinda said, 'I was thinking – perhaps the colonel is right, Josh. If I were you, I think I should get another rider. Someone with more experience. I've been thinking—'

'I thought I heard the wheels going round in your head and I thought that would be the next thing you said!'

'Well, it would only be fair to Goosey.'

'At the moment there is only one goose in this horse box, and I'm talking to her.'

'OK. As long as you're sure – I promise I'll work.' Melinda stared ahead grimly. She would work. She would work, and work and work. She would show Colonel Simpson that Melinda Merriott could be as good as anyone else on the circuit.

'You've changed, Mel, since – you know.'

'I know.' Melinda nodded, still staring ahead. 'You know' meant her mother leaving her father, all of them having to cram into Keeper's Cottage, Mums getting pregnant again. She had indeed changed. And no wonder, really, when she came to think about it.

Who would not change if she suddenly found that her parents wanted to divorce, her mother had no money and was expecting yet another baby, and that she herself was secretly in love with the son of the man who now loved her mother? It was enough to change anyone, surely?

'I know. I've become harder.'

'No, not harder . . .' Josh hesitated as Melinda still stared ahead, frowning. She felt harder. 'No, more determined, I think that's it.' Josh nodded, obviously agreeing with himself. Melinda smiled and offered him a peppermint, and then they both shut up, thinking about different things, as they so often did, but not needing to talk.

Melinda loved being in the horse box. To her just being in it was like a holiday. The sway of the cab, the smell of the horses behind, the knowledge of all the work ahead of or behind them – there was a sort of magic to it all.

And the slowness of it was good too because it allowed for concentration, and thinking. So now she turned to Josh and added, 'You're right. I'm not harder, just more determined. After all, I have to be now, don't I? I mean, supposing my mother dies in childbirth? It will be up to me to bring up Letty, and the next one, whoever it might be.'

'Your mother won't die in childbirth. Women don't die in childbirth any more, Mel. This is not the Victorian age. Your mother won't die . . .'

'Let's hope not,' Melinda agreed, after a pause during which she tried not to remember Hope's account of her dream, and how she had suddenly clung to her eldest daughter after she had recounted it to her, and how frightened Melinda had felt, not wanting either to believe in the dream or to see how vulnerable her mother had become since the fall in their fortunes and her unexpected pregnancy.

After another small silence Melinda continued, 'But, none the less, Josh, it has to be faced. Should something happen to Mums now, it will be up to me to look after the rest of us, because Dads simply isn't interested in us any more. I mean he couldn't even remember my birthday. Nothing – not even a card. Nor Claire's last birthday either. Claire cried her eyes out as soon as she realized, although I don't know why really, except I do, but that's how things are for us now, Josh. *We* are not hard so much as *it* is.'

'I don't understand why you are – not of any interest to him any more. I really don't.'

'Well, you wouldn't, Josh, would you?' Melinda laughed suddenly.

'Why – why wouldn't I?' Josh looked quite as suddenly hurt at her laughter, as if she was mocking him.

'You wouldn't understand, Josh, because – you – are – a – boy. If any of us had been boys, just one out of the four of us, Mums told me, it seems our grandfather would have been willing to leave us all a fortune, or anyway leave Dads it, but with us all being girls and so not real Merriotts in his eyes it will all go to someone else, a male Merriott not a female Merriott. But now, well. Dads is so hopeless at business he's had to run off with a rich widow who will let him have any number of posh cars and a private jet and who knows what else? I mean, maybe he's *right* to leave us all, Josh. If private jets and expensive cars mean more to him

321

than us, maybe he's right to abandon ship – or take to a yacht!' she ended, smiling ruefully.

'It doesn't seem . . .' as so often with his hesitation Josh stopped and Melinda waited, and then, 'it doesn't seem right to me – Mel, in fact it seems really wrong.'

'Well, I know, but there we are. As a friend of mine at school was always saying, *God did not choose to come down on earth as a woman but if He had it might have made things a bit easier, if not for Him at least for us!* No, in case you hadn't noticed, Josh, it's still a man's world.'

Josh lowered his voice while reaching for another peppermint. 'All right, all right, but don't tell Goosey, OK? I don't think she realizes she has to have foals no matter what.'

They both laughed at that, feeling relieved that the truly serious moment had passed, and Melinda once more looked more cheerful.

Josh shifted gears as the old wooden-sided horse box pulled them up the last hill, almost groaning with the effort of making the steep, steep ascent, until at last the view told them that down below in the green and the dark of the end of day lay the Mill House, and home.

Hope was saying, 'Letty's no trouble, Jack, really. She's as easy as anything. I don't mind if you leave her with me while I have my rest, really I don't. I quite like it if she plays near me.'

'I am taking her for a walk and you are staying

322

for some peace and quiet. What's the matter, don't you trust me?'

'Of course I do,' Hope lied, but she put on Letty's coat and waved goodbye to them from the cottage door until they had quite disappeared up the garden towards the gate, as if by watching her out of sight she could prevent anything untoward happening to Letty.

Nowadays Hope was so far into her pregnancy that she had reached that point when she could hardly remember a time when she had not been pregnant, and yet her worry over Letty would not be abated, despite the fact that she knew that once she was in hospital, or home with the new baby, she would have to delegate responsibility for Letty to Jack and the girls anyway.

She lay down on the cottage bed and stared at the ceiling.

Even now, the violent change in their circumstances sometimes did not seem possible. To go from the big old house to Keeper's Cottage, from being married to being separated, from being unpregnant to being pregnant. It sometimes made her head reel to think of how their lives had changed since Aunt Rosabel had come to stay that Christmas. It was less than two years ago, but it felt like a thousand.

Yet it was not so long that Hope did not still find herself, at night – before she put on her bedside light – looking round for doors and rooms that were Hatcombe, or turning, when she heard someone coming in, expecting to see Verna or Aunt Rosabel. It took a moment to remember that they, and Hatcombe, were quite gone.

The moment a person dies a place seems to change, not within weeks, but within hours, and where once such an object was placed there, or flowers arranged over here, or a picture changed so that it will catch the light better, and beds made with specially hand-ironed sheets and the bedside tables covered with sweet-scented leafy geraniums, those things die too. But not within days, as one might expect, but at that moment. The person who has gone seems to take their very essence with them, perhaps because they owe their purpose to them. And in a second the life of a place has vanished, and it is all over. The plants may remain, the beds stay made up, the paintings hang in the same place, but the imagination that placed them there, the intention behind them, once so vibrant and giving, just goes.

Someone had said that to Hope, long ago. Was it her mother? Was it someone she had once known and would never see again? Or was it simply something she had read, somewhere, by someone, and they too – like the geraniums and the paintings and the hand-ironed sheets – were gone, their sweet kindness never to be replaced?

Keeper's Cottage with three teenage girls, despite everyone finding themselves part-time work or signing on at local colleges, was beginning to feel unsurprisingly more crowded by the minute, and yet the less Hope was able to do about it the more she worried about the effect that the arrival of another baby in such an environment might have, which really did not make sense, for she was already far, far too late into her pregnancy to worry. But then neither did her proud refusal to move in with Jack make any sense. (It was a refusal based on the knowledge that Josh, Tobe and Cyndi, while still living at home, must not even begin to sense that their father's attention might not be wholly focused around them.)

Then, abruptly, the Merriott sisters' situation at over-crowded Keeper's was suddenly made sense of by Rose.

'Mums?'

Rose scratched at the door. Despite the fact that Hope had just dropped off to sleep, she sat up immediately. 'Come in, come in.'

'Mums.'

'Rose.'

She took Hope's hand. 'This is not going to sound right, but there is no other way of putting what I have to tell you – I am going to London. I had a letter this morning from Aunt Rosabel's old friend, Hugh Reilly? And he's made me an offer to lodge in his house, and I simply can't refuse. You see, it means, while I'm beginning to go for auditions and go up for RADA and all that, I can be on the spot, and if other things come up, you know, small roles and stuff, walk-ons, whatever, I can go up for those too. Which will be brilliant. But I have to go up to London the day after tomorrow, if I'm going, because he's going out on a tour and he wants everything fixed up before he goes. You know?'

Hope stared at Rose. It was not really a surprise. Yet now the moment had come it was still a shock, because it spelt yet another end to everything that had been only a few seconds before. Suddenly it seemed that even the last hour was in some way an end, as if every minute of every hour that passed was just that, an eternal end to something which had been before.

She could see at once that very soon there would be no Rose to laugh with, to watch dancing about the place, to see cheering on young, studious Claire to make herself more glamorous – contact lenses instead of glasses, New Year diets, do-it-yourself yoga.

Soon Rose would be gone from them, and with her departure her dark beauty, her ringing laugh, her zest and her humour, and soon after that she would be only a set of photographs, or a voice down the telephone saying, 'How are you, Mums?'

Hope wanted to beg Rose not to go to London, not to try her hand at auditioning for drama school, not to be independent of her, because she loved her so much. She loved all of them so much, she just wanted them to stay for ever as they were, where they were, all of them together at Keeper's. Laughing together, cheering each other up by making cheap but warming meals out of spices and vegetables from recipes in magazines, drinking hot chocolate to keep warm before huddling together in the little bedrooms above the tiny living rooms that made up Keeper's.

But it was not possible. And besides, even to hint at such feelings would mean, Hope knew, that she was a bad mother.

All her daughters must leave her, and with things so bad for them – sooner rather than later, she knew that; so there was no point in pretending either to them or to herself. No-one could stay at home, they all had to take their chance. It was just that Rose happened to be taking her chance *first*. Inwardly Hope breathed in and out, willing herself to sound cheerful and accepting.

'I'm so glad, darling, that you have decided to go to London, and to audition for drama school, you know that? I never wanted you to stop dancing, Rose. It wasn't me who wanted you to give up your place at Park Lodge.'

'No, I know. Don't worry, I realized that, long afterwards. Dads shouldn't have blamed you! I don't know how Dads has been able to treat you as he has—'

'No, darling, you mustn't criticize your father. It takes two to tango and I am just as much to blame for our break-up as anyone.'

'Oh, come on, Mums.'

'No, not *come on, Mums* at all. Really. My fault. I should never have agreed to come to Hatcombe, to live in the country, saying yes when I meant no. Not telling the truth. No, I was just as much to blame for our drifting apart as Dads. I was weak and stupid, always trying to cover up when I should have stood up. Remember that, Rose. For my sake, never say 'yes' when you mean 'no'. Not ever. Do what Jack says the farmers do round here – take a year, two years, what you will, before you come to a decision rather than say yes when you mean no. Now. End of lecture, you'll be glad to hear!'

Rose looked down at her mother's hands. They looked suddenly careworn, and although, with the pregnancy, and Jack's attentions, she had bloomed, Rose would have liked Hope not to be pregnant, to be back in the dear old days once more, at West Dean, where they had all seemed so happy, and not to be facing having yet another child.

But there, it was all over and done for now, and Rose had to go to London, get organized, audition, *kick on* as Mellie would say.

'Anyway, I thought I'd better tell you first – you know, before I started to spout large chunks of *Saint Joan* at breakfast and you began to wonder what was happening.'

'You're an angel, do you know that, Rose?'

'Of course,' Rose agreed briskly. 'But this angel must leave you to have a zizz while she learns to play a saint!'

Telling her mother of her plan to leave Keeper's and go to London was dead easy for Rose compared to telling Mellie and Claire that she was leaving Wiltshire for good, and what was worse doing so in only a couple of days.

Perhaps it was because Rose had not really thought out the effect it would have on her sisters and so had just blurted it out. Or perhaps she herself had not really thought it out, and it was only at the actual moment that she made her announcement and saw the expressions of real loss on the faces of her two sisters that the reality hit Rose.

She was leaving home, and them, and although she said, jokingly, to them, 'It will mean there's a bit more room to swing a cat, and even Minou is in need of more room at Keeper's,' she could see that room was not exactly what the other two most wanted, for the fact was they had all, despite their adversities, or perhaps because of them – as Claire had said, all the time – *just like the war when everyone got on so much better and didn't grumble* – grown a great deal closer, if that were possible.

Small wonder then that the other two wanted Rose to stay with them and not to go to London, but to go on trying to make them laugh with her send-ups of her audition pieces, helping them both get through this really scary bit of their lives, when their parents' marriage was breaking up and they all needed each other so much, if only to share a magazine and a mug of hot chocolate, or a good gossip about people in the village, if only to stop themselves from bursting into tears every other minute that God sent.

Now they both stared at her, not really believing that Rose was going so suddenly and so soon, that she had already found a room in a house with a mad old actor, someone whom Aunt Rosabel had used to know many, many years ago and whom, just before she had died, the old lady had got it together enough to write to on Rose's behalf, knowing that Rose had quite set her heart on what Aunt Rosabel always called *that acting thing you want to do.*

'This Hugh Reilly. This old actor friend of Aunt Rosabel. He will give me a room in his roof, an attic room, in return for doing his housework and the other lodgers' ironing. Apparently it's got the use of a shower on the same floor – I only heard about it all this morning. And I would have come and told you straight away, but I thought I ought to tell Mums first, or else she might be upset.'

There was a long silence during which no-one had anything to say, so Rose went on, 'And Mums has said yes. I mean, she's agreed that it's a pretty marvellous opportunity thing.'

Claire turned away, clearing her throat and pretending not to be upset, which was always Claire's way.

'If you're going to be doing all the laundry you'd better learn to separate the coloureds from the whites,' Melinda joked, as she saw from her turned back and hunched shoulders just how upset Claire was at Rose's news. 'Blimey,

Rose, your ironing's not exactly brilliant.'

'I thought you could coach me,' Rose told her, smiling and pulling a droll face, although she suddenly did not feel like it at all, but only wished to go to bed and pull the duvet over her head and not get up again, ever. 'How about now, for instance? You're not doing anything, are you? We could improve the shining hour with a spot of the old ironing. I mean if I don't learn to get stuck in, I'll be out on my ear. Although he did say it would mostly be sheets, which is a relief, particularly when you remember how many of Aunt Rosabel's petticoats I burned, not to mention – ugh – Dads's shirts.'

Melinda raised her eyes to heaven, still pretending to be bored and intent on teasing Rose, if only to give Claire time to get over her feelings. 'Oh, all right,' she groaned, and she caught Rose by the arm, pulling her towards the tiny cottage kitchen as if Rose was reluctant, which they both knew she was not, thereby giving Claire not just the time, but the space, to finish being upset.

'What was that you said?' Rose had heard Claire muttering something.

Claire, her back still turned, said, 'Nothing, really. Just that thing Aunt Rosabel used to say. You know. *If you feel sorry for yourself there's nothing for anyone else to do.*'

'Oh, I don't know.' Rose cleared her throat. 'I've spent most of my life feeling sorry for myself. I actually don't think one should give other people the privilege.' She raised her eyes to heaven, as if talking to a saint, and added to her departed relative, 'Sorry, Aunt Rosabel, but you know what I mean. There's something so lovely and slushy and damp about feeling sorry for oneself! Like having a warm bath after a cold walk!'

'Right.' Melinda set up the ironing board. She had always seen to Rose's dancing things for her, ever since she was quite tiny. Loving to make her look as good as she could, just as nowadays she loved to spend hours grooming the Grey Goose and making her look her best. 'So, what you should do with shirts is this. You start at the back of the collar, right? Like this . . .' She turned over a large shirt that happened to be in the ironing basket, and then wrinkled her nose. 'Oh no, don't let's do this one – it's Dads's old one. Yuk.' She threw it back, took out one of her own riding shirts and began again. 'Start at the back of the collar, you see?'

Rose nodded, but she stood for a second staring at nothing even so, utterly shocked at Mellie's reaction to their father's shirt.

God. It was so strange that Mellie should hate Dads now as much as Rose, did when Mellie had always been his favourite. As Claire often said, *Mel was the only one he didn't mind being a girl, because he still thought there was time to have a boy, you know?*

And yet look at Mellie now – she could not even bear to iron one of his old shirts.

'Do you hate Dads now, Mellie?'

Melinda looked up from spraying the shirt with starch. 'What?'

'I said do you hate Dads now?'

'No. Not really. I mean hatred is such a waste of time, don't you think?'

Rose twisted her mouth into a funny shape and then took in a great gulp of air before letting it out again. Then she asked in a low voice. 'Do you think Dads was always the way he is now, Mellie?'

Melinda nodded, still concentrating on her ironing demonstration. 'Oh, yes. Always. It's just that we were all so busy trying to pretend that he wasn't, that he was our darling Dads, the only man in our lives, we couldn't see the wood for the trees. That's why it's so important to see things clearly, not to try to pretend, because if you don't, well, you end up like Mums. Don't forget that when you're in London, and you're not getting anywhere. Whatever happens, it's better to – you know, try at something, even if you don't make it, even if you never make it, even if you drop dead from trying – it's better to – you know, *kick on*.'

They stared briefly at each other, both knowing what she meant. Rose must not be weak as Mums had been with Dads, always giving in to his whims when she should have stood up for herself.

'Funny.'

'What?'

'That's just what Mums herself just said.'

Melinda wanted to say *A bit late for that, isn't it*,

considering? but that would have been unfair, and anyway they both wanted to get on with the next few days, *kick on* as Colonel Simpson kept telling Melinda as she and the Grey Goose prepared to take off over some new obstacle, *kick on*.

To cover the moment, and to get them both over the difficult forty-eight hours before Rose's departure, Melinda plumped for being facetious about Rose's leaving home. They had always loved sending up well-known platitudes – *little nuggets of wisdom that will never do anything except drive you raj bongo* was how Rose sometimes put it – whiling away the time on long dull journeys by making them up, and then, naturally, finding them excruciatingly funny. So now Melinda thought up a couple on her own, both to get over her own desolation and to cheer Rose when she might be finding the going a bit tough in London.

Life's just a cross country course, full of obstacles, but great when you complete! She wrote this on a piece of paper which she secretly put on the top of Rose's clothes before shutting her suitcase for her. And again to make her laugh, she placed another at the bottom of the suitcase for Rose to read when she finished unpacking the last of her things when she arrived in London.

Life's just like a dressage test, no-one really understands it, but everyone pretends that they do, even the horses!

After which they tried to keep their goodbyes what Rose called *cheap and cheerful* because, in the event, as Claire agreed in her deep little voice, when they finally waved Rose off at the station, 'It is best, really it is, Mel. Like people in black and white films, you know? Best to keep crisp. Like *Brief Encounter* and those sorts of things.'

As for Hope, she stayed at home. She could not face goodbyes any more. And yet she could not have said why.

On the train to London Rose herself thought long and hard about what Melinda had said. And as the lovely countryside stations and the green fields retreated, and the villages became towns, and the back gardens became oblongs bedecked with lines of brave washing rather than fields with small ponies, it seemed more and more to Rose that Mellie could only be right. It *was* no good pretending around a relationship, or a person, or a job for that matter; whatever happened, she must not do that. She must face life in London head on, no pretending her geese were swans, no holds barred, she must call the soot and the grime black not grey.

But, of course, the moment she did actually arrive in London she forgot all about her good resolutions, and instead of seeing the great, blackened, grimy city as the trap that it was, held to ransom by traffic, filled with people who had rather be at home resting than in its moiling embrace working for great profits for someone else to enjoy, instead of seeing the pale, grim faces that passed her or stood beside her on the Underground platform for what they were, unhappy people who would give anything for another way of life, if they could find it or afford it, Rose saw only excitement, and bustle, and felt only wonder that she had at last become a part of this great city full of people reaching out for what it had to offer.

For growing up in West Dean Drive, although it was technically London, none of the Merriott sisters had ever really known London *proper*. They had lived on a quiet suburban avenue on the edge of a large green park where they had known everyone, and everyone had known them, but it would have been ridiculous to suggest that it was the real London. It had been no more London than it had been Paris.

And so it was that as Rose found herself trailing her suitcase from the taxi to the flight of steps that led up to Hugh Reilly's front door she felt that unique sensation that only cities can bring, namely that come what may she was a stranger to everyone who passed, and as yet still a stranger to everyone living at Mr Reilly's large Victorian house so near to Clapham Common, but so far from the West End.

Now, unlike Hatcombe, or even West Dean, no-one knew her at all. She could do what she wanted without comment. She could be quiet or noisy, fat, slim, talented or a complete dud, and no-one would really be in the least bit interested.

Anonymity was an intoxicating sensation after the smallness of country life, and as Rose rang the bell, quite suddenly she knew it and it was like a sea breeze before you actually saw the sea, or the scent of flowers before you rounded the corner and saw them growing, or music heard very, very far away, but clearly enough to make you want to grow closer to it, to run it through you, to feel it and all its compulsive yearnings, despite the fact that those yearnings made you restless, longing for something that perhaps might not happen, could not happen, and had never happened, not to anyone or anything. That was what it was like knowing that you were no-one who wanted so much to become someone.

'My dear girl, do come in. Can I help you?'

Hugh Reilly stood by the dark red door of his large Victorian house with its Edwardian tiled floor and its dark brown walls and looked at Rose with interest as she dragged her over-large suitcase into his hall, but he made no move to help her, only lightly brushing the sides of his reddish-fronted white hair with his fingertips as he watched her. When he had seen her into the hall, he closed the door behind her.

'Rose Merriott. How do you do?'

They shook hands, and Rose could sense at once that he liked her for observing an old-fashioned 'Aunt Rosabel' sort of form in introducing herself to him. He withdrew his hand, and yet again his fingertips brushed each side of his hair, first one side and then the other, and he walked ahead of Rose up the dark-carpeted stairs, slowly followed by Rose, dragging her suitcase and carrying her handbag.

Up and up they went, Rose panting behind him, while every now and then Hugh Reilly stopped, as if in concession to the weight of her suitcase and the height of the climb, but he never referred to her luggage, or turned to look at her, only waiting, one foot poised, one hand on the banisters, until Rose was once more behind him.

Her room was revealed to be everything that an attic room should be, its walls covered in a flower-printed wallpaper, matching curtains on its high windows whose views were only of chimneypots, the floor covered in hessian, and the cupboards of lightly painted pine.

'So.' He paused, and then remembered to smile, and as he did so, for no reason she could think of – except perhaps that his smile was so detached, almost bleak – Rose felt a tidal wave of homesickness sweeping over her.

Here she was, all alone, in London, her heart's desire, but for some reason home suddenly seemed so far away it might as well be Mongolia, and to her shame she found herself longing to be back with her sisters. Her mind went back to the hens that Mellie had bought for Keeper's and the way they sheltered by the door from the rain, fastidious in the finery of their feathers. She longed for the sound of the millrace when they walked past Jack's house on a Sunday afternoon and up to the fields behind. For the sudden sound of the wild Canada geese flying overhead on a quiet, warm summer morning. For the foxy auburn of autumn leaves when the dying year seemed to have turned the trees to a ballet of colour. For the smell of the wood fire burning in the cottage grate and the hiss of the logs as the flames warmed the damp wood.

'I have some sheets for you to iron, but they can wait until you have unpacked your little suitcase.'

Her landlord smiled again, and then with one last gesture which incorporated the inevitable finger-combing of his side-swept hair, he was gone. Rose raised her eyes to heaven, and in her imagination she wagged her finger at Aunt Rosabel in heaven on a cloud. *Hugh Reilly* had always sounded, when he was referred to by her great-great-aunt, somehow Edwardian and important, broad-shouldered, perhaps corpulent, with a quite definite eye for the women, not at all the man she had just met.

As Rose opened her suitcase, it came to her that Aunt Rosabel had probably not seen Hugh Reilly since they were both in their twenties – in which case it would hardly be surprising if he had changed a great deal, and those parts of him that had once been concealed by the glories of youth were now all too evident.

Having laughed at both Mellie's jokes, she put everything away in the cupboards and went

339

downstairs to find the kitchen, which she discovered at the back of the house overlooking the garden. It was also full of sheets.

Not just one, two, or three sheets, but pair after pair, doubles, singles, pillowcases, some striped, some white, some yellow, but all waiting for her attentions and all piled one upon the other, any old how, in a way that made what they had to have done to them seem even more arduous.

As she stared at them, and the ironing board, another thought occurred to Rose. Mr Reilly must have been left in the lurch by some rebellious soul who refused any longer to be his domestic drudge, and the hurry to have someone replace this luckless person was everything to do with getting the laundry done for free and very little to do with his going away to Ireland on a very important tour.

Quite against her will, and to her shame, as she plucked the first of the double sheets from the pile beside the ironing board Rose's eyes filled with tears, but she quickly blinked them away. After all, she was a Merriott, she was made of sterner stuff. To prove this to herself, just before she began on the sheets, she took the pieces of paper with Mellie's jokes written on them out of her pocket and read them again, to encourage the shaming lump of self-pity that she could feel in her throat to disappear, never to return, and so that she would see for herself what a damp squib she was to make a fuss over ironing, of all things. After all, as Aunt Rosabel often said, *Well, never mind. It's not the war, after all, is it? There were no doodlebugs falling today at any rate!*

Claire stared dismally around her room. She had always, come rain or shine, whether at West Dean or at Hatcombe, or now at Keeper's, shared a room with Rose. Now, next to her book-strewn bed, there was one neatly stripped of its sheets, covered over with a counterpane and left with only a small forlorn teddy on it, and no Rose.

Claire picked up the teddy and, climbing into her own bed, tucked it beside her. She had forgotten the bear's name – Rose had so many – but she thought it was Biddy. Something very like that, anyway. She put her arm round Biddy and stared up at the cottage ceiling. Somewhere, far, far away in London, Rose would already be beginning to have a really exciting time.

Claire stared at the ceiling, imagining her middle sister with her tall figure and dark hair, her beautiful long legs and her dark eyes, perhaps in the outfit Aunt Rosabel had bought her – the glittery top and the swishy skirt – making an entrance into some party, or some restaurant, where all eyes would be turned on her. Every man in the room would want to come straight to her side and seduce her with their words and their looks, forcing her to choose which of them she would allow to take her out to dinner.

'Crush them beneath your heel, Rose,' Claire whispered into the teddy's ear. 'For me and

Mellie, and you and Mums, crush them under your heel!'

She was only a year behind Rose, and so, as she clutched the borrowed teddy and stared up at the white-painted ceiling, it was hardly surprising that the thought came into her head that she too must soon be going to London, and for all the same reasons as Rose. Hatcombe and the country had nothing to offer her. The towns and villages were full of many delights, but none that were of the slightest interest to Claire.

She wanted to study art. She wanted to see the works of great painters. She wanted to work in an art gallery. She wanted to meet new and talented people. She could do none of these things living at Keeper's Cottage, near Pensbury, Wiltshire.

Her heart sank at the idea of how far she was from what she wanted. She still had innumerable tests and exams at the local college before her treasured 'A' in History of Art came about, but when it did she would follow Rose to London without a second's hesitation.

For a moment her mind dwelt on Melinda, alone with Letty and Mums at Keeper's, but then it swiftly passed on, because, after all, Mel really loved the country, and riding. The Grey Goose and she were 'an item', as Claire and Josh were always teasing her. They were not horse and rider any more, they had become one great big flying spirit. With all that, not to mention Josh, Mel would not need Claire around. It was just a fact.

Claire fell into a contented sleep, suddenly aware that Rose was just a front runner, or a fore-runner, well, some kind of runner, for Claire herself. She had gone ahead to London, that was all. Claire would shortly follow.

Chapter Twelve

By the time there was no disguising Hope's pregnancy and Claire seemed to have crocheted more layettes than the baby would ever need – all in yellow and white so that it would not matter what sex the new child was – Alexander seemed to have disappeared without trace from all their lives, for good.

Jack, who had an endearing love of gossip, eventually found out that Muffin Hatherleigh was not only rich, but dominating, and that her previous husband had died in not-so-mysterious circumstances – driving their Range Rover into a loch in Scotland while under the influence of more drink than was normal even at that time of year, having previously attended a Christmas party at a well-known distillery famed for its single malt whisky.

While this had been most regrettable, it was generally agreed that, given the uneven tenor of his life, not to mention his wife's famously bad temper, his death had in fact been more than merciful. It had been a relief.

Armed with this information, Hope was quite able to face the rest of her pregnancy in the knowledge that while they, at Keeper's Cottage, might be having to what Claire called *make and do*,

Alexander's life would be one long round of pleasure, while his soon-to-be second wife exacted payment for such luxuries as private helicopters and homes staffed by hovering butlers and crisply uniformed maids, not to mention the use of chauffeured cars and jet travel to exotic foreign locations, in the shape of his peace of mind, if not his happiness.

'Apparently she has the temper of the devil and is impossible to please, having been both a beauty and rich all her life.'

Hope could not help smiling at that. She was sitting beside Jack in the Mill House sipping a glass of elderflower and soda while Jack talked and played the piano. 'Well, never mind that now.'

Jack stopped playing and stared at her. 'Never mind that now!' he teased her. 'Never mind that now! After the way he's treated you! You haven't heard from him except through his lawyer for the whole of your pregnancy, have you?'

Hope shrugged her shoulders. Had it been Alexander's child she was expecting, how different she would feel. But as it was, knowing that it was Jack's child, and that they had an emotional future together, she could only feel benevolent towards her former husband.

'He's putting you through a quickie divorce, he's gone off with everything and that's all you can say – never mind that now?'

Hope started to laugh as Claire came in with

some dips she had made for them all, and they stopped talking while she told them about her day trip to the Tate Gallery, and showed them her postcards.

'That girl lives for art.' Jack shook his head and went back to playing a new theme he was working on. 'That's the good thing about our lot, they all know exactly what they're going to do. We're very lucky.'

This was true, and did make bringing up 'their lot' a whole lot easier than it might have been, particularly given the radical change in Hope's circumstances.

Rose had applied to go to RADA, and they were all keeping their fingers crossed for her. Claire had found herself a temporary situation as a mother's help in a nearby village house while she took an early A level in History of Art, and Melinda and the Grey Goose were already making a fine fist of their eventing partnership thanks, Melinda insisted, to the brilliance of their coach, 'dear old Stricty-boots', as the colonel was now called by her.

Meanwhile, Josh, Tobe and Cyndi – 'my lot', as Jack in his turn always affectionately referred to them – spent all the time they could spare between work, university and school at home in Jack's studio in the Mill House grounds, making music. But whenever he could repossess it, Jack made sure he was back in there, secretly trying out a love song he was writing for Hope.

He had said nothing to her, but it seemed to him that the composition of this song, its reality, making it beautiful for her, was more and more important as every day of every week went by. It was many years since he had actually been around a pregnant woman, and now he was filled with the kind of anxious pride that he could only vaguely remember feeling about Josh, Tobe and Cyndi.

And so, to take his mind off everything, he would wander round the studio discarding things, tidying his music sheets, even, on occasion, washing the floor.

'You're like one of those birds out there – fussing about with a piece of straw in your beak one minute, an old leaf the next.'

Jack was momentarily embarrassed, because he knew that Hope was right. He was like a nesting bird. Too late he remembered that men nested too, although the realization did not stop him. And while he knew that Hope was right not to move in with him until they were married, he also guessed that their 'secret' was probably not a secret from Hope's girls, that they probably all knew, if only from watching him with Hope, that he was in fact the father of her baby.

He actually wanted to compose a new song for the new baby, but he was too superstitious, thinking that to do so would be to invite calamity.

Nevertheless, to help himself get over his anxieties, he could at least write a song to Hope, and as each day crept by he knew not only that he could, but that he must.

At first he felt so anxious about her that nothing would come, and he would find himself day after dreary day just shifting about the studio, not only unable to compose a note, but quite unable to be on his own too, for the worry of her. As long as he was actually with Hope, as long as he could see her, he felt that she would be all right, but of course he could not be with her all the time. That would be ridiculous. He had to leave her alone sometimes, if only to rest, or to have some peace and be with her own children.

At last, as the final weeks shook themselves inside the kaleidoscope of time, and all the reds and the blues and the greens and the oranges became confused but starry patterns, Jack's love song to Hope came to him. Not as his songs usually did, in a rush, the notes pouring from his fingers, but little by little, as if the gods, feeling for his state of loving anxiety, only let inspiration come to him on a daily basis in order to distract him from the reality of what was about to happen to Hope. Take his mind off the danger that might be to come.

For herself Hope was only too relieved when the heat of summer was at last over, and so it was that with the weather less warm, and the date set for her Caesarean section, she found herself on the way to the County Hospital to have the baby.

'Don't forget I don't want to know the sex,' she reminded her outwardly optimistic gynaecologist. 'I just don't want to know until it's all over and I'm awake again, and he or she is in my arms.'

'By the looks of the scan, it is in very good shape. In fact, perfect shape.'

Hope was on her way back to her room, for an evening of anxiety spent free of anything except water, and the gynaecologist heading for an evening, doubtless, spent with her husband and children, with nothing more to think about than the cooking of dinner, a little gossip, perhaps a glass of wine or two.

As she unpacked her overnight case Hope found herself wishing that she could swap places with the surgeon, or the hospital porter who had just passed pushing someone in a wheelchair, or the man with the umbrella that she could just see in the street outside, with anyone, in fact, rather than be herself waiting for yet another Caesarean.

'Sometimes my life seems to have been one long Caesarean section,' she said to one of the nurses, who gave her a comforting squeeze on the arm. Hope's answering smile was wan, her courage at rock bottom.

Soon however Jack was along to see her, bouncing about her room, telling jokes and humming something in little snatches, before stopping and telling her, 'I'm not saying anything but I think I'm on to something here.' He had called at Keeper's Cottage on his way to the hospital, and brought Hope up to date on the supper eaten by Letty, the continuing good health of their Burmese cat, and the telephone call from Rose in London, wishing her mother luck.

Melinda had jumped a clear round at Colonel Stricty-boots's menage, and the moorhens in the reeds beside the Mill House had at last revealed themselves, 'and there are *ten*, would you believe? *Ten!*' His manager had rung to tell him that someone was interested in making something or another into a musical and would be interested in Jack Tomm doing the music – 'only small, but could be fun.'

Hope tried to smile as she watched him, but she could hardly attend to what he was saying. All she could think of was the seemingly endless possibilities that she faced, and tomorrow.

Meanwhile Jack took turn and turn about Hope's room and Hope stared at him and thought of nothing except that he was looking strangely pale, despite the cheeriness of his tone.

'I'll be all right, Jack, you know that, don't you? I'll be fine.'

At which Jack turned away to the window and cleared his throat. 'Yes. Course,' he agreed. 'Course. I know that, Hope. Just, you know.'

His voice tailed off and there was nothing more either of them wanted to say, and so he kissed her forehead one final time and left her with the light over her bed still on, for comfort, burning through the night, lighting up her face, which was composed yet unsleeping, waiting, just waiting for those early morning hours to come when she would hear the bustle of the starched aprons, feel the pre-med injection, listen to the wheels on the trolley as she was pushed towards her nine o'clock date with surgery.

'Good luck, Baby,' was the last thing she remembered saying before, together with the anaesthetist, she started the slow count down from ten to nought, inevitably only reaching six before darkness snapped out the world and all its worries.

'Good luck, Mums,' Claire said out loud as the hand on the old mahogany kitchen clock at Keeper's Cottage reached nine o'clock. 'And good luck New Baby, whoever you're going to be.'

'Good luck, Mums,' Melinda said out loud as she cantered through the woods behind the Mill House on a strangely excited Grey Goose. 'And good luck to you, Baby.'

At the hospital Jack arrived to find a porter sweeping a floor, nurses gossiping about last night's charity ball, and an elated nurse emerging from the operating theatre.

'Mr Merriott,' she declared, 'I am happy to tell you you have a son, a baby boy.'

Jack walked on for a second, and then stopped, raising his eyes to heaven before turning back. Of course *he* was 'Mr Merriott'. He swept the still masked woman round and round, despite her laughing protests.

'Where is he? Where is he?' he demanded. 'I must see him, and how is Hope? Where is Hope?'

'Another twenty minutes before she comes out of surgery, but she is just fine, Mr Merriott, just fine, and so is young Master Merriott.' The eyes above the mask sparkled, and pointed Jack in the direction of the baby unit. 'Over there.'

Jack crept across the hallway, as if had he made any noise he would have woken Hope from the anaesthetic, and peering through the glass he looked for his newest son.

'Merriott?'

Jack stared down at the little face wrapped in the blanket and hardly more than a few minutes old. He looked – well, he could not say what he looked like.

'It's a boy. He's a boy! Mums's had a boy! Well done Mums!'

Claire danced round the kitchen and she could not wait for Melinda to get back from riding, and when Rose called she too danced round the kitchen, but it was Hugh Reilly's kitchen, and much as she loved London she ached at that moment to be with the other two, and having put down the phone she dabbed at her eyes and rushed to her purse to see how much she had left of her student grant which she could put towards flowers to send to the County Hospital.

*   *   *

For herself Hope knew she would never, ever, forget the moment when her son was placed in her arms. Not because he was her son, but because he was alive, and whole, and all right, and with his eyes tightly closed and his little tonsure of dark hair he looked so perfect. She stared down at his face and then up at the happy smiling face of her gynaecologist who was walking so fast beside the bed upon which she was being pushed along, and then at Jack's proud face, and then down at the baby again.

'He looks just like you, Jack.' But that was as far as she could get before she frowned and her eyes moved away from her baby's face and up to Jack's.

'Hope, are you all right?'

Hope nodded, her eyes smiling up into Jack's. Of course she was all right. She was out of surgery, she was fine. How else could a mother who had waited so long for a son feel other than not just all right, but possibly as happy as she had ever been?

'Oh, yes, Jack, I am so all right.' She laughed. 'Yes, so all right.'

Hope's large eyes stared back for a moment into Jack's, and she could see his lovely face, his eyes which were large and blue and beautiful and full of a strange but peaceful kindness, as if Jack had been on this earth before and learned so much that the gods had decided to send him back down again, to have another go. Hope loved Jack's eyes, but she blinked as she stared up at him. She could no longer see him very well.

And although she could feel her baby's finger, she could not feel it as well as she had, could not really squeeze it.

And yet she could still hear that dear gynaecologist saying to Jack, 'It went much better than I could have hoped, Mr Merriott. The operation went really very well.'

Hope wanted to tell her, 'Jack's not Mr *Merriott*, he's Mr *Tomm*, and he's not my husband, he's my lover, and perhaps my next husband, who knows? But he is the father of my baby. My son.'

Hope blinked her eyes once more, slowly. She could definitely still hear everything, Jack and the gynaecologist, a nurse laughing when Jack teased her about something, the baby, very distantly, but as she tried to refocus, assuming she was experiencing some after-effect of the sedative, nothing was happening. Everything was dark.

She blinked her eyes again slowly, but it was no good. Everything was going away from her, and quite fast, as if she was a train retreating into a tunnel. There was definitely too great a distance between her and her baby. He should be right there, but she was going away from him into the tunnel.

She heard someone shout 'Quick!' at least that was what it sounded like. And then there was a pain, a searing pain, like no pain she had ever known before, a screeching, tearing, numbing pain which turned everything red, except that she could just see a hand and feel it too, and it was reaching out to her, holding her, trying to stop her falling into what was now red, and then black.

Jack saw Hope's eyes seeming to fade from his, and her expression of love turning to the look of someone who was gone into the next world, unseeing, blank, and as he lost her, a second after giving such a gasp of pain, he heard a strange thing, he heard himself shouting, but he had no idea what he was saying. He knew it was his own voice because it was a masculine voice and there was only himself and the gynaecologist and a female nurse present. It was his own voice, but it was so strange!

'Nurse! Nurse!'

It definitely was his voice, and someone else's voice, it was everyone's voice and they were all calling to each other, everyone's voice except Hope's. Hers was nowhere to be heard among that medley of calling people, and someone was handing him the baby and he was holding it to him as the chorus grew stronger and more urgent, all saying, 'Quick, quick, emergency! We must get her into Intensive Care!'

And the trolley on which only Hope was now lying, motionless without her baby, was being wheeled backwards once more, and re-set to go down another strange corridor, and then another, well away from her room. And all the time, because he could not help it, Jack was running alongside, looking down at her, wondering, *Is she dead?*

On hearing the good news from the hospital Melinda had fairly sprung out of the door of Keeper's Cottage heading for the Mill House stables and the Grey Goose, singing to herself at the top of her voice one of Jack's old songs, one of his evergreens, which just happened to be very apt since it was entitled 'Welcome Baby'.

After all the months of waiting and worrying, the whole strange ethos of the nine-month wait for a baby suddenly seemed to make sense. It was as if nature knew that unless humans waited, they would not really appreciate their young. And the very idea of having a new baby, a baby brother called James, was somehow a light shining directly down on them all after what had been such a hard dark time.

Now everything was pretty brilliant, and she could not wait to tell Josh. She could not wait to tell Tobe and Cyndi, either, as a matter of fact. But most of all she could not wait to have Mums and the baby home, and to take care of them both, which was ridiculous, because there would be nappies and bottles all over Keeper's Cottage and they would both be up nights and heaven only knew – but she had been so awfully worried, all this time, always thinking, after Mums's dream, that something would happen to her, that there would be some terrible event which would leave

Melinda all alone, as in Mums's dream.

She was hardly out of the door, heading back out into the air, its bracing cold lifting her elated spirits, so that it seemed to Melinda that she could see them above her, that they were in fact a hot air balloon, floating away from Keeper's towards the Mill House, Goosey and the end of a long and anxious nine months, before the telephone rang once more.

Leave it. The telephone is for your convenience, not the caller's.

That had always been Aunt Rosabel's sage advice, and it was sage, if Melinda thought about it, inasmuch as a telephone ringing is only a – what was it Aunt Rosabel always called it? Melinda frowned as she tried to remember. Oh, yes. She always said the telephone was *a caller without a card*.

Remembering all this Melinda still hesitated. If the phone rang and rang, and rang, and rang, it had to be Rose ringing from London wanting to know more than Melinda had already told her about the new baby, about Hope, about everything.

It did ring, and ring, and ring, and although Letty was out walking with Mrs Shepherd, and there was no real reason to turn back, nevertheless Melinda did turn back, but as she reached the front door once more it stopped. She was glad. She felt as if she had made every effort, and that being so she could now go out riding and forget all about telephones, and feel only the marvel of Goosey as she started to gather a bit of speed, started to enjoy a welcome blow after their fifty minutes of concentrated dressage the previous afternoon.

'Keep her mind open, Mellie,' the colonel had kept advising, but then he would pat the mare's neck and smile up at Melinda and say, 'Actually, I don't know what I'm talking about. She knows best, don't she? They tell us, don't they, Mellie? They tell us, not the other way round. We humans, we think we know it all, but it's *they* who know it, not us!'

Colonel Simpson had become Melinda's 'father figure'. Jack, because he was Josh's father, could never be so to her. Not that she minded her mother being in love with Jack – she could quite see the attraction, for both of them. But Melinda was wise enough to know that trying to replace a father with another man was just plain dumb. She and Claire had enjoyed a long conversation about it only two nights before.

Claire said, 'I *am* looking for a father figure, Mel, but that's because Dads and I never bonded – yuk. Well, I got on his nerves really. So I am – you know, in the market for a father figure. But I agree with you, it can't be Jack, because Jack – you know, he's *Jack*. And he loves Mums, and that's fine, because she's been miserable pretty well since we came to Hatcombe, wouldn't you say? But you know what I mean, I can't see Jack as this other person, this dear daddy guy. That doesn't mean I don't love him to pieces, because I do. But only as an older guy who loves Mums. What I actually need is someone to love me who happens to be older. Or someone who will pretend he loves me because he's older, or something like that. Well, you know. That's what I feel. So.'

Melinda felt quite differently. She knew, in a way, that she had been very much her father's favourite, and as such would never forgive him – well some time perhaps but not now, not this minute – for going off with this Muffin Hatherleigh woman. On the other hand, for her too, Jack was, and always would be, Mums's.

Not that Jack did not also belong to Josh. And to Tobe and Cyndi, naturally, but he could never be what Dads had been; and there again Dads could never be what he had been to her now that he was Mrs Hatherleigh's oh-so-kept man.

She and Josh never really discussed their parents. It was a no-go area, into which they did not stray conversationally, touching only on practicalities and instinctively leaving their parents to be quite separate from their friendship.

Just as Hope had known that it would be quite wrong for her to live with Jack at the Mill House until the older children were gone, so Melinda knew that to touch on any future that she and Josh, or Hope and Jack, might have together would be insensitive.

So it was only to Claire that she had ever really spoken of how she felt, and now that she was once more mounted on Goosey and turning her towards the fields and meadows behind the Mill House, Melinda made up her mind that she would leave it like that. She would talk only to Claire about Jack and Mums, not to anyone else.

She sat down and loosening her rein she let Goosey down a notch or two. As always when on horseback, she wondered why she had ever dismounted, for when the wind blew a little and the sun shone a little, and the fields were lit with a still autumn light, was there anything to touch it?

'What the hell is the matter, Tomm? And how did you get our number? I never want to speak to you again!'

Alexander had frowned with impatient anger as Muffin handed him the telephone, mouthing the words *Jack Tomm for you.*

'Oh, so my soon-to-be ex-wife has had a baby, has she? Pull the other one, Tomm! No, don't tell me another girl! Well, if it is – it's yours, Tomm, yours, because four is my quota, believe me.'

He was in the process of making a little moue at Muffin and at the same time sliding his free hand across her pretty little backside, giving it an appreciative pat, when he stopped, pulled a face, and said, '*What!*'

Muffin had started to kiss his fingers but when he said '*What!*' she stopped and stepped back. Staring up at Alexander questioningly she mouthed the word *What?* back at him.

Alexander covered the phone with his now free hand.

'It's Hope. She's had a stroke.'

For some reason the fact that the gynaecologist was a woman made whatever had to be said seem better, or at any rate, less worse. Not that anything could be better, or worse, or anything really, Jack thought dully as he stared at her calm face, wondering what it must be like to deal constantly with other people's tragedies. To spend your whole life contemplating other people's minds or bodies in some sort of state of extremis.

'We did the MRI scan yesterday, Mr Merriott—'

'Tomm. I'm not her husband yet.'

'I am sorry. Of course. Tomm. Mr Tomm—'

'Jack.' He held out his hand to shake hers, quite ridiculous really, as if they were at a party, not in a hospital standing outside a room where the love of his life lay in Intensive Care.

'Polly.'

She seemed to appreciate the moment, if only because it gave the poor woman a breather, a small pause in which she could summon up yet more energy to deal with someone else's life, someone else's problems, someone else's decisions. Decisions which, whatever anyone said, must haunt those who had helped to make them.

'As I say, we did the MRI scan yesterday, Jack, and while we are still looking at it in detail, the prognosis is not good, I'm afraid.'

'How bad is not good?'

'Your— Mrs Merriott is in a very deep coma, Jack.'

They had suddenly run into a protocol cul-de-sac. Hope had obviously not called her gynaecologist Polly, so now, with the requirement for permission to call someone by their first name being strictly observed, everything they were saying sounded so odd it was almost laughable.

Had the news not been so grave, had Hope been there in person, Jack would have laughed so much. It was the kind of moment that always made him break up. For a second, almost wilfully placing himself in an agony of heart and mind, Jack imagined how Hope's eyes would have lit up if she had been standing beside him instead of lying in the room to the right of them, and how her laugh – the laugh which was always so delightful that Jack did not need to be in the same room to smile when he heard it – would have rippled in unison with his, and they would have turned to each other and she would have caught at his hand with delight at the ridiculousness of it all.

He could still hear Hope saying, *Oh, my goodness, that is so funny!* when Polly continued, 'There is very little chance that Hope will recover from a stroke as apparently traumatic as this one. Even if she should, to be realistic I would have to say she would be an invalid for life.'

Now that she was saying 'Hope' instead of 'Mrs

362

Merriott' Jack wished that Polly had stuck to being more formal. *There is very little chance that Mrs Merriott will recover from a stroke* would have made it seem as if it was someone else besides Hope, whereas as soon as she had said Hope's name Jack knew that he could not possibly, even for a fraction of a second, pretend that it was someone else. It was beyond Jack's powers to pretend that this woman was trying to talk to him about some other woman, someone with whom Jack was not passionately in love, someone who he did not now know would be, in whatever state, the love of his life, for ever.

He flailed about mentally within himself for a few seconds, hardly able to think that what she had said could possibly be true.

Finally, the words seemed to blurt out of him and he said, 'I thought, dear God! I mean I thought you people were meant to be able to do great things for stroke victims nowadays? I thought you were on top of all this stuff, what with all these advances in technology and brain scans and all that stuff. I thought that nowadays you never gave up on stroke victims?'

'That depends on the initial damage, Jack. The scan indicated that this was a particularly damaging embolism, resulting in heavy bleeding. It would be unrealistic to expect any more than partial recovery. From talking to my colleagues here—'

Polly stopped. She had elected to break the

news to Jack because it was she who had, after all, looked after Hope, and knew Jack, if only by sight, enough to say hallo to him and pat the little girl that Hope and he sometimes brought to the clinic on the head.

'Will you have help at home when we send the baby home, Jack? With the little one and a new baby, and Hope in here, you really are going to need help.'

Polly thought it best to try to steer the conversation away from the immediate fate of her patient, and for a second she could see that the poor man, who looked wrecked, was indeed distracted by the practicalities of what might lie in front of him as father and stepfather.

'Oh, yes. Of course. Yes. We have plenty of help. Mrs – er – Shepherd, I think that's her name, at the cottages at Hatcombe, where Mrs Merriott used to live with her husband's great-aunt, and then of course there are two daughters still at home, and of course I have brought up three children myself. So, yes, I think we can manage. Until Hope gets better. Because she is going to get better. She'll be back with us. As soon as you can say – well, anything. She will be back. I know it.'

'It must be very hard for you to accept what has happened—'

'Hard? I don't accept it! I simply will not accept that Hope will not come back to me. It's as simple as that. I will not accept that she will be lying in there instead of coming back to talk and laugh with me as she always has. I will not accept it, so don't expect me ever to leave her side from now on, not ever, do you hear? I will not leave her. She will get better! She will!'

Jack turned towards the door behind which Hope lay, and flinging himself through it he fought his way past his tears to his love's side, not caring that the duty nurses were seeing him, Jack Tomm, a grown man, crying.

But once in the room he found that it was not just his tears that made seeing Hope so difficult. It was everything. The quiet, and the seeming dark of the room, and the tubes and tubes, and more tubes, and bottles, and things going 'blip, blip, blip'. But he didn't care, not a hoot, not a jot.

He took her hand. She was his Hope. He would never leave her. Not ever!

PART THREE

The Way is not difficult; only
There must be no wanting or
Not wanting.

Chao-Chou

Chapter Thirteen

Jack Tomm's devotion to Hope Merriott was the talk of the hospital. When they came to take blood from her he liked to make little jokes which the nurses and everyone found touching, although not as moving as the sight of this man who would not leave the side of his so dearly loved love, who sat holding her hand for hours on end, sometimes reading to her, sometimes playing music to her, always telling her that he was there.

Today when they came for some blood he said, 'Watch it, darling, here comes the Frankenstein mob again,' and when they went away again, he said, 'I hope you didn't feel that, darling?'

From inside the peace of her silver-green shell Hope smiled to herself. Jack was so funny! She loved to hear his little jokes, listen for his voice, waiting for it to reach her where it would echo into her silver-green shell and tell her about all manner of things, about precious things that she had always held dear in her life when she had been with him on that far distant shore where she was no longer, but where he was, from where his voice was coming to her in her peaceful silver-green shell.

* * *

But sometimes, like today, Jack could not stay as long as he wished, and so Melinda came in with Letty, and they sat beside her and told her of their day, and on other days Claire – whose temporary job had come to an end – came in, and she read to her. It was an erratic family routine which had established itself, if only to get Jack to realize that he did have to go home sometimes and change and bath, and sometimes even shave, before he bolted back once more 'to be with my Hope'.

Of course it had been Jack's idea to keep talking to her, or reading to her, or playing music to her, and perhaps because of this Melinda and Claire had felt shy at first, self-conscious, not really knowing whether or not they should be treating Hope as alive or dead, but they had quickly got used to what was required. Not so Rose who, when she came down on her one day off, temporarily freed from looking after Hugh Reilly's house, had been petrified of even sitting with her mother.

'What are we meant to be *doing*, Mel?' she kept asking.

'You're not in a play, Rose, for goodness' sake,' Claire grumbled. 'You're going to see your mother. You can't look for Mellie to direct you, as if you were in some production or other, you know. I mean, you just have to go and sit there.'

'I'm dreading it!'

Claire and Melinda stared at Rose, at first in furious, outraged horror, and then Melinda started to laugh, and although Claire did not, she did at least smile in understanding.

That was so Rose, somehow. She was always the one to say exactly what she felt, and then wait for everyone else to tell her off, which they inevitably did, while all the while knowing that she had merely said what the rest of them had actually been feeling.

'We felt just like you, at first,' Claire agreed, 'didn't we, Mellie? But after a couple of visits we were fine. I mean it's not like being with someone who's dead, it's like being with someone who's very much alive, just doesn't speak back, if you know what I mean?'

Rose had found that there were two chairs either side of the bed, and Melinda directed her to the far one, and she sat on the nearer one, and while at first Rose just could not look at her mother, after a minute or so, allowing herself to look, bit by little bit, she soon got accustomed, and she sat in on Mellie reading to her from one of Hope's favourite books and that somehow soothed Rose.

As she said to Claire later, 'There is something about favourite books that has that effect, and the special moments seem even more special because you know that they are coming, and in this case, in a hospital room, they spread themselves out, like a garden, all those somehow familiar words that you have never learnt but which you nevertheless know, and it's suddenly all right, everything is all right, and you're not frightened any more. Anyway, that's what I think.'

After that Rose had gone back to London, but she telephoned every evening, and that was when they had all started to pretend that it was all a sort of game, really.

They pretended that looking after Letty and the baby was a hoot. They pretended that nappies and bottles and getting up in the night was the same. They made jokes about setting fire to disposables and, because they were so expensive, they called them 'fivers'.

'How many fivers have you set fire to today, Claire?'

'Fourteen fivers – *and* they wouldn't burn. Imagine!'

Neither of them wanted Rose back, which was good, both for her and for them. It would be hell for her, and hell for them, and they all knew it, so the subject never came up, but she sent them money, another subject which never came up between them, except as a joke, because everything was in such a muddle that what else could they do *except* joke?

'Something will happen to change everything,' Rose confided to an ever more desperate Claire one evening.

'Do you think so?'

To Rose living in London on hope and cream crackers, Claire was sounding more and more desperate. Claire herself did not know it, but because the voice is such a sensitive conveyor of the state of a person's feeling, Rose heard her sister becoming less and less confident until her voice was almost a monotone, and it seemed to her that it was almost too hard to bear, to be there at Keeper's as Claire was, and yet not want to be there at all.

The young doctor stood by the desk in the pale yellow room, which, like so many official rooms everywhere, was bare of detail, a sort of void of a room which seemed to have nothing to do with hospitals, or patients, or sickness, or anything really except forms, some of which were attached to his clipboard which he now put down on the desk, making it seem almost obscenely untidy, and the clipboard pathetic, as if what it said was already past and did not matter, would never matter, not really, not the way Hope mattered, and Jack didn't matter at all, not to himself anyway.

To her who was still with him, he was sure he mattered to *her*, but not to himself, not any more, for he was in that state of tiredness where his whole life had become an out of body experience, all the time looking down on himself, wondering at what a strange kind of guy he was – that fellow – Jack Tomm.

'What is love, do you think?'

The doctor looked astounded. 'I beg your pardon?' He stared at the tall, bearded, rambling shambles of a man in front of him in his crumpled although obviously expensive clothes, with his strong good looks, his bright blue eyes and his controlled restlessness – which meant that although he stood still, and his hands and body were quite relaxed, he seemed to be moving inside, climbing and climbing to some height which the doctor could only sense, but which none the less frightened him.

'I asked you – what is *love*, do you think?' Jack raised his fine arched eyebrows and, what with his bright blue questioning eyes, everything in his face demanded an immediate answer of the white coat with the bland expression who now shifted, puzzled, almost hurt that someone should be asking him something that was not in a *form*, that did not have a *box number* attached to it, or could not be answered by pointing to an *X-ray*.

'I really don't think I, er, know, really, Mr Tomm—'

'You must have some sort of idea, surely?'

'No. I'm afraid I don't, and I don't have much time, either, Mr Tomm, much as I would like to debate such a question with you. I have very little time for such discussions thanks to the National Health reorganization, and the cut in our working hours.'

'How can you be a doctor if you have no idea, not even an inkling of an idea about love? Without love you would have no people, and without people there would be no-one to cure, nothing for you to do, no fulfilment.'

'Look, Mr Tomm—'

'All right, let's begin again, shall we? Do you know what Gertrude Stein asked before she died?'

'No.'

'She asked, *What is the answer?* And when no answer came, she laughed and said, *In that case what is the question?*'

'I really have very little time—'

'And no questions, hmm?'

There was a short pause, during which Jack's eyes remained on the doctor's face but his mind bent itself to trying to understand this other mind that did not want to contemplate the greatness of that greatest of all emotions, in all its forms. Then Jack snapped back to attention as the doctor spoke.

'I'm afraid Mrs Merriott, my patient—'

'My great love—'

The doctor managed to look both embarrassed and shocked at that, which was probably why he cleared his throat.

'I'm afraid there is no real news about her condition, Mr Tomm,' he went on carefully, picking his way across his words as if he was afraid that the waiting Jack would suddenly pounce on him. 'I have run a few checks on Mrs Merriott—'

'My beautiful Hope—'

'As I say, I ran a few checks on her, and I am afraid there is really nothing at all to indicate any change in the depth of the coma, which is very disappointing.'

'Nothing to indicate it yet.'

'Well, precisely, nothing to indicate it, yet.'

'Except your tests—'

'We can only do tests on Mrs Merriott, Mr Tomm. We can't do anything else.'

'You could. You could exercise some humanity around her. That is another alternative, besides tests, I would say. Quite a positive alternative.'

The doctor stared at Jack, almost dreading what he would have to say next, and yet at the same time filled with a curious fascination, as someone might be who sees someone standing without clothes in the middle of a busy high street, a harmless sight, and yet none the less exercising a strange fascination on the clothed.

'For instance, yesterday,' Jack went on, and he found himself breathing in deeply and then breathing out slowly, to control something inside himself which might become uncontrollable, which might burst out of him, and cover the room which was so bare of humanity, so devoid of anything, with red raw humanity and feeling. 'Yesterday, and this was not a *test*, doctor, this was a human reaction, I squeezed Mrs Merriott's hand and I swear I felt some movement. So.' He nodded and the look in his eyes was replaced by wonder at the memory of what he had felt. 'So. You see. So you see, you must be just a little behind with your *tests*, doctor. Or do your tests not allow for human reactions, only rats'? And by the by, why is it always rats and beautiful gentle guinea pigs whom you people carry out all your experiments on? I mean whoever thought that a rat or a guinea pig's reaction was the same as ours? I have actually got to know both extremely well at different times, and I can tell you neither of them are like human beings, not in the least. They are gentle, clean, non-destructive and do not bear the slightest likeness to ourselves. So why do you people think they are so like us that any reaction of theirs will have any bearing on ours? Why condemn them to lives of torture and agony when – doctor – we are so totally unalike? You must tell me. It's something I have always wanted to ask someone. And now I have.'

The doctor looked down at his clipboard, waited for a few seconds and then began again, obviously determined not to pay any attention to the madman in front of him.

During those few seconds Jack imagined the doctor going home to his wife that evening, having put in the statutory hours laid down by management – perhaps even *clocked out*. He might use that expression, who knew? He imagined him saying to his wife, who would momentarily lower the switch on the telly to hear, *My God, if today was a fish I would throw it right back! Remember that woman I was telling you about, the one on the life support machine – been there for weeks. Well, I had the boyfriend in. What a nutter! Blabbing on about rats and guinea pigs and I don't know what. I'm glad they're not all like him, I tell you.*

'Mr Tomm. I know you are going through a great strain, but really, I must ask you not to be quite so demanding, if you don't mind, to try to see things from a medical point of view. I know it is very difficult—'

'Life is demanding, doctor, death is demanding, the only thing that is not demanding is you, which surely is wrong? Medicine and philosophy are as one, are they not? Should it not be you people, most of all, who should be asking the questions?'

'Mr Tomm! I am trying to explain what the chances are of Mrs Merriott's surviving, and since her husband has not come to the hospital since she was brought in, and there is only you in daily attendance, I must explain to you despite the fact that you have no actual status! What I am trying to say is that I do not have to be here, and I do not have to have this conversation with you. You have no status in law, but because you are obviously in love with Mrs Merriott, I am quite willing to take you into account! Now either listen, or I will leave.'

'It is you who have not been listening – either to the questions or the answers.'

The doctor came up for air, took a breath, and gave it one last go.

'No matter what you think of doctors, we try, Mr Tomm. We really do. And if I may say so, if you don't like the way we do things, you try being us, and see how you get on. It's not easy. Believe me.'

Jack opened his large eyes wider, and then he shook his head slowly, and his voice lowered itself so that it was hardly audible. 'You want to turn off her machine, don't you?'

The doctor looked at him and for the first time a look of compassion came into his eyes. 'Yes.'

'And you want me to agree?'

'Yes. Although, as I said, there is no question of your having a status in law, you have . . .' the doctor gave a half-smile of great gentleness, 'you are devoted.'

'You want me to go and tell Hope's daughters that we should switch off their mother's life support machine?'

Jack knew straight away from the look in the doctor's eyes that he was there in one.

'Why don't we both sit down?'

Jack sat down and as he did so he seemed to collapse.

'Are you all right?'

'No. Of course not. Would you be?'

The doctor looked at him. He could not allow his emotions to become involved, it would be unprofessional, but it was difficult to prevent some feeling for this great rock of a man creeping into his dealings with him, for who could not feel moved by someone who so loved this woman on her life support machine that he would only leave her for a few hours at a time? Besides, he had, when he was at school, read of people who had gone mad with grief, and perhaps that was what had happened to this man. He was mad with grief.

*　　*　　*

Rose must be there, of course, so she must be summoned home, or back to what passed as home. And Melinda, and Claire, but not Letty, really she was too small, Jack thought dully as he drove home. Just too small, little Letty, to be told anything except euphemisms. For a second Jack wished that he too was too small to be told anything except euphemisms, and he remembered, long ago, holding his father's hand as they walked together by a river in Cumbria where they had lived, and he thought of how gentle his father had been, and he wished suddenly, for a few weakening seconds, that he was that small boy once more.

The nurse reached up and adjusted the light above Hope's head so that it did not shine directly into the patient's eyes, a pair of apparently non-reacting orbs which Dr Teal was holding open with the aid of two small steel fixtures.

'We shall get a proper picture once we get a scan,' he said, addressing the young doctor who had just been dealing with Jack Tomm. 'However, I have to say that you are quite right. So far is not so good. There is very little definite physical re-action to light and the surface of the eye would appear to be insensitive to touch. I shall know better when I remove the clamps and test deliberately for involuntary blinking, although such a test is not the be-all and end-all. The system could still be in total shock, as you are possibly aware.

Which means these stimuli tests can often be misleading to say the least, and is why a scan will be altogether more revealing. Even so, I doubt if any messages are getting through to the brain. We would certainly have no lung function were we to turn off the ventilator momentarily, as we have already seen -- though again that could still be due to shock trauma. That too is standard in such cases. Once the blast wave has passed, so to speak, we often find responses return and the initial damage is nowhere near as severe as originally diagnosed. However, as I say . . .'

Carefully he loosened the two eye clamps and eased them out of Hope's sockets.

'As I say, so far is not so good. I have to confirm your diagnosis and prognosis, and it is, as you surmised, an obvious one. Mrs Merriott has suffered a cerebral embolism, one which has left the right hand side fully paralysed and the left partially. What we will obviously need to confirm for a second time is the damage done to the brain. How much bleeding, how much oxygen deprivation. The good thing is we shall be doing an MRI scan, not a CAT, so we're going to get a very clear picture indeed.'

'Yes, well, that is something we really are going to need, not just for Mrs Merriott's boyfriend, poor guy, but for her husband.'

The specialist stared at the young doctor.

'He is coming this afternoon. Although they are divorcing, or were, but still are. Or whatever.'

'Bit of a muddle—'

'You could say.'

'Nice woman, I should have thought.'

They both stared momentarily down at their patient and then looked at each other, each knowing without saying what so many patients told their doctors and nurses – namely that the state of the unconscious, for some reason, does not preclude being able to hear.

Later that afternoon the same doctor who had addressed Jack on the subject of Hope's machine's being switched off found himself facing Alexander, newly arrived in Muffin Hatherleigh's Range Rover. It was a surprise to him to find Mrs Merriott's husband waiting for him, and as soon as he entered the room he found that he had taken a powerful and irrational dislike to the handsome, self-satisfied man introducing himself as 'Alexander Merriott, Hope's soon-to-be, or was soon-to-be-going-to-be ex, you know? But I had to come, had to find out what the prognosis might be, for everyone, myself included, of course.'

'It may help you if we backtrack a little,' the doctor suggested, looking up from Hope's notes, once they had shaken hands and sat down again. 'Do you know whether or not there was any family history of strokes, pulmonary embolism, deep vein thrombosis – anything related like that in your wife's family?'

Alexander hardly bothered even to give the question much thought. He simply shook his head and tried to look sufficiently serious.

'Your wife's blood pressure was apparently perfectly normal throughout the pregnancy, she was a non-smoker, there's no history of diabetes, or heart disease – none of the usual risk factors.'

'More importantly, doctor, if I may say so,' Alexander wondered, 'as well as more pertinently, since there's no point as I'm sure *you* know in shutting stable doors once horses have bolted – what precisely is the damage? And the expected span of recovery? If there is a hope of recovery, which I most surely hope there is.'

'We did yet another MRI scan a few hours ago, Mr Merriott, and while we are still looking at it in detail, the prognosis is still not good, I'm afraid.'

'How bad is not good?'

'Mrs Merriott is in a very deep coma, Mr Merriott. There is very little chance that she will ever recover from it.'

'But if she were to?' Alexander wondered.

'She won't, Mr Merriott, believe me. She won't.'

'But miracles have happened and continue to do so.'

'Yes, although I wouldn't necessarily call them miracles. Medical misunderstandings leading to unexpected results is the way I would put it, Mr Merriott.'

'That at least is honest. Most doctors would

rather not admit to *misunderstandings*.'

'This must be very hard for you to accept, Mr Merriott, I realise that. Very hard indeed.'

'It certainly isn't easy, doctor,' Alexander replied. 'I loved my wife. I don't like to think of her dead, as I am sure you will appreciate. But of course I have to think of the future of my daughters, I must think of them.'

There was a small silence as Alexander stared at the doctor who yet again wondered what it was about medicine that brought you into contact with such dilemmas.

'The situation,' the doctor began again, 'as I understand it, is obviously pretty complicated, but it cannot be allowed to influence any decision we make in here about your wife.'

The doctor suddenly saw, and all too clearly for even his peace of mind, that for this self-satisfied man in his cashmere coat and Rolex watch, his crocodile shoes and his hand-made shirt and silk tie, life would be a helluva lot easier if his wife was totally ex. If the machine was switched off. Dead people had very few rights. It would just make things simpler for him, more straightforward somehow. All this technical hanging about for a man like him was irritating. Not more, the doctor would not have thought. Just irritating. Like waiting for his private plane to land or take off.

'If your wife was a divorcée the final decision about the switching off of the machine, the absolute say, would be with her children. As your wife's heirs, it would be, in law, up to them to say whether or not the machine should be switched off. It is not within the rights of her boyfriend, who has no legal status, but in the circumstances I would have said it is the moral right of those of her daughters who have achieved their majority to say what they want done about their mother, since you are, or were, in the process of divorcing. I should have thought. I mean I am not talking legally here, Mr Merriott, I am talking morally. That is how I would see it. But of course what I am saying is off the record. I am only putting my own spin on things. A lawyer would tell you quite differently, because until you are legally divorced, you are still her husband, and she is still your wife.'

Following a small pause the doctor nodded at Alexander Merriott, and picking up his notes and clipboard left him.

How much better was the lover, he thought to himself. And how right poor Hope Merriott had been to leave the one for the other, for the husband was quite simply what his own wife would call '*not* a nice man'.

For, while the lover was difficult, and hurt, while he was wrecked by his sorrow, he was a complete man, the way, it seemed to the doctor, that a man should be, whereas the husband was at best a lightweight, at worst a destroyer.

* * *

Feeling oddly isolated, Alexander went into the room where his wife lay. To Alexander, Hope was already dead, removed from reality, resembling only someone or something he had seen on one of those ever present, absurdly popular hospital series on television.

He stared at the sight she presented to him. There hardly seemed to be one part of her body which was not wired or tubed to some machine or other – there were tubes into her mouth and her nose, into her arms, and some even running out from under her bedclothes. There were pads with wires on them attached to her throat, her chest and her arms, their leads running up to an array of monitors and other machinery set on various shelves above and away from the bed. From large shiny steel stands hung drips, saline, aqueous and medicinal, Alexander supposed, while wondering *All for what?*

For keeping someone who was no longer alive half alive. Just one pull of the plug, one turn of a switch, and the whole pretend business of her being alive would be over. That's all it would take. Someone just had to switch Hope off and that would be that, there would be no more – anything. Just him and his new life, just fun with Muffin, and forget the rest.

He sat back on his chair, pushing his long legs out under his wife's bed. This was one scenario he had not imagined. Death, yes, but not this. For a second he was frightened, because as he stared at her amid all the paraphernalia of late twentieth-century medicine it seemed to him that she moved, or that she was about to move, and he pushed the chair he was seated on backwards suddenly, his heart beating, his nerves suddenly feeling red raw. And while he still went on re-assuring himself that she was unconscious, he sprang off the chair.

But the thought would come into his head, and it terrified him. *What if her eyes open and she turns her head and stares at me? What if she dies and becomes a wraith and leaves her body for a while before I can leave the room? What if she sits up and stares at me, or speaks to me?*

He stepped back towards the door, unwilling to turn his back on her in case she might suddenly spring from the bed and somehow surprise him. Or he might hear her laughter, that light laugh of hers that suddenly seemed to be coming back to him so clearly, the way he had used to hear it all over the house in the old days, before they moved to Hatcombe. The days when they had used to laugh at funny things and she would always be asking him, *Are you all right? Are you all right, Alexei?*

Finally he shot out of the door and closed it behind him, and all the way out to Muffin's Range Rover he found he was repeating to himself that one word. *Yes.*

Yes, he was all right. He had a private jet. He was all right. He had two Range Rovers. He was all right. As soon as he was free he was going to marry a beautiful woman with three large houses and a villa in the south of France. He was all right. *Yes*, he was all right, all right. Of course he was. He was just so all right. Which was strange, because as he drove off, too fast, from the hospital car park, if he was so all right, why was he crying?

From inside the peace of her silver-green shell Hope smiled. Jack would be here soon and she would hear his voice, only his voice. Jack would be there on the shore, or Melinda, or Rose, or Claire, or little Letty – some voice which would echo into her silver-green shell and tell her of things, of precious things that she had ever held dear in her life, in the times when she had been there with them on the shore, that far distant shore from where sometimes she could hear their voices carrying to her over the waters, down into the dark, and into her peaceful silver-green shell.

On his way out Alexander had momentarily stopped at the reception desk in IC.

'If there is the slightest change, even the tiniest indication, make sure to ring me at once on any of these numbers.'

The two nurses on duty had watched him as he removed an immaculate card with all his reachable numbers in Scotland, London and Paris on it, and then when he left one turned and smiled at the other and sighed loudly.

'A bit of that I would not mind,' she said, sighing.

* * *

Jack had called all the girls over to the Mill House. They had resolutely refused to what Melinda called muddy the waters with us tramping about your house since Hope had been in hospital, and even now they arrived in their best clothes, all brushed and beautiful, carrying the baby in his Moses basket, as if they were visiting a relative with whom they must be on their best behaviour.

Seeing how posh they looked Jack felt unaccountably hurt, as if they did not trust him any more, the way they had when Hope was still about in all their lives, as if now they had to dress up to see him the way they might dress up to go to meet someone they did not know.

'How's my son?' Jack stared into the basket while they all stared at each other, briefly, and then carried on into the Mill House, walking in an embarrassed way, maybe wishing that he had not said anything, that he had not verbally laid claim to him, or even, perhaps, not believing him?

They all sat down in his drawing room primly smoothing themselves, or so it seemed to Jack, as if they were in church, not at the dear old still familiar Mill House with its exuberant colours and its abstract paintings, with its memories of them all together, Hope, and him, and all of them.

'Would you like a mineral water with elderflower?'

Jack could see that they quite definitely would, and so he poured them all out their preferred drink, and himself a Scotch and water, and sat down opposite what might be in some ways a jury, he thought, or a tribunal of some kind, which in others ways it was.

'Right. So. Best to come right to the point, or rather the person. Hope. The outlook is not good, kids, as you probably know?'

They nodded in unison, their eyes staring almost blankly at him as if they were about to be bored by what he had to say, or as if they had already guessed why they had been suddenly called over to the Mill House.

Taking that presumption as a given, Jack therefore continued, 'As you know, there is talk among the doctors about switching off your mother's life support machine, and there is a case for this, of course. Although James is my child—'

Rose put up her hand. 'And you are therefore responsible for why she is like she is!' she reminded him.

Jack was just about to point out the relevant fact that it takes two to tango, or make love, when he stopped.

No! No, he thought, both his eyes twitching with fatigue, while the Scotch he was sipping was filling him with a warmth that was almost shocking, as if it was a furnace, so long was it since he had trusted himself to have a drink and not burst into a torrent of tears that might never cease.

He must not emphasize his role in Hope's life, or Hope's role in his. These girls were *her* daughters, not his, and as in all moments of life and death, she, in their eyes, belonged to them, not him. He had to be careful to tread the line between commitment and possession, a line that he recognized as being so fine as to make the gossamer threads that ran at dawn between the wild flowers and leaves, over the grass and around the spiders' webs, seem as thick as tow rope. He just had to find that thread and keep himself close to its weaving path, for Hope's sake.

'Of course I am responsible,' he agreed, 'there is no doubt about that at all. I am responsible, as the father of James, for Hope's condition.'

He paused, and for a second the black guilt of it all smothered him, and he could have wept and wept, but he sipped at his Scotch again hoping against hope that they had not noticed that his lips were trembling as much as the hand holding the glass.

But of course they had all noticed and Claire frowned at Rose, and Rose felt terrible for what she had said. As usual it had burst out of her in a way that was so her, and so wrong. And now it was agonizing just to sit there in silence while a grown man like Jack, whom Mums after all had loved to pieces, looked like a forlorn little boy, his lips trembling so hard, and his hand holding his glass too, that she thought he might collapse completely.

'I am the reason that darling Hope is in a coma.'

There, it was out, and as soon as it was the girls

all tried not to look at Jack, only stared at their feet, or at the baby, knowing that Jack had a lump in his throat which was probably the size of the ice in his Scotch, and that it was only with the greatest effort that the words he had just said had been uttered at all, as if they had been cut out of him, not spoken.

'But we have to accept what is, and try to make the very best of everything. That is all, absolutely all, that is open to us.' Melinda looked round at her two sisters. As usual she could be relied upon to be reasonable without being as tactless as Rose.

'Yes,' Claire agreed, in her deep little voice, 'the past is the past, and no mistaking it for anything else.'

Aunt Rosabel had used to say that to Claire, which was why she thought to say it now, and she was quite glad that she had when she saw how relieved Jack looked that she was not going to blame him as much as he had perhaps thought she might.

'What do you think, Jack?' Melinda put her finger into the baby's tiny hand, and felt his strong grip and smiled down at him, by way of distraction. 'What do you think we should do?'

'I have no status here. It is for you three to say, no-one else.'

'If we leave everything as it is,' Rose put in suddenly after a short, awkward pause, 'well, there is nothing to lose, but if we just – if we—'

'Switch off the machine?'

'Yes.' Rose nodded at Claire. 'If we do that, then

wouldn't we always wonder if we should have? Whereas if we leave it for a while longer, to see, just to see if there's not something there, she might come back to us, mightn't she? I mean that is what this is all about, really, isn't it?'

'Yes, I think so.'

'Mellie?' Rose stared at Mellie really hard because she seemed so distracted, as if she was not really with them all in the room, which perhaps she was not, perhaps in her mind she was really at the hospital sitting beside Mums, talking to her, as Claire had told Rose she was so often, just talking and talking to her, the way she had used to sit talking to her in the kitchen at West Dean or at Hatcombe in the garden while Hope did her needlepoint.

'Yes, I think we should hang on in there for a few more weeks, or months, not do anything just yet. She might be still wanting to stay on. Or she might, who knows, suddenly defy them all, and wake up!'

The others had not really taken this idea into account, and so now they stared at Melinda.

'Mums might wake up?'

'Yes, why not?'

'Because people don't, do they, after such a long time, people don't wake up, do they?'

'Yes they do,' Rose put in. 'I was reading about just such a case, only the other day. After a year, this woman woke up and spoke to her family. One boy woke up and was perfectly all right after a

393

terrible car accident and after everyone had given up on him. He woke up.'

'That's it, then.' Melinda looked Jack straight in the face for the first time since they had arrived. 'We have decided, Jack. We'll leave Mums as she is.'

Inwardly Jack sighed with relief. Yet he said nothing of the little squeeze of his hand that he had been convinced he had felt, not wanting to raise their hopes. He just prayed that he was right.

Chapter Fourteen

Before she left for London once more Rose, brought in by Jack, had visited her mother alone, no longer frightened to be with her, and taking with her a bunch of freesias. As she went into the room she realized that she was actually on tiptoe, creeping towards the bed, really afraid of disturbing her, which was truly pathetic.

Meanwhile, as Rose visited Hope, Jack was down the corridor talking with a specialist. Someone called Marcus whom, he told Rose on the drive in, he had known years before and had, in light of the girls' decision, brought in for another opinion on Hope's case.

Rose carefully placed the freesias in a vase beside Hope's head. They looked too small and too few for the vase which the nurse had found for her, but they smelt nice.

'Guess what, Mums? I've got an audition to RADA at last, next week,' she told her mother, speaking in a perfectly normal tone. 'Isn't that great?' she went on, feeling for her mother's hand. 'I'm supposed to be doing a short piece from *Saint Joan*, and also a little bit of Gwendolyn from *The Importance of Being Ernest*, a complete contrast. So that should be pretty nerve-racking for a start.

Then. Well, then the following week I have another audition but this time for LAMDA, oh and Guildford, I thought I'd try for that too, just for starters.'

As Rose was telling her mother all this, Marcus was saying to Jack, 'She hasn't got a chance, Jack. Sorry.'

'No chance of what, Marcus?'

'No chance of anything, Jack. Hope is technically dead already.'

'No, Marcus,' Jack said, in warning. 'No, don't say that. You don't know. You think you know, that's quite different.'

'Jack. As I understand it there is no hope. Really. I am the *second* second opinion you have brought in – and believe me, if I could I would have it quite otherwise, but I can only look at the facts as presented, and there they are.'

'I won't accept it.'

'You don't want me to fill you with false hopes, old friend, now do you?'

'Define no chance. Give it a definition.'

'All right. Before MRI came along I'd have said you were right. CAT scans, you see, they couldn't differentiate properly between the white and the grey matter in the brain, but they're as clear as daylight with MRI. It shows damage graphically, Jack, and completely distinctly. As I said, that was a big one, and people don't recover from those.'

'So far.'

'It just isn't humanly possible, Jack. With that amount of brain damage even the smallest, tiniest logical thought is impossible.'

Jack did not reply. He would not believe it.

'Hope is brain-dead, Jack. And I am very much afraid that she always will be.'

'But you don't know.'

'No, Jack, I don't know. I agree. I am not God.'

Jack paused and then, flippantly, he asked Marcus, 'Do you know the difference between God and a doctor?'

'Yes – God doesn't think he's a doctor. But don't you see, Jack? There is no point in all of you continuing in this agony?'

That is such a lovely smell, Rose, not that I can actually smell anything, but I can imagine! I can imagine what your flowers smell like and that imagining is stronger than you could believe possible. Thank you for bringing them in for me, and putting them so close by me. They say blind people have deeper senses and although I am not blind, because I can see inside my shell of silver-green, yet I have learned to feel more with my spirit. My spirit has heightened senses, senses that can only be felt and not described, so beautiful are the sensations, so strong the feelings.

'I do hope you can smell these, Mums,' Rose went on, still holding Hope's hand in hers. 'Because these are special. They're from Mr Parsons – you remember Aunt Rosabel's gardener from

Hatcombe? He grows them in his greenhouse, and he brought me a bunch for you just as I was leaving Keeper's. He wanted you to have them most particularly. He's so kind and gentle. And such a good gardener. But you know that. Here. I am just going to hold them very carefully under your nose, now. There. I know you can't smell, but you might be able to sense them, mightn't you?'

As she placed the flowers beside her mother Rose sang softly to her, 'Ah but I should never think of spring, for that should surely break my heart in two.'

'It is so lovely to hear you sing again, Rose. You were singing even before you danced. I loved to hear you. Most especially in the early morning.'

Marcus's eyes were full of compassion for Jack, but his voice remained firm. 'So finally, those patients who are found to have this amount of damage – their life support systems are closed down.'

'You mean they are killed.'

Marcus shook his head. 'You cannot kill something which is not alive, Jack. Life support systems create false life. They do that so that we – the doctors and so-called experts – may be sure that all proper and natural life is dead. Life support systems create life where there is, if you will, already death. They make a patient breathe mechanically. Shut the ventilator off and there is no message from the brain to tell the lungs and the heart to work, so the patient is already dead. When we turn off the ventilators, we are killing an electrical circuit, not a person. We are stopping a machine, not a life. The people the law tells us we may do this to are already dead and gone. They are only being kept alive artificially.'

'Sure,' Jack nodded, agreeing. 'But that is, I maintain, only as far as you know. You see, I, on the other hand, I know that Hope is still in there, I know that she is still not brain-dead. Don't ask me how, but I know.'

'Shall we begin again, Jack?' Marcus nodded to him, and they both sat down, as if they had been jousting but had now decided to talk as friends instead. 'Perhaps it might help you if I explained where I think we are at, as it were. The medical profession bases the criteria for diagnosing what is known as brain death on the determination of the irreversible damage to the brain. We also look for persistent deep coma, an inability to breathe independently if the patient is taken off the ventilator, and the absence of what is known as brainstem function. This can be assessed by ascertaining whether or not the pupils react to light, whether or not the patient responds to painful stimuli – such as a needle being inserted into a limb, or the touching of the naked surface of the eye to see if there is any sign of involuntary blinking. The responses to these tests give us clear evidence as to whether or not the brain is alive or dead. Now, while an EEG is not really required—'

'Which is?'

'An electroencephalogram. An EEG records the tiny electrical impulses produced by activity in the brain. And as I say, this is not a requirement, but it can confirm or deny the results of the other described tests. Provided the results of all the tests are scrupulously monitored there is no chance at all of a wrong conclusion being reached. All that is then required is to gain the necessary assents. That is the procedure.'

'And her daughters will not, at this stage, give those assents. I have asked them, we all talked – they are quite firm in their opinion that we should not, as yet, do anything, not yet. And while I have no status as far as Hope is concerned I am very glad that is how they feel. Naturally. Very glad,' he ended abruptly.

'Very well, then we must proceed as we are. Comas are very unpredictable. However, for all your sakes, I would advise a set period of time to be agreed upon with the team here. Perhaps a month might be reasonable? During this time Hope will be monitored quite closely, always remembering that the brain is a vast unknown subject, and we can nurse a hope that somewhere there may well be another part of the brain that is still alive and working.'

'I thought of playing her favourite sorts of music to her. She loves Strauss, and Chopin, and

Verdi, of course – Puccini, naturally. I thought that might be a good idea.'

'Excellent,' Marcus agreed. He smiled at his childhood friend while inside he sighed for the heartbreak he could see in store for him.

Jack began again, 'Hope had a book, you know, about this kind of thing, or rather based on this sort of thing, you know, the brain? She told me all about it once, she told me that if you coloured the little bit of our brains that we use and then saw how very little it was, we would be ashamed. While if we could learn to use just twenty per cent more, just think what a brilliant world we would have.'

'Maybe we will?'

Jack smiled briefly. 'Yes, maybe we will. Before our sun burns out in four or five billion years, maybe we will have learned to love each other, cure each other, even understand each other.'

'And even then we may only be using a half of that old grey matter. Just think of that, Jack.'

'I do, Marcus, all the time.'

Before he left the hospital, and after Rose had left her room, Jack went to see Hope for himself.

'It's OK, darling,' he said, holding her hand. 'I will not let them do it to you, you understand? You just keep fighting on, dearest soul, and I shall see you back here in a couple of hours, after I've taken Rose to the station. After I've seen her onto the train. She's a good girl, by the way, they all are.

They're going to come through for you, and you're going to have to come through for them, and for me. For us. Now. Don't move! I won't be long, and when I come back it will be with music for you. Things you really like. I've made a tape.'

Yet again, and his own heart nearly stopped, Jack could have sworn that he felt a slight movement from one of Hope's fingers, but as he drove Rose to the station he said nothing to her, not wanting to raise her hopes, and knowing, in his heart of hearts, that he could well have been mistaken.

It was no good denying it, least of all for Rose to deny it, once more, as she saw London's soot and London's grime creeping towards her at the end of her journey, she could have cheered. Here it all was again, and grimy and sooty and sweaty as it was, she loved every little bit of it.

As it happened, once on the Underground, she found she had to stand all the way to her stop, so to take her mind off this she found herself thinking of all the problems that she had left behind at Keeper's Cottage, and wondering once more at Melinda's ability to cope with them. She was thankful that it was not her having to deal with them all, and immediately felt selfish. Still, since there was no way that she would want to go back to live in Wiltshire again, there was no way that she could help Mel.

Moving to Hatcombe had seemed to be the start

of all their problems. Indeed, as she looked back at all the disasters it would seem that more than anything the move to Wiltshire had proved fatal for all of them. As she swayed on her strap and tried to avoid a very respectable-looking City gent's hot hands, Rose found herself thinking of the old days at West Dean and remembering how her parents had seemed to be so happy there. She stared at the darkness of the tunnel they were going through, remembering them dancing in the kitchen, laughing together. All that had gone when they moved to Wiltshire.

She frowned. She had to snap out of the habit of looking back. Instead she looked forward – dreading the inevitable mound of laundry that she would be facing when she got back to Saintly Street.

But having inspected the kitchen for notes from Hugh Reilly as to what chores she should or should not be doing, and having found no ironing, a miracle in itself, she found herself instead passing a new face on the stairs.

They smiled, Rose with her usual assumed confidence, he with a sort of shy diffidence.

'Hallo?'

She had already well passed him, her room being right at the top of the house. 'Rose Merriott!' She waved to him, from above him now, not wanting to stop running up the stairs because it was part of one of her many breathing exercises, running to her room while quietly making 'humma, humma' noises to herself to help improve her diaphragm and make it stronger.

'Charles Felbrigg.'

'Of Felbrigg Hall?' Rose asked facetiously and immediately regretted it because it was obvious, from the faint sigh that he gave, and the slightly resigned way he stared up at her, that he was well used to this reaction when he introduced himself. 'Oh, God, I am sorry. Come up and have a tisane with me later, and I'll say sorry a great many more times to make up for being so crass.'

'I would love to take a tisane with you,' he said simply.

Rose stared down at him briefly. She was just so glad to be back in London, not to be facing all those problems that everyone at the Mill House and Keeper's were facing, and yes – not to be sitting beside her mother willing her to be back with them the way she was. Perhaps it was the depth of her relief to be somewhere else that made her realize something else too. Something lyrical and marvellous, and that was that Charles Felbrigg, *not* of the Hall, was beautiful.

Not only was he beautiful, but so was his voice, light and musical and agreeable, in fact everything about him was aesthetic and pleasing, from the long slender fingers carrying his books to the curve of his mouth as he stared up at her and said 'tisane', as if the modulations of the word pleased him as much as just looking down at him, from her great height above him, pleased Rose.

'Tisane, then. Nine-ish. Got to study, alas.'

She continued with her 'humma, humma, humma' all the way up to the door of her room, whereupon she fell against it and closed her eyes. Charles Felbrigg was just so beautiful, impossibly beautiful, like a painting, like a song, like a poem.

And he had to be a professor, looking as he did, soft-collared shirt, white, much laundered, with a silk scarf falling down either side, which actually Rose usually hated, but which looked somehow endearing on such a young man, as if he was trying to look older, for some reason.

And then he had been wearing what had looked from above, from where she had been standing, like a sort of sleeveless cardigan, and those wide-bottomed trousers that people in old films always wore and which came in and out of fashion as regular as a battery clock. And this was all before she saw his shoes, which were the right kind of loafers, discreet, and not too highly polished.

'Nine would be fine,' she had heard him finally call as she shut her door.

'Nine would be fine, nine would be fine, nine would be fine,' she started to sing out loud, before beginning to learn yet another of Shaw's long, long speeches, from *Major Barbara* this time, a speech so long that she was sure, as she took turn and turn about her room, making a fist of one hand and pounding it against the open palm of the other, and repeating, and repeating, that had she not agreed to give Charles Felbrigg a tisane she would have collapsed on her bed and fallen fast asleep.

It was as if she was so relieved to be back in London that she could not wait to fall asleep in order to wake up again and find herself once more besieged by aeroplane noise, by the sound of cars far below, by the knowledge that there were fascinating people everywhere.

Not finding her progress with Shaw's speeches satisfactory, Rose put that particular play back on her shelf and plucked down Ibsen's *The Wild Duck* instead.

She had bought it, but she had never read it, and somehow as she opened the title page she had a feeling that she should have read it, because right from the moment that her eyes fell on the title page it seemed to be speaking to her, telling her something, as if it had streaked across a night sky, or suddenly appeared and fallen, like the falling stars that she and Mellie would sometimes watch for, standing outside Keeper's Cottage during the darkly bright nights that came around in autumn, ripping through the night sky.

Perhaps *The Wild Duck* could be a play to which she could attach a star? Perhaps she could be like those very stars they had seen, brilliant, scintillating and wondrous, lighting up the stage with Ibsen's words?

'Good evening, *professor*.'

He smiled in amusement, knowing at once,

without being told, that she had already given him a nickname. And Rose saw, with some triumph, that she had been right, that the cardigan he had been wearing earlier under his jacket was sleeveless and made of a very fine silk cotton, very long, and, although done up correctly, had pockets, into which he now thrust his hands. But he remained by the door while smiling across at her, waiting for her to invite him in, which was rather touchingly modest.

'Come in, come in.'

She realized once he had stepped into her room, carefully shutting the door behind him, that he was very tall, but the look to his eyes even while he was smiling was strangely vague, as if he was not quite focusing on Rose, which was immediately a challenge, because Rose liked people to focus on her, at any rate when they were with her, for goodness' sake.

'I was just wondering how you run up these stairs, so often,' he said, 'and all the time making your yoga noise, or whatever it is.'

This was getting better. This meant that he had noticed Rose before, perhaps because his door was ajar, or perhaps he heard her 'humma, humma, humma'ing all the way up to the top of the house all day long, between auditions for drama schools, and laundry.

'Don't have to go to the gym, can't afford to anyhow. And it's not a yoga noise, it's a breathing noise. Hugh O'Reilly gave it to me. It works, actually, you'd be surprised how much it works.'

Rose smiled and waved a hand for him to sit on one of her two cane sofas.

'Sit down, Charles Felbrigg, and tell me your choice of tisane. There's Rose, Lemon flower, Peppermint – actually they all taste like shampoo, but you can choose anyway, and if you don't like it, keep it for the final rinse!'

He laughed, and then, shifting a little in his seat, he stared at the cushions, and then at her, and asked, 'Why do landlords in Clapham and Battersea always insist on furnishing rooms as if they were in Spain?'

Rose made their two teas with little bags in two nice china cups and sat down opposite him, at the same time offering him a plate of small lemon biscuits.

'For the same reason I am offering you a tisane and bikkies – m o n e y. *Merney!*'

Charles sighed, suddenly and loudly, and stared at the mean cane sofa upon which he was trying to pretend that he was comfortable.

'If you always rented rooms in London you would think there were no other kinds of furniture besides patio chairs and sofas, wouldn't you? Once someone becomes a landlord and lets out rooms it seems it becomes a religion with them to furnish the world with cane. Cane should be banished from this sceptred isle for ever. If only someone could be found who could prove it was harvested from some diminishing resource – or from some reed bed where its harvesting could be proved to be endangering the life of a newt – then we could all take to the streets in protest.'

Rose laughed, and so did he, and she was glad to notice that he had nice even teeth, which meant that he was not just quite beautiful, Rose realized with an inner sigh of satisfaction, he was very beautiful, even down to his teeth.

'Listen, professor. I didn't ask you for tea to discuss furniture.'

'OK, so I'll give in, and ask. Why do you call me professor?'

'Because you look like a professor.'

He squinted down at himself, soft linen shirt, sleeveless cardigan, reading glasses around his neck on a cord. 'I suppose I do.'

But he said nothing of what he did, and so Rose said, 'What do you do?'

'I am dreadfully afraid that if I tell you you will not want to go on having tea with me.'

'Well, as long as it's not . . .' Rose considered for a minute. 'As long as it's not anything to do with animal research or making cosmetics out of something unspeakable, or pulling down trees, or torturing people for information they don't possess, I'm pretty sure I won't mind.'

'I am afraid you will. No, I can't tell you what I'm doing at the moment, it's just so uninteresting.'

'Please!'

'I'm writing a biography of a very obscure

French novelist for a European paperback house who will have not the slightest interest in it once I deliver, which is why I too sit on cane furniture and suffer the slings and arrows of Hugh's horrible cane furniture.'

'Oh. But that's quite exciting, isn't it, writing biographies?'

He smiled. 'If the person is exciting, it is exciting, if the person you have chosen is a pill – and the man I am writing about at the moment is just such – it is exactly like spending too much time with someone you don't like on a very, very long train journey, with no stops. Now,' he leaned forward, suddenly earnest, 'you must tell me, why is it that you make those funny noises going downstairs and upstairs all day long? Or, at least, most of the morning, anyway?'

Rose smiled mischievously. 'Because, professor, I am learning to be what my great-great-aunt Rosabel used to call an *aahctress* and *humma, humma, humma* is a breathing exercise that strengthens the diaphragm and therefore helps the voice. I don't just want to be a telly actress, you see. I want to be a great actress, the kind that fills a theatre with her voice, that can project to the back of the Upper Circle, not just mutter in a TV studio – *know-what-I-mean?*' She lowered her voice. '*Know-what-I-mean-love?*'

Charles Felbrigg smiled, and his smile was genuine, and dazzling.

'Right,' he said, 'Rose Merriott. Let's see. You

410

must always try out stage names, do you know that? As if announcing them, or as if – well, anyway, let's try it for size. Ready? Right. You want to be a great actress. Let's see – *Dame Rose Merriott*. Mmm. Yes. It does go, actually, doesn't it?'

Rose looked at him, startled. 'Do you think so?'

Again the dazzling smile. 'No doubt of it, Dame Rose Merriott.'

'Another tea? Or rather, I should say – would you like a change of rinse, prof?'

'No, really. No, I think I'll stay with Peppermint, if you don't mind.'

Rose frowned and stared at his hair. 'Yes,' she agreed slowly, 'good, because it seems to be doing your highlights the world of good.'

Charles smiled and unconsciously put up a hand and passed it over his thick dark hair. 'The dame and the professor? Makes us sound like a couple of Mafia types, doesn't it?'

Rose laughed, and then she leaned forward and said, 'Actually, I suddenly thought, if you're so clever, and so bright, and if you write, surely you can help me, can't you? Because I am reading Ibsen's *The Wild Duck* at the moment, and – well, you could help me work on it, couldn't you?' She sensed at once from the calm look to his eye that this was just what he wanted to be asked, that ever since she had said she wanted to be an actor he had been intrigued.

'We could read it together,' he agreed. 'But

don't expect too much of me, will you? At the moment I am only a biographer.'

'You're clever, that's enough for me,' Rose told him, and going to her bedside and picking up the book she settled herself artlessly beside him, which they both at once realized could be going to be a mistake.

'Would you prefer it if I sat opposite you?'

'As a man – no. As your professor – yes.'

Rose changed her place and sat opposite him. But that too, although she did not know it, was a mistake, because it meant that Charles noticed even more how her thick dark hair caught the light, and how fine her eyes were, and how pale her skin, and how long her legs.

He quickly held up the copy of the play to block his vision of her. 'Right, Act One, Scene One.'

He started to read, and as he did so Rose realized afresh that it was not only actors who possessed lovely voices.

Melinda stared at their mother who just lay there, eyes closed, arms straight down by her sides, her breath regulated by the ventilator which stood to one side of the bedhead.

'She looks so young like that, doesn't she, Claire? She looks more like our sister than our mother.'

'I thought only old people got strokes,' Claire murmured. 'I thought only old people like Aunt Rosabel got pegged by strokes. I didn't know people as young as Mums could get one.'

'No, I know.' Melinda nodded. 'Me too. Until Jack explained. He knew someone even younger than Mums who had a stroke. A friend of his ex-wife's. She had it while she was having a baby as well.'

'Did this woman recover, Mellie?'

Melinda looked across at Claire, and at once began to rearrange some more flowers. 'I don't know – I don't really remember,' she lied, remembering her mother's dream, her saying over and over to Melinda, *'You see the baby was there, Mellie, in my dream, a boy, a baby boy – and you were walking with him to the church, and Jack was with you, and you were all there, and I wasn't.'*

The fact that Claire knew Melinda was lying became enough reason now for her to slip her index finger into her mother's tubed hand.

'There's something else, but perhaps I shouldn't say it,' Melinda began, looking at her comatose parent. 'It may not even be true. Aunt Rosabel told me, so it probably wasn't.'

'Her hand tightened,' Claire put in suddenly. 'I swear I felt Mums's hand tighten just as you said that name – *Aunt Rosabel*. And again. I did, I felt it.'

'It can't have done—' Melinda hurried back to the bed.

'Mellie? She's not dead!' Claire whispered. 'See? If she can squeeze her hand in mine, Mel, she's not dead after all!'

Chapter Fifteen

From inside her sea-green shell Hope knew that Melinda was back again, because the music on the tapes had been stopped, and she could hear her talking.

'Anyway the weather's broken, which means I've been able to gallop Goosey at last. We had our first really proper serious piece of work last week and she feels amazing. She just loved it, Mums. She really stretches out now, and of course all that racehorse speed – if I can control that cross country and use it properly, she's going to be sensational. Oh – I nearly forgot – though I don't know how – she won her first dressage last Sunday! How about that? There were two inter-mediate horses competing, and one Open, and Goosey beat them all! She really has come on in leaps and bounds. Well, I told you last week how well she was going, so seeing that we've got her ground work so good now, we might have a good round at Aldon.'

For a while there was not much more to say after that so Melinda quickly put the music back on for Hope, and held her hand instead, because they had all agreed it was stupid just to talk for the sake of it, and that it was much better to stop when there was nothing more to say.

As Claire said, 'Just as you would talking to someone on the telephone. If you've run out of things to say, you stop. There's no shame to that. It doesn't mean you love her less, or anything, does it?'

So for the next few minutes Melinda just sat with Hope, holding her hand, and listening to the music on the tapes that Jack had so painstakingly made for her while wishing that her mother could answer her back.

Of course there were things that she could tell her, but which she did not like to touch on, such as the fact that Jack had hired a nanny for James and Letty, and reorganized the rooms at the Mill House so that they were all there together. They still came back to Melinda and Claire on Nanny's day off and for half of the weekend, but Claire and she were able now to get on with things a bit better. Although at first Melinda missed having Letty and James around all the time, and found herself looking round for them every five seconds. Or waking fearfully in the night, thinking that she had heard the baby crying in the next door room, she would run in to him, only to find his room empty, and herself feeling an idiot as she remembered, too late, that he was now at the Mill House.

It was pathetic, but for a while she even missed things like making up the bottles and setting fire to the nappies in the back garden, so used to the routine of looking after them both had she become. But it was ridiculous to pretend that they were anything but fine and not missing life at Keeper's Cottage at all, and in the end, that was what mattered.

Besides, Jack had given Letty two baby rabbits, and what with the large garden and the indoor swimming pool there was so much more for her to do that Melinda was now giving that attention, that time, which she had once been giving to her young siblings, to the Grey Goose.

'I think my seat is improving,' she said after a while, wondering how long she could keep up what little news she had to tell her, especially since Hope had never been interested in horses, and was always what the colonel would call 'a bit of a foot follower' when it came to stable news.

After a minute or two more, talking of jumps made, and jumps down, and spreads, and various kinds of bits that she was trying, Melinda stopped suddenly and sighed. What was the point? Mums had never been that interested in horses. A bit, but not much, and just because Claire had thought she felt Hope squeezing her hand did not mean that she necessarily had, it did not really prove anything. And it had never happened again, so doubtless it had just been her imagination, her wishing that she had felt it.

To her shame Melinda found herself thinking, *What are we all doing this for day after day after day? Perhaps we are all mad? Should we not listen to her doctors and switch off her machine?*

Only yesterday she had found Jack fast asleep, his head on his hand, still at Hope's bedside, still hoping, not giving up. And although he awoke with a smile she thought she saw, for the first time ever, that having passed from madness to commitment he might now, like her, be journeying from commitment to defeat. There was something in the back of his eyes, and in his voice, that was not as strong or as certain as it had been, something that had disappeared.

'We'll win through, see if we won't, Mellie,' he reassured her, looking all too apologetic that she had found him asleep and that he had awoken sounding and perhaps looking dejected. 'I know we'll win through. It's just a question of—'

'Kicking on?'

'That's right.'

'Your friend Marcus said another month and then we'd talk. It's now—'

'Don't let's talk dates, Mellie.' He turned away, at the same time squeezing her arm lightly. 'Don't let's get too narrow, talking dates. Being with your mother all the time, I hardly know or care what the day is!'

Melinda felt a sudden surge of possessiveness. Yes, Hope was her mother, and not Jack's mother, and Jack might be James's father, but was not yet Hope's husband. He had to wake up to that fact, not always be there, in the hospital, busy owning her the way it seemed to her that he sometimes was, as if he was the only one who truly cared, as if none of them cared as much as he did.

But as quickly as the thought came, Melinda rejected it, feeling ashamed, for she knew that Jack had actually been a tower of strength, and that Hope had wanted to have the baby as much as they had all wanted her to come through it all right, that she need not have had it, that finally, really, it had been her decision, and not Jack's fault.

'No, OK, sorry. No. We won't talk dates. I hardly know what day it is either, at least I wouldn't, if it wasn't for the Grey Goose. I say, Jack, she's really coming along well, you're going to be proud of her, one of these days. The colonel, everyone at Locketts Farm – you know, the place where we school her? They can't believe how well she is coming along.'

'Great. By the way – good news. Josh is coming home tomorrow.'

Josh. Melinda could not say anything, least of all to Jack, but she somehow could not face seeing Josh. Feeling as she had before about him, now that their parents had actually had a baby together, and in such terrible circumstances, she could not see that how she had felt about him was not in some strange way wrong.

It was ridiculous. But being with Josh, she and Josh, did not seem the same at all, now that so much had happened between their parents. It was almost embarrassing. No, not almost – it was embarrassing. Besides, Josh had not even written to her once from South Africa, where he'd been sent to study farming methods – not about Hope, not about James, nothing, which only went to prove that he must feel the same – really embarrassed. As if their parents having a baby together meant they were somehow related, even though they were no such thing. It was stupid. It was pathetic. It was everything. But there it undoubtedly was. Things could not be the same, and probably never would be.

'I am boxing up to go to see the colonel.'

'Fine. Josh will drive you, be happy to, I'm sure he would.'

'No, don't worry him. Please. I'm being driven, it's a share, two of us going for some show jumping, dressage, the lot. It will be a long day.'

'I'll tell him anyway. If he wants to come he can call you, eh?'

'OK, but really, there's no need.'

But as it happened, the next day came and went, and Josh did not call, and Melinda thought she knew precisely why.

Rose was frowning at the professor. They had reached an understanding over *The Wild Duck*. His interpretation had won hands down over hers, and in consequence, on his advice, she had changed her audition pieces and was now waiting to hear if she was called back. Which she would be if he was right, and could not be if he was wrong. Because she had completely changed all her ideas about acting because of him.

'Supposing I don't get in anywhere, supposing no-one wants me, prof?'

'You will, but—'

'But?'

'Once there it's simply a question of deciding – do you or do you not want to *stay* there. That will be your particular problem, I would say.' He smiled at her. 'You are so gifted, Rose. You were gifted from the moment you were born, it's quite obvious. But sometimes people get to places, colleges, drama schools, universities, what you will – and bingo. They don't want to be there any more. They find out that what they need to nourish their talent is just not there, and that it would be harmful to stay. That is what happens. Sometimes. Maybe not to you. But sometimes, to other people. It happens. And then.'

'And then?' Rose demanded impatiently. 'And then, prof, please tell me?'

'Then, Dame Rose, you leave.'

'After all this sweat, no way!'

'You'd be surprised.' He tapped the page of the play he was holding with his pencil. 'Now take it from Act Two, Scene Two, please.'

They had progressed to buying two of everything to study, and so Rose frowned down at her copy of *The Winter's Tale* and started to read. But she could not, not with this *thought* hanging over her, so she stopped before properly beginning.

'If I was talented, I would not have needed so much direction from you, would I?'

'On the contrary, talent is always humble, it looketh not for praise, but for help, it seeketh not reward except in getting it right. Now, are you *ready*?'

'Aye, aye, sir.'

Nevertheless, deep down inside her Rose sighed.

It was such an exquisite problem, really – seeing the professor each morning, working together on her pieces every night, but not *doing* anything about anything, about each other, because, quite simply, they could not. There was no time for being in love, or anything even approximating to it, at least not at the moment.

Sometimes it was so difficult, trying not to fall in love with him, because Charles was so beautiful, so finely made, he reminded Rose of an exquisite drawing, and she found that not only was it difficult not to fall in love with him, but she worried over him if she heard him coughing when she passed his room, or if he looked pale because he was working too late, and she wanted to do and say all sorts of things. But it was not possible. There were other things in life that were far more important to her, one of which she thought about all the time – success.

She had to succeed, for herself, but most of all for Hope. Somehow she had it in her mind that if she succeeded in making herself into a star, Hope would come alive again. The last time she had visited her she had told her so too, but unlike

Claire, Rose had felt no response, Hope had not squeezed her fingers.

Of course it might have helped if the professor had not been so kind. To be so kind and so beautiful was too much really. And he went to such trouble to pretend that he was not being kind, too. Coming down to the kitchen in the very early mornings and talking to her when she was ironing, pretending that he had not known that she was there all the time.

And he would make coffee for them both, and it was just so nice, to have coffee and talk, that Rose always forgot that she was ironing, and at the same time realized that he had come to see her in the basement kitchen for just that reason, so that the tedium of the ironing would zip by and he would take her through speeches, and all sorts of interpretations, because he believed work done in the morning had twice the value of anything done after twelve noon.

Sometimes he said with a smile, 'I'm *hot-housing* you, you know that? I'm making sure that you're full to the brim before you go before those frustrated people who sit in on drama auditions. You must be so fully developed and confident in your talent that nothing will shake you. You must not care at all what they say or think. You will be you, the actor we both know you are. That's the best way. As a matter of fact it's the only way.'

'How shall I thank you?'

'I don't know, we'll think of something!' he

would joke before wandering off to his room.

Although they had never kissed and their hands had only touched as he passed her a pencil, or she passed him his inevitable peppermint tisane, although they had only worked together, and lived on different floors, it was as if they had been lovers, so finely tuned to each other had they become from working on her pieces, from reading plays and listening to music together, from talking. Until finally Rose awoke, late, to the realization that the professor was really always more interested in what she was doing than in who she, Rose, actually was.

Yet each time she tried to remedy this, balance everything up, ask him questions about himself, try to personalize how they were together, he deflected her in his wry way, sometimes teasing her, often making fun of himself.

'Oh, but please, just, well – at least tell me when your book will be published . . .'

'People talking about their books are so dull.'

'I don't think so.'

'Yes, of course you do, Dame Rose. But – and this is a big but – you are about to do something exciting, so you will make up for both of us. At the moment.'

But for someone who did nothing exciting the professor's telephone rang a great deal, and he had a volume of mail, and large envelopes containing manuscripts would come and go with a flustered middle-aged woman who called punctiliously three afternoons a week, departing with dictation tapes, which made Rose wonder if there was not another side to her professor. Some secret side that she knew nothing of, and of which he did not want her to know.

Not that it mattered, for in reality she did not want to find out too much about Charles Felbrigg, not just yet. She only wanted to listen to him as he helped her to come to some understanding about so many of the plays she studied for parts, but which, as a whole, sometimes eluded her; most especially *The Wild Duck*.

He had only to start to explain, to take a scene in a play apart, and it seemed to Rose that he was not speaking, but that his words pirouetted and spun, danced and waltzed with knowledge, not just of the play they were reading, but of life.

'I don't want to see life, like this, somehow, I just don't, not yet anyway,' she begged him, once or twice.

And once he had left her she would go back to her magazines, to the well-worn lightweight novels that stacked the shelves of her bedroom, and which had been left by some other lodger who also had not wanted to see life as Charles and the great playwrights saw it. 'I just want everything to be – well – nice.'

'But it's not. Life is not nice, you can see that already, you know that.'

'I know, that's why I want it to be, don't you see?

I just want what we read to be ugly, to be fiction, and real life to be – well – fantastic.'

'It's both. That is both its glory and its tragedy.'

'You sound like Oscar Wilde.

'Now there is a case in point. A life of tragedy which fashioned the greatest comedy of all time, and written in a week.'

'At Hove. Brunswick Terrace, actually.'

'Thank you, Dame Rose, for that piece of fairly useless information.'

'Don't call me that. Don't call me Dame Rose any more.'

'Why not?' He looked startled by her sudden intensity.

Rose sighed, and then bit a nail, suddenly confused. 'I don't know. It makes me feel like a *déjà vu*. As if I have already had my career, as if it is all over already. I mean, I read the other day that Laurence Olivier said the worst moment of his life was when he went to the National and there was the theatre named after him – the Olivier. He said when he saw that he realized that he might as well have been dead. You know, no point in going on, once your name is on a theatre, you must feel you're no longer an actor, but a building. I felt just that, a minute ago, when you called me "Dame Rose" I felt just as he must have done, as if I have already been an actor, played all the great parts, and that it was over already.'

Charles smiled, and gently removing her chewed finger from her mouth he smiled at her, and when Rose looked up at him she saw that the expression in his eyes was kind, and that he recognized that this was just a form of nerves.

'A little touch of petulance is only to be expected. You will be brilliant at your audition tomorrow.'

'I want so much to be!'

But she was not. She was terrible, and when she came home, she did not make 'humma, humma' noises all the way up the stairs to her room as she would normally have done, and neither did she knock on his door and tell him how it had all gone, but crept up to her room and hid until it was dark, and after it was dark she refrained from putting on a light, or eating, or doing anything. She just lay on her bed, and thought, *How* could *I have been so terrible?*

Josh did not call, and Josh was never around when Melinda was up and doing with his father's mare, but really, in so many ways Melinda could only feel thankful. She thought she knew, absolutely, how he was feeling and she was feeling the same, and so it seemed to her that they had reached a sort of truce, avoiding each other, not really wanting so much as to catch sight of each other, such was their inability to deal with the awkwardness that their parents had, inadvertently, created for them both.

It had to be faced. Their friendship, nearly romance, must be, and was, over, so when it turned out that he had touched base only briefly before going off to India with Cyndi, all that Melinda felt was not hurt, but huge relief.

Claire never asked Mellie about Josh now, thank God. In fact they both found that when they were together they really only talked about future things, and about what they were going to do, and how they were going to do it. Melinda was going to win something simply brilliant on the Grey Goose, and Claire was going to London.

'Going to London?'

Claire nodded, taking off her specs and putting them on her head and clearing her throat, and standing tall to give herself a feeling of authority, which she sometimes found that she had to do with Mellie, Mellie being the eldest and now seeming almost to be standing in for Hope, as it were, what with one thing and another.

'Well, I must, really, Mellie. I mean there's nothing for me here, not now I have my pathetic little A level in History of Art.'

'It's not pathetic, it's brilliant and you know it. You studied and studied for that exam, and you passed. But I thought you were going to do Open University now?'

'Not much point, Mellie. Not here. There are so few people and until I've passed my driving test like you, what can I do? And now that Letty and James are all snug up at the Mill House, what on earth should I do going on being here? Much as I like farmers they don't have many paintings or anything, and no-one round here is friendly, not like in London, where Rose says everyone can find someone they can get on with. Big cities aren't lonely at all, they're where it's at, Mellie, really. Particularly if you have my interests. I liked it here at first, but I don't any more. Not now Aunt Rosabel has died and Dads – *Alexander*, rather – has gone off with Muffin Hateful, and poor Mums is still not better. The trouble is, really, I thought sitting with her was going to bring her round, but I don't think so any more, not really, Mellie.'

Claire stopped, not able to go on with what she might have said, which none of them could bring themselves to say, about turning off the machine, about what to do.

'Jack still believes she's there, that she's still with us.'

'So did I – you know that; particularly that once when I thought I felt her squeeze my finger. But let's face it, it only happened that once, Mellie, it never happened again, so now, well, now – now I think it must have been just my stupid imagination and I really should not have raised all our hopes that way. I felt quite bad about it, really I did. I should never have said, not really.'

Melinda shook her head. Finishing her elderflower and water she looked at Claire for the first time since she had begun talking to her, really looked at her, in the eyes, as if she was a barrister about to cross-question her in a court, which Claire hoped devoutly she was not going to do, but her tone was suddenly so serious, and the look on her face so solemn, that Claire could not guess at what was coming.

'You should never say that, Claire.'

For a split second Claire thought it was actually going to be one of those rare moments when Mellie lost her rag. She was really not looking forward to that. But far from it.

'You were quite right to say what you thought you felt. Just because nothing else happened after that doesn't mean that it *didn't* happen, or it *did* happen. It just means that you thought you felt, or perhaps did feel, *something*. And of course you have to go to London. It's important that you do. Goodness, there's nothing round here for you, and if I didn't have the Grey Goose and really love the country, I would be going with you.'

'And leaving Mums?'

There was a pause, and then Melinda nodded. 'Yes, Claire, and leaving Mums. Really. There is no point in pretending. I have to be truthful. I would be doing just like you, if I was you. Or Rose. But I'm not. You see, I do love the country, Claire, I really do, every little thing about it gives me pleasure. The dawn, the night sky, the getting up and the going to bed, and all the in-between times, they all make me so happy. But that doesn't mean that you and Rose have to like it too, and let's face it – most young people *don't* like it, because what they want to do is definitely not going on in the country, is it? It's going on in cities all over the world, but not in the countryside where things are just growing and being, nothing more, and nothing less. Of course that's what I like, the feeling of being part of all that growing and the seasons coming and young life in the fields and paddocks, all of it inextricably inter-linked, part of something so beautiful, somehow. And when I ride out I can go so quietly on Goosey that nothing moves, everything, all the rabbits and the deer, and all kinds of birds, they all just think that she and I are part of them, and we *are*, for that hour or so, and it feels as if it is all flowing through me – you know, the way that the water flows over the reed beds to purify them, so it sometimes seems to me that we should be a sort of reed bed to nature, so that whatever happens we are helping, we are making things better. So. That's why I love the countryside, because that is how I feel.'

'Of course; and because of your love for horses.' Claire let out a little sigh. She had tried to like horses when she was young. She certainly liked looking at them, but she had never been much of a rider, and now that she was grown up she knew that she never would be. When she watched Mellie riding she knew that it was a real gift, that Mellie just felt marvellous *to* the horse when she was up, that she did not just have balance, she had everything, gentle hands, intelligence. She knew all this from watching Mellie having lessons with the colonel. She and Goosey learned so quickly that even the colonel – old Stricty-boots – was surprised at just how fast they both were at picking up on what he wanted.

Claire knew almost nothing about dressage, less about things like 'bascules' – which she had only lately discovered was making a rounded shape when a horse jumped – and less again about what should be done to count strides when horse and rider faced the most terrifying-looking jumps across country, but she did know when something looked right.

Mellie and Goosey looked so right together, just one organism, not separated, just horse and rider as one. And Goosey, as a consequence, took such care of Mellie that not even Claire, who worried about nearly everything, ever worried about her. Which was probably wrong, because, after all, anything could happen, but somehow when Mellie was up Claire felt it was not going to. She inspired confidence.

'You're a brilliant rider, Mellie.'

'Oh, no, I don't think so, Claire. But I might have a brilliant horse.'

'No, really, I think you're brilliant. Aunt Rosabel always called you a "natural". She said you rode like her mother, she often said that. Same way of looking on a horse, she said. She thought a lot of you, Mellie, you know that, more than of us. She thought a lot of you.'

They both knew that Claire was trying to cheer Mellie up about Claire's leaving, and that pretty soon she would be confessing to having found a room in London, in a house, nowhere near Rose but much the same sort of set-up, and that she would go on to tell Mellie that she had also found a job, and that there would be all those kinds of conversations that people had when they were pretending that they were interested in something that they did not really want to happen, when they were not saying what they would really like to say, which was, *Wish you weren't leaving me alone* and *Wish I wasn't leaving either, but what can I do?*

More than that, they were both saying, *This is goodbye, isn't it? We're not going to be so much to each other now, other people, other things will come between us. We'll still be sisters, but it won't be the same.'*

And of course, in so many ways, Claire was not just saying goodbye to her eldest sister, she was saying goodbye to her mother too.

'I'm going to London, Mums, but that doesn't mean that I won't be thinking about you all the time, and rooting for you, and I mean really. I have a sort of job interview thing, and I have joined a secretarial agency which means that I can pay my way until I get a good job, and also means that I can send a bit home to Mellie for flowers and things for you. Because just to begin with I won't be coming back every weekend. Train fares are too expensive, and I haven't passed my driving test, but as soon as I have the money I shall be coming back to see you, don't you worry. And I shall buy myself a Mini or something, and I will be simply whizzing down the motorway to see you, and Mellie, and we'll all be together just like we have been these last days and weeks since James was born. I know you were thrilled when I told you about passing my silly little exam thing, I don't know why, but I just know you were. Just as I know Mellie will be coming in, and of course Jack never leaves you for more than a few hours. He does love you so, Mums. It is so nice, that, to have a man love you as much as Jack loves you. And now you both have James, that's quite something, isn't it? Quite something, Mums.'

That was enough really, Claire thought, getting up and going to the door, but she came back for one more thing.

'And Mums, I do love you. Just because I'm going doesn't mean I don't, you know. And another thing. I'm going to make a great big success of London, for you. Just like you always said, *Got to make something of yourself, Claire, or else what is the point?* I didn't really know what you were on about then, but I do now, and Mums – I'm on my way!'

The house to which Claire had been directed was a tall London house, perhaps six storeys, she thought, squinting myopically up at it, with the basement, or was it seven? Whatever it was in all, as she rang the doorbell she could not help feeling relieved that she was not going to have to clean it for Mr Crawford Haye, that she was only going for an interview for the post of part-time assistant, because his long-time secretary had fallen ill.

'Come up!'

The voice on the intercom was immediately boyish, and warm, and yet older, because having said 'Come up' he then added, 'Come up, do, third floor. Lots of stairs, but you're young, you'll manage!'

There were some houses, and Claire had only visited a few, that from the moment you stepped into them embraced you. From the moment you walked in they put their arms around you, and their colours and their paintings, their flowers and their plants, everything, shouted a welcome. Not grand, not standing on ceremony, but somehow perfect. And you knew immediately that you never wanted to leave, that you wanted to stay in or around them, and that to leave them at all, like parting from some enchanting friend, would be to suffer a sense of loss, to be left with the feeling that something had been taken away from you. As if you had been given a present, and then someone had run after you and taken it back, thinking you not deserving of it.

That was exactly how Claire felt as she climbed the stairs to meet Crawford Haye. So that by the time she reached the third floor and he was waiting for her, smiling, older, tall, and distinguished, she was already in love with him. And she knew it, just from climbing the stairs of his house, from traversing his hall and seeing his paintings, from looking at the carpet on his stairs, and that being so, it followed that she had to impress Mr Haye, because if she had fallen in love with him, she had to get the job.

Of course she could not say as much to him, and naturally, as soon as she followed him into his offices – cream walls, more paintings of the most beautiful kind – she felt inadequate.

Not that Claire was down-at-heel by any means. Before she left Keeper's she had gone to great trouble to see that all her clothes were mended and her shoes soled and heeled. And Mellie had been brilliant to her, giving her some truly 'London' clothes, things that Aunt Rosabel and Dads had brought back that day so long ago, which, Mellie said, she had no use for now, not really, since she was never out of jodhpurs. Nevertheless, in her plain-cut navy-blue jacket and skirt, as she stood in the high-ceilinged elegant room Claire felt that she knew just how some messenger boy from a postal service might feel in his serge clothes, with his biro at the ready for signing. Plain, ordinary, serviceable, and no part of this other life that she sensed around her. This life where every object had a value of its own. Where perhaps William Morris's exhortation to surround yourself with something beautiful had been not absorbed, but inhaled. Here in this room not to be beautiful would be to stand out.

In fact, Claire realized, as she shook hands and

sat down – feet together, ankles not crossed – here in this world that Crawford Haye had created, everything was in reverse of everything that happened in real life. Out there in the street if you were beautiful people turned to stare, or lingered to look at you, not quite able to believe that you were real. Here everything was decorative and fascinating. Here – and at this realization Claire gave an inner sigh, the sigh that someone might give who had searched and searched for some kind of truth and at last had found it – here was perfection.

Crawford, on the other hand, not knowing how Claire was feeling, could only stare in satisfaction at what he saw before him. His secretary, Marjorie Vickers, his adored right hand dogsbody, was away nursing her sick mother, and her stand-in, sent by some footling agency, had proved so unsuitable for his particular needs at that moment that it was laughable. He needed someone for a specific purpose, now.

Not tomorrow, not the next day, but now.

And here she was, and unbelievably she was not in the least like the last one they had sent, skinny-bodied, multi-ringed, with a satin tan and a tight little body in a microskirt, not to mention blond locks and a dazzling white-toothed smile – she was round-eyed, a tiny bit plump, bespectacled and wearing navy clothes such as nannies in parks wore.

In short, Miss Claire Merriott was perfect for

436

what he wanted, in every way. Not only in looks but in manner, her obvious out-of-town innocence contrasting delightfully with her direct look, a look that had a touching defiance.

'I don't want to know about your word processor proficiency, I don't want to know if you know a Constable from a Miró, I only want to know if you can be trusted to be discreet, Miss Merriott,' he told her, after the usual preliminaries. 'That is what I need to know. Can I trust you?'

Claire shook her head. 'No, I wouldn't say so,' she confessed. 'I find it terribly difficult to keep a secret, so if you want me to keep one, well I can't. I always want to tell someone. I can't help it. I think it comes of having sisters and always telling each other things.'

Crawford stared at this young bespectacled girl in front of him. Was she really *that* trustworthy, was anyone? 'I'm sorry?'

'Well, so am I, actually. I really can't stand anyone telling me a secret, so if you want to tell me one, please don't. It makes me feel as if I've put on weight. I mean I go around feeling the weight of it all the time. I find myself waking up in the morning thinking, *Oh my God, someone's told me a secret! Supposing I forget it is a secret and tell someone I shouldn't!* No, I'm sorry, Mr Haye, I can tell a jolly good lie, as good a lie as the next person as a matter of fact, but I can't lie about this. I can't, simply can't, keep a secret, so please don't ask me to.'

Crawford opened his mouth to say something, and then, frowning, closed it, only to open it again to laugh with genuine amusement.

'Miss Claire Merriott, you must be the only person – besides my secretary Marjorie, that is – whom I find I may be able to trust!'

'Yes, but why do you need to trust me? You mean because of all the valuable things here? I mean, if that is it, well, yes, you can trust me, because I am immensely reliable about things, especially beautiful things.' She nodded at the mallows in their beautiful china bowls, at the small maquettes on tables, dotted about the room, at a collection of Chinese figures of infinite delicacy, at the lamps with their silk shades. 'I have lived with beautiful things, just for a little while, in my great-great-aunt's house, and so I am all right around them. But don't tell me a secret, because I just can't live with those.'

Crawford noticed that once she had actually stopped talking she sat quite still, composed, and there again, the odd contrast between her obvious naivety and her ruthless honesty was suddenly strangely affecting.

Encouraged by this, he crossed from behind the desk to sit down on her side, and he leaned back in his chair, amused and delighted by her, and once he was closer to her Claire could see that this was so, at which she blushed and hoped that he had not noticed, but of course he had, and it made him smile again, because Miss Claire Merriott was not only everything that he wanted for his particular purposes, she was more. She was perfect. Straight up from the country, clean and pressed appearance, polished shoes, her long hair held back by a tortoiseshell Alice band.

'Now. Let's see. We should begin at the beginning—'

Knowing her *Alice*, Claire promptly murmured, '—and go on until we stop.'

Crawford's smile broadened. 'Very good. I always think you can trust people who know their *Alice*.'

'But not with a secret,' Claire insisted.

'We have, I think, established that,' he agreed, and Claire saw at once that he was getting just a little tired of her insistence on her inability to keep a secret because his foot went up and down and he crossed his legs and tapped a small, smooth stone which was on the desk beside him a trifle impatiently.

'Sorry. But I just don't want to let you down.'

'You won't.'

Claire stared at him. His eyes were of a grey-blue that she normally would not have really liked but, in contrast to his blue-grey hair, they were very attractive.

'Here's how it is. You don't know me, and I don't know you, but I have to trust you, because quite frankly I am desperate. Now if I tell you I am an art dealer, or that I deal in art, then I think it is very likely that you will probably instantly despise me, or lose respect for me anyway; but the point is, and it is a point, we are not all the same. And I have honourably distrusted my business life all my life. It just so happens that sometimes I – well, sometimes I find something, and thereby hangs my reputation. Sometimes, through completely fair means, I know that there is a painting which I must acquire, which, perhaps, I have always wanted to acquire, and which sometimes I acquire to keep, but – and here is the big *but* – such is my reputation, if I go to the auction, if I bid for it, or if my secretary Marjorie bids for it, since the rest of the art world knows myself, and Marjorie, we will lose it.'

Claire stared at Crawford. This was more than a secret, it was a conspiracy and she thrilled to the very idea of it, most particularly because a conspiracy was something which, in her mind anyway, was somehow shored up against secrecy. You could not be even remotely tempted to give a conspiracy away, simply because whatever it was would not then happen. Quite different from a secret where it had already happened, and you simply must not let anyone else know that it had. She could not even be tempted to tell Mellie about a conspiracy, because it would be the end of it. Like telling someone you had fallen in love.

'That is why I have to trust you, you see, Miss Merriott. I am so well known that the moment I wave my paddle the price will go rocketing, and . . .' He paused, giving her a considering look, wondering whether or not to play this particular card. Deciding that he would, he finished, '. . . and the painting will be lost to England for ever.'

'That would be awful,' Claire agreed diplomatically. 'We must keep our art in England. Always.'

'I think we must.'

'Too much has been lost. Successive governments have ripped the art world apart, and it is time they were made to see they can't!' she added with a flourish.

'Precisely my feelings. But I must come clean about this particular painting. I shall not be donating it to a museum quite yet. What I shall be doing, I am sorry to tell you, is a great deal less altruistic. If I manage to acquire it I shall be hanging it on the wall, over there, where I can see it and enjoy it.'

'Which is what the artist would have wanted. Entertainment on walls is what pictures are, according to one of our leading painters.'

Crawford frowned. He had never thought of art in precisely that way, but there was no reason not to think of it like that. After all, whether the picture be the *Annunciation of the Virgin Mary* or a bath scene by Bonnard, the ideas behind it – the love of life, devotion to Christianity, or in Bonnard's case a woman – were all the same kinds of themes that filled cinemas, or theatres, or concert halls, and everyone always happily described those as 'entertainment'.

'You have thought a great deal about these things, haven't you, Miss Merriott?'

'It's living in the country. All that time on your hands!'

Claire started to pull on her gloves. Precious leather gloves that she had bought especially for the interview, knowing that they could give the right impression, that they would reassure, in case the rest of her should fail to do so.

'Wiltshire?' He glanced down at her CV and for a second Claire's mind raced back to Keeper's Cottage where Mellie was, and then to the Mill House where the 'littles' were, and from there to the County Hospital where Aunt Rosabel had died and where her mother now lay.

They were all so spread out now, all of them in different parts of the country, and all waiting for something to happen to them. Mellie with the Grey Goose and Mums with her struggle for life, and Jack with Mums, and Rose in London, somewhere quite near probably, auditioning for drama schools – everyone, just waiting for something to happen.

So when Mr Haye said that one word 'Wiltshire' it was no longer a county, it was a whole pattern of life. It was people. It was waiting.

'Yes, the Marlborough Downs, Pewsey Vale, all that,' Claire murmured while wondering if he could read her mind, or follow it, as helicopters followed cars from above, or trains whizzing down rails.

If Mr Haye had been able to follow her train of thought, what would he have thought? He would not have thought Claire was some quite dull girl in navy-blue clothes, he would have thought of her as being complicated and highly strung, or as how Aunt Rosabel used sometimes to describe people – *nervy*.

'So here's how it is, Miss Merriott, because we had better get on with the business of the day. I want you, as you are, nothing changed, to go tomorrow and bid for a painting for me. It should not be very expensive. Perhaps at most five thousand pounds. But – and this is the catch – the five-thousand-pound painting might not be the painting we are buying. However, if you manage to acquire this quite cheap painting for me, I shall personally see that you are amply rewarded. The facilities between my bank and the auction house are all in place, so you need have no worries on that score. All you have to do is take your place, sit quiet and bid, but be sure not to throw yourself around. Don't look at anyone, try not to attract any attention to yourself *at all*.' He paused. 'Now. Have you got all that? I mean have you followed me so far?'

Claire nodded, and then, after a second during which she stared at him, holding her breath, not quite able to believe what he was asking her, a complete stranger, to do, she said, 'Yes.'

'Good. The painting is number fifty-four in the catalogue, and will probably come up mid to late morning, which will be to our advantage. It is a genuine country house sale, held out of town, and there are a number of exquisite and very valuable Persian rugs at the start of the sale, and they will be attracting the most interest – in fact they will be attracting all the interest. The paintings are not considered to be much, but there is some very fine china, which always goes for a great deal if it is, as these pieces apparently are, in perfect condition. Try to sit somewhere in the middle of the room, about ten or twelve rows from the front. Do not come in too early in the bidding. Wait to see if there is any interest elsewhere in the room, or from telephone bids, but make sure that when you do bid, you catch the auctioneer's eye. If the weather is bad, which it is forecasted to be, you may well acquire the painting for under five thousand. But if you don't, don't worry. Do not look too keen, do not overbid, do not take enormous leaps in the bidding and above all try to look casual, as if – take it or leave it, you don't really mind whether it falls to you or not. But whatever you do, come home with it!'

Armed with the catalogue, ten minutes later Claire found herself on the way back to her basement room in a house in Pimlico hardly able to believe what she had just been told she was going to do. She knew of course that genuine country house sales always attracted international interest, but once back in her bed-sitting room sight of the

444

catalogue proved that this was more than an ordinary country house sale. Since the family that were selling off their effects, not to mention their house, had once been international financiers, this was less like a country house sale and more like the selling up of a small kingdom.

Several items had already attracted press attention, and the following morning, having bought her daily paper from a local newsstand and walked home with it held in front of her face, absorbed by the importance of the sale and its prominence in the newspaper, she at once realized from the report that the house in question was in Hertfordshire and that it would take the car that Crawford Haye was sending for her quite a time to reach its destination.

Not wishing to risk failure by so much as a misplaced hair, Claire dressed exactly as she had the day before. Navy-blue jacket, navy-blue skirt, white blouse, black shoes, leather gloves. The hire car called for her promptly.

'Tell your sister I'm here for her, will you, dear?'

Claire stared at the driver. 'I am my sister,' she said, just a little crossly.

The driver stared. 'You don't look more than fourteen.'

'That's because I have not finished dressing. If you don't mind waiting. I shall not be more than a few minutes.'

That was a lesson in how she must look, all right! Claire bolted back into her bed-sitting room and flew to the drawer that held what little make-up she owned. Having applied it with as heavy a hand as was possible without looking clownish, and after only a couple of minutes' concentrated work, she was able to stand back and stare at her image with some satisfaction. Now there stared from the cheap mirror someone who, there was little doubt, would undoubtedly be considered to be a much older person than she was. The brightness of the lipstick helped, of course, and the mascara. Satisfied that she looked more like a person who might be able to bid for a painting costing five thousand pounds, she then seized a charming and quite modish hat that had once, fleetingly, belonged to Aunt Rosabel, which Claire had brought up to London for no good reason except that she could not bear *not* to bring it with her, reminding her as it did of their summer at Hatcombe, and crammed it down on her head.

The driver opened the door and having ushered her into the back he settled himself into the front of the old Rover and commented, 'That's a bit better. You look old enough to run for Prime Minister now. As a matter of fact, there's a bit of a coincidence today. I went to the preview of this thing, a couple of days ago. There's been so much talk in the press and that, and you know – what with all that stuff on TV I thought I'd have a butcher's at what's on offer. Some quite nice things, really, quite nice.'

Remembering the secrecy that was so important

to her mission for Mr Haye, Claire smiled as vaguely as possible.

'Yes, some quite nice things,' he went on. 'I suppose since you work for that Crawford Haye, you know he's on the telly sometimes? Talking about paintings, and that. Quite an expert. Course my firm, we've been driving him about quite a lot, to this and that, particularly lately. Quite a nice man, and knowledgeable of course. Very knowledgeable. Extremely knowledgeable, I'd say.'

He paused and, since the traffic had come to a standstill, he glanced at Claire in the mirror and smiled. 'I expect you're bidding for something important, though, aren't you? Not like me – just loo brushes and that, or Nanny's old rocking chair!'

'No, nothing very much, not really.'

He grinned. 'Oh, and keeping your trap shut too!'

Claire smiled, embarrassed by his curiosity, and only too relieved when, the traffic having moved off, he turned up the radio and they listened to Classic FM all the way to the Mountfort Sale.

The sale started late. The crowd was bigger than forecast, and the atmosphere, as at all genuine sales, excited and interested. Claire made sure to look at several pictures, but most of all she looked at Lot 54. It was so ordinary that it was almost breathtaking, just a dull-looking gentleman and his horse. So ordinary that she suddenly knew that behind this very ordinary painting there must be some work of great genius, some work that only

Crawford Haye knew about, which he had sent her to acquire for him.

As the men in their dark suits, and the women in their uniformly dark charcoal-grey suits with bands of pearls at the neck, or dark ribbons edging their lapels with velvet, took their place, as the crowd became one large impatient audience, waiting to make their bids, eyes down, catalogues in hand, paddles ready to wave, Claire realized that she was literally sick with nerves. She must not fail Crawford Haye. She must not let him down, and yet the divide between success and failure at an auction was notoriously slender. She might bid too early and send the price up, she might bid too late and lose it.

As predicted, the bidding for the rugs and the china was intense and exhausting, such was their known value, and telephone bids for them were particularly intense. However, again as predicted by Crawford, the paintings came up just before lunch, which was to their advantage quite simply because the call of the bar was stronger than the attraction of various small paintings attributed to minor artists. Indeed, as the auctioneer ripped through the sale of small painting after small painting, time, having hung heavy, started to break into a gallop, so that by the time Claire heard the words 'Lot number fifty-four, a small eighteenth-century portrait believed to be attributed to John Coleshill the younger, *Mr Jennings and Bashful*' it seemed to her that this was no longer the painting she had been sent to acquire, but a dream, and that she was sitting back listening to other people's bids and somehow the whole thing was nothing to do with her. It was just like waiting to come into a room where you knew there were people who did not like you in the least, but it had to be done. And now!

'Three thousand pounds, am I bid three thousand pounds?'

Claire caught the auctioneer's eye and up went her paddle.

'The lady in the seat in front of me in the straw hat is bidding three thousand pounds. Three thousand pounds, am I bid three thousand five hundred pounds? I am bid three thousand five hundred pounds by the gentleman in the back row.'

Claire just knew that he must be a professional, some hard-headed art dealer hiding away in the back row, but she did not care or dare to look round, judging it to be better if he did not see her face, remembering the driver saying, *Tell your sister I'm here for her, will you, dear?*

In her head, the bidding seemed to have assumed the same noise as her train waiting to pull out of the station only a week earlier, when she had left Mellie – waiting to pull away from her, to leave her behind. And there would never be enough time to put her suitcase into the luggage place or say goodbye properly, or do any of those things which were so necessary, four thousand pounds, four thousand five hundred pounds.

What would she do if it went up to six thousand or seven thousand? Crawford Haye would be so disappointed. But she might have to go well beyond six or seven thousand, she might have to go to ten thousand, and he would never *trust* her again. She would never trust herself again.

'Five thousand pounds, I am bid five thousand pounds by this lady here, and five thousand five hundred pounds, and six thousand pounds from the lady in the middle here, six thousand pounds. Six thousand pounds. Any more bids for this fine little portrait of *Mr Jennings and Bashful*? Very well, going, going, gone. Gone to the lady in the middle. Thank you, madam. Now my next lot is a small painting entitled *Pug with Ducklings* by a well-known Victorian dog painter, Yarwood St John. Four hundred pounds, I shall begin the bidding at four hundred pounds—'

Claire rose to her feet. Her head was pounding, her mouth was dry, and her legs felt as if they were going to give way under her. She edged her way out of the row in which she had been seated and made towards the exit, anxious only to be away, to collect the painting and go, worried too that it had cost so much more than Mr Haye had wanted her to pay for it.

But as she started to hurry up the side of the auction room the man in the back row, the man she knew had been bidding against her, straightened up, stood up, and followed her. When she saw who it was, Claire's plans to leave with the painting changed immediately, and she quickly made sure that he lost her in the crowd struggling towards the luncheon tent.

Chapter Sixteen

There – it sat beside her on the taxi seat, carefully wrapped and put into a cardboard box. A not very large painting, medium-sized in fact, meant to be eighteenth-century, attributed to John Coleshill the younger, and yet Claire already felt that it was something else, not just an ordinary portrait of this Mr Jennings and his mare Bashful but something really out of the ordinary. And as the taxi drew away from the station, weaving its way slowly in and out of the traffic, and she watched small children walking home from school, and the street lights coming on, and the other thousand things that spring in town seems to herald – awnings being pushed up, dustbins put out, café chairs and tables with tourists bravely seated at them – Claire continued to turn over in her mind the possible provenance of the picture.

The whole experience of the day had left her with feelings that were at once ridiculously euphoric and strangely fearful. As soon as she had realized that the man she had bid against, who it would seem had lost the painting to her, appeared to be following her, Claire decided to take no risks, and instead of taking the hire car back to Knightsbridge as she should have done she had escaped to a payphone and ordered a station taxi to collect her from the back drive of the house. Finally, taking delivery of the painting and clutching a plain cardboard box with it carefully wrapped inside, she had found herself hiding from the hire car driver, realizing that due to the tensions of the day she had most likely become totally paranoid, seeing the most respectable people as potential thieves.

But before slipping off to meet the taxi she had forced herself to ring Mr Haye and give him the bad news that she had spent a thousand pounds more than he wanted her to spend.

There was a long silence, and then he laughed. 'Miss Merriott, just get home in one piece, that's all. I shouldn't have cared had you spent three thousand more. You're sure it's number fifty-four?'

'Oh, yes, it's number fifty-four all right,' Claire agreed, and she wondered whether to tell him that she was not coming back by the hire car, but thinking that he might worry at the idea of his precious work of art travelling on public transport she said nothing.

She had barely had time to say her name into the entry phone when the buzzer clicked and the door swung open.

'Come up! Come up! And make sure to shut the door behind you!'

Five minutes later Claire was sitting in a small

old leather-covered armchair with a fresh cup of coffee while Crawford Haye stood by the window carefully examining the painting she had just bought on his behalf. Even though she hardly knew him Claire could see that he could hardly believe his good fortune.

'Good,' he said, finally, and he shook his head. 'Very good. Now tell me what happened.'

Claire had always found that when she told stories to some people they just did not understand, not deep down, why something was funny, or something else was strange, or why you had felt something at a particular moment. And with that realization, try as you might, you petered out, unable to interest yourself, let alone them; such was not the case with Crawford Haye.

She began at the beginning and she went through right until she stopped, and he was quite silent all the time she was talking, seeming, or so it appeared to Claire, to be appreciating everything, her nerves, the crowded tent, waiting for fifty-four to come up, waiting to pay for the painting, waiting for the station taxi.

'You didn't come back in the car?'

Claire shook her head. She might as well be honest. 'No, Mr Haye. I expect you're going to go bananas, but I took a taxi to the station and came back on the train. I am sorry, but you see, I had this idea. Don't laugh. Although I don't blame you if you do. I had this idea that the driver was after the painting. I don't know why, but I just had this idea, because of all the publicity and you being who you are – you know, the man with the X-ray eyes who can see the original painting behind a fake – I thought, supposing – well, just supposing someone knows that I'm bidding for you, they might follow me, or something. And the thing was—'

'Yes?'

'The driver did.'

'What?'

'The driver did try to follow me.'

She had his full attention so it was quite fun to make him wait to hear what had happened.

'And you know what, Mr Haye? That driver – he was also the man who bid against me!' She paused, and then shrugged her shoulders. 'Probably just being cheeky, I expect.'

Claire took a taxi back to Pimlico, by way of a sort of posh gesture to herself. At the end of this day which she knew she could never forget, she felt as if she had done something particular. Better than that, perhaps – that she had been something which she had never thought she could be. She had been brave. Hitherto she had always suspected herself of lacking courage, not being horsy like Mel, or balletic like Rose, not being anything but a bit of a bookworm, really. But now she felt she had almost done something physically brave, going to an auction and bidding on behalf of the famous Crawford Haye.

She let out a sigh of such loud satisfaction that she was surprised that the taxi driver did not hear. Because, quite apart from the painting being whatever it was, it was such a great story. And as soon as the painting was cleaned, which would probably take months, she would be able to find out the end of that story, the whole marvellous history of the painting would come to light, and that would be a story in itself.

Inevitably she found herself watching everything from the window of the taxi through a mist of appreciation.

Yesterday, before the auction, she had felt like a child, perhaps even thought like a child, but now all her childhood seemed to have vanished, to have become sorted and set into images, as photographs are sorted and carefully pasted into an album. Images of apples in a store, the blue and white china that her mother used to collect and set out on their dresser back in West Dean, the dew on the spiders' webs which draped the bushes at Hatcombe in early morning, lit by the slowly waking sunlight. Mellie galloping past her on Goosey. Rose dancing in the barn to make her laugh and cheer them all. Letty staring into James's face sucking on two fingers as Claire gave him his bottle. They were all there in her album, never to be forgotten.

But now too she knew that they were shut away in her private album, to be replaced by cosmopolitan images. Bustling strangers, red buses, tree-lined avenues, smart shops, galleries and clamour, and the drone of the traffic thrumming endlessly past everything, the fumes on the early evening air still rising, people outside the windows of the cab still walking, but this time away from their offices, back to the homes they had made in the honeycomb of the city. Somewhere their rooms too would be filled with their pasts, their hopes, and their futures. And she was part of it all at last. All around her the noise and thrust of a life of which she had, in the past few hours, become quite suddenly a part, because Crawford Haye had offered her a job.

An hour later, changed and brushed, Claire was back in Cheshire Street with her new employer and waiting in the upper studio for him to choose a tie.

'I hate ties, but since we are going out of town to celebrate this marvellous buy of yours . . .'

Claire smiled. It was hardly *hers*.

She had pressed the bell and as usual he had called to her through the intercom, but this time it was to come up to the 'top room'. Doing as she was bid she had climbed the stairs, up and up, and up again until suddenly she had found herself standing in an immensely light room with a curving conservatory roof up to which stretched indoor trees and exotic tropical plants, tracing beautiful patterns against the walls, and towards the shining glass above them.

Off this room was a dressing room in which Claire could now see her host and employer, standing fully dressed except for a tie.

'You choose,' he ordered her, holding up two ties in front of him for Claire to inspect. 'I am hopeless at choosing ties. Marjorie usually does it for me.'

Claire stared at the two ties, which to her seemed identical, before looking at her employer's shirt and suit, his face, the colour of his eyes and the tone of his skin.

'I suppose it is being a bit obvious, but I should say that the bluish one would set off your eyes,' she murmured, because in some ways she had only just noticed that Crawford Haye was handsome, slender of face, and tall and slim with an athletic figure set off by expensive tailoring.

'Ah, right, so this is your first choice?'

'Yes.'

'You know what they say about first choices.' He expertly flicked his collar up and started to tie her choice while walking back to his dressing room.

'No, I don't know what they say about first choices.'

She waited for a put-down. And as she did so, for no reason, she could hear her father's voice coming to her from long ago. *Really, Kipper, you are so slow on the uptake. Really, Claire, you should know your own mind! Poor old four-eyes, never knows what she likes!*

'No,' Crawford called cheerfully back, 'neither do I!'

They drank one glass of what seemed, to Claire at any rate, to be perfect white wine from expensive flute glasses before he rang down to the basement to tell his housekeeper that they were leaving. They walked through a small garden planted with shrubs set about in pale aquamarine-painted boxes so that Crawford could collect his car from his garage. He instructed Claire to wait in the alley for him, and there was a sound which, to Claire, was more reminiscent of a jungle animal than a motor car. A moment later Claire found herself being called to 'climb in' to a Ferrari.

'My indulgence!' He looked suddenly boyish and conspiratorial, smiling at her as if he had kept his car a secret from everyone except her. 'It's a Daytona Ferrari. I've always wanted one. And, well. We only pass this way once, don't we? Know anything about cars?'

'About as much as I do about nuclear science.'

This was a remark that Jack sometimes made, but the first time Claire had tried it out on anyone. The results were gratifying, because Crawford laughed. 'Never mind, anyway, this is an experience you will always remember. Second only to driving a Daytona is being driven in one.'

'Where are we going?'

'Somewhere very special. Such a celebration. New car, new acquisition – which by the way is starting to be cleaned tomorrow – thanks to you, the race is on. So. We must celebrate, and some-where very special.'

Wherever this *somewhere* was, it was miles out of London, a destination to which Crawford drove Claire not like a boy racer, but in the manner in which she was slowly coming to realize he did everything, elegantly and expertly.

It was a journey that Claire knew was always going to be memorable. It just had that feeling. Not just because she had landed a job, or bought the picture, not even because the great Italian car seemed to have a life of its own, but because Crawford Haye turned out to be the most delightful companion, seeming to have a story for everywhere they passed, until at last they reached the Cotswold countryside, leaving the main Banbury Road, and finally turning into the small courtyard of a beautiful old country house built on a bend of the River Windrush.

'This,' Crawford said, looking around and smiling at everything as if it was all familiar, 'is not just the best restaurant in England, it is one of the greatest restaurants you will find anywhere.'

He was greeted as an old friend, which perhaps he was, Claire thought, glancing round, and then instantly turning back as she saw another couple arriving.

'Something the matter?'

She shook her head. 'No. At least, yes. Are we going straight in?'

She must have looked tense, because Crawford

answered quickly, 'Of course,' ignoring the fact that he had just asked someone to bring them a bottle of champagne. 'Don't let's bother with champagne now, we'll have it with the pudding,' he went on easily, following her into the well-lit restaurant with its views over the river. 'And shall I ask the waiter to put whoever it is you're trying to avoid in the next room?'

'Thank you.'

Claire had shot ahead of him, and now, having seen her seated, he left her, and 'had a word'. She stared at the river outside. Of all the worst luck, on an evening like this to see those two, of all the luck.

But happily Crawford was too well known not to have influence with the staff, and so the room remained serenely unoccupied by any but themselves and an elderly couple celebrating their golden wedding, and they were able to eat crab done in some way that was light and delicious, and then sole, equally light and delicious, and after that little tranches of lamb on a bed of vegetables, without Claire once feeling that she was being watched, or that she could not carry on as if that wretched couple were not dining under the same roof.

During one of the pauses Crawford said, 'You don't have to call me "Mr Haye", you know.'

Claire smiled and then wondered if it was not a little early to first-name an employer, and a second later she heard Aunt Rosabel's voice intoning, *Once you have been invited to first-name, you take it*

up, and not before, that is the rule, Claire dear.
Everyone has the right to be called what they wish, even
if it is Fishface, not what someone else wishes.

But despite this comforting memory of her old
relative and although she dropped saying Mr
Haye she could not bring herself to call him
Crawford. She probably would, in time, but at that
moment it seemed strange, just not quite right,
somehow.

'Tell me about the painting.' She found she had
lowered her voice, as if anyone hearing might
know immediately to go to Cheshire Street and
find it. 'Why do you think – know – that there is
this other one underneath it? Why are you so
certain that it's been over-painted?'

They were pausing before cheese and a
pudding. Crawford smiled at her serenely, not
only a man well dined and wined but a man who
had accomplished something at a time when he
most needed so to do.

'I mean, I know you have the reputation of
having X-ray eyes—'

'Oh, that rumour! Mind you, I have no intention
of discouraging it. It drives my competitors mad,
I promise you.'

'It must,' Claire agreed, but she was too curious
to leave the matter alone. 'So how do you know
about this other one? I mean, obviously you can
tell it's *over*-painted by textures and things, but
how do you know that it might be *this* one that is
hiding beneath?'

'Easy, really. And nothing to do with X-ray eyes, alas! You see . . .' Crawford paused for a second. 'You see, art discovery is only research, but occasionally when you think you have researched a provenance accurately, for some reason or another you find that you have actually got it wrong. At other times, as with this, you more or less *know* you've got it right.'

He paused once more, and ordered them both a pudding and some sweet wine to accompany it before continuing.

'I actually knew about this painting by chance, which is really the best way. I was told all about it by one of my aunts, of all people. You see, she was a great friend of the former owner of Mountfort – the house where you were today. This friend, Zelda Francks, had inherited the painting from her father, a banker. The father was a man of great character. Not only did he love art as much as he loved to live, love, eat and drink, he loved this country. But not our tax system. So, although he remained domiciled in England, he went to great trouble to hide some of his wealth. He hid it all over the place. Switzerland, Austria, America – wherever. But not his precious paintings. He simply could not part with those. Consequently when this country faced the threat of a Nazi invasion he had many of his greatest paintings over-painted.'

Claire nodded. Of course. Hide a great painting behind a lesser fake.

'Quite. A good idea, don't you think? And of course, being a very rich man, he had them *very* well faked. No problem. Well. Happily we were not invaded as had been forecast, but unhappily he died very soon after the war, and Zelda, his heiress and only child, naturally set about selling the hidden treasures or restoring them to their former glory. And very skilfully too, I may say. Except, halfway through this process of restoration she remarried and went to live in Italy. As it happened, at that time – I'm not boring you, am I?'

'No!'

'As it happened, at that time my unmarried aunt, Penny, was Zelda Francks's closest friend, as well as her personal assistant, so she knew all about this, and she always swore that there were still at least two paintings at Mountfort that had either not been restored, or were still labelled with their wrong attributions.'

'So, there is another?'

'Yes, I just don't happen to know which that is! As a matter of fact I was only interested in this one – and if I am right, it will do fine.'

'Who do you think it is?'

Crawford leaned forward and lowered his voice and Claire leaned towards him, dying to hear Renoir, Degas, Monet, Manet – what?

'Cozens.'

Claire straightened up and smiled politely, experiencing a feeling of searing disappointment. Unable to lie, she shook her head and confessed,

'I'm dreadfully afraid that I don't know him.'

Crawford smiled warmly. 'Not many people do. He was actually better than Constable, so Constable thought, but he died too young to leave enough behind him to ensure his popularity. But a true genius, someone that undoubtedly deserves to live for ever. But there. Genius does die young. And when you think, so many of us so ordinary people just go *on* and *on* and *on*. Which all goes to show something!'

'What will you do, if you are wrong?'

'Laugh!'

At which they both did, and then he asked her just what instinct had made her take the train home rather than coming back in the hire car?

'It was probably stupid, I know. But I just felt safer. And I had one of those funny feelings as if there was someone behind me pushing me to take the train, on my own. As if, should I take the car back with that man, he might rob me, and then dump me. It was just a feeling, but not one I could ignore, although I expect you thought I had gone bonkers, didn't you?'

'Not at all! I like people who listen to their inner voices. That's what I've spent my life doing, if you can imagine? I think you did the right thing, coming home by train. Of course, we'll never know if the driver was just bidding you up out of devilment – acting out the Jack the lad – or if he was working for someone else, or if he really fancied buying the painting, and had the money!

But still, you did very well to assume the worst.' It was his turn to stop. 'It very often is,' he finished, and he suddenly threw back his pudding wine in an uncharacteristic gesture of defiance, before signalling to a waiter to bring them two more.

Claire stared. She did not want to say to her new employer *What about the breathalyser?* but – what about the breathalyser?

He smiled, apparently reading her anxious thoughts immediately. 'It's all right, I've booked us both in here tonight!'

This statement cast a cloud as big as the planet over Claire's side of the table, but she smiled nevertheless while allowing her anxious thoughts to take a new and wholly different turn. He must have sensed sudden anxiety.

'Don't worry if you've come unprepared. The management will have laid on everything – tooth-brushes, soap, whatever – and they keep dressing gowns and slippers and all that in every suite.'

After that, her confusion being so evident and herself so suddenly anxious, she refused more wine, inwardly turning over and over in her mind, as she listened to Crawford talking about one of his earlier, justifiably famous finds, just what she was going to do – *if?*

Over and over the potential embarrassment of the moment presented itself, over and over she mentally rehearsed the inevitable words *I like you very much but . . .*

And as she did so, her heart sank, thinking that

it would cost her every bit of her wonderful opportunity, until she remembered her new-found courage, the one that she had accidentally discovered at the Mountfort Sale, and she finished by thinking, almost triumphantly, *I will do as I must always do, I will say what I think and feel, and that is an end to it. All my life I must follow my own desires, never let go of my integrity, never let anyone force me to compromise on what is right or wrong, make up my own mind.*

The evening having come to an obvious conclusion Claire followed Crawford to the reception desk, her mind so firmly made up, and her little speech so carefully prepared, that she really did not care if he had booked a honeymoon suite, but before Crawford could ask for their keys – or key – a voice spoke from behind them.

To Claire it was a very familiar voice. It belonged to the man that Crawford had so kindly helped her to avoid earlier in the evening, someone Claire had hoped would have left the hotel by now, and be well on his way back to London.

'What are you doing here?'

She turned slowly, unsurprised, but nevertheless appalled, because the one thing she had hoped, prayed, for all evening was that, since she had been to such trouble to avoid him, her father would have the decency to ignore her.

'What are you doing here, Clair-oil?'

That had always been his insulting name for her when he was cross.

467

Claire looked very directly at Crawford, and once she found his eyes her own begged him not to say anything. She would handle this.

'Same as you . . .' She was about to say 'Dads' when she hesitated. '*Alexander*.'

She had not thought the use of his name would be such a bucket of cold water over him, but she saw at once that it was. It did not matter, because in her eyes he deserved to be hurt.

Muffin Hateful was standing so near her she could hear her intake of breath at the intentional rudeness, and although she could see the momentary pain in her father's eyes Claire really did not care. Alexander had left them all for this elegant woman in her Armani dark red suede and silk evening suit and her expensive patent leather slippers, and that was his business, his life. But he could not expect to do what he wanted and everything stay the same, he could not take his daughters with him into his new life, not with their mother still lying, all those miles away in that hospital, neither dead nor alive.

'Are you staying here?'

Another anxious glance towards Crawford, and suddenly he did seem to be Crawford and not Mr Haye, and she nodded. 'Yes, I am staying here, with Crawford. Are you?'

A glance at Muffin and then, 'No.'

Of course! Claire remembered. How stupid of her to ask. Muffin had yet another house just nearby somewhere. She remembered it now, but

468

she remembered it in such a way that it was as if she was waking from an anaesthetic, as if for the previous minute she had been put to sleep.

'Well, goodnight.'

Claire nodded.

Crawford had taken charge of two room keys. Claire saw this immediately with a strange mixture of relief and disappointment, but not Alexander. He was too busy frowning down in disapproval at his daughter, still making a feeble attempt at trying to frighten her, but with her new-found courage Claire just stared right back up at him, hoping, hoping – hope against hope – that seeing her apparently about to stay the night in an hotel with a man as old as himself he might experience just some of the hurt that she had felt when they discovered just how much he had deceived them.

No-one said anything more after that. What was there to say? Alexander turned away, pushing Muffin ahead of him, obviously itching to say something to Crawford, but not able to think of what it could be, or even perhaps what it should be, given the circumstances.

Claire walked ahead of Crawford clutching her key, and without a backward glance made her way up the old staircase to bed, followed, some paces behind, by a puzzled Crawford, who realized that he had just witnessed something but was not at all sure what it was.

And so it was that at the top of the stairs,

when they had turned safely out of sight, he turned to Claire and asked, 'Who on earth was that?'

Claire was silent for a second.

'That,' she said, 'was nobody.'

Chapter Seventeen

Still there was nothing. Still the page was a blank. Yes, there were plenty of words there, words all over the place – and notes too. Clusters of notes, crotchets, quavers, minims and semi-breves – and the whole thing didn't add up to as much as a teaspoon of beans.

Jack sighed and shredded yet another manuscript. It just would not arrive, this feeling that he so much wanted to express, and, it seemed, the more he wanted to express it, the less it arrived. It had happened many times before. After his wife deserted him, leaving him with the kids to bring up. After his father died, when Jack had seemed quite unable to settle to anything, not for weeks, but for months. After his second American tour when he had been too exhausted to know his own name. At all sorts of times and in all sorts of places, his creativity had deserted him, and he had wanted to lie down and forget the urge to express himself musically for ever.

But then he thought of Hope, lying there all alone, perhaps listening for him to arrive, for someone to arrive, but locked into that state of consciousness which tells the outside world *I am not here* while all the time being there, all the time knowing about everything and everyone and not being able to speak to them.

Pause on the stairs, he said to himself. *When you're trying to say something important, musically, always pause on the stairs.*

He sat with his head resting on the top of his piano. He was exhausted. He did not think that he had ever felt so tired, or so useless. Nevertheless the sounds of the house came to him, softly creeping up his own state of semi-consciousness. The wind rattling the doors of the house, the water going through the millrace outside, the sound of the sheep that were grazing somewhere up the fields.

He paused on his own particular imagined stairs and, his eyes still closed, he found himself falling asleep while at the same time imagining his emotions, colouring them until they took a shape that was more than real, it was surreal.

After a while the sound came towards him, but this time it had a musical shape, and he no longer felt tired, he felt exhilarated, and he knew exactly what his song had to do. He knew precisely what he wanted of this song, at last he had the sound, he had found the sound.

But while Jack had finally found his sound, Rose Merriott had lost hers.

'I have passed into drama school, I have done what I wanted to do, I thought I would be over the moon, that I would be walking on air,' she confessed to Charles, 'and all I have is this feeling that in going to drama school, I am doing completely the wrong thing.'

'It's only to be expected. Particularly after you thought you did so badly, which obviously you didn't. But auditions are very cold experiences, I'm told by friends who've been through that particular mill.'

They were sitting drinking wine, and Rose kept ploughing her hands through her hair, and, unforgivably, chewing at one of her fingers. Every now and then Charles found himself hitting her lightly on the knuckle.

'I thought that audition I gave was a perfect pill, but no, they thought it was great, so it seemed, and now I find that because they thought it was so good I am accepted – and I don't want to go! I have lost respect for them. If they think that was good, then I don't want to know. How pathetic can you get?'

'What do you think has particularly changed you? There must be something.'

Rose fell silent, and then she cleared her throat, and looked at the professor, her dear professor.

'You!'

Crawford hated anything dull, and for many reasons his life, after Claire left in the evenings, had become dull. The painting was being slowly restored, about two inches of the old paint had been removed, enough to see a fraction of what was underneath. That was all very satisfactory. What was not satisfactory was how lonely he now found himself in the hours he was bereft of the company of Claire, the long, long hours before she arrived back for work the following morning.

He was miserably lonely when she was not at Cheshire Street running up and down the stairs, making his coffee all wrong so that, without her seeing, he had to nip downstairs and make it all over again. It was not that he was in love with her, it was nothing like that at all, he kept reassuring himself. Love was not a possibility. It was that in this, the late afternoon of his life, she was his Indian summer. She was also his fawn.

He loved to watch her running about the place, which she always did, never doing anything at half speed. He loved to hear her laugh, to watch her from an upstairs window as she swung down the street to fetch his suit from the cleaners or on her way to the delicatessen for something for their lunch. He liked everything about her. He had always had Marjorie to look after him, but perversely now, of all times, he found that he wanted to be with this one person for the rest of his life. That he lived for the sound of her knocking at his door, that he spent most of the day trying to think of good reasons why she should stay behind for a drink – friends coming in, someone to hand round the eats, anything.

Even his paintings had become just so much paint on canvas, and while he knew they were beautiful, since she had arrived in his life he did not *feel* they were beautiful any more. He had never anticipated this. He had not anticipated looking forward to seeing another human being with such a passionate intensity.

Crawford Haye is not like this, he reminded himself, in the middle of the night, early in the morning, when he showered, when he ate breakfast, over a late night whisky, at a concert. *He is simply not like this. Not at all*. It was as if he was his own best friend and that this dear, close friend had turned out to be quite the reverse of what he had thought him to be, as if he had been betrayed by this person called Crawford Haye.

Of course the restoration of the painting was fascinating, would be fascinating, and would add a great deal to an already glittering reputation in the art world, but since – well, since lately – this painting, this perhaps Cozen, had become just another work of art to hang eventually in some great gallery for a scattering of tourists to pass it at carefully timed intervals, and say, 'Oh, yes, I read about that being discovered.'

While the girl with the laughing eyes who stuck her spectacles on top of her head whenever she was in a hurry, the girl with hair that seemed always having to be scraped back from her forehead by her tortoiseshell hair band, the girl with the navy-blue clothes and the eternally white shirt – she was what art only imitated. She was the real thing. She made him feel more alive than the

475

discovery of a thousand Cozens would ever make him feel.

But besides the company of Claire there was one other thing for which he found himself pining – his beloved Bryndor.

Josh was back from India, but he had not come back alone.

Jack did not want to say to him, amid the chaos of Letty and James, *Actually, old son, I've just finished the song which I have been waiting for months to be able to write, and I really haven't got time for you!*

Because there was something so affecting about children when they were grown-up but still needed you, he found himself setting about looking after both his son and his unwanted guest – a bug he had picked up in India – rather than going off to stay with his old friend Rusty Naylor in Wales where she now lived in darkest seclusion, willing someone, somewhere, to drag her on and make her sing their next hit.

'You'd better keep away from the littles,' Jack advised him, but saw by the look on Josh's face that it would have been better not to have advised this, so he stopped and began again. 'Look, Josh, I know it's difficult for you – you know, with Letty and James here where you and the others once were, but – and this is a big but – you know you three will always come first with me, don't you?'

Josh nodded, pale-faced and disbelieving. He

476

had lost a ton of weight in India, and was quite rightly feeling very sorry for himself.

'It's your life, Dad,' he said miserably.

Jack started to say, 'Yes, it is, old son,' and then stopped. Josh did not need that. Neither of them needed to say those things to each other, those half things which were really just little fencing statements made to mark time and defend your own point of view. What they all needed was to grow up and get on with things.

'OK, so here's how it is.' He smiled. 'You are going to be moved up to my old games room and into the guest suite in the wing. Those can be yours, from now on, and that will leave Nanny and the littles to get on with their routine, here, with me, in the main house, while you get better. That'll be your space from now on. So. Independence. Your own thing, no-one around, just you.'

He knew that Josh had been after the games room and the adjoining suite for himself for years, and while it was a wrench for his father to make the rooms over to him, it was nothing compared to the smile Jack received from his patient in return.

'Yes, and you can play endlessly, and pointlessly, with and on anything you wish. You have my full permission, I promise. There is one proviso, though, and it is a very strict one.'

'Which is?'

'You get better.'

Following this short exchange Jack felt quite

able to leave for Rusty Naylor's house in Wales the next day, armed with his song, his hopes absurdly, pathetically high.

She lived beside a lovely stretch of water, in a dip of mountains, opposite a beautiful hotel which was both a folly and a tourist attraction, which meant that she could boat across for dinner when she felt like it, or just lie in seclusion overlooking the water when she wanted.

Like so many women who have independent means and have lived for their careers all their lives, her house reflected her interests and her individuality in a way that sprang up and cried *This is me!* from the moment Jack arrived and parked his car, perilously close to the edge of the water, an inlet from the sea.

'It means that you never get fed up of looking at it, you know?' Rusty nodded towards the water. She was slim, trim as a blade and her hair was no longer dark but white, her skin tanned from being out of doors 'messing about in the garden' as she put it, but for the first half a day Jack spoke of everything and anything with her, except music.

Finally unable to bear the tension of not talking about their careers, as they sat up into the small hours reminiscing, Jack found that he had to open her up. He could not bear to leave again the following morning and not know if his song had some sort of chance.

'Rusty—'

'Mmm?'

'We haven't talked music—'

'No.'

'Are you still singing?'

'Sometimes, alone in the boat. Makes the dog howl if I sing in the house!' She laughed and kissed the top of her bearded collie's head. 'He's a bit of a *wusser*. Singing frightens him!'

'Start again. How many song writers have you had after you, these last few years?'

'Do you want the truth or a lie?'

'Oh – a lie, please. Preferably a big fat one.'

'OK so. None.'

'That's what I thought. So I'm just one in a long queue to your door, aren't I?'

'Not a word of a lie, this time. Yup, Jack, you are.'

'Don't you *want* to sing any more, Rusty?'

'Not really. I like living too much, you know?' She wrinkled her nose at the idea of singing again, pausing before elaborating. 'Here's how I see singing nowadays, Jack. You sing, and you sing, and you sing. It kills you but you do, and finally the thing's a hit, you have a hit. And what happens? All your family come after you for your money – and I mean *all* – and after you have given it to them you have to go out and sing some more. You go on gigs, you get exhausted, the record company's making millions to your thousands, you get bad press because your secretary says you owe her money, or you've trashed an hotel room, or not paid your housekeeper, or *something*. And your family still comes after you, for more and more and more. Because it's never enough. And while that is happening, every few months – because the whole world knows you're rich now – someone tries to sue you, or your lawyer says you should sue *someone*, because *he* wants more and more and more, and it's never enough for him either. And none of them likes you! And so finally you think, who needs it? I mean really. Who does? Life is for living. Let them all go away and earn their *own* money. So that's what I've done. I've let them all go away, leave me alone, and earn their own money. And I stopped singing. It's as simple as that, you know?

'Course, there are other things. I mean I actually like being here, on my own. I like watching the water as darkness falls. I like listening to the wild duck, or getting up early to see the dawn and breakfast by the sun rising. I like everything here, but I don't like singing any more, because singing is people, and people ain't been kind to me. See? I'm a loner. I always have been. I always will be. I like the feeling that no-one will call, no-one will visit, and no-one is going to. Except, of course, you, Jack! But then you always were different, weren't you, Jacko? Jacko the maverick they called you, didn't they, boy?'

There was a short pause while Jack sighed inwardly as he realized his chance of getting Rusty to even look at his song had just vanished down the plughole.

'Funny you should mention wild duck. Hope's daughter has just been cast in a film, a remake of Ibsen's *The Wild Duck*. She's been cast in the title role.'

'Hope being?'

Jack looked at Rusty. She would not do his song, he was sure, so why tell her about Hope? Because the song was not just all about Hope, it was for Hope. Why tell her?

But then he gave in and told her anyway, because, when all was said and done, they went way back, and Rusty Naylor had made his first hit single, and when you have done that together you don't just go back, you go deep.

And after that he played her his song, not well, because his nerve had well gone after everything she had just said and anyway it was two in the morning and two in the morning was not his time of day any more.

Still, it seemed silly not to play it to her, after coming all that way.

How Rose had been cast in the part of the Wild Duck, an unknown in the title role, albeit for a small-budget film, was one of those stories that even in the telling, however many years pass, never quite lose their wonder. In fact it had all happened so quickly, she had had so little time since it happened – since the professor had put her up for it, and she had been cast – that only her eldest sister Mellie knew the full story.

But being cast in a part, while it brings many things, does not bring in the bacon, so when a girl lodging in the room below her offered her an opportunity to actually earn some cash, Rose jumped at the chance.

The Wild Duck did not start shooting for a month, and although she did not need to eat, and her work at Saintly Road covered her day to day living expenses, she did need some new shoes. About three pairs, actually.

'It's just running about on a racecourse wearing a suit that makes you look like a kind of poncey air hostess, smiling, and coming home again, that's all. Nothing you can't manage, you know. Oh, and you have to wear a sash that's got some kind of a sponsor's promo on it, but that's not a problem. The real problem is usually avoiding his wandering hands. Old blokes! You just have to shut your ears to anything they say to you. I usually sing the national anthem, that makes them think I'm daft, and they shoot off after someone in the bar.'

All this was being said as Lily, the girl from down under on the floor below, was driving Rose to the racecourse.

'What a shoot though, yesterday.'

Because Lily's normal profession was modelling her stories were often hilarious, and she loved to tell them to Rose, seeming to revel in the ridiculous.

'How'd it go, yesterday?'

As always Lily needed little prompting. 'Don't ask! No do. Wait till I tell you. You won't believe this. One of the male models, from Frisk Models, you know? He choked on his moustache. He was meant to be posing in a bathing suit with a sombrero, and he did it, he sneezed and inhaled his moustache, burst into tears and had to be given first aid. Well, that was just after ten. By midday the die-rector had punched the producer – couple of cokeheads *if* you like – and so by two we were down to three and shooting with the second assistant and a PA who kept bursting into tears – I ask you! And this is England! Whatever happened to British cool, may I ask?'

'Mums said it went out with rationing.'

'*My* mother sent me to England to get what she calls "polish". She's a real Melbourne Lady, if you know what I mean? Well, since I got here all I've met is aggro and hysteria and—'

'Australians?'

Lily laughed. 'You're one hell of a funny lady, aren't you?'

They parked, met the promoters, changed and, hoping not to see anyone they knew, crept out of the ladies' cloakroom and onto the racecourse. Happily they were both tall and so the sashes that said *Simply Say Strachan* did not look as bad as they might have done, at least Rose thought not, until she saw the winner of the second race and had to walk beside her into the unsaddling enclosure, smiling, just smiling.

483

'Please God make sure she does not see me,' she prayed.

But she did, and she laughed, and laughed. God might not have been smiling on Rose that afternoon, but Muffin Hateful was certainly laughing at Rose in her bright pink suit and her yellow satin sash with *Simply Say Strachan* on it, and so was Alexander. They doubled up with laughter at the sight of her.

Rose turned away.

'Who's that?' Lily nudged her. 'Who's taking the so-and-so out of you, then?'

Rose shook her head.

'No-one, just no-one,' she said.

Rusty Naylor had a friend. She said, 'Well I would, wouldn't I?' and laughed when Jack looked quizzical.

Despite her defensive speech, despite everything she had said to Jack, and more than once, she could not resist taking him to her friend's house, and Jack, now needing no urging, played while Rusty sang his song through for her friend – Mandrake – and they all agreed that it had to be recorded, and of course, just by chance, by sheer coincidence, Mandrake had a private recording studio and so the unimaginable happened and, after a week's commuting between their two houses, they had recorded Jack's song.

Just like that, just as if they had all arranged long ago that they would, just as if they had all known they would come together and make a hit.

'This is a hit all right, Rusty. And let's face it, the voice is better than ever. The long lay-off, the good Welsh air, Jack's song, everything has conspired to make the voice deeper, more rounded. You are not only back, Rusty, you are back on top, and if this is not a hit I will eat my socks.'

'It's not a hit yet, Mandrake, you hysterical old fool.'

But as he left after his over-long stay Rusty hugged Jack so hard that he suddenly knew just what a comeback would mean to her, just how much, despite everything, she really wanted that hit, even if it did mean that her family would be back with their begging bowls, and her lawyer too. She wanted that hit so much she could taste it already.

'So. And where for you now, Jack?'

Jack held up the tape which Mandrake had just handed to him. 'Me? I'm off to play this to the person I wrote it for. It's to her, and for her.'

Rusty nodded, understanding. 'Oh, Jack.' Her eyes filled with tears. 'I'm crossing everything for you.'

Jack smiled. 'Sure. But first, you know, cross them for her, kid, cross them for her.'

PART FOUR

Even nights when I sleep alone
I set the pillows side by side;
Holding it close, I sleep.

Japanese Folk Song

Chapter Eighteen

Melinda had been Hope's sole visitor for over ten days now. She did not mind. Calling in at the hospital had become part of her day, and she would no more have missed doing so than she would have missed any other part of her day, grooming Goosey, going for lessons, show jumping, all the bits and parts of her new life spent so much on her own.

'He's now been clear three times, Mums – three times in a row,' Melinda said, flicking through the copies of *Horse and Hound* she had brought with her. 'And I mean at Longleat – well, to be honest, everyone thought we were robbed. And I think we were. I do wish you could see this picture of her . . .'

Melinda folded the magazine in two at the Horse Trials page, where there was a spectacular photograph of 'The Grey Goose with Melinda Merriott up' jumping out of the water complex on the fine cross country course set out on the estate surrounding Lord Bath's historic house.

Having stared at the magazine herself, Melinda went on, 'They printed a picture of her even though technically we were second. It was ridiculous because we finished faster than the winning horse, but because we were fourteen seconds faster than the optimum time and the other horse was ten seconds slower it won. It's all these funny rulings in eventing. Anyway, the great thing is she has stopped knocking down her show jumps. That's four clear rounds now, and it's all down to old Colonel Stricty-boots. And give him his due, he really has made a difference. Goosey now gets right to the bottom of her jumps, really jumps off her hocks, instead of just racing round trying to hurdle them. So, Mums. So. Chepstow here we come.'

She glanced at her mother and the feeling came to her that Hope really could hear her. Or maybe it was that she really wanted her to hear her?

'It's only a novice championship, Mums, but apparently half the course is Intermediate size. But of course the thing is it's a two day event, it's the novice two day event, so really, if we get placed, it would be quite something. And the thing is, Mums, I want *so-o* much to win it, for you, Mums! I want to win it for you.'

Melinda smiled down at her painfully thin mother and squeezed her hand, after which for a single blissful second she too felt what Claire had thought she felt, her mother's finger imperceptibly moving.

Jack had arrived back from Wales to a message from Marcus. He wanted to come over and discuss recent developments, for not only had both daughters, and Jack, thought they had felt a slight movement from Hope's finger, but some of the nurses had thought they noted a slight movement in one of the eyes.

'At first everyone was determined that no-one could recover from the type of stroke which Hope suffered, simply because they know of no cases where this has happened. Certainly not fully. Several cases I know of have made it from her state to the unconscious state, what is cruelly known as the vegetative state, and a small number to full consciousness, but accompanied by total paralysis. Which to my mind is far worse than death. I think we would all hate to deprive Hope of a dignified exit while condemning her to a life in the cabbage patch.'

'There was one stroke victim I read about who not only recovered, but learned to paint, because he had been using *the other side of his brain . . .*'

'I remember that case, but he was not as bad as Hope, Jack.'

'The point is he'd had a stroke, and you lot had written him off as scrap!'

'You know I am as delighted as you that Hope has survived this far.'

'But.'

'But. Exactly. But.'

'Now you must run more sensory tests—'

'Exactly. But we will then see. And.'

'And.'

Marcus dropped his gaze, not wishing to see the

hope in Jack's eyes, not wishing to see how much his happiness depended on the outcome.

Jack stared out of the window at the ordinariness of life below. Someone passing a car, someone else stopping for their dog. Two old women greeting each other, just life trickling by, little by little, while inside the hospital room in which he was standing it seemed to him that his own life had momentarily stopped. Yes, they had registered that her eyelids moved; yes, they had registered that she had responded perceptibly to sound, and now Marcus was talking to her, holding the hand that Jack had been holding for what now seemed to him to be years.

'Squeeze one for yes and two for no.'

The two men's eyes met again but this time Marcus had no need to avoid looking at Jack.

'She had no such reflex as this before, Jack.' Marcus straightened up and looked round at the rest of the medical team as he spoke. 'We have had no such definite response before.'

'And now?'

The medical group standing round Hope looked at each other. Understandably, they could not believe what they were hearing.

'Now she has responded.'

'Which means?'

'Which means that she is self-respirating.'

'Which means?'

'Which means, Jack, that Hope is technically alive.'

'And?'

'We can switch off her life support system.'

'Which means?'

Marcus smiled. 'That something has happened that we had not thought possible.'

'She is alive.'

'She is alive. Technically. But that is all.'

'All!'

Jack turned away. All.

Perhaps the roses already knew the good news, because they were out on Bryndor when Crawford and Claire climbed out of the helicopter which had ferried them across from the mainland on a cloudless morning. Far below the sea had divided itself into turquoise, midnight blue, deep green and near-black by strange turns, making half moons of the colours so that as Claire stared at them she fell to wondering what it was that so fascinated in the sea, its mystery, its tranquillity, its capacity to subjugate, finally, perhaps, to overwhelm.

This morning there was no feeling of threat to it, and yet its ability to destroy was evident in the marker buoys which noted the wreckage of some ship which had paid the final price of jousting with this other world. Only a light westerly blew as they started to descend to Bryndor, causing the lazy early summer day to allow the tall grasses around the lakes to bend and sway as if in greeting to the visitors.

Outside a freshly painted wooden outbuilding, about the size of a stable, with a glass window at the front, a wooden hut stood proudly welcoming, and boasting a sign which proclaimed the small grassy field to be 'Bryndor Airport', and to the side of that stood a minitractor and trailer onto which Crawford hoisted both their suitcases.

'I would love you to come to Bryndor with me. It's owned by some friends of mine, lived there since they were married – John and Maisie Fellowes,' was how Crawford had framed the invitation for a week away with him. 'Family party, no strings attached,' he had added, pulling a face so straight that Claire knew that he was teasing her, and had sensed her fear that night at the hotel.

The tractor pulled its visitors through paths that were lined with wondrous shrubs whose flowers were large and scented, colouring their silent journey along the dark paths and stopping every now and then to drop off someone, or something, a holidaying couple, a parcel, a pair of garden shears, and as they journeyed deeper into the island it seemed to Claire that not only did the shrubs flourish more profusely than she had known, but in the hedgerows exotica bloomed in full and magnificent growth, large and lush thanks to the warmth of the Gulf Stream.

And birds, too – they passed more birds of more variety than she had thought possible in such a short time.

'They have nothing to be afraid of,' Crawford said as she remarked on this. 'John and Maisie allow no shooting, you see.'

It seemed the island was populated by sea birds, wild duck, geese, swifts and swallows, not to mention song thrushes and blackbirds so tame that they followed the visitors down all the paths as if they were shepherding them to the very doors of their holiday destinations.

Only minutes from their arrival, the tractor took a sharp right and suddenly there was the house, a large handsome building with a courtyard and large iron gates through which the minitractor took them, and they climbed down from their wooden seats to see that it was set about with flowers in tubs, and climbing plants festooning the calm exterior of the house.

'My dears!'

'This is Maisie—'

Seconds later, 'Welcome!'

'And that is John.'

Their hosts stood in welcoming array in the doorway of their house, their kaftans billowing about them in the mild early summer breeze.

'They've never quite recovered from flower power,' Crawford murmured, and bossed his eyes slightly in Claire's direction.

To Claire, who was used only to older people who wore tweeds or faded Barbour topcoats in greens and browns, the Fellowes, appearing as they did in their multicoloured African robes, their silver jewellery and their sandals, were delightfully exotic.

'I know you're Claire Merriott, I've heard all about you and how *brilliant* you were – the auction, the painting, everything. But,' Maisie Fellowes went on, 'I just hope, my dear, that Crawford warned you about us, didn't he? I'm sure he did. You see, we have lived here for a year and a day, and have drifted into these sort of habit-things. We *kaftan up* from the first week of May until the first week of September when the storms start, at which time we dart inside and start wearing seamen's knits and wide-bottom bells. So. That's just how it is here, I'm afraid, but I dare say you won't mind,' she finished, 'because Crawford said you're awfully nice and don't stand on form and couldn't disapprove if you tried.'

Claire smiled, feeling the warmth, not just of the sun on her back but of Maisie Fellowes' smile, and then she glanced back at Crawford, sensing that he was staring around him unable to quite believe that he was where he was.

'I can't tell you how nice this is,' he murmured to his friends, and they both hugged him again. He stared down at them. 'It's been too long, hasn't it?' he asked, and it seemed to Claire there was something apologetic in his voice.

They smiled at him. 'We knew you'd come back, some day.'

*   *   *

The house was set in grounds made up of terraces on different levels and lawns that led to rougher terrain and trees in amongst which were scattered guest cottages, each individually named after musicals.

'I'm an old musicals nut,' John told Claire as he showed her into Camelot, and Maisie walked Crawford off to unpack in Carousel. 'I don't think you could better the good old days of the great sweeping musical, I don't really. The thrill of the great velvet curtains, the orchestra tuning up, the arrival of the conductor to scattered applause, and then – moment of moments – the opening bars! What a moment! What excitement! Nothing like it now, is there! You can't come out humming a cat miaowing!'

He proceeded to hum a few bars from what must have been a popular number when he was a child, and Claire watched him, smiling, thinking that islands must breed very special people, people who were not afraid to be themselves, people who – perhaps, like the birds, because they felt safe – retained their childish enthusiasm.

'Leave you to unpack. Cocktails on the terrace, then luncheon and a siesta, although knowing Crawford, always was a glutton for punishment, he'll probably want to take you for a bicycle ride or something hideous later. Take your time, wash up, as the Americans say, and then see you on the terrace.'

Claire had so few summer clothes that she had

been forced to beg Melinda for a loan of some of her things, so putting two and two together she had enough to hang up in the curtained chintz-fronted wardrobe which stood on the other side of her bedroom, the bedroom itself leading to a small sitting room and on to a tiny kitchen where she could make her own breakfast and lounge about in peace.

'So awful to see anyone at breakfast,' John had explained before leaving her.

Claire showered and changed into some shorts and a plain T-shirt and a pair of espadrilles that she had newly bought in the King's Road to match the T-shirt.

'I feel so ordinary beside you, I'm afraid,' she told Maisie when she found her on the terrace before lunch. 'I wish I had some kaftans.'

'Oh no, don't wish for any such thing! Kaftans are such a bad habit! Truly. The moment one gets into the way of them, you see, that's it, one can never see a reason for not wearing one. Kaftans pass as day clothes for eccentrics like us, and uniform for flower children, and night clothes for insomniacs, and party clothes for simply everyone. And although one does of course see the point of other clothes, one never really goes back to them. Kaftans keep the skin so airy and free and the body so relaxed that quite frankly they turn one into a total naturist. So don't whatever you do adopt one. Adopt anything, but not kaftans. They are not a way of life even – they are a drug, like pasta or jazz, or handsome young men, or collecting paintings. A drug!'

Seated on the terrace at a wooden table Claire could admire a view of the sea from across the lawns. The gardens were full of shrubs and trees which must be rare and fine, judging from the various name plaques and carefully placed netting surrounding them. She had been seated for no more than a few seconds when she became aware that she was the focus of attention of more blackbirds and thrushes than she had yet seen.

'I wish I had something for you,' she murmured to two of the boldest of the thrushes, putting out her hand.

'Don't wish that!' John called to her as he approached carrying a silver tray on which were placed refreshing-looking drinks and small toasted nuts and olives.

'No, don't wish that,' Maisie agreed. 'They are all without manners, and within seconds you will look like a scarecrow in a field, with birds all over you, sitting on your head and your shoulders, and you will wish you had never given them the time of day. They won't even scare! Look!'

She clapped her hands sharply together, but the birds only looked at her, interested.

'They're like Ben Weatherstaff's robin, aren't they?'

'Just like him,' Maisie agreed and her eyes looked suddenly shrewd as she stared appreciatively for a second at her young guest. 'Good,' was all she finally said, but she smiled.

Crawford appeared a little later and he too smiled at Claire, at everything, but he warned her, 'Don't ever be tempted by John's cocktails. They belong to another era when men were men and women were too!'

Home-made lemonade was the order of Claire's day, and while the Fellowes drank cocktails that Crawford described as 'lethal' he had only wine, and later they ate pasta salad under the spread of cream linen umbrellas on the upper terrace, after which Crawford commanded Claire to follow him and they went in search of bicycles so that he could show her round the island.

'Each cottage has a pair of bicycles for itself. We find that's best,' Maisie explained, 'you know, for people to be able to take off on their own. Much the best.'

Claire found that her cottage boasted a lady's five-speed bike, a much more sophisticated machine than the one on which she had been used to ploughing her way around Hatcombe and its lanes.

'I'm not used to such a posh lot of gears,' she moaned to Crawford, struggling after him as he set off in front of her, his trousers tucked into his socks.

'Someone your age, I thought you would be a flash cyclist,' he teased her, pushing ahead of her with accomplished elegance. 'I, on the other hand, am the Alain Prost of the velocipede. In fact I was odds on favourite to win the Tour de France one year, and only an ingrowing toenail prevented me from bringing the trophy back to England.'

With that he engaged gear and swished off down the track with elegant and impressive ease, followed considerably less stylishly by a wobbly Claire.

There were three roads in all on Bryndor, but as no cars were allowed the swish of their wheels along the track seemed to be the only sound to accompany their cycling efforts, the wheels and the glorious birdsong.

Taking one of the two inner roads first and cycling slowly and steadily past nothing but fields full of wild flowers and trees full of birds, Claire imagined that she must be in paradise. Beyond the meadows the blue sea shimmered in the afternoon sun, while the waves broke silently on the bright sanded shores.

Halfway along the track they passed a deserted farm, a small low-lying white-painted house with a few outbuildings surrounded by paddocks. Further along another deserted and much older building still stood, despite everything that time and the weather could throw at it, and beside that a tiny stone dwelling which had long since lost its roof.

'A prison, would you believe?' Crawford had stopped and he turned and looked at Claire. 'The Fellowes think it's early sixteenth-century and used for either mutinous sailors who were brought ashore or as an isolation cell for those with contagious diseases.'

'They just left them here to die, is that what you're saying?'

'Probably, but don't look at me. Go and ask John and Maisie. They own the island, I don't.'

'Just imagine always living here, though?' Claire sighed and stayed staring out to sea for a minute.

'Oh yes, but imagine the boredom.' Crawford stared at her straight-faced.

'You could never become bored here, surely?'

'I could become bored anywhere,' he announced defiantly.

'Not here. This is heaven,' Claire said solemnly.

He looked down at her. 'No, you're right. It is heaven.'

Following which, as if the admission was too much for him, he flung a practised leg over his bicycle and cycled off from her too fast for her to catch him. Claire pedalled furiously after him, calling 'Stop, stop!' which was exactly what had used to happen back at West Dean when she was little and always pedalling madly after Mellie and Rose.

'I have such trouble with finding the right gears,' she confessed as he slowed down for her.

'Right, I'll call them out for you.'

She followed him at an ever-growing distance, but nevertheless, since Bryndor was so quiet, his voice came back to her on the afternoon air, 'Second, first, third, second, first.'

Claire realized that they made a strange little procession, what with Crawford calling to her, and herself desperately trying to follow his calls, inevitably finally losing sight of him altogether. She contented herself with slowing down to a steadier pace, more suited to a person who had little idea of gears, and allowed herself to indulge in a fantasy where she lived on Bryndor for the rest of her life, with only wild flowers and birds for company.

She did eventually catch up with Crawford, finding him lying on a large flat rock overlooking a beautiful white-sanded cove, where the sea lapped crystal clear, calm as a pond, and sea birds dived and called to each other and lacy tops to waves frilled towards the sand below.

'Are you all right?' she asked, dropping her bike on its side in the sand. 'I didn't know where you'd gone.'

'Don't worry, you won't lose me. Not on this island.'

'You cycled off so quickly.'

'Sorry. I thought I saw a puffin.'

'I've never seen a puffin.'

He glanced at her briefly and then out to sea. 'We'll go out in a boat tomorrow. To Puffin Island. There aren't nearly as many puffins as there used to be, thanks to the Spanish fishermen. Maisie was telling me all about it. Apparently, John says they are a bane because they trawl with these tiny-mesh nets, illegal of course, and kill all the food the puffins and other rare sea birds need. That's why we're losing all our sea birds. The colonies are half the size they used to be.'

'How awful.'

'Yes, it is. Terrible. Now, let's get bicycling, Miss Merriott, or we won't be home in time for a pre-dinner swim, which I am sure you would like. To be followed by what John calls "teenies", except they are far from being so. His martinis are so good, though, I know that tonight I shall not be able to resist them – but you, young lady, must.'

Claire nodded, only half hearing. She was far too busy trying to concentrate on her gear change.

And so, in happy, and much slower, formation, they cycled back to John and Maisie's house to the sound of Crawford's voice, 'Down to first, right, now up to second, and third!'

The next day Claire awoke as she had when she was still a child, far, far too early. As she made herself a cafetière of coffee and sat out in the agreeably warm early morning air, she remembered how Rose and she were forever banging their heads on their pillows when they were little, to try to wake up early on the first day of their holidays. It was always such a thing for them both to be up early, to explore, which looking back was inexplicable really, because later would have done just as well. But they always had to do this early exploring, although she now realized it was really more to do with being up early, and alone. That was what it was, really. If she thought about it.

This morning was no exception. Claire wanted to be up early and alone. But, more than that, she wanted to swim.

Dressed in a towelling dressing gown and her new espadrilles she set off with a towel round her neck to find the sea. It was further away than she had expected, as the sea always seems to be.

At last, there it was. The sea, and opposite another island, and around her clumps of coarse grass growing through the sand. Feeling strangely daring, she took off everything except her bathing suit and crept down to its shallow, cold edge, dipping first one toe into it, and then a foot, and then two feet, until, rubbing her arms to give herself courage, she found she was going deeper and deeper, and then suddenly very deep indeed.

Pushing the water away from her she imagined it to be folds of silk, and thrusting her legs out behind her she thought that she must know what it was to be the only person on earth. The water was so cold it made little hissing sounds around her neck, and so calm that there was no reason to stop.

'I am the water, and the water is me,' she said, out loud, which she knew was something that lonely people did – talking out loud to themselves, which was strange because she knew she was neither lonely nor alone, that below her was a whole other life, whole worlds over which her body was passing.

Warmed up and as happy as she had ever felt, after some minutes she swam back to shallower waters. She started to dive in porpoise-like movements through the waves, loving the sensation of the glistening shards of clear sea splintering over her head, and again that cold hissing sound as she settled down to swim again towards the horizon, only to turn back and head once more for the shore.

And suddenly there was a figure on the shore, and he was waving, but instead of feeling disappointed that she was no longer alone, as she might once have done, as soon as she saw who it was Claire stopped swimming and waved, treading water and breathing out as she did so.

'Come in!' she called. 'Come in! The water's wonderful, cold but terrific!'

But Crawford only shook his head and waved back to her, and she, thinking that perhaps he could not swim, contented herself with one last dozen strokes before heading back for the shore, leaving that exciting world over which she had just swum, leaving behind her the feeling that the sea was her, and she the sea.

He handed her towelling dressing gown to her, and together, laughing and talking, they went back to their guest cottages and Claire made breakfast for both of them, which they enjoyed sitting out on the grass in front of their doors, 'like natives in front of their huts', Crawford said, but Claire noticed that shortly afterwards he went inside, and left her to read and sketch the birds that would keep coming up to the table for crumbs.

John and Maisie were going to visit a friend on another island, and so they left Crawford and Claire alone for the next few days.

'You are to do exactly as you want and when you want, and when we come back we want to find that you have drunk all our drink and eaten every scrap of Amy's food, or else.'

So they dined alone each evening at a small table on the terrace, lit by candlelight, and served by the ever faithful Amy, housekeeper and, Crawford said, 'the real mistress of Bryndor. Because no-one says or does anything without Amy either knowing, or giving her approval. Isn't that right, Amy?'

Amy, small, round, and with a neat bun of white hair pinned to the back of her head, nodded severely. 'You are a bad boy, Mr Crawford, but then you always were.' She stopped at that. 'Yes, you always were. A terror for teasing everyone.' She shook her head, thinking back, and then removed their plates with an eagle eye as to whether or not they had 'eaten up'. 'Your appetite is still good, too,' she added approvingly. 'That is good. Best to feed you up now that you're here.'

'Have you been coming here since you were very young?'

Crawford nodded.

'He used to be part of the place, Miss Claire,' Amy called back, before serving a cold lemon soufflé with a lime and mango coulis.

Crawford sighed suddenly after she had left them. 'I have a sort of open invitation, always have had. The Fellowes and my family are inextricably interlinked, as it were . . .'

He sighed again, and his face seemed to darken. Sensing that she might have blundered, Claire said nothing more, only smiled and made a 'mmm' noise, because the pudding was so delicious.

'I should have come back before, and now, in some way thanks to your buying the picture, and – well, I have made time, I have come back. And I am so glad that I did. It's forced me to realize a lot of things about myself, and about the past, forced me to come to terms with things.'

Claire nodded at the tablecloth, and although she was feeling shy, sensing that he was feeling sombre, even sad, she said in her hesitant way, because she did not really want to talk about things that were very near to her, 'Sometimes it's very difficult, isn't it?' She was thinking of her mother. 'To come to terms with things, I mean, and make – well, make it all fit back again. It's just as if – well, it's just as if you've dropped a plate and you try to stick it all together again, but it comes out quite a different shape. I'm beginning to think that it's actually, probably, better to leave the plate dropped. You know, just carefully pick up all the pieces and make it into something else. You know how people do with mosaics, they pick up all those smashed pieces, all kinds of things – and then they make a beautiful floor of it. They make sense of all that chaos that surrounded them. And when you stand back and look at it, there it is, smashed bits no longer, but a beautiful floor full of colour and somehow with much more to it than if there had been no broken plates at all. That's what I think, anyway. Probably stupid. But that's what I think we have to do with life.'

Crawford lit a cigar from a thermidor laid on the coffee tray and stared at Claire through the candlelight. 'You have some sadness, too, haven't you?'

Claire nodded, 'Oh yes. That's why I've been thinking, really, about everything, about making sense of things.'

'It's understandable.' Crawford smiled. 'Don't stop! More for tomorrow, please, more thoughts.'

He finished his cigar in silence, and shortly afterwards Amy reappeared and they took leave of her, and each other, and thanks to Bryndor's clean air, Claire had hardly climbed into bed before she fell fast asleep, dreaming that she was swimming on the back of a dolphin while Crawford held up a torch for them to see their way through the dark.

*   *   *

The weather stayed brilliant, and so the next day, after a breakfast of eggs and bacon and home-made saffron rolls and honey, and cups of delicious coffee, Crawford suggested that they take a picnic to one of the other islands. He had hired a boat and the services of one of the local fishermen.

'Only an idiot would imagine that he can steer his way around these islands,' he said to Claire as they clambered on board the sturdy little blue-painted fishing boat. 'Some of the most famous shipwrecks ever have occurred round here, and it's not just the tremendous currents or the unseen rocks. It's because the weather is so changeable – calm as a millpond one minute and the next as rough as a storm in the Aegean. You have to have been born here to sail here.'

Once away from the shore, Jimmy the fisher-man headed almost purposefully, or so it seemed to Claire, towards a ring of wicked rocks, which she realized surrounded most of Bryndor. A passage of sea ran between the row of needle rocks and some much larger granite ones, one or two of which were big enough to be classed as islands themselves, although from the boat they looked unassailable. But it was worth the hazards for here were the bird colonies that Crawford had spoken of, communities of guillemots and fulmars, terns, cormorants and kittiwakes, screaming, diving, calling and fishing in the now gently swelling seas. But nowhere were there any puffins.

There were some seals, but fewer in number than Crawford remembered from years gone by.

'Got any fish on you?' he asked Jimmy.

'Some bread.'

'They'd eat brown paper, this lot.'

Claire tossed them some crusts, watching how they seemed to love basking on the rocks warmed by the Gulf Stream, and how their expressions close to were filled with friendliness, and how little they shifted their positions, except when tempted by the bread. They stared at the newcomers with big limpid eyes.

'They are so beautiful,' she called to Crawford and Jimmy over the increased engine noise as Jimmy finally eased the boat away from the rocks, revved the engine up and slid it into reverse, swinging hard to port to steer well clear of one of the seals who had slipped into the water searching for scraps.

'Now let's go in search of the vanishing puffin.'

Claire would have spent all day watching the seals, but since Jimmy was offering her the helm of the sturdy little fishing launch she forgot about seals in the excitement of heading the boat towards a vast rock a mile away.

Now they were away from the protection of the island and its reef the seas were slowly building as the tide turned, so with Jimmy's help she kept the craft headed directly into the wind and the swell. Above them grey and white gulls with black-tipped wings circled and swooped, filling the air with their call of *kittiwayke*, while cormorants and shags dived from the cliffs straight into the seas for food already espied.

'Look!' Claire cried out to the two men excitedly as suddenly four birds flew off the side of the rock, their short wings beating over-fast and their bright orange legs stuck out behind them like rudders. 'Puffins!'

'They're so unlike anything else,' Crawford called back to her, shading his eyes to watch them. 'Even the way they fly.'

'They're auks, aren't they? I was reading about them in a book at my cottage this morning.'

'That's right. But then so are razorbills, the black and white birds we saw back there with the guillemots.'

'I wonder what the great auk was like?'

'Aukly nice, I should think. Sorry, terrible joke.'

Crawford grinned boyishly, and with that Claire abruptly understood that deep down inside him, until now, he had been followed by a shadow. But quite suddenly it had gone. She could feel it in his aura, as she could feel his happiness and contentment as the puffins flapped their way across the seas in search of food and the shags dived sharply and swiftly into the dark blue depths about them. She could feel the only shadow that was following him now had been cast by the sun.

He turned back to her. 'I can't remember feeling happier, do you know that?'

*   *   *

Day after sunny day followed this first boating and fishing expedition, days during which it seemed to Claire that Crawford grew more boyish, and she grew more mature, as she realized just how unwell he must be.

The knowledge, like so much that is kindly, came to her very gradually, although she had first been alerted by Maisie Fellowes' saying *Take care of him, won't you – I know you will* as she left, as if Claire was in on the same secret as the rest of them, as if she too knew what there was to be known.

Thereafter it was Amy who, although careful to be nonchalant around 'Master Crawford', nevertheless by her care of him, and even more by the way her eyes turned to look at him when he was not looking at her, made Claire increasingly sure that Master Crawford was coming to terms with a shorter future than she would have wished him.

'I think the Fellowes are leaving us Bryndor,' Crawford joked as they set off on yet another expedition, this time to an island with a famous restaurant. 'I think they've run off and left us, and we'll soon find that we have to run the place for them while they sun themselves elsewhere.'

Claire smiled at Crawford, and then at Amy, who had just joined them on the terrace with their picnic basket.

'No picnic today, Amy,' Crawford told her. 'We are lunching at the wonderful Skiffys on Mintoul.'

'You'll take the basket with you, Master Crawford, or there will be no dinner tonight for you, and that's my last word on it.'

She handed the basket to Crawford, who raised his eyes to heaven. 'There never is any arguing with you, Amy, and there never was.'

'There's elevenses there for the two of you, hot coffee or home-made lemonade, ginger snaps and chocolate chip biscuits, made with plain or white chocolate. And Jimmy's lunch is egg mayonnaise sandwiches, sardine and cucumber sandwiches, sausages with herbs and accompanying mustard, and a cheesecake; lemon also. And for his luncheon, ginger beer, but nothing alcoholic for we have no wish to see him crashing into the rocks.'

She said this every morning about the ginger beer, as if it was a prayer that would keep them safe.

'Do you always spoil everyone like this, Amy?'

Amy looked back at Claire and then over to Crawford. 'The world could do with more spoiling, couldn't it?' she asked. 'There's too little spoiling if you ask me.'

Reaching Mintoul by boat took them all morning, but only because Crawford insisted on stopping everywhere they could to watch yet more birds diving, catching, flying and diving, endlessly delighted by their activities, so much so that when they landed it took Claire a few minutes to be able to walk steadily, so much had her body lost its stability with the motion of the waves and the rocking of the boat.

514

'Look – people!'

Crawford glanced down at her, and he himself was surprised at the cultural shock that the sight of his fellow human beings, tourists like himself, presented after the tranquillity of Bryndor.

'They only really come here for the restaurant. There's little else here, just Skiffys and the sea.'

But *just Skiffys* was rather more than a restaurant, as she found out once they had climbed up to it.

It was a white-painted building which, when seen from the outside, might have been a restaurant on a Greek island, with chairs set about and a vine-covered entrance through which live music could be heard playing. But inside the atmosphere was somehow neither Continental nor Greek, nor British. It was just, as Claire said afterwards, 'its own person, like him, really'.

Skiffy was a tall man with an amiable smile and a soft voice. He moved from table to table, greeting old friends, patting children on the head, joking, handing out glasses, menus and napkins, seeing to everyone and inspecting every dish as it came from the kitchens. Not a moment was missed by him, and not a dish placed that he had not scrutinized first.

'Ah, now, Mr Crawford, we have never met, but John Fellowes warned me that you were coming and that you liked your fish.'

Crawford seated himself after Claire and then smiled across at the restaurateur. Claire saw that there was a moment of immediate recognition between them, a moment that said, *You like to eat, and I like to cook!*

'I like fish very much indeed,' Crawford nodded.

'I have some sea bass today.'

Crawford closed his eyes momentarily. Sea bass, his favourite, his eyes said when he opened them again.

'Just caught, and chef is even now preparing it. In half an hour, say? With a bottle of the Heugel Traminer?'

'Maître Skiffy. Just run through how it is prepared, for my assistant here, Claire Merriott. I'm afraid she still has L plates on as far as food and wine are concerned, but she is learning very fast.' Crawford looked at Claire affectionately.

'The bass is caught by our own fisherman, and cooked in the following manner. It is cleaned and prepared and then laid upon a bed of lemon slices, seasoned with thyme and oil and salt massaged into it, also a good handful of herbs inside – all this placed in foil and sealed. We bring it to the table as soon as it is cooked with a sauce made from the herbs which has been fiercely boiled. Delicious.'

It was delicious, and before it they ate prawns simply done in butter, but so large and juicy that finishing by dipping fresh bread in what remained of those juices was a mouthwateringly rhapsodic moment.

'Eating and drinking well is so important. England is only now after hundreds of years coming to terms with the puritan ethic that to do either was somehow wrong. Terrible to think of all those white-faced British children being thrown tasteless food and stoking up on chocolate because they are given nothing to eat that actually has *flavour*.'

Claire looked round the restaurant. It seemed to her, at that moment anyway, to be filled with people enjoying themselves eating and relaxing in a convivial atmosphere, and she saw that Crawford had to be right, because the restaurant was packed, but not just packed with couples.

'You must be right, because all the families who are here with their children are all eating and smiling and laughing, having a great time. There's not one person who doesn't look happy here, who doesn't look as if they wouldn't swap places with anyone.'

'It can't be that difficult, can it? To give people food that tastes of something?'

The sea bass, 'that noble fish that the Italians literally worship', Crawford told Claire, when it arrived was as noble and tasted as delicious as promised by the admirable Skiffy. It was followed by a ricotta pudding served on a sauce of pistachios and kirsch.

Afterwards Claire smiled at Crawford. Placing her spoon back on her plate she sighed with the sheer pleasure of the moment. 'Wow. That was just to die for!'

Oh, to take back that moment, for her mouth to have remained as closed as when she had been eating! As soon as she had said it Claire quickly dropped her napkin and, happily, by the time she had straightened up she felt that the moment had passed. But it could not be denied, it had been a moment, and unbearably, for a few seconds, she saw that the cloud that had followed 'Master Crawford' had come back, so that he was silent for the next few minutes, his eyes gazing out to sea, to the sparkle on the water, to the wind pushing the waves towards the shore, to the distant horizon which seemed to go on for ever.

After black coffee and home-made Turkish delight, it was too hot to walk round the island, and they were too well lunched. Instead they chose to wander through the ornamental gardens, stopping at all the most exotic plants, whereupon Crawford would patiently explain where they came from and how they had been brought to Mintoul from practically every corner of the earth by the man who had originally built the restaurant as a house, a banker turned sailor turned explorer turned horticulturalist.

'The Victorians were amazing people, much underrated and derided in the last fifty years. Heavens knows why, for the fact is that they were some of the most highly inventive and cultured

English generations yet produced. Outside, that is, of their propensity to over-paint masterpieces.'

They were sitting by one of the large ornamental ponds whose clear waters were filled with rare water lilies and small bright red goldfish. Over them in the soft sea breeze waved the branches of a tall palm, while far out on that same horizon which had so taken Crawford's eyes over lunch, vast ships moved at a snail's pace.

'I wish I never had to leave these islands.'

Crawford looked across at Claire and for one wonderful second she thought he might be going to tell her that she did not have to leave, ever, that they were both going to stay on Bryndor, so dreamy and out of this world had the past days been. Instead he just smiled at her briefly and turned back to the sea once more, preoccupied.

On the boat trip home Claire came face to face with the reality that she had been avoiding since they had arrived on Bryndor, and that reality was that she had only to go into Crawford's bathroom to find out the truth about him. Perhaps sitting with her mother for the past months, or perhaps being with Aunt Rosabel, had given her this second or third sense, as being with older people sometimes does, but there it was. She knew exactly what she would find if she went to the bathroom of Crawford's guest cottage.

There would be reality in the form of tablets, medicines, bottles with indecipherable names typed on tiny labels, and they would be called things that started with *chl* because so many medi-cines for grim illnesses seemed to do so, or ended with *dyl* or *lyl*, and the dull truth would be there for her to see in all its starkness, the truth about why Crawford would turn away and swallow things with glasses of water, or look suddenly, unaccountably fatigued, despite his outward gaiety. The dark shadow that he had, for these last days shaken off would be identified and she would be able to give a name to that reality.

But what was the point? And again, what was the *point*?

Later, when she was helping Amy prepare a simple supper of ham salad and fruit, the old housekeeper leaned across the kitchen table and confided, 'You're doing Master Crawford the power of good!'

Claire looked away, pretending to search for an oven glove, knowing just what she was not saying, and in truth not wanting to know any more.

'For him to come back here, after all that happened, is a miracle indeed.'

At that Claire did look at her, she could not help herself, for of course the housekeeper's words prompted the thought *After all* what *happened?*

Amy must have seen the blank in Claire's eyes because she straightened up and demanded in a low voice, having glanced quickly over her shoulder, aware that Crawford might be ambling in from the terrace outside, 'You surely knew about the awful business of his young wife, did you not?'

Wife? Claire could not imagine Crawford married. He seemed so much the loner, the man apart, far too sensitive for the maelstrom of marriage.

'She came here with him every year. They were married so young. Master Crawford, he was brought up here, by Mr Fellowes, old Master John Fellowes that was, that is. Young Master Crawford, he was a cousin of the family, and his parents having been killed in a motor accident he came here and was brought up with young Master John as if they were brothers. Well, then he married young, of course, for he was very handsome and she was a beautiful French girl whom he met here, and of course there was no stopping either of them, but then it happened.'

Claire widened her eyes. She didn't mean to, because she was actually trying to look casual and just carry on mixing the salad, feeling just a little guilty that she was listening to gossip about Crawford, but quite unable to stop being interested.

'The accident. They were out in a boat, and what with those demon rocks out there they met with one of those sudden storms that happen, you know? Somehow he came back, but she was never found, not for weeks, and when she was her parents came for her body. They blamed Master

Crawford, and took her back to France and buried her as one of them, and Master Crawford never came back to Bryndor. So you can imagine? It would have been a terrible thing, as things are for him just now, if he had never come back here. And for Miss Maisie and Master John, too, for they always loved him, you know. Always kept in touch, while understanding his not coming back, of course. They perfectly understood that the memories would not go away, as why would they? But now I think all is healed, for which God be praised indeed, all things considered, for he needs to find peace, poor fellow. Well, we all do.'

She sighed, and nodded, finishing with another 'Indeed' and turning back to her magnificent old black cooking range.

Up until that evening their meals taken together on the terrace had been jolly affairs, conversation flowing, both at ease with each other. But that evening, without realizing it, Claire must have been quieter than usual, because quite suddenly Crawford downed his fruit knife and jumping up announced that they should go for a bike ride because the moon was more than usually bright, and it was not to be missed.

One of the many entrancing aspects of Bryndor was cycling round the island after dinner, for as the moon came out the dark sea seemed actually to slow under the weight of the night sky above it, forcing the sea to a steadier pace, and as the small cottages at the side of the shore put out their lights and their owners went to sleep, Crawford and Claire would cycle slowly down dark paths illuminated only by the great orb above them, making their way back to their guest cottages the long way, reluctant, as always, to say goodnight to this entrancing place to which Crawford had at last returned to make his peace.

Tonight, as she cycled behind Crawford, Claire could not stop herself from thinking about the tragedy at the centre of Crawford's life and imagining the awful scenes out there in the dark water somewhere, imagining a young carefree Crawford blaming himself for the rest of his life for what had happened. Perhaps waiting on the shore for days and weeks, always longing for the impossible to happen, for his wife to come back, and then finally unable to come back himself.

'Do you want to come in for a drink?' He smiled down at her as they propped their bicycles against the walls of the cottages. 'I should take ruthless advantage of my generosity if I were you, because your days here are numbered. Only two more nights before you must go back to London, I'm afraid. Marjorie rang this morning, and she is yelling, not calling, for help.'

Claire was there in one as soon as he said it, understanding at once what he was telling her. She was silent for a few seconds. She was going back to London. He was *not* going back to London.

It was like an exercise in French, or Italian. *We*

are going back to London, they are going back to London, the whole world is going back to London, but not Crawford. Crawford is staying on Bryndor.

'Come in for a nightcap?' He repeated his invitation.

'That would be fun,' she said, careful to keep her voice even, not to sound surprised or disappointed, and for no reason she thought of all the birds they had seen during their stay, seagulls wheeling, ducks waddling across the sands, wild geese flying in formations as precise as military guards.

Lucky things. They have dangers, yes, but no worries. No such things as fears for the future. No. Why have I got this pain, am I going to be out of a job tomorrow? No pills in bottles, no medicines ending in dyl, no haunting tragedies, just eat and live and feel. And then die.

Claire sat down in a chintz-covered chair in Crawford's cottage and found herself staring ahead of her, much as Crawford had done after lunch. Only now that she was leaving him did she realize just how much she loved him. It was startling and strange, and yet at the same time it made sense. She loved him for his kindness and sensitivity, for his elegance – even more perhaps for his melancholy, a sadness which she realized somehow matched her own underlying sorrow over her mother. Perhaps it was that more than anything that had drawn them together in the first place, not just the painting, the auction and all that, but those other things about which neither of them could speak, and of which they probably would not speak again, because there was no point.

Some things are better not said. Hope had said that quite often. *Just better not said.*

There were no goodbyes, just looks.

Crawford looked at Claire and she stared back at him, willing him to know how much she had grown to love him, and he smiled suddenly, a dazzling smile of great certainty, as if he knew. A second later the pilot made a circular motion with one finger in the air to indicate to Crawford that he was intending to lift off, running his last checks on the helicopter, while Claire pressed her face to the window, watching him walking away out of the danger zone, his hands in his pockets.

The moment the pilot began to increase the engine revs he turned back to watch the craft take off, and Claire raised her hand, putting it back to her lips and blowing him a kiss. The man on the ground returned the kiss and waved, and kept waving until the little red helicopter had lifted itself higher and higher into the sky so that the man on the ground became smaller and smaller, and then a dot, and then nothing at all.

He walked back to the house, leaving the tractor behind to pick up John and Maisie who were due in an hour later, and as he followed the earth path he turned once to see if he could catch sight of the helicopter, but it had disappeared completely from his sight into the beyond, leaving the island silent once more, hushed except for the morning birdsong and the sounds of the sea and the trees.

Two hundred yards further on he stopped by one of the lakes and skimmed a pebble across the mirror calm of the waters, watching it duck and drake until it finally lost its impetus and sank swiftly out of sight. He watched a moment longer as the ripples closed and died over the lost stone, then he turned and walked on.

Chapter Nineteen

Her worst nightmare was realized the moment Melinda saw who was down to judge her dressage test, and her second worst was when she saw out of the corner of her eye who had arrived at the last minute not just to watch that same dressage test, but to film it. The first and worst bad dream was Mary Dandridge, a woman with a face like a Sherman tank and a body to match who had a stack of prejudices as far as marking dressage was concerned that would have built a cross country fence.

The second bad omen was Josh Tomm, whom she had assiduously and successfully avoided ever since his return from India. But since there was nothing that Melinda could do about either of them, she turned her attentions to who mattered most at that moment, namely Goosey, and began her warm-up before entering the dressage area, before she had time to think too much. And of course, as always, the moment the Grey Goose started her dressage she became a star. It was as if she was saying, *Listen, I may have been a squib on the racecourse, but this I can do, just watch!*

And she was good. Melinda knew it, and her groom-for-the-day Barley knew it, and it seemed to Melinda that Goosey knew it. They had been good. No, they had been better than good, they had been almost brilliant. Not Olympic standard, but what Jack would call 'coming very close, Mellie'.

'Want to see it? I've – I've – I've got Dad's video in the back of my – of my – of my van?'

Melinda had forgotten about Josh's hesitation, and looking down at where he was standing to the side of her and Goosey, she found that she had forgotten a great many other things about him too. She had forgotten how like a young Jack he looked, and how sweet his expression was – always so anxious. Most of all she had forgotten, in all the hurly-burly of the past, just how kind he was. People did forget things, but then they suddenly came back again, the whole niceness of someone, it came back, and this was what had happened to her, she had forgotten that whole rounded niceness of Josh.

'Sure, I'd love to see the video.'

Melinda would have loved to pretend that she didn't want to see it, of course she would, because she had pride, and she had been hurt by Josh's not coming round to see them when Letty and James were at Keeper's, or writing to her about Hope, all those things that can make someone feel un-reasonably hurt when they are being hurt by everything so much. But now that Josh was walking beside her and they were going back to join Barley at the box, and then to walk together to view the video, all the hurt seemed to have gone away, and she found that there was nothing to say any more, about anything, and what she might once have said was unnecessary anyway.

Some things are best unsaid, some things are better just left.

She frowned. Someone she knew had often said that to her. Aunt Rosabel, was it? No, of course – Mums. She often said that, and it seemed, now that Melinda thought about it, that it was true. Some things *were* better left unsaid, perhaps for ever.

'All right, let's do some unbiased judging, shall we?' Melinda turned to Barley and shrugged her shoulders. 'What mark would you give us?'

The tall, good-looking blonde also shrugged her shoulders, hesitating, and then said, 'Well – I'd say nineteen and that's being tough, really. Being normal I'd give you both a seventeen, I think.'

Melinda was quiet for a second. Barley was a good judge. She was pleased. Goosey had been brilliant. 'Josh?'

Josh gave his sudden smile. 'Whatever you say, boss! I know – nothing.'

Melinda smiled, while at the same time raising her eyes to heaven. 'You wait for Frau Kleb and her method of marking. I expect it'll be forty.'

Josh followed them both, all the while humping his camera with him. 'Uh huh, I always forget that the low marks are brilliant and the high marks are crap in dressage,' he muttered.

Electing to walk the show jumping course with them he listened as the two girls sighed over the twists and turns and changes of rein and direction that would be needed. As with most event tracks horse and rider were being asked everything, and that was all before the cross country.

To make matters worse, as Melinda was warming Goosey up in the practice ring the skies which had been clear until then slowly began to darken and in the distance thunder rumbled over the hills.

'This is all we need, Goosey,' Melinda muttered, with an eye to the heavens as they trotted round. 'A rainstorm and slippery ground. Thanks a lot, God!'

Sure enough the moment the bell rang for them to start their round, the heavens opened. But this was no ordinary shower, this was a storm of monsoon proportions, the heavy rain falling in sheets, whipped up by a sudden wind so that on certain sections of the track Melinda could hardly see the jumps. Yet somehow the miracle happened and the mare jumped clear, never even touching timber nor once losing her footing in the atrocious conditions. And as the announcer proclaimed their clear round the rain stopped as suddenly as it had begun. The sun shone on the rest of the competitors in Melinda's section.

'And many thanks again, God!'

Despite the harsh dressage marks the partnership had been in sixth place, which with exactly three hundred and fifty horses competing was better than any of them predicted. Now with the show jumping phase over and the scores posted on Friday evening, Melinda found that she had moved up a place and was now lying fifth overnight. Both the leaders had also jumped clear to stay on their dressage scores of seventeen and nineteen respectively. At this point Josh went back to the Mill House to report back to Jack and try to sleep, while Melinda and Barley stayed the night, having borrowed a friend's box, a luxurious affair, complete with cooking and showering arrangements.

Melinda and Josh walked the cross country course early the following morning. It was Melinda's second time, and as they walked silently round she kept chewing her finger nails and silently counting between the jumps while staring at the ground. The fact was, the course was so difficult, it might as well have been Intermediate, not novice.

Halfway round Josh removed her nails from her mouth, quietly but insistently. 'You won't have any fingers left to ride.'

'Not biting, just eating, really.'

'Chewing.'

'If I get round, if we get round, I will give up chewing for ever,' she promised.

'D – deal.'

'Deal.'

By now they were standing at a combination with two arrowheads.

'There's no way anyone is going to make the time going the safe route,' Melinda went on. 'It's got to be the sorry route.' She tapped the arrowhead. 'And let's just hope we won't be. Sorry, I mean.'

Two hours later, having been despatched by the starter on the Roads and Tracks and Steeplechase section, Melinda was glad to be off at last. In fact the word 'Go!' and the sight of the starter dropping his flag was the greatest. No more chewing anything, nails, fingers, the cud – she was off and so was Goosey, but only a second after Melinda had set her stopwatch.

Since she was an ex-racehorse the main problem with the mare was control. She had to go fast not to get any penalty points, but if she got her head and took over when Melinda shook her up, there could well be chaos on what was meant to be their sedate walk and trot back home.

The first steeplechase fence was one of the worst and had already claimed several victims, being built on a rise with a sudden and very real drop on the landing side. Since the run to it was uphill, to the novice horse it would seem it was being asked to jump into space, so it took skill and courage on both the rider's and the animal's part to jump it quickly and accurately. For one moment, one heart-stopping palpitating moment,

Melinda felt Goosey check and thought she was going to refuse, so she gathered the mare up just slightly, taking her back in her hands, squeezing firmly with her legs so Goosey just kept up her momentum. In answer the grey mare flew the fence, landing well clear of the drop.

The next two fences she flew. And after that, the fourth, where other horses had skidded and had to be checked in order to find the line, thus losing precious seconds, Goosey went round the corner on wheels and flicked over the fence.

Hooking left again after the fourth, to line up for the long straight run to three more fences and the finish, Melinda knew the point had come to press the button, so sitting and squeezing she allowed Goosey to run; and run she did, true as an arrow, picking off the last three fences at full racing clip before galloping flat out for the finish, which was not that easy, seeing that they were meant to slow down and pull up just the other side of a narrow farm gateway. Yet when she sat back and asked the mare to come back, miracle of miracles, Goosey did, albeit giving an enormous buck of celebration as she did so.

'Behave yourself, you great grey goose,' Melinda muttered, reaching forward and pulling at the mare's ears. 'You are now going to have to start to walk like an old lady with a shopping basket.'

Of that nonsense Goosey was not having any, and she promptly proceeded to walk out on the homeward section of roads and tracks as if she had just come out of her box first thing of a morning, overtaking other competing horses, and coming onto the racecourse and into the park proper with her tank still brim full, and as far as her support team could make out – as they hurried to welcome her into the ten minute box – no penalties.

Ten minutes. That was all they had to cool the horse down, rub her off, grease her legs and prepare her for the stiffest part of the trial yet, namely nineteen cross country fences.

The night before, Jack had shaken his head at Josh's description of just the preliminaries. 'Only the good old British cavalry could invent something like eventing to train their horses for battle. No wonder they were the best in the world!'

As they fussed around the Grey Goose it was Barley who spotted it first, only a moment before Melinda was to be legged up.

'She's lost a shoe!'

Somewhere on the roads and tracks section she had lost a shoe, and there were only three minutes left.

'Quickly! Josh! Find a farrier!'

Barley and Josh ended up flying in opposite directions, Josh to collar the large and amiable farrier who had just finished reshoeing another competitor's horse, and Barley to intercept one of the officials who was on his way to the start box. Explaining what had happened, Josh, his hesitation at its worst in the excitement of the moment, persuaded the man to drop the mare down a place, which was well within the rules but quite without his ideas of what should happen.

'I think I ber – ber – bored him into doing it!' he told Melinda later.

Back to the mare and Melinda, and now Josh plunged his hand inside his Barbour and brought out a twenty pound note.

'Can you sher – sher – sher – shoe . . .'

'In five minutes?' Melinda put in as Barley flew back across the grass with the spare set of shoes they never travelled without.

'For twenty quid?' The farrier stuck the note between his teeth and carried on talking and shoeing at the same time. 'For twenty quid I can shoe her in four!'

Goosey stood as still as she had ever stood as the farrier pulled off one shoe and started to fit the next, but even he was beginning to sweat as Melinda called out the seconds and minutes, until finally, it was done, and everyone seemed to be legging Melinda up at the same time, and the start box appeared fifty miles away not fifty yards, and Barley was shouting up to her, 'Don't forget your watch! Remember what happened at Longleat!'

'I know, it was me riding, remember!'

'Kick on coming up the hill.'

'Horse number 213!' an official called from the start box, and they were all patting Goosey's rump and shouting various forms of 'Good luck.'

'Coming, sir, coming!'

'Ger – ger – good luck!' Josh called.

'Five seconds . . .' the official warned.

Melinda reset her stop watch.

'Go!' She pressed start on her watch and was gone.

She had never really stretched the Grey Goose, always leaving something in reserve, because once she started jumping she was so naturally quick and nimble at her fences for a big horse that her racing pedigree gave her a good three or four seconds' headway over her rivals without ever having to notch her up into top gear.

But for Melinda, today was different. The optimum time of four minutes fifteen seconds set was more than challenging, it was the fastest time the pair had so far had to meet, so if all went well they were really going to have to go for it, and some.

The first five fences – Busby Start, Ratso Kegs, Titus Drop, and the rest – presented no problem, although when Melinda got a good view from behind the mare's head at Ogilvy's Barricade, she momentarily trembled inwardly. But the mare made nothing of it, barely checking her stride, and taking off without Melinda's having to ask, landing well clear of danger and picking up as soon as her feet touched the ground.

With that Melinda's confidence returned and together they flew, Melinda knowing that anything was possible, and all she had to do was to keep Goosey in her hands, keep her balance, find the right stride, and *go*.

Jack had been away from Hope for so long, yet now he was back and beside her again he felt so depressed at seeing her still where she was that his confidence deserted him and he felt too self-conscious to play her his song. In fact for days now he had been with her in hospital, back to his old routine, and not daring to play it because, in his heart of hearts, he felt it just was not good enough.

It was Hope who had brought back his confidence in himself, it was Hope who had made him feel he could go back on tour again, face real people, real audiences, but it had been with old songs, and the people had been old fans, and they had come to hear their old favourites, his 'evergreens', and this song was new. No-one except Rusty and Mandrake really knew what it was like, and now that Jack was no longer with them he had lost his confidence again somewhere on the road.

And so he talked to her and played her many things as he sat with her, but not his song. It just was not good enough, not now that he was back with her, not now that he was sitting with her. His song for her that had been meant to be so brilliant now seemed to him to be lacking in everything he had wanted it to be, lacking even in the one ingredient with which he had so longed to fill it.

He walked restlessly up and down the hospital room thinking about all this, and wondering in the next second how Melinda and Josh were getting on, and in the following second how Letty and James were liking their nanny and whether she was too old for them, but finishing up, as he always did, by reassuring himself that having an older person to look after them was good because it meant they were growing up with all ages, and Hope had always said that was good.

He stopped.

That was probably the matter! Hope had said so much to him, all of which he remembered, but she had never said what she thought of his work, she had only ever smiled when, his confidence returning, he had started to play to her. 'La Giaconda' he had used to call her, saying she had a smile just like the painting. He looked across at her. Oh to see her smile again, just once.

Melinda could not believe how well the mare was going.

'You are a genius!' she called to her after they had been through the water complex, over Nylands Copse, down Roberts Salmon Steps, making nothing of Zan Ski Jump and Midges Table. It seemed they had flown the course so far with hardly a check, passing the beautiful ruin of a Palladian mansion and flying off the steps, and according to Melinda's stop watch they were still within the time.

But perhaps they had become too confident, lost their concentration for a second, for suddenly as they approached Richards Rails Goosey lost her impulsion and her stride, shortening up into the fence and losing her footing, so that as the mare took off Melinda found herself without stirrups and round the mare's neck. With a second arrowhead marking the next jump coming up, she had no chance.

'Stay on, Mellie, stay on!' she heard a voice that was not her own saying. '*Stay on for me, Mellie!*'

Mums. Dear God. She had to stay on, if only for her.

The mare must have heard Hope too, because instead of running out to the right at the second part of the fence, which ninety per cent of horses would have done, she not only righted herself but jumped the rails clean, all by herself, unaided by Melinda who by now was hanging halfway down the horse's shoulder.

With Melinda clinging on grimly and without stirrups, their troubles were by no means over. With Jason Tyres looming before them and Melinda still fighting for her balance and trying to get at least one foot back in her irons, while using the reins to keep herself on the mare rather than steer her, the natural consequence had to be Goosey's galloping straight, unchecked, thereby losing precious seconds until Melinda could right herself.

'Whoa, Goosey!' Melinda yelled at her horse.

And miraculously for a moment Goosey slowed her gallop, checking with a bounce as she did so, and very nearly catapulting Melinda, but this time out of the side door. But, feeling the mare stopping, Melinda used the check to the very opposite effect, pushing against the mare's neck, and allowing the momentum to throw her backwards. The moment she felt herself going in that direction, even before her backside hit the saddle, Melinda gathered her reins and hauled right, hard. The Grey Goose turned, changing direction as if on a sixpence, her sudden swing causing Melinda once again to bounce back up out of her saddle – but at least by now they were straightened and as Melinda's feet still searched desperately to find their irons, she yelled once again, 'Go, go, go!'

Goosey went. In fact now that they were clearing Jason Tyres, although there were still no irons, Melinda had a moment of inspiration. She kicked her left foot free of the stirrup for which she had been feeling and finding herself perched exactly where she knew she should be, at the point of balance, and giving just enough rein, she leaned back, easing the pressure on the mare's mouth as she landed.

And they were over, after which there was just enough time for Melinda to pitch forward and tap the irons back onto her toes.

Now they were back on track, and in so many ways Melinda settled herself – not just into the gallop position, but into the knowledge that whatever happened after that, they could surely survive anything?

'That cost us four seconds, Goosey,' she cried, 'we are going to have to kick on,' and as she did so she felt the mare remember her past on the racecourse and slip into top gear, eating up the ground as she went.

All right, so he *would* play his song to her. After all, he had written it to her, and so he must take his courage into his hands and play it to her. And if it was terrible, it was terrible, what did it matter?

But of course it did matter enormously to him that the song should sound as he wanted it to, that it should be as he wanted it to be, for her whom he loved so much.

'I'm going to play you my song, if only to keep my mind off how Melinda and Josh are doing at that blasted event,' he finally confessed to Hope. 'Your daughter is mad, and so is the whole horse world, but there you are, she's doing what she wants to do, and thank God Josh and she are friends again, because for a while that relationship seemed to be staying on hold, and some.'

Having kicked on Melinda expected to find the tank empty once she came to the last set of fences, and it would not have been surprising had she done so, but far from it. The mare not only found more under the bonnet, but she went into overdrive, as if she herself knew that she had to give more than she even knew she had, flying the second last and galloping up to the last in a fashion that was simply breathtaking.

Josh and Barley had watched many horses falter towards the end, but now they stood by the finish seeing the Grey Goose seemingly lengthening instead of shortening over Duff's Trakaener and flying Teresa's Tops with such a leap that the fence judges whooped in amazement and the small crowd of onlookers cheered.

'Go, Goosey, go!'

Melinda sat down into the saddle and rode as hard as she could for the line, and they flew past the finish where those right on the line spun round in semicircles as the grey mare flashed by them.

'Yes!' Melinda cried, checking her watch as she began to haul the horse in one-handed. 'Yes, yes, Goose, you've only gone and done it!'

They were one second inside the optimum time. It was literally unbelievable.

Jack put the tape away again. He could not play it to her. And it was nothing to do with Hope and himself being on their own, with her still being there, with his confidence suddenly ebbing, it was all to do with something else. He stopped, and then started up his thoughts again.

It was all to do with his thinking, all the time that he was with Rusty in Wales, all the time that he was with Rusty and Mandrake, on the long drive there, and on the long drive back, all that time he had kept imagining that somehow or other, somehow, with this song, he could bring about the miracle. But now, faced with playing it to her, his courage faltered, and he realized he could not face failure. All his hopes for Hope fading. And his song just being a song that had brought him and Rusty together again, but not Hope and himself. He sat down beside her, and put his head in his hands. He was too afraid to do anything and yet at the same time in such despair that to do nothing seemed to be almost worse.

Melinda flung herself off Goosey, and straight into Josh's arms, and as she did so that daydream of long ago came back to her – herself flinging herself off the newly arrived Grey Goose into Josh's arms.

It was only a delighted hug, and of course there was one for Barley too, and the two girls danced delightedly round in a circle for a moment before turning back to the horse, while Josh looked on and laughed at their unaffected exuberance, knowing that they were celebrating long days and weeks of hard work and dedication, of belief in the teeth of despair, of loyalty to an ideal. It was different for him. Melinda's hugging him that way was quite different, that was rather more than a celebration of a sporting achievement, that was more about making something of a future that might be spent together.

'So now, now we wait.' Barley loosened Goosey's tack. 'This the worst bit though, isn't it?' she asked the mare, pulling at her ears and pulling a face at Melinda at the same time. 'The very worst bit, the waiting, I always think. I hate waiting.'

'Yes, me too.' Melinda looked away and for a moment the delight in her eyes faded and she could no longer concentrate on the timing of her round, or on what Josh was saying about other rounds, or make sense of anything. Something had happened in the last minute, and for no reason she remembered the last part of her mother's dream, the picture of them all together.

'But I couldn't see where I was, Mellie!'

The moment Claire opened the door of 38 Cheshire Street, she knew. As usual she arrived a good half an hour before Crawford's secretary, Marjorie, but despite her not having yet arrived, nevertheless Claire knew that something had happened, and so when the telephone rang and she heard Marjorie's voice it was as if she had been given that half an hour to prepare herself to take the news calmly, so that when Marjorie arrived she was waiting to comfort her.

The previous evening Rose had returned from the studio knowing without any doubt that do what he would Sir Godfrey Brimpton could never shake her performance. He might be playing the lead, and Rose Merriott might have been cast against his wishes, but nothing, nothing that he could do would shake her confidence in how she should play the title role of The Wild Duck.

The atmosphere on the studio floor had started

off only vaguely interested the first day. The technicians on a small-budget 'art house' movie were always more anxious just to get it done and over with, Perry Francis the director told Rose, than to get it done brilliantly. But from the moment everyone on set realized that Sir Godfrey was preparing to throw the book at the unknown ingenue playing opposite him, they lined up to watch what they would undoubtedly have thought was going to be more of a major attraction than the film itself, namely an old star making mincemeat of a young player.

But the old actor could not shake Rose. He tried to, of course. Yet, hours though he kept her waiting to play their scenes together, days that he complained volubly and incessantly that she was 'not giving him anything', all were as nothing before Rose's almost supernaturally unshakeable confidence.

'Perry's seen the rushes,' Charles told her, day after day, and day after day the message was always the same. 'He's delighted. Sir G may be still throwing the book at you, but you are doing nothing to his too much!'

Rose sighed with delight, while the professor's arms went round her, and they kissed, because they had become lovers.

'I have been in a sweat. I didn't like to tell you, you know, but the thought of letting you down, after all that work on the play together. *Figure-toi!*'

'Don't mind me, it's you doing it, you must

forget your professor, put me out of your mind, once you're on the floor.'

'Forget the person who put me up for it? After all those other actresses had read for it, to walk into a film part on one reading, all thanks to you, and you tell me to forget you? I carry you with me to the studios, in my heart!' Rose pointed to her chest dramatically. 'Right in there, and you know it.'

'Your reading was so intelligent you had to go up for it, and besides, I knew Perry was looking for someone completely fresh.'

Rose stood up. '*And* you arranged for Perry to read me last, you cunning old thing!' She stopped and slowly, slowly, sank into the splits, which she could still just do, miracle of miracles. 'But are you sure Perry is really, really pleased with me?'

Charles smiled. Over the past weeks he had come to realize that Rose, while gallantly always assuming an outward confidence, actually needed propping up at every turn – although not, it seemed, once in front of the cameras.

'Quite sure. I am quite sure that he is not only pleased with you, he is thrilled.' He paused. 'Now it's my turn. How come, and from where, did you finally put together your performance? Because Perry told me it *is* quite unshakeable, that the old man simply can't live with you, can't go your speed, he has to sprint behind, which he is not used to doing at all with young actors, it seems.'

'No, and nor shall he catch up with me, the old

devil.' Rose looked up from bowing her head over her knees, her arms, swanlike, over her head. 'But if you want to know the story of how I came to sew up my performance, set it in stone, if you will, it is actually quite simple. The other week I went off with Lily – you know Lily? – course you do. Well, I went off with her to do a really drench-making promotion girl thingy, at the races. So there I was in my divinely horrible suit and a sash with a promotion logo on it which says something so perfectly embarrassing that I can't even repeat it, when who should win the second race but my future stepmother, and my father. Of course as soon as I realized this and saw them swanning up to take their prize, I hid.'

Rose folded both her legs and arms solemnly in front of her now, looking, it seemed to Charles, exactly like something out of a story illustrated by Arthur Rackham, with her long hair, streamlined body and serious, almost mystical expression.

'But you can't hide from my father. Never could. I don't know what it is, but he's one of those people who always seems to find you, wherever you are. And as soon as he and this woman – this Muffin – as soon as he saw me in this awful suit with this promotion sash across me, he started to laugh, and much worse – she did too. And I mean they didn't laugh, they *cracked up*.'

Rose stopped again, remembering the pain.

'It was just so shaming. You can imagine? First of all seeing them there, and then to see them laughing at me. And that's when I realized, in one, what you had been on about all the time we were working on pieces together, what you had been on about when we read *The Wild Duck* together. About the selfishness of the father, and why he's always hiding himself in his dark room, and why the daughter goes to save the wild duck and why she ends up shooting herself, sacrificing herself. And why the father will go on being just the same, in spite of everything, that it won't change him at all. I understood it in a flash, and I mean that deep down understanding that you really need in order to become someone else, to inhabit the character properly, I understood it all, because of standing there that day and seeing my father laughing at me. It came to me at once, and no-one can take away that feeling of pain. And you know what?'

Charles shook his head but Rose waited, so finally he said, 'No. No, I don't know what. What?'

'I take my sash to the studio every day, and every day, before I'm needed, I stand quite quietly at my dressing room mirror and I drape the sash around me, and all those feelings come back, and when I finally take it off and go out there, there's nothing that hateful old devil can do about my performance, he can't shake me, I *am* the Wild Duck.'

'Of course you know he has left you the painting? The Cozen? He did so want you to have it, I know.

As soon as it is finished being cleaned – months and months yet – he wanted you to have it. He told me so, and since I am his chief executor I shan't forget his wishes in a hurry, of course I shan't. Good heavens, he will never leave me, not for a moment. Even though he has gone, I will always hear his voice. He was so brave, though, wasn't he? Always so brave and so cheerful, and pretending to everyone all the time that he was just the same as he had always been. Died in his sleep, you know, quietly and beautifully. What a dear man. Never will I meet such a dear man again, so dear.'

Marjorie was rambling on as people in shock are prone to do, her plump, pretty, middle-aged face reflecting her devotion to Crawford Haye, and as she did so, walking round the great top room where Claire and Crawford had first had drinks that first evening when she had been to the auction, it seemed to Claire that she could see Crawford smiling at them both from somewhere in the room.

If he was he would certainly find Marjorie drinking his best brandy at eleven in the morning amusing. *Look at you, Marjorie, at eleven o'clock drinking brandy like a barge woman!* Claire imagined she could hear him saying. *Anyone would have thought that you were in love with me!*

And of course the truth was that Crawford had *It*. The thing that Aunt Rosabel was always talking about, that quality that made someone so

549

fascinating to people that they would always want them around, so it was natural that Marjorie would always imagine that Crawford was around her. Besides, she loved him, Claire could see that, which was why she had stayed with him all those years, despite knowing, which she must have done, that he would never marry anyone, after losing his wife that way.

'Just one more thing I think you should know, my dear.'

Claire looked across at the secretary, waiting for her to confess that she had been in love with Crawford. In her head she started to write the words that she thought she might use. *I was in love with him, you know, my dear? All my life I was in love with him.* Words that older, elegant women in black and white films seemed always to be using.

'Just one more thing, my dear,' Marjorie said again, topping up her brandy glass for the second time. 'As you probably knew, Crawford was long aware of what was happening to him, knew all about his illness, and so on, and although he made several wills over the years, in this last one, during his last weeks on Bryndor, he changed his mind about some things, and kept other things the same. Oh dear, I am rambling on, I am dearly afraid it must be the brandy!

'What I mean to say is, he left the business to me, which was so very sweet of him, in gratitude for thirty years here, and, as well, the use of this house, as tenant, for my lifetime, after that to pass to the Fellowes' boy, his godson. His paintings are left to various galleries and so on, all perfectly proper, but there is one more thing.'

Marjorie looked across at Claire nursing a lemonade and mineral water.

'He has left you his little – and it is only little – his little art gallery, dear, the Kingsettle Gallery. It's in Hampstead. It's only small, but it is freehold and he thought you would like it. And as a matter of fact, I thought so too.'

None of them could bear to watch the score sheets being written up, and yet to leave the tent where they were posted was worse, and so yet again, and agonizingly, Melinda, Josh and Barley watched more score markers coming in with a fresh set of cards collected by a team of small volunteers on sturdy ponies.

'Is this the best that they can do in the computer age?' Josh asked Barley, but she just smiled and lit a cigarette.

From afar the markers' backs seemed to be deliberately hostile.

'I can't look,' Melinda muttered, but she too rushed forward to gaze up at the boards.

'Here we – go!' Josh said quietly as the last scores were written up. 'Mellie! Walden Wonder's had a stop! A refusal – that puts you second!'

Melinda made a fist of her hand and bit it.

'You are second! You have to be second!'

'You might even be fir – fir – fir – damn it, you might even be first!'

'No way, Josh, look.' Melinda pointed to Blake's Epiphany which was now being posted for the cross country phase. 'Clear, see? No penalties.'

'No, look,' Josh said suddenly and clearly, 'look, they've got time penalties. Five time penalties. They've finished on twenty-seven. You are only twenty-six.'

'Josh. Barley. Mums! I've won!'

Chapter Twenty

Jack had made up his mind, long before he left home, that today was to be the day. He arose in the morning, and, putting on a clean shirt, he shaved off his beard and packed his guitar into the back of his four wheeler, knowing that today was definitely to be the day that he would sing to Hope. Yet long before he could walk to her side, in that room which he knew as well as any room in his own house, he sensed that there was something different in the ether. A profound change, a change which he had somehow already anticipated.

And yet.

There was no sign of anything different. Hope still lay as she always lay, supported on two pillows, flat on her back, her arms by her sides.

And yet.

As he placed his guitar down by the side of her bed and kissed her forehead he knew that there was something different about her. Normally he would sit down and start to talk to her, telling her about what was happening back at the Mill House, or about Letty going to play group for the first time, or James's new weight. He knew that Melinda had been in the day before telling her all about winning. That would have really thrilled her. It was wonderful when he knew that the girls had been in, that they had told her things like that.

A few weeks back it had been Rose rushing in to tell her about getting the role in the Art movie. Then there was Claire down only yesterday on a flying visit to tell her all about this art gallery some bloke had given her. Given her, would you believe!

But they were the things that Jack knew she would want to know, and the girls themselves always seemed to want Hope to be the first to know about them too. That had not changed the whole time she had been lying there. To them, as for Jack, Hope was still alive. No question of it, she was still with them, part of their lives as much as if she was sitting in the kitchen at Keeper's, waiting to hear all their news.

'Now, darling, today I have brought in my guitar, and I'm going to sing you a song, which has actually been recorded by Rusty Naylor. You remember her, way back a little? She was never off the airwaves. Well, she thought she'd retired until I made her sing this, and it is good, this song, especially the way Rusty gives it her special treatment. But I wanted to sing it to you myself, because I wrote it for you, Hope, and to you, and so here it is. I won't do it as well as Rusty, but here goes anyway.'

He put his guitar across his knee and began.

All of my life all of my life
I've been searching for
A love like ours
Somewhere to stay
Somewhere safe
In your arms
I was so sure.

It seemed to Jack that she was moving, but that could not be, because – well, it just could not be.

But it was. Hope was moving and she was sitting up and her eyes were opening and she was looking so beautiful. Her hair was blowing back, it must be from the breeze coming from the window, and she was smiling, and everything was just as it had always been, and she was reaching towards him and putting her arms round him, and Jack could feel her hands wiping the tears from his face as he sobbed out his gratitude at the sight of her.

'Oh, Hope, I knew you'd come back to me, I just knew it. I told everyone I'd bring you back and I have. I have sung you awake!'

She slipped off the bed and he started to waltz her around the room, saying, 'I've sung you awake. I knew I could. I just knew it.'

'Oh, Jack, once more. Sing to me once more.'

Hope stood in front of him, and picking up his guitar Jack prepared to sing to her again. Hope sat leaning towards him, her hands clasped in front of her. He continued:

Don't leave me this way
Don't tell me it's over
We've only begun
And love is so young
You're leaving me nowhere
Don't leave me this way.

He was singing it so much better now, so strongly, and with her eyes on him the last lines became triumphant.

'Oh, Jack, I am so glad that you love me!'

She smiled at him, and Jack, unable to bear the moment any longer, the sheer euphoria of it, ran out of the door to fetch someone, anyone, to tell them all that Hope was back.

'Nurse, nurse, doctor – she's come back. She's all right. I said she'd come back, I said she'd wake up. I sang to her, and she came back!'

As Jack ran down the corridor towards two nurses who were hurrying towards him, the sun became brighter and brighter until it filled the whole of the room where Hope lay.

'We're coming, Jack, we're coming!'

The nurses smiled but they looked so anxious that Jack stopped and stared at their hurrying.

'It's all right,' he called, 'she's all right. Really.

She's come back.' He frowned as one of the doctors passed him too. 'It's OK, really. She's all right.'

Seconds later he was still standing in the same place when they came back out to him and the doctor walked towards him. 'Jack. I am so sorry.'

Jack stared at the young man and frowned. Why did he have tears in his eyes?

'Hope has gone, Jack.'

'No, Hope has not gone. She spoke to me.'

'No, Jack, Hope has gone.'

'She can't have gone. I tell you, I was there, singing to her. Do something. Bring her back. What the hell's it called – when you use electricity? Use those electric things on her! Do something!'

As he was imploring him the doctor was walking Jack gently back down the corridor and into Hope's room.

'Look,' he said, pointing to the monitor above the bed. 'It's there on the monitor. Hope died minutes ago. There's the time, see? Blood pressure, heart, everything's recorded from in here to out there. It all stopped, suddenly, five minutes ago, out there, and no-one noticed. You get this with even the best monitors – everything stopped. That's why there were no alarms sounding, and it was only when one of the nurses noticed the fault—'

Jack stared. 'But I was singing to her, and we were laughing and talking, and she was fine.' He looked at the monitor above the bed and then back at Hope. 'I was singing to her and she danced and I held her in my arms.' He was silent, and then he said again, and his voice was full of gratitude, 'She came back to me.' He looked at the doctor. 'She came back to be with me while I sang to her. She came awake with my song!'

They buried Hope in the graveyard of the little church that was so near to Keeper's and the Mill House that the children could put flowers on her grave any time they wanted. The sun played on their bright hair as they walked up to the church, and there was a light summer breeze which moved and swayed the roses against the side of the church walls, while high in the sky a song thrush sang.

Jack had filled the place with musicians, because, as Melinda said, 'She really only had us, when you think about it.' And they too came to the little church on that bright summer day with their violins and their cellos and a Yamaha piano. And Rusty Naylor came, as she said, 'just with me voice'.

The three girls helped Jack to choose her music. Among much that was beautiful, they chose Jack's song, which meant that Jack kept saying, 'You don't have to have it, you know, just because I wrote it.'

As for Jack, he chose 'Morning', which Richard Strauss wrote on the eve of his wedding to his so-great love, a sublime evocation of tenderness and purity, because, as he said, when his time came and they were reunited, he liked to think that they too would be married.

After everyone had left, late in the afternoon, as the sun was preparing to set and the evening breeze was ruffling the leaves of the willows, they all went down to the river that ran past the house and one by one they threw the petals from the roses they had made into a bouquet for her and Jack sat under the trees, watching them and playing his guitar, playing, for the last time, the love song he had written to the woman he loved.

Epilogue

Jack still went to see Hope every day and told her everything that was happening and what he hoped might happen too. Visiting her and talking to her was as much part of his day as it had ever been, and she as much part of his life as she had ever been.

But it was Aunt Rosabel who momentarily rendered them all speechless. Her lawyers, having extricated Hatcombe from the dubious orphans' charity, subsequently discovered, and her safe revealed, that having died seemingly penniless, she had in fact squirrelled away a positive fortune in as many as twenty different accounts.

'I think she was hiding it from Alexander. Goodness, Mums would laugh, wouldn't she?' Melinda shook her head, staring at the card that Aunt Rosabel had left her, forwarded to her by her great-great-aunt's solicitors. It transpired that Aunt Rosabel's money was to go to Rose, Claire and Letty, while Hatcombe was to go to Melinda. Paradoxically, the card depicted an idealized Victorian family Christmas, but the riddle was explained when on opening the card Melinda saw the greeting. It read, *With love from the Spirit of Christmas Past.*

Together, Melinda and Jack decided that Hatcombe should become the home of not just the soon to be married Mellie and Josh, but of the two youngest children too, Jack deeming it better that they be brought up with younger people, and Josh and Mellie welcoming the idea of a ready-made family. With Jack in residence only a few miles away at the Mill House, and Rose and Charles, also heading for the altar, living at Keeper's Cottage at weekends, there would be no shortage of relations on hand to help them.

And so it was that with all the unhappy memories banished, Hatcombe prepared to put on its finest and host a wedding for the young couple. Not a grand wedding, but a splendid one, with flowers and music, and food made by them all in the kitchens of the old house.

By the time another June was preparing to set to and bring on high summer, the wedding arrangements had necessarily gathered momentum. The fitting of the bridesmaids' dresses – gowns made of lawn with fresh flowers at gathered sleeves, and underbusts in the Regency style. A cream and pistachio-coloured cake to match the marquee that Jack had chosen to be pitched on the big lawn, south of the house. The picking and arranging of dozens of pale cream roses and brightly coloured leaves from shrubs in neighbours' gardens. And the bride's dress, a simple but beautifully fashioned gown of cream pleated silk matching the pale cream roses in her hair and her bouquet. It seemed that everything was ready.

But one more event gave the wedding an extra and special blessing, for no sooner had it been decided that Melinda's wedding was to be held at Hatcombe, than a pair of linnets began to build their nest in the roof of an old greenhouse in the grounds.

They were brought to Mellie's attention by Mr Parsons, Aunt Rosabel's old gardener.

'They're rare now, Miss Mellie. Very rare,' Mr Parsons whispered as he took Melinda to see them. 'All but extinct in some parts, yet when I was a boy they were a common garden bird. What them's doing building in the greenhouse I don't know, since they nest in bushes usual, or thickets. They's special birds, you know, and not a lot of people do. For they have a mantle of luck about them. They say if linnets nest as you wed – well, 'tis for a lucky couple, that's what they say, Miss Mellie.'

So, whenever she was at Hatcombe during those last weeks before she and Josh were married, Melinda would creep down to see the linnets nesting, finding not only eggs, but in time a chick, which, as the preparations for the wedding gathered pace, feathered and fledged until it was a perfect tiny bird.

Up bright and early on the morning of the wedding itself, Melinda paid a hurried call to the greenhouse only to find Mr Parsons there cutting flowers, but the nest empty.

'Oh, no. What happened?'

She turned to Mr Parsons, who ignored her, continuing to snip at his precious blooms before looking out to the skies beyond the open door.

'She's flown, Miss Mellie. She's flown. First thing this morning as I was opening up I saw the mother on the greenhouse roof with her baby, then as the sun got warm they spread their wings and up they went to the skies.'

'I'm so glad . . .'

Yet she couldn't help feeling sorry, too, seeing the empty nest.

'So you should be, Miss Mellie.' Parsons turned to look at her. 'That's how it is with linnets, see? The old tale has it that if the young fly on the day that you're wed, you'll be happy for the rest of time. It's what the bird represents, see? It's all to do with what the little bird represents.'

'Which is? What exactly does the linnet represent?'

'Why, did you not now know, Miss Mellie?' He smiled for the first time. 'The little linnet, she symbolizes hope.'

THE END

DEBUTANTES
by Charlotte Bingham

'A big, wallowy, delicious read' *The Times*

A century ago marriage, and marriage alone, offered a nicely brought-up girl escape from the domination of her parents. Indeed, it was the only path to freedom. That path led her to a Season in London and, the ultimate goal, Coming Out as a debutante. But along the way she had to survive a terrifying few months, a make-or-break time in which her family's hopes for her could only be fulfilled through a proposal of marriage.

For Lady Emily Persse, Coming Out means leaving her beloved Ireland, and its informalities, for England's stricter codes. For Portia Tradescant, released from the boredom of life in the English countryside, it means trying to get through the Season despite the best efforts of her eccentric Aunt Tattie. For beautiful May Danby the Season is an entrée to a whole other life, worlds away from her strict convent upbringing in Yorkshire.

Debutantes, Charlotte Bingham's delightful and stylish saga, centres around a single London Season in the eighteen-nineties. But it is not just about the debutantes themselves. It is as much about the women who launch them, and the Society which supports their way of life. It is also about the battle for power, privilege and money, fought, not in the male tradition upon the battlefield, but in the female tradition . . . in the ballroom.

Available in Bantam Paperback
0 553 40890 9

GRAND AFFAIR
by Charlotte Bingham

'Extremely popular' *Daily Mail*

Unaware of the misery that surrounded her birth, for the first four years of her life all Ottilie Cartaret knows is love. And when her mother, Ma O'Flaherty, moves her family to what she believes will be rural bliss in St Elcombe in Cornwall, their fortunes seem set fair.

Tragedy strikes when Ma dies and young Ottilie soon finds herself in unfamiliar surroundings. Adopted by the Cartarets, the wealthy couple who run the Grand Hotel, she grows up pampered and spoilt, not only by her adoptive parents but by all the visitors – with the exception of their mysterious annual guest, nicknamed 'Blue Lady', with whom Ottilie is unknowingly and inextricably linked.

But as times change, and the regulars to the now-decaying hotel die off, the Cartarets find they are unable to adapt to modern ways. Only Ottilie has the means to save the Grand, even though she may sacrifice too much of herself before learning once again the power of love.

Available in Bantam Paperback
0 553 50500 9

A SELECTION OF FINE NOVELS
AVAILABLE FROM BANTAM BOOKS

THE PRICES SHOWN BELOW WERE CORRECT AT THE TIME OF GOING TO PRESS.
HOWEVER TRANSWORLD PUBLISHERS RESERVE THE RIGHT TO SHOW NEW
RETAIL PRICES ON COVERS WHICH MAY DIFFER FROM THOSE PREVIOUSLY
ADVERTISED IN THE TEXT OR ELSEWHERE.

50329 4	DANGER ZONES	*Sally Beauman*	£5.99
50630 7	DARK ANGEL	*Sally Beauman*	£6.99
50631 5	DESTINY	*Sally Beauman*	£6.99
40727 9	LOVERS AND LIARS	*Sally Beauman*	£5.99
50326 X	SEXTET	*Sally Beauman*	£5.99
40803 8	SACRED AND PROFANE	*Marcelle Bernstein*	£5.99
50469 X	SAINTS AND SINNERS	*Marcelle Bernstein*	£5.99
40429 6	AT HOME	*Charlotte Bingham*	£3.99
40427 X	BELGRAVIA	*Charlotte Bingham*	£3.99
40432 6	BY INVITATION	*Charlotte Bingham*	£3.99
40497 0	CHANGE OF HEART	*Charlotte Bingham*	£5.99
40890 9	DEBUTANTES	*Charlotte Bingham*	£5.99
40296 X	IN SUNSHINE OR IN SHADOW	*Charlotte Bingham*	£5.99
40469 2	NANNY	*Charlotte Bingham*	£5.99
40171 8	STARDUST	*Charlotte Bingham*	£4.99
40163 7	THE BUSINESS	*Charlotte Bingham*	£5.99
40895 X	THE NIGHTINGALE SINGS	*Charlotte Bingham*	£5.99
17635 8	TO HEAR A NIGHTINGALE	*Charlotte Bingham*	£5.99
50500 9	GRAND AFFAIR	*Charlotte Bingham*	£5.99
50501 7	LOVE SONG	*Charlotte Bingham*	£5.99
40072 X	MAGGIE JORDAN	*Emma Blair*	£4.99
40615 9	PASSIONATE TIMES	*Emma Blair*	£5.99
40614 0	THE DAFFODIL SEA	*Emma Blair*	£4.99
40373 7	THE SWEETEST THING	*Emma Blair*	£4.99
40372 9	THE WATER MEADOWS	*Emma Blair*	£5.99
40973 5	A CRACK IN FOREVER	*Jeannie Brewer*	£5.99
50429 0	KITTY AND HER BOYS	*June Francis*	£5.99
40820 8	LILY'S WAR	*June Francis*	£4.99
40730 9	LOVERS	*Judith Krantz*	£5.99
40731 7	SPRING COLLECTION	*Judith Krantz*	£5.99
40945 X	FINISHING TOUCHES	*Patricia Scanlan*	£5.99
40947 6	FOREIGN AFFAIRS	*Patricia Scanlan*	£4.99
40942 5	PROMISES, PROMISES	*Patricia Scanlan*	£5.99
40962 X	MIRROR, MIRROR	*Patricia Scanlan*	£5.99
40944 1	APARTMENT 3B	*Patricia Scanlan*	£5.99

All Transworld titles are available by post from:

Book Service By Post, PO Box 29, Douglas, Isle of Man, IM99 1BQ

Credit cards accepted. Please telephone 01624 675137
fax 01624 670923, Internet http://www.bookpost.co.uk
or e-mail: bookshop@enterprise.net for details

Free postage and packing in the UK. Overseas customers: allow £1 per book
(paperbacks) and £3 per book (hardbacks)